Sweet Pursuits

Sweet Pursuits

Pauline Wiles

Author's Note

In keeping with its English setting, this novel uses British spelling and grammar conventions.
You can find a glossary of British terms at the end of the book.

Acknowledgements

I had a blast writing *Sweet Pursuits* but novel-creation is a marathon process. As always, reader feedback spurred me on and was just as vital as consuming plenty of cake while typing. Thank you to every single person who has let me know you enjoy my work: there are many days when you keep me going.

For *Sweet Pursuits*, special recognition is due to Nancy True who was the winner of my contest to name a Cambridge college. Thank you, Nancy, for the convincing suggestion of Trewe College.

My superstar team of beta readers included Joanne Phillips, Martha Reynolds, Julie Valerie and Jean at DelightfulRepast.com. They provided the ideal blend of critique and encouragement that hopefully took this novel from almost-baked to perfectly done.

Once again, I'm grateful to proofreader Jude White, who was both patient and thorough in her checks for errors and consistency. Any remaining blunders are mine.

Finally, my skill as a writer falls short of finding the words to thank my husband, Darius Wiles. Without his steadfast tolerance and encouragement, *Sweet Pursuits* would not exist.

Sweet Pursuits

Prologue: July 2009

With hindsight, buying my dream wedding dress before Owen had actually got down on one knee may have been a mistake. But it was so exquisite, and such an incredible bargain at sixty per cent off. And I was so certain that one day soon I would be walking up a peony-scented church aisle towards him, that I took the gamble. It was the sensible, economic thing to do, after all. Weddings are expensive and, on his meagre academic salary, I knew Owen would appreciate my thriftiness.

Except *appreciative* didn't exactly describe his reaction.

'Bella, what in the name of God is that?' He threw the Vera Wang gown, still in its garment cover, on our bed.

'Oh!' I was admittedly unprepared for this conversation. He rarely, if ever, delved into the airing cupboard. 'You've found it.'

'It looks,' he said, backing away as if it were a white tiger which might spring up and attack him, 'like a wedding dress.'

'Er, yes.' I sensed from his tone that the timing of this momentous discovery might be off. I attempted distraction. 'What were you doing in the airing cupboard?' Ironing pillow cases and placing them neatly on the slatted shelves next to our aging boiler was not Owen's scene.

'Looking for a suitcase,' he said, his face as pale as the dress.

'Why do you need a suitcase?'

By now Owen was pressed against the wall, in a curious impression of a man on a cliff ledge. 'Job interview.' He'd barely taken his eyes off the gown.

'Where?' I asked, at precisely the same moment he said, 'Is it yours?'

'Well, yes,' I laughed. 'With two bachelor brothers, it's not like I'm storing it for them.'

I saw him swallow. Twice.

'So, where did you say?' I asked again, thinking he wouldn't need to stay the night in London or Oxford, so it must be further, like Manchester or Leeds. I wasn't sure how I felt about moving away from Cambridge.

He didn't answer.

'Owen,' I tutted. 'You're being all strange. Where's your job interview?'

Finally he looked at me, his expression a blank mask. 'California.'

~~~

He got the job, of course. My brilliant geneticist boyfriend spoke in monosyllables for two days, then flew off to America where he wowed the interview board with his British accent, Prince Harry hairstyle, and unmatched knowledge of the proteins of the influenza A genome. Within seven weeks, he'd packed his essential belongings into half a dozen enormous boxes, nipped down to London to get a precious embossed visa in his passport, and was gone.

I was left with a flat too big for me, a collection of unmatched socks, two chipped Garfield mugs, and an unworn wedding dress. Plus a broken heart.

I got rid of the mugs and socks, eventually. But even though I never told anyone about it, I kept the dress. Every time I moved I concealed it, furtively, so I wouldn't have to explain why a thirty-five-year-old spinster needs a Vera Wang gown in her wardrobe.

And alongside it I also stored the hope that one day Owen and I would get a second chance.

Chapter 1

Valentine's Day, 2014

My involuntary squeal reverberates around the small, high-ceilinged office I share with my boss, Gertrude.

'What is it now, Bella?' she asks, as if I'm the one prone to dramatics, not her. After all, she made an unseemly fuss of the red roses which were delivered to her this morning.

'Nothing. Sorry.' My fingers have clenched. 'Just, uh, cramp.'

I'm lying, of course. No need to tell Gerty I've stumbled upon the news I'm certain will change my life.

Unable to sit still, I pace to the window, pretending to stretch. Turning my back on my caustic supervisor, I gaze out at the inner court of Trewe College, reminding myself to breathe. Below is a scene of classical perfection, a quintessential Cambridge vista of genteel buildings, the colour of pale tea, aged by centuries of academic endeavour. These are arranged around a flawless square of grass, so lush that it looks unreal. At least, I assume it's real: I've never actually touched it. No mere mortal is allowed to walk on this grass, only the Master of the college and his chosen few.

But I'm not looking at the lawn today. Nor do I notice the wisteria clinging to the opposite wall, barren on this February afternoon, but soon to bloom in cascades of purple. Instead, I'm forcing myself to count down from twenty, and wondering, when I go back to my computer, whether it will still be there.

'I could just fancy a cup of tea,' hints Gertrude from behind me.

Since she's senior to me, it's unofficially my job to make refreshments around eleven and three each day. Clearly, colouring cells on her spreadsheet is thirsty work.

'Right,' I say. 'In a minute.' I'm not going near hot water until this even hotter wave of elated disbelief has subsided. It wouldn't be safe.

Feigning nonchalance, I sidle back to my desk, which naturally is devoid of Valentine flowers. Then, hoping Gertrude isn't watching, I let my eyes creep to my screen, and the article from the *Cambridge Evening News*.

Marin Genetics are latest Science Park arrival

The headline itself is nothing to get my knickers in a twist about. It came up in my Google alert because it contains a reference to Trewe.

'While Marin Genetics will continue to maintain a significant presence in Berkeley, California, we are excited to be locating one of our research teams in Cambridge where we look forward to deepening our collaboration with both the public and private sectors,' said Jasper Lyon-Bowles, head of the new team and an alumnus of Trewe College. 'Cambridge has a world-class reputation in health care innovation and it makes perfect sense for us to be at the heart of this change engine,' added team member Owen Rigby, also a Cambridge graduate.

I skip over the rest. I know PR gloss when I see it: part of my job in the Development Office at Trewe is to come up with similar superlatives describing the work of our faculty and students. I'm also supposed to monitor online news feeds for anything relevant to the college, so we know what the media is saying, and to glean information on prominent – or wealthy – alumni.

Gerty sighs loudly and examines her watch. I take the hint and get up to make tea. She'll get grumpy if she's thirsty, and I don't want any extra attention on me today. I might even share those heart-shaped shortbreads I baked for Valentine's Day. I wasn't going to give one to Gerty, but now I see it may be in my best interest. I need to be left in peace to read and reread that article.

With tea duty accomplished, I scour the internet to make certain it's the same Owen Rigby. Then I indulge in a montage of delicious reminiscences of our time together. From the day we moved into our flat and blew the fuses cooking dinner to our first foreign holiday – with skinny dipping – in Malta. From the day we got the giggles in Ely Cathedral to the time Owen attempted a barbecue on the balcony and ignited the window box too.

Naturally, I finish off the shortbread before searching the web again to see if I can find an up-to-date photo. I make yet another pot of tea, and stare poignantly out of the window a little longer.

And after I've done all that, I start planning how to get him back.

Chapter 2

'Right!' says my aunt Amelia. '*Thelma and Louise,* or *Charlie's Angels*?' She holds the two DVDs as if asking us to pick a card, not a movie for sad singletons on Valentine's Day.

'I don't suppose you've got something like *Notting Hill* or *Four Weddings*?' Grace asks from Amelia's cream sofa.

'Grace, darling,' Amelia sighs, 'tonight's about girl power, not lame romantic encounters.'

I don't know exactly how old Amelia is, but she's glamorous, sassy and oozes feminine mojo. She owns the thriving Saffron Sweeting estate agency and treats every encounter – romantic or otherwise – as a scintillating adventure. Grace works for her, but she obviously doesn't have the same pizzazz.

Thanks to my auburn-haired aunt, it's now a Valentine's tradition for the single women of Saffron Sweeting to sequester themselves in her small but stylish house. We scoff finger food, swig wine and pretend we couldn't possibly be having a better time. But it's a small showing this year. My best friend Sophie is all loved up with her guy, Tom. They're both qualified pilots and have flitted off in a little plane to one of the Channel Islands. And my culinary chum Lorraine, who runs the village bed and breakfast, has gone on a last-minute bargain cruise.

'Grace doesn't get it,' I say mildly, 'she's not single.'

'I am tonight,' Grace shrugs. 'James is at a conference. Great timing.'

'Is he?' Amelia says. 'Where?'

'Las Vegas.' Grace, who's about my age, grimaces as she answers, and I notice a look pass between her and Amelia. I wonder what's wrong with Las Vegas. Grace, in fact, used to live in America, but moved back to England a couple of years ago and chose Saffron Sweeting. I don't know her well, but the fact she picked our little village when she could have settled anywhere makes me think she must have her head on the right way round.

'Ugh.' My housemate, Morgan, screws up her face. 'I can't stand that place.'

Grace, who so far this evening has chatted happily with Amelia, a little with me, but hardly at all to Morgan, turns to her. 'Where did you say you're from?'

'Houston, originally,' Morgan replies in her clear, confident voice. 'Then Yale, before Trewe.'

Unlike Grace, who only lived in the States for a few years, Morgan is American from top to toe.

'And Bella said you're working on your PhD?'

'Yeah. I'm here for a semester, maybe two.'

'That's terms,' I translate.

After Sophie moved out, her room was empty for a bit, then came a tedious episode with a tenant who swore she didn't smoke, but every time I came into the living room, she was standing by the window with one hand dangling outside. So she had to go. My Uncle Mike, who's my landlord and Amelia's ex-husband, came back to live for a while, but he soon got itchy feet and set off on his next moneymaking quest. And now I'm sharing a bathroom and a fridge with Morgan, who talks at top volume, does nothing that looks like PhD research to me, but instead is leaving a trail of broken hearts around Cambridge.

'Y'all, do we have to watch these?' Morgan says now, with characteristic bluntness. 'I've seen them.'

'Of course we've seen them,' I reply. 'That's the point.'

'Well, no,' says Amelia. 'We can talk about our love lives instead,' she adds, with a slight edge.

Morgan doesn't get the hint. 'I had two offers of dates tonight,' she says. 'I turned 'em down. One's a post doc in Environmental Sciences.'

'And the other?' I can't help asking. I've never been asked out twice in one night, let alone on Valentine's Day.

'Tax attorney.'

She makes gagging motions, but both sound pretty eligible to me.

Owen generally resisted going out on the fourteenth, rightly saying that restaurants were a menagerie of couples faking devotion. And the last February we were together, he was so miserable with the flu he didn't even get me a card. I tiptoed around him, offering hot toddies and toast.

'How about you, Amelia?' Grace says. 'I bet you've got a few admirers.'

Amelia gives a throaty chuckle. 'None that I'd say yes to.'

Grace shakes her head as though she doesn't believe her. Then she looks across at me. 'And you, Bella? Anyone you want to tell us about?'

'Actually...' I run my tongue over my top teeth as my smile widens. 'There is.'

'Oh?' says Amelia. 'Who?'

I savour the moment and push my hands under my legs to try to keep them still. But I'm rocking forwards and backwards just the same. 'Owen.'

Amelia's head jerks up. 'Owen...?' The cogs are turning in her brain. 'Not *Owen* Owen? The one you lived with?'

I nod, aware my face is glowing. 'He's coming back.'

Grace sips her wine. 'Okay, so who's Owen?'

She appears politely interested, although of course she has no idea who he is. Morgan, though, has picked up her phone and is scrolling.

'The one that got away–' I begin, but am interrupted by Amelia.

'Let's see,' she says. 'Where to start?' She puts her index finger to her cheek as if pondering how best to explain. 'Owen lived practically rent free with Bella for eight years while he finished his PhD, treated her like his maid and personal assistant, and conspicuously failed to ask her to marry him.'

'Six years,' I interject. 'Not eight.' I jump up from the sofa and cross to the fireplace, where I hassle the coals with a poker.

'Then,' Amelia continues, 'he got a juicy job offer in America and sodded off to the States with barely a goodbye.'

Grace looks at me for confirmation.

'The job was in genetics. Aimed at curing cancer,' I say quickly. 'It was only right he should go. I understood completely.'

I've repeated those last three words so often over the years, I almost believe them.

Grace's eyebrows twitch, but she's too polite to say anything.

'Sounds like an asshole.' Morgan pulls a face.

'He's not an asshole!' I flush, but rush on. 'He's lovely. He's clever, and funny, and really good-looking.' I always thought, for a scientist, Owen was strikingly attractive. And once I got used to his uncompromising sense of humour, he was entertaining too. 'I'm going to get him back and I need you all to help.' For emphasis, I jab at the smouldering log.

Morgan reaches for the nearest platter. 'That,' she drawls, 'sounds kinda lame. Are these pigs in blankets?'

Amelia folds her arms. 'We call them sausage rolls.' Then, to me, head on one side, 'You were gutted when he left, darling. Are you sure you want him back?'

'Yes! Of course I'm sure!'

I never tried to hide it: I was a mess when Owen left. In the hours since that news article popped onto my screen, I've thought of little else. That's why I'm so sure this is fate working now. I turn to Grace, hoping for some support.

She shrugs. 'I think it's quite romantic.'

You, I think, are my new best friend.

Morgan's chewing, while Amelia looks like I'm trying to sell her double glazing. 'Bella,' she frowns, 'as your aunt I feel compelled to tell you, you can do better.'

'Well, I haven't done better, have I?' I shoot back. 'In the – what – five years since Owen went to California, I've been out with a bunch of nitwits.' I go back to the sofa and flop down next to Grace.

Amelia grins. 'They weren't all losers, surely.'

I glare at her, refusing to be drawn. If she's referring to her sexy friend from London, he only wanted a one-night stand. And later, I heard mutterings of something between him and Grace, before her husband turned up. I am *not* getting sidetracked into discussing Scott, or any of my other dating disasters.

'Losers,' I repeat. 'Except Owen.' My tone softens. 'It's always been Owen.'

No other guy has queued in the rain to get me tickets to a Jeremy Northam play. Nobody else has salvaged my whole day just by impersonating the donkey from Shrek. No subsequent boyfriend could crack an egg in each hand at the same time.

'Maybe that's why it never worked with anyone else,' Grace says, 'if you weren't over him.'

Morgan tuts and picks up one of the DVDs. I'm irritated that a movie she's seen before is now more interesting than my love life.

'So, if I'm not mistaken, you said you want us to help you.' Amelia pours more wine.

I dip my chin. 'I want to, er, make some changes. To improve my chances.'

'Changes?' Grace says gently.

I look at the soft rug under Amelia's reclaimed wood coffee table. 'Well, clearly I need to lose a bit of weight.' I was far less chubby when Owen left. I suck my stomach in, wishing I hadn't eaten so many mini quiches tonight. 'And Amelia, I was hoping you could maybe come shopping with me?'

Grace makes a small sound and when I look up, I see she's smiling. But her expression isn't directed at me, it's more like she's just remembered something.

'And you two, Grace and Morgan –' Morgan's on her knees by the DVD player and doesn't look around. 'I was hoping you two could give me tips on what American girls are like. Owen's probably been out with a few, I don't want to come off badly in comparison.'

Amelia, perched on a low chair with a subtle cheetah print, twirls a patent shoe on the end of her foot. 'Darling,' she says, 'are you sure this is what you want?'

'It's not what she wants.' Morgan tosses her long black hair. 'Bella, forget him and move on with your life.'

'That's all very well for you to say,' I reply. 'I didn't have *anyone* ask me out tonight.'

Grace looks sympathetic. 'I'm not sure I can help much. I'm not too good at this stuff.'

I'm not one for judging other women by their outfits, but now I take in her faded jeans, polo neck sweater and trainers. Not what I had in mind for seducing Owen. But at least she's willing.

Amelia shakes her head, but in the way someone does when they mean yes rather than no. 'Honestly, Bella, I'm not sure about this. But if you want to feel better about yourself, I'm hardly going to refuse.'

'Thank you.' I didn't think my beloved aunt would let me down. Distracted, I reach for a sausage roll.

Meanwhile, the DVD comes to life and Morgan chooses that moment to turn back from the TV. She points at my midsection with the remote control. 'I thought you wanted to lose, like, twenty pounds?'

'Morgan—' Amelia begins, but my housemate is oblivious.

'What?' she says. 'You said so.'

My cheeks flame. I should have realised sharing my goal of getting Owen back would expose me to public scrutiny.

'Bella's fine as she is,' Grace says quickly.

I'm grateful but I know I'm *not* fine as I am. My favourite jeans are tight, and only this week at work I bent down to file something and a button popped off my skirt.

'You are,' Amelia puts in. 'You have lovely hair and a totally sweet face.'

My hair, it's true, is long and soft. But it's a shade too

dark to be truly blonde, and I know I could do more with it than my habitual clip or ponytail.

'I hate my nose,' I say. It's pointy, out of character with the rest of me.

'So get a nose job.' Morgan's attention is on the screen as the trailers begin.

'Fine,' I snap. 'I will.'

'Nobody needs a nose job,' Amelia says smoothly. 'Bella, you have gorgeous blue eyes and terrific boobs.'

Grace grins. 'Lucky thing.'

'But you could dress more appealingly,' my aunt continues. 'Of course we can go shopping.'

'How long have we got?' Grace asks. 'Is he here already?'

I shake my head. 'I'm not sure how long. The newspaper suggested soon.'

'And he's with Marin Genetics?' Amelia says. 'I know their HR people. I'll make enquiries.'

'Oh, please don't.' I'm horrified that my romantic hankerings are going to be known all over Cambridgeshire.

Amelia looks at me quizzically. 'I'll be discreet, darling, of course. But do you want Owen back, or don't you?'

I glance at the others. Morgan's studying the remote control, but Grace nods encouragement.

'Yes,' I say. 'I absolutely want him back.'

'Well then,' says Amelia. 'Let's make it happen.'

Chapter 3

It's one o'clock on Monday and I'm having lunch with Joey at a tiny cafe tucked between King's Parade and Peas Hill. Well, he's having lunch; I've ordered carrot sticks with hummus.

Joey's not normally the perceptive type – unless he's looking through a camera lens – but my sigh when our meals arrive is loud enough to get his attention.

'Why are you eating rabbit food?' he asks, a two-inch-thick sausage sandwich poised in both hands.

'Oh, you know,' I say vaguely, 'trying to trim down a bit.'

Over the weekend, I launched into my mission with gusto. I went to the tiny Saffron Sweeting library and stripped the shelves of dieting advice. Actually, that amounted to just four books, but they gave me loads of ideas and encouragement.

At the behest of *French Women Don't Get Fat*, I embarked on thirty-six hours of cleansing, where my only food was a thin leek soup. In between slurps, I purged my half of the fridge of anything which might lead me astray. I bid a fond farewell to a pot of clotted cream, plus some leftover blackberry crumble. But I did eat the chocolate mousse I'd made on Thursday: that was too good to waste and surely didn't undermine the magical properties of the leek soup.

'Hmm,' says Joey, 'my sisters are always on some kind of diet.'

Joey's family is large. As I recall, he has three – or is it four – sisters, all with similar sounding Italian names.

'They spend several days eating nothing but grapefruit, getting increasingly tetchy with everyone around them, then they capitulate and stick their face in a tub of gelato,' he finishes.

'How silly,' I say, pushing thoughts of leek soup and chocolate mousse aside. Now I think of it, I have been somewhat grumpy since Saturday. Not to mention tired. 'Anyway,' I declare, 'I've lost two pounds already.' I twirl a carrot stick in the hummus and chew slowly. Maybe I can still bake carrot cake as part of my healthy eating regime?

'Nice,' says Joey, with the enthusiasm of someone who never goes near the bathroom scales. 'Not that you need to,' he adds hastily.

I pause. I wasn't going to tell him. But he and I go way back. He behaved appallingly with Sophie, of course, but he's worked hard to redeem himself since then.

'I'm trying to win back the love of my life,' I say.

'Are you?' Joey whistles. 'Cool.'

I relay the edited highlights of the Owen situation, playing down the bit where he moved to California.

'I know!' Joey's enlivened by this new topic. 'Ask him over for dinner.'

Joey's always shown heaps of appreciation for my cooking. It's one of the reasons we get on so well. And I've caught him eying my cleavage on more than one occasion. Maybe a male perspective *would* be useful here.

'And cook what?' I ask.

'Steak,' he says, without hesitation. 'Or that beef thing you do. The posh one, in pastry.'

'Beef Wellington?'

'Yes,' he says. 'And sticky toffee pudding. I'd marry you for your sticky toffee pudding.'

'Aww, thanks, Joe.' My stomach rumbles at the thought of soft sponge, dates and golden syrup. I crunch down hard on a carrot instead and change the subject. 'And how about you? How's business?'

Joey has a studio now, in a village on the south side of Cambridge.

'Good.' He looks away modestly but his grin spreads. 'Really good.'

'Oh, yes?' I'm pleased: Joey has his faults but he's

passionate about photography. 'What's up?'

Having finished his sandwich, Joey crams two of the accompanying crisps into his mouth. I hear the crunch and can't help licking my lips in envy.

'You mustn't tell anyone,' he says.

I lean in, the crisps forgotten.

He looks over both shoulders, confirming that no one is within earshot. 'There's a feature film shooting in Cambridge,' he says. 'A period drama.'

I nod. Cambridge has been used many times for films and television, but I especially adore period dramas. Maybe Joey has a tip on where I can see some filming.

'It's starring Brendan McKinley... and Tasmin Fellows.'

I sit up straight. Brendan McKinley's name is only slightly familiar to me, but Tasmin Fellows is a megastar. She got her break in a Jane Austen television adaptation, then went off to the States where she landed the lead in a massive blockbuster. But her personal life has been in the headlines even more: she's rumoured to have dated Prince Harry, dumping him for a married US Senator. The Senator then left his wife, causing a huge scandal. But Tasmin was already bored, and moved on to one of Madonna's ex-bodyguards.

'Wow,' I say. 'She's huge. The tabloids adore her.' I mimic Joey in looking around for eavesdroppers.

Joey grins again. 'I know,' he says. 'And guess who's been hired to take publicity shots?'

My eyes widen as I catch his meaning. 'You?' I mouth.

'Yup. Yours truly.' He's finished his food and crumples the paper napkin as he sits back and folds his arms. 'This is it, Bella. I think I've made it.'

~ ~ ~

By Tuesday afternoon I'm so hungry, I'm as cranky as Gertrude. She's prodding the shop-bought Bourbons, miffed about the lack of homemade biscuits.

'I told you,' I say, 'I'm trying to lose weight.' No way am I baking cookies just for her.

'Humph,' She looks me up and down critically. 'Well, yes, you are a bit tubby.'

I flinch. It's fine for *me* to tell people I'm fat, but not in the least bit fine for them to agree.

Gerty dunks the Bourbon in her tea. 'That reminds me–'

I'm saved from further criticism as our office door opens.

'Professor Palin!' I'm genuinely pleased to see him. Yes, he's doddery, but so are most of the faculty. Palin's always been kind to me and the Bursar hinted that the Professor's vote helped me get this job.

What's more, he reaches happily into the proffered biscuit tin for a Bourbon. I shoot Gertrude a look: if they're good enough for the Professor, they should be good enough for her. She shakes her head and looks away.

I used to work part time for the Bursar, organising the many conferences held at Trewe. But then this position came up in the alumni and fundraising office, and Professor Palin was on the interview panel. Gertrude, who'd hoped her daughter might land the job, was livid when they offered it to me. My official title is Development Assistant, but I help the alumni team too.

'Now, Bella,' Professor Palin has finished two Bourbons, showering the floor with crumbs, 'I wonder if I might prevail upon you?'

'Of course,' I say.

'I'm having a bit of trouble with my *email*.' He draws out the last word as if it's a form of witchery.

I hide a smile. Poor old Prof: he probably can't open an attachment, or he's forgotten how to print again. Despite my protests, he insists on printing every message, writing his response in red pen, and then laboriously typing it all in again.

'Shall I come and have a look?'

'Would you? I'd be most awfully obliged.'

By the time I get back, half an hour has passed and I reach for my coat.

'I need to leave early tonight,' I tell Gertrude, logging out of my computer.

'Why?' Her tone is overly sharp. 'We're very busy.'

We're not. And I know for certain she was playing solitaire while I was gone.

'Morgan's taking me to CrossFit.'

'Cross what?'

'CrossFit,' I repeat. 'It's a fantastically efficient way to get in shape. Cameron Diaz swears by it, apparently.'

As does Tasmin Fellows, I add silently, remembering I'm not supposed to talk about her.

Gerty snorts, but I ignore her and pull on my gloves.

Owen tended to admire svelte women, not cuddly. I have work to do.

~ ~ ~

Morgan's waiting outside the Trewe gates. There's a nip in the February air, and it's almost dark. Why someone thought this was a good month for Valentine's Day, I'll never know. But I do consider it a glorious omen that I found out about Owen's return on the fourteenth.

'Ready?' she asks.

I nod. 'Shirty Gerty didn't like me leaving early, but she'll get over it.'

'Why've you nicknamed her that?'

'Because she's so grumpy.' We head towards the bus stop. 'Shirty – it's a word for bad-tempered.'

Morgan doesn't comment on the strangeness of the British language, but stops at the corner of Pembroke Street. 'Are you sure about this, Bella?'

Despite her snarky comments the other night, my

housemate has in fact been mildly constructive. She told me to help myself to her low-fat Greek yoghurt from the fridge (I haven't), and removed her bounteous supply of Jaffa Cakes from the kitchen to her bedroom, so I wouldn't be tempted (I have). On second thoughts, that may have been so they're easier for her to eat in bed when the urge strikes her. She denies this habit, but I've seen the telltale chocolate on her sheets.

But her most generous gesture was agreeing to take me along to her exercise class.

Now she says doubtfully, 'It's a real workout. Not for beginners.'

'That's great!' I beam at Morgan, dancing from one foot to another like a boxer. 'No pain no gain!'

I'm going to have a film star body in no time.

Chapter 4

My bravado wavers when we arrive at Morgan's fancy gym in Chesterton, an echoing cavern which reeks of willpower and fresh sweat. It triggers unwelcome flashbacks to my pudgy schooldays and weekly humiliation in what was then called PE.

'Hello! You're new?' The instructor bounds into the room, wild orange hair escaping from a headband.

I nod. 'I'm Bella.'

As she looks me up and down, I notice her bulging biceps.

'Great! I'm Sheila. Have you trained before, Bella?' she asks in a thick Scottish accent.

I bet she's never encountered trouble walking home from the pub in Glasgow on a Friday night. At least, none she didn't start herself.

'Oh, yes,' I say, jiggling my shoulders in a pantomime of limbering up. Well, I went to some aerobics classes in college. And a bit of Pilates at the village hall last year. They both count, surely?

'Cool,' says Sheila, then turns to the class, assembled loosely at the front of the room. 'Okay, you lot: dynamic warm-up!'

At this cryptic command, the class – who I notice now average ten years younger than me – all turn to the right and begin lunging their way across the room. I follow, trying to keep my balance as I drop one knee and then stride forward with the opposite foot. Almost immediately, a pain shoots up the front of both thighs, but I can't stop or the guy behind will crash into me. Eyes watering, I keep going. We reach the far wall, and the whole group turns to lunge back the way we came. By now my legs are killing me and there's a funny twinge in my ribs too. But I continue my wobbly progress across the room, dipping each knee far less now.

I swear the opposite wall moved while I had my back turned: it takes me much longer to reach it. But there's no rest: on an invisible command, the class turns to face the front of the room, then gallops sideways like demented crabs. This looks easier. I try to mimic their movements and am relieved that no new muscles snap or pull. But I'm awfully hot and wish my T-shirt wasn't so thick. Morgan is wearing a cropped top which shows off her toned abs; naturally there's no way I'd show the class my midriff, but it would be nice not to feel so sweaty already.

'Knees up!'

Mere seconds have passed and the others, like a well-trained platoon, pivot again and begin prancing, legs flying up towards their chests.

'Come on, Bella!' Morgan hisses as she passes, and I join in carefully.

This one isn't too bad. I'm panting with the effort, but nothing has twanged yet.

Famous last words: either someone just stabbed me in the buttock, or I've found a new muscle there too. I jog pathetically to the far wall, where I stand, hands on hips, breathing hard.

Sweat is trickling down my face and streaming down inside my T-shirt. I have a stitch, a twitching thigh, and now a throbbing bum.

'Good work!' shouts Sheila, and a few of the class reach for the water bottles they were wise enough to bring. 'Okay, you lot. Let's start!'

'Start?' I cry to Morgan in a panic, 'I thought we had started?'

'That was the warm-up, honey.'

Oh, God, I think. I'm toast.

~~~

'I told you it was tough but you insisted,' Morgan whispers unsympathetically as we lie face down on adjacent mats. Well, I'm lying down, letting gravity ease my muscles and enjoying the possibility of finding more oxygen down here. Morgan, on the other hand, is doing something called a plank.

'Now raise your left leg!' Sheila shouts.

I turn my puce face to see Morgan supporting her entire body weight on her hands and one foot.

'You too, Bella!' calls our instructor and I groan, then make a half-hearted attempt to raise my midsection off the mat. This will be worth it when Owen falls in love with me again.

'And right leg up!' Sheila passes down the line and I sag back to my mat in relief. I bury my nose in the comforting blue plastic, not caring who has breathed – or sweated – all over it before me. All I want is to be left alone here, to pass out in peace.

'Twenty press-ups,' comes the command, and Morgan begins bobbing up and down, her body still in perfect alignment.

'Try them on your knees,' she mutters, and I wait until the rest of the class reaches about eight before struggling to my knees and making vague attempts to lower my weight on my elbows. My T-shirt is clinging to me and there's a coppery taste in my mouth.

'Good!' hollers Sheila. 'Stay strong, Morgan.'

Morgan grunts and doesn't answer. Even she's finding this hard. What on earth was I thinking?

'And... rest!' Shelia strides to the front of the room and begins writing on a whiteboard. From my prone position on the mat, I raise my chin enough to see a strange shorthand taking shape.

'What's that?' I ask Morgan in an undertone. 'Aren't we done?' I, for one, am done in, I'm sure of it. Images of Owen and his unbridled lust for my new body are fading fast.

'Five minutes!' Sheila shouts. 'As many reps as you can,

at your own pace. Remember, you're only cheating yourself!'

Miraculously, the class gets to their feet. I thought half of them would be unconscious on their mats by now.

'What are they... doing?' I lumber up, clinging to the wall for support.

Morgan has started inelegant, repetitive squats. She gestures at the blackboard. 'Ten squats, sprint, ten burpees. Repeat.'

'What the heck are burpees?' I stand, bent double, as the strongest of the class stampede to the opposite wall and back again. Then they start flinging their bodies around like breakdancers on an ants' nest: arms fly up, then down. They drop to the floor, legs kick out behind them, then they spring up again. Their faces are blank masks of determination, like an elite fighting force.

Still grasping the wall, I make one last effort, bending both knees and letting my weight sink down into the prescribed squat. There's a terrible rasping sound and for a moment I think I've done irreparable damage to my spine. But it's not my back. It's my leggings. Purchased yesterday in a hurry in Cambridge market, my clothing is no more up to the challenge than I am. I put one hand behind me to confirm what I already know. I'm now displaying my cotton knickers – the ones with printed pink daisies, no less – to the rest of the group.

'Whoops! Maybe leave it there for today, Bella?' Sheila's voice booms louder than ever.

All heads, whether in the middle of a squat, a sprint, or a burpee, turn to me.

I have two choices. I can slide down this wall, close my eyes and never move again. Or I can muster the last of my energy and flee. I pause for what seems like an eternity. Then, as my stricken lungs summon enough oxygen for one rasping sob, the white-hot flames in my legs abate just long enough for my lurching exit from the room.

Chapter 5

The next day, I swallow my guilt and call in sick to work. It's not my usual style. I'm far more likely to drag myself into Trewe with a streaming cold, whereupon Shirty Gerty makes a thing of shuffling her chair as far away from mine as she can. Then she'll march to Boots in her coffee break and buy an industrial sized bottle of Vitamin C, and use my illness as an excuse to leave early in case she's coming down with it too.

But today, while I haven't contracted anything, I simply can't face it. Gerty knew Morgan was taking me to her exercise class and if I turn up, she'll crow with delight at the outcome.

'Sorry,' I croak to her voicemail, 'food poisoning.'

As I roll out of bed my legs feel like lead, and when I reach to pull the cord for the bathroom light, the pain in my arm makes me wince. The ultimate humiliation comes when I try to get up off the toilet: I wobble and gasp as my thighs screech in indignation.

I stagger back to bed and take three aspirin, then snuggle under the covers to indulge in half-conscious dreams of Owen.

When I wake and drag my limbs downstairs, Morgan is mixing up one of her New Age smoothies.

She eyes me as I slump in my dressing gown at the kitchen table. 'You look like you ran a marathon.' Her tone is devoid of sympathy. 'Up Mount Rushmore.'

'Umph.' I rest my head on my forearms, quietly resenting her for taking me to her torture class.

'Try bananas,' she suggests, spooning Greek yoghurt from its container. 'They're good for muscles.'

'Okay,' I say, thinking that if we had any ice cream, whipped cream, chocolate sprinkles and cherries, I'd be happy to give bananas a try.

'And stretch,' Morgan says. She's adding spinach now.

Yeah, right. 'Before or after a dozen burpees?'

'Jeez, keep your hair on. CrossFit was *your* idea.' But she passes me a mug of coffee.

I know it was. I know. 'Sorry...' I mutter. 'I just...'

'What?'

I let my head loll, noticing the pricking sensation behind my eyes. 'I just really want him back.'

Morgan pauses. 'Yeah. Well, like I said. Bananas.'

I look to see if she's being funny, but there's no trace of a smirk on her pale face.

~ ~ ~

Morgan has just left for the day when the post clatters through the letterbox. There's a catalogue for bras in large sizes, a gas bill, and a wedding invitation from my cousin. I sit at the bottom of the stairs and savour the crisp white card and swirly grey text. It informs me that Eleanor and Edwin are getting married in early May. The ceremony's at Trewe and I'm supposed to bring a *plus one*. Normally, I love weddings – admiring tiered cakes on Pinterest is one of my favourite pastimes – but today, my heart doesn't lift.

Still, this seems an ideal time to check on the Vera Wang dress, currently hidden under my bed in a heavy-duty garment bag. I hobble back upstairs and unzip it.

Today, more than ever, just peeking takes my breath away. From the simple Chantilly lace bodice to the tulle mermaid skirt, every soft, sleek inch proclaims quality and class.

And spinsterhood.

Resisting the urge to shed a tear ten weeks before cousin Ellie walks up the aisle, I make the only reasonable choice and head for the fridge. But it's devoid of comfort food and offers little more than milk, eggs and Morgan's yoghurt. Undeterred, I shuffle to the larder. Into an ovenproof dish goes rice, sugar, nutmeg, and most of the milk. I've made this so often, I could do it with my eyes shut. I slip the dish into the oven and settle down with a novel while I wait.

Two hours later, it's ready: warm, creamy, a little stodgy, delicately scented like the rainy Sundays of my childhood. With a whimper of longing, I grab a spoon to sample the rice pudding I've baked.

And a few minutes after that, it's all gone.

~ ~ ~

Naively, I expect to feel better the following day, but my legs are even worse. It's as if someone opened up my limbs while I slept and stuffed them with nails: both heavy and sharp, stabbing me every time I move.

'Sorry,' I say to Gerty's voicemail at dawn, 'it might be flu, not food poisoning.'

I make coffee and check the fridge. My diet plan specifies half a grapefruit and a hard-boiled egg. I guzzle those, then trudge back upstairs for a hot bath.

When I emerge from the thirty-minute soak, my muscles do feel looser. Maybe Morgan has a point and I should try to move around gently. Nothing like actual stretching, of course, but I could wander into the village. With luck, Violet at the post office will have bananas in stock. And chocolate sprinkles.

My stomach growls approvingly at the thought.

It's not much of a morning for a stroll and hardly anyone's about. Saffron Sweeting is a lovely village, with a long main street flanked by centuries-old cottages and a few grander houses, but, like most of England, it looks bleak at this time of year. The sky over the patchwork rooftops is an ominous slate, and an east wind nips at my coat as I walk. I'm grateful for the temporary protection as I skirt the walls of our poor malt house, which has been Amelia's pet project for over a year now. She's president of the recently-formed *Friends of Sweeting Malt House* and is determined to formulate a cost-effective plan to renovate it.

Now that I'm out, the air is refreshing and I decide to take the indirect way to the post office. Violet, our postmistress, keeps threatening to retire, but she secretly adores being the lynchpin of village communications. I turn left, passing a row of gorgeous thatched cottages with snowdrops nodding bravely in their tiny front gardens. Near the village hall I bend to the right, and before I can question my route, I find myself outside the bakery.

I pause for a second, pretending to watch a robin hop along the pavement, whereas in fact I'm peeking into the shop. But Brian spots me and waves from behind the counter, so I decide it would be unforgivably rude not to go in. As I'm enveloped by the smell of fresh bread and chocolate cake, I check his cabinet to see if he's made anything this morning with bananas as the main ingredient. He hasn't, but after we chat for a few minutes, I see it would be a grievous snub to the baker not to buy something.

And since one Eccles cake looks pathetic in the bag by itself, I agree to Brian's suggestion that he add a Chelsea bun. At this point I decide Morgan was quite magnanimous this morning, and that I'll thank her with something reminiscent of home. That fresh apple pie, golden and glistening in Brian's display cabinet, will do the trick.

'Bella,' says a cheery voice, 'how are you?'

And with my arms full of sweetly guilty calories, I turn to find Grace.

'Hi!' I jump visibly and use my only functioning muscles to attempt a smile. 'I'm fine.'

Grace, bundled in a puffy winter coat and long stripy scarf, greets Brian like an old friend. Our baker is a popular man. Then her eyes flick to my cargo of pastries. 'How's Project Owen?'

'Great!' I say automatically. But my face crumples.

Grace and Brian trade glances.

'Okay...' she says, inching away from me. 'That's good.'

I put my bags back on the counter and lean as heavily as I dare against the glass cabinet. 'Actually,' I say, 'not fine. Awful. Bloody awful. I tried to get fit and can barely move. And I went on a diet and ate a whole rice pudding – and –'

Grace looks at the pastry bags again. 'Right,' she says. Then she tugs off a glove and reaches into her bag for her purse. 'Brian,' she says, 'I think Bella and I need some custard tarts.'

'I don't need custard tarts!' I wail. 'I'm fatter than ever and if I buy custard tarts I'll – well, I'll eat them.'

Brian looks puzzled and is no doubt about to say that's the whole idea.

But Grace takes my arm gently and shakes her head. 'They're not for you,' she says. 'We're going to see Amelia.'

~ ~ ~

I don't tend to visit Amelia at work: she's usually ferociously busy with the phone and paperwork, or sweet-talking clients into the merits of investing in property.

'She won't mind,' Grace says. 'Anyway, I need to drop off more business cards.'

Grace explains that on first coming to Saffron Sweeting, she worked for Amelia for a while, and still helps out part time. 'My main thing now is corporate relocations, but I'm slowly getting my interior design business off the ground.'

Together, we cross the wind-ravaged street from the bakery to Hargraves Estate Agency. Grace walks like a normal person, while I do a combination of a limp and a waddle, wincing as I negotiate the two small steps down into Amelia's office.

'Look who I found,' says Grace, by way of a greeting.

Amelia waves from behind her desk, her phone tucked under her ear as she leaves a message for someone. Apparently an offer has been increased to two million but must be accepted within twenty-four hours. Serious money, whatever the property.

Grace pulls business cards from her bag and begins restocking a holder near the door.

I lower myself gingerly into one of the visitor chairs and drop the bakery bags on the coffee table.

'Bella,' says Amelia finally, getting up and coming towards us, 'you look ghastly!'

'Thanks.'

'What happened?' Amelia looks at Grace, as if I might be too delicate to explain.

'CrossFit,' I say.

Amelia looks blank, but Grace puts her head on one side. 'I've heard of that.'

I give them a gloomy rundown of the class, my shameful split leggings, and the aftermath.

Amelia throws back her head and laughs. 'I like the daisy knicker part.'

I shake my head. 'I'm not sure I'll ever walk properly again.'

'Of course you will,' Grace says. 'I tried jogging once or twice: deadly, the next day.'

'And I lasted five days on my diet...' The past tense is clear.

Amelia spots the white paper bags. 'Good for you,' she says, but I notice her lick her lips.

'I hate myself,' I say, also looking at the bags.

'Oh, Bella,' Grace begins, 'don't say that. It's hard when you're feeling down. You can't count calories in a crisis.' She looks at Amelia, as if this is a mantra they've shared before.

'Absolutely!' Amelia nods vigorously.

I droop further. 'I'm just so exhausted. And hungry.'

'Well, you will be,' Grace says, 'if you did CrossFit on an empty stomach. Did Morgan take you?' Then, as I nod, 'I thought she looked scary.'

'Are all American women like that?' I ask. 'I need to know what I'm up against.'

Grace considers the question. 'I really can't generalise,' she says. 'But the one who tried to pinch my husband was pretty scary, yes.'

For a moment I forget my own anxieties to gape at her. I'm dying to know more, but don't like to ask.

'Of course they're not all like that,' Amelia says. 'Most of my clients are sweethearts.'

'You would say that,' says Grace, 'you're flogging them houses.'

Amelia's property business owes much of its recent success to the influx of Americans to Saffron Sweeting. But she herself is so foxy and confident, she's almost like one of them.

'I'm serious,' I say. 'Am I kidding myself I even have a chance?' I gesture desperately. 'Look at me.'

Grace shakes her head. 'Don't be silly.' But she looks at Amelia for support.

'Absolutely, darling,' Amelia says. 'If you're sure you want him. We'll just spruce you up a bit.'

'But the first thing to do,' Grace says, 'is to eat something. Amelia, we brought custard tarts.'

My aunt doesn't hide her glee. 'Did you, darling? Bloody good show!'

Grace grins. 'I'll put the kettle on.'

Twenty minutes later, when Amelia has demolished two custard tarts and Grace and I have agreed Morgan really *doesn't* need that whole apple pie to herself, I take a deep breath.

'Okay,' I say. 'I do feel a bit better.'

'Of course you do!' they exclaim in unison.

'Morgan told me to try bananas,' I say. 'I'm not sure whether I was supposed to eat one or rub it into my legs.'

Amelia eyes the remaining pastries. 'I had a chocolate massage once. Frightful waste.' Her phone starts to ring and she ignores it, but then clicks her fingers as if reminded that time is money. 'Right. Back to Project Owen.' She looks at me intently. 'Bella, darling, are you *sure* you want him back?

You don't think you can do better?'

I nod my head at the first question, then switch to shaking. 'Yes. No. I do. I mean, I don't.'

I might look and feel like something the cat dragged in, but I've never been more sure about anything. 'I still love him. I always will.'

My aunt gives a low whistle, but Grace nods and leans in. 'Right. So. What do we know?' she asks.

Amelia sits back and begins circling an ankle in its shiny brown boot. 'I spoke to the HR manager,' she says. 'Owen starts work at the Science Park the first Monday in March.'

I gasp. 'Oh my God. That's, like, ten days away.'

'Wow,' says Grace. 'Fast.'

'You know how these American companies are,' Amelia says. 'Once they make a decision, they don't dillydally.'

I'm silent, digesting the news that Owen will be back on English soil so soon. Apart from the failed CrossFit attempt, I've done nothing practical to prepare. Extensive daydreaming hardly counts. Nor does allowing dozens of non-cake wedding images to creep onto my Pinterest board.

'There's more.' Amelia waits for me to look up. 'They're putting him in Grey Stoke House.'

Grace sniffs. 'Those are the new short-term apartments,' she says to me. 'They're at your end of the village, on the road to Grey Stoke Farm. Corporate clients love them.' Then, in an aside to Amelia, 'I can't believe they got them done so quickly.'

'Got to hand it to Scott.' Amelia nods. 'Whatever you think of it, Grace, they did a nice job.'

Grace frowns, but I don't want to discuss my misguided one-night guy or his boring building project. I'm reeling from this news. 'You mean,' I say, 'Owen will be *living* in Saffron Sweeting?'

'Yes,' says Amelia. 'Arriving any day.'

If CrossFit made me sick and dizzy, now I think I might pass out. I put my hands over my face.

'I'm not ready,' I say. 'I can't see him yet.'

Amelia picks up the phone. 'Darling,' she says, 'you'll be ready. But I think we all agree, there's no time to lose.'

Chapter 6

The next evening, I'm staring into the fridge and wondering how many calories are in a Welsh Rarebit – millions, no doubt – when Amelia turns up, brandishing a roll of black bin bags.

'Right, darling.' She marches straight up the stairs. 'Let's see what you've got.'

Having hurled the contents of my wardrobe onto my bed, she gestures at the pile. 'Either it makes you look gorgeous, or it doesn't. If it doesn't, out it goes.'

I thank my lucky stars the Vera Wang dress is concealed back under my bed.

But nothing else is safe. Not wasting a minute, my aunt begins holding clothing up against me, passing verdict at breakneck speed. Every so often she makes me try something on, but in general the death sentence is handed down instantly.

'What are you doing?' I panic. 'I need that!'

'No, you don't.' Amelia flings my favourite black T-shirt on the discard pile. The bigger pile, incidentally. 'It's drab.'

'I wear those to work,' I say, as she holds up two perfectly serviceable skirts.

'And you look like one of the bedders, I expect,' she retorts, referring to the college staff who used to make the students' beds but now do general cleaning around Trewe. But she puts the grey one on the 'keeping' pile.

Preoccupied with hiding the special shoebox in which I've saved every birthday and Christmas card Owen ever bought me, I turn to find her dangling my Cath Kidston pyjamas between pinched fingertips.

'No!' I say. 'Not my floral PJs.'

Amelia pauses, one hand on a hip. 'Okay. But if you get to the point where Owen's staying over –' she waits for emphasis, then continues, 'you are *not* to wear these.

Understood?'

I nod. Part of me is horrified at the growing pile of rejects, another is quietly relieved to have someone take charge. And I'm secretly fascinated by her choices.

'Those are for fat days,' I say, as she stretches the waistband of my sensible navy trousers.

'Not any more they're not. You're losing weight, right?'

I don't like to tell her I did lose a bit, but then put it all back on after the CrossFit fiasco.

Later, we open a bottle of wine and I compromise by making us toast and Marmite, with no melted cheese in sight. Amelia lugs three black bags of clothing to the front door, ready for donating.

'Well, that was a good rootle,' she says. 'Important to work out what you've got, before filling in the gaps.'

'Gaps?' I reach for more Marmite, hoping it's a lower calorie choice than honey or Nutella, which are what I really fancy.

'Gaps, darling,' she nods. 'You're riddled with them.' She swirls the wine in her glass, gesturing with the other hand as if the offending holes are all around us. 'Tomorrow I have to work, but you're going into Cambridge to see Fabiana.'

~~~

The name sounded familiar, and when I get to the small shop on Bridge Street, I realise why. One of Joey's three sisters – fortunately, the one obsessed with fashion, not the plumber – has a Saturday job at a boutique. The tiny space is brimming with accessories.

'Amelia sent me,' I say.

'We know,' chorus Fabiana and the shop's owner.

'She told us what you need,' says the owner, who's called Bo and is clearly sizing me up.

'And you'll get my employee discount,' adds Fabiana, a

hint of Italian in her accent.

'Great,' I say, immediately anxious for the health of my current account.

But I can't think of a way to back out, and before I know it, they're festooning me in hats. A fedora, a trilby, a beret and a knitted cap are all tried and rejected, before a baker's boy style is proclaimed just right.

'You look like Keira Knightley in *Love Actually*!' cries Fabiana, making my insides flutter in gratitude, even though I'm sure I don't.

'Agreed!' says Bo. 'But take this felt one too.'

Fabiana claps approval. 'English women don't wear enough hats.'

Well, I think, it's easy for her, she's half Italian. She was born looking stylish, probably donning designer sunglasses before her first nappy.

The hat attack is followed by scarves of all colours. Unfortunately I can't pull off either a long Doctor Who shape or the square Audrey Hepburn kind. I must have a short neck.

'No problem, try this.' Bo drapes soft cobalt blue around me.

'Oh,' I say, 'that's gorgeous. Is it cashmere?' I brace for a three figure price tag.

'Nope!' replies Fabiana. 'Brilliant imitation, though.'

'I'll take it.' I decide that until I can have Owen wrapped around my neck, this will do nicely.

'It comes in this pistachio too,' adds Joey's sister. 'Good with your hair.'

Five minutes later, I'm sporting an armful of bangles and a couple of necklaces.

'This one's on a cord.' Bo demonstrates. 'You can adjust the length.'

'Make sure...' Fabiana gives a coquettish smile, '...that it hangs at your cleavage. That'll draw his eye.'

'Oh.' I squirm. 'Amelia told you?'

'No,' Fabiana grins. 'Joey did. We're all rooting for you!'

I nod awkwardly, not sure whether to be pleased to have so much support, or nervous at the additional pressure. What happens if Owen wants nothing to do with me? Will half of Cambridge know I've been rejected – again?

'Okay, final thing.' Bo brings us back to business. 'Fabby, you wanted to give Bella one of your bags.'

'I did! I do! Bella, come over here and pick something *magnifico*!'

'No,' I say, 'I couldn't possibly.'

But she insists. 'You must. Haven't you heard the theory about bags and shoes?'

I hesitate. 'I don't think so.'

Fabiana gives a saucy wiggle in the middle of the shop. 'Great shoes show off your hips and bum. Whereas a beautiful shoulder bag is like jewellery for your boobs. Both places men love to look!'

'Okay...' I'm blushing now. Of course I want Owen to notice me, but I'd like him to notice more than *those* parts.

Then again, with my wobbly stomach and thighs, maybe those parts would be just fine.

~ ~ ~

'It's like being caught in a typhoon at Paris fashion week,' I say to Grace on Wednesday after work. 'So many clothes have been flying around.'

I'm sitting, nerves jangling, in one of the fancy swivel chairs belonging to Amelia's scary hairdresser.

'Just a trim, please,' I beg, as he sizes up my head through narrowed eyes.

Grace, who claimed she happened to be shopping in Cambridge but was probably dispatched by Amelia to make sure I turned up for the hair appointment, shakes her head. 'Don't worry. She sent me here too. You'll come out feeling wonderful.'

'Really?' I say, as Jean-Claude prances away. 'You too?'

Grace leans in. 'He's awfully good.' She throws her magazine back on the pile. 'Has Amelia taken you underwear shopping yet? Watch out for that.'

'Underwear? No.' I pause to wonder why Grace needed to be taken underwear shopping, but decide not to ask. 'Everything but.' I fill her in on Friday's wardrobe massacre and Saturday's visit to Fabiana.

'Then on Sunday,' I say, 'she dragged me to Debenhams and made me buy a new coat.'

We hurtled into Cambridge in Amelia's green Mercedes, parked across two spaces, and within minutes I was modelling coats. My aunt's logic was, with at least two months of winter left, there's a good chance that when I do bump into Owen, I'll be wearing it.

'What colour?' Grace asks.

'Owen's favourite,' I say. 'Blue. He supports Chelsea. Amelia said it matches my eyes.'

And I hope it doesn't bankrupt me at the dry cleaner's.

Grace nods. 'You have nice eyes.'

She really is a kind person. Maybe I'd enjoy getting to know her better, even if she did have a fling thing with Scott. But that doesn't matter, I tell myself. I'm totally over him and focussed on Owen now.

'Then,' I say, 'Amelia did a smash and grab in Next. I came out with four colourful new tops.'

Jean-Claude's back, brandishing scissors.

'And shoes?' Grace asks. 'She has a thing about shoes.'

'Actually, she seemed mildly satisfied with my footwear.' I quite like my feet and, when other clothes look awful on my plump frame, shoes are more gratifying to buy. Amelia approved of my burgundy slingbacks, bronze loafers and zebra-print ballerinas. 'The only thing missing, she said, was boots. She frogmarched me into Russell & Bromley, picked out a stunning pair of grey suede Chelsea boots, and declared them an early birthday present.'

'When's your birthday?'

'Not until September. I'm a Libra,' I say. 'Last but not

least, she's been onto some friend in Scotland who's a cashmere wholesaler. Not sure what she ordered for me; it hasn't arrived yet.'

'Well,' says Grace, as Jean-Claude steps back and surveys his work, 'one thing we know about Amelia: when she's on your side, she's really on your side. Like a fairy godmother, almost.'

'Yes,' I say. 'I'm incredibly grateful.'

But what I don't say, as I move my head carefully and notice how light it feels, is that I'm not sure I need a fairy godmother. I think what I need is a cupid.

Chapter 7

I open the pub's dishwasher, and through the steam I see a silhouette which looks like Owen.

I'm full time now at Trewe College but for a while, when I was only employed part time, I used to work for Fergus at The Plough. He's been clobbered by the horrible bug that's going around, so I'm helping tonight as a favour. It's no hardship: the pub is cosy, convivial, and steeped in the aroma of my favourite comfort foods. Plus, Joey once told me the dim lighting is supremely flattering.

Wait: it *is* Owen.

'Oh my gosh. I don't believe it.' I grab Sophie's arm. 'Don't look!' I squeak this last part as, inevitably, she turns towards the door.

'Considering you've spent the last couple of weeks in a total tizz with precisely this moment in mind, I thought you would believe it,' she replies.

I tut. She never used to be this pernickety. Inseparable as childhood friends, we lost touch when we went to different universities and only met again at her aunt's funeral a few years ago. After that we were housemates, which I adored. She was far nicer than Morgan, and only marginally more messy.

My eyes dart around the pub, then back to Owen. It's him. In the flesh. Not only back on English soil, but back in Saffron Sweeting, mere yards away. I could vault this sturdy wooden bar and be in his arms in two seconds. Well, all right, maybe not vault it. Maybe run around it instead.

'What do I do?' I hiss to Sophie. My palms are clammy and gleeful dread swirls in my chest.

'Act natural,' she says. 'Do what you've been doing. And I'd like some salt and vinegar crisps, please.'

I pass her a packet, but my gaze doesn't budge from Owen. The jukebox is playing Mariah Carey and the scene before me takes on a softer focus.

'He's still gorgeous,' I murmur, and Sophie turns surreptitiously on her barstool.

'Which one?' she asks.

Incredibly, she's never actually met him. Owen had already gone to the States when Sophie and I reconnected. And apparently she wasn't paying attention to all the photos I made her look at last week.

'The tall one,' I reply, drinking in Owen's appearance. 'With the muscles.'

He looks like he spent the last few years on the beach in California, not in a research laboratory. He's wearing a dark, long-sleeved T-shirt, but it's tight enough for me to see he's in fantastic shape. His sandy hair has the perfect amount of messiness, flopping forward when he moves.

Sophie nods and turns back.

'I'm not ready to see him.' Having waited so long for this moment, now it's here, I want to hide. 'You need to take over.' I eye the trapdoor behind the bar which leads to the cellar.

'You are ready,' Sophie mutters. 'You look fab. Stay where you are.'

I truly wasn't expecting to see Owen tonight, but I've been heeding Amelia's advice and dressed carefully anyway. I'm wearing a periwinkle cashmere sweater – newly arrived from her friend in Elgin – dark jeans and my new Russell & Bromley boots. My haircut has been a hit with everyone, including Sophie, who wouldn't normally notice. Even my boss, Gertrude, said it looked 'nice', which from her is high praise.

'I shouldn't have eaten those pancakes,' I say.

Yesterday was Shrove Tuesday and I suddenly regret the extra calories I consumed. Even though I made them wafer thin, and rolled mine carefully with lemon and a sprinkling of sugar, I wish now I'd shunned them altogether.

'Don't be daft.' Sophie, my partner-in-pancakes the night before, licks her lips as if remembering. She, of course, slathered hers in golden syrup and wolfed them ecstatically.

I grab a glass, which is perfectly clean, and begin polishing it. Perhaps he won't come over, I think. At least, not yet.

But not many people walk into a pub unless they want a drink, and in England, the only way of getting that drink is at the bar. From the corner of my eye, I see Owen heading my way. I know I'm already pink as I duck my head and focus on my glass polishing. It's so shiny, I can see my reflection in it.

As he clears his throat in the time-honoured way of signalling to a British bartender you'd like a drink, without actually coming out and saying so, I force myself to look up. Here, at least, I have a tiny advantage from spotting him first.

'Two Adnams please.' He's looking down at his wallet, pulling out a note.

'Hi, Owen,' I say, in a voice which is strangely breathy.

He looks up and does a double take. Clearly, he was not expecting to bump into the woman he'd lived with for six years, tonight.

'Wow!' he says. 'Yeah. Hi. Wow.'

My cheeks tug upwards as joy washes over me.

'It's good to see you,' I say, editing my thought just in time. *So damn good.*

'Yeah. Wow,' he says again. Not exactly smooth conversation, but understandable in the circumstances.

'Two pints of Adnams,' I confirm, and turn to get the drinks. My hands are wobbling and I think I might be holding my breath as I pull the pints, concentrating so I don't present him with a mass of foam.

I place the beers gingerly on the bar, take his money and find change. Frankly, he could have paid in dollars and I wouldn't have noticed. 'There you go,' I say, and wipe my hands on a bar towel, not because they're beery, but because it gives me something to do with them.

There are slight laughter creases at the corners of his

eyes, which are the sparkling blue of an alpine river. But they're not a cold blue. He can melt me, just by looking.

'You work here?' he asks, staring incredulously.

'Helping out,' I say. 'I live in Saffron Sweeting now.' When we were together, we had a flat in Cambridge. 'Hang on, I'll come around.'

This last bit is so we don't have the barrier of the bar between us. Maybe, if I join him on the other side, he'll take me in his arms like I've been yearning for. Or at least give me a friendly hug.

'Oh. Right. Wow.'

Hmm, that's three wows in a row. Is that a sign he's happy to see me?

'Er, this is Sophie,' I say, once I'm on the correct side of the bar. The embrace was not forthcoming and we stand at an awkward British distance from each other.

My friend is sizing Owen up through narrowed eyes. They shake hands.

'Owen,' he says.

She nods. 'Bella told me about you.'

I brace myself. Is she going to mention that I'm glammed up solely for his benefit? That I've barely slept – let alone eaten – since the news of his impending arrival? Or is she planning to tell him off for living with me for years and then leaving me high and dry?

Fortunately, she does none of these, just reaches for a crisp and bites it thoughtfully. I notice she doesn't offer one to Owen, which means she's reserving judgement. Sophie's careful about sharing her crisps.

'So... this is Jasper.' Owen half turns to the short, plump man with him. 'My boss.'

I know this: Jasper Lyon-Bowles was mentioned in the news article, which of course I can recite in my sleep. Sophie and I murmur polite hellos.

Then Owen finally reaches out and places a hand on my shoulder. 'And this is Bella,' he says to Jasper.

My whole body quivers from the light pressure. I don't

know if he feels it, but he smiles at me, and my heart lifts as I glimpse the old Owen – the one who used to bring me cups of tea in bed and write silly poems for my birthday.

'And what brings you to Saffron Sweeting?' Sophie asks Jasper, although naturally she's been briefed by me.

While Owen's boss gives two sentences on their work and the stint at the Science Park, Owen releases my shoulder and looks down at his phone. I take the opportunity to regain my composure and get my shallow breathing under control. Another moment and I'd have been tempted to nuzzle his hand with my cheek.

Jasper's accent is American, though he attended Trewe College as a student. 'I'm real thrilled to be back in Cambridge,' he says. 'Can't think of anywhere better to go head to head with the human rhinovirus.'

Sophie pauses before speaking. I know her brain is whirring. There's a distinct danger she's about to crack a joke, possibly involving horns.

'That's colds,' I say quickly, to divert her. I'm proud to have remembered the scientific term. 'You know, sneezing and... stuff...'

I trail off, trying to hide my surprise. Although this was Owen's original specialism, I thought his work in America was battling malignant tumours, not sniffles. The rhinovirus doesn't sound right at all.

'And you, Owen? Are you pleased to be back?' Sophie asks.

I've been staring openly at the love of my life, and am caught out when he looks up.

'Huh? Yeah. It's great.' He pockets his phone. 'Really great.'

I have to work to stop a big smile spreading across my face. All right, his tone was a little flat, but he was looking at me as he said that. He's surprised, but pleased. I know he is.

'Oy, Bella.' The interruption comes from further along the bar. 'What does a chap have to do to get a drink in here?'

'Sorry,' I call to the village postman, 'sorry, coming.'

As I move away to take the postie's drink order, I look back towards Owen and Jasper and see them heading across the bar to an empty table. I'm disappointed, but perhaps it's for the best. Owen might not want Jasper to know I'm his ex, and I was struggling to think of any conversation which wouldn't reveal my extensive online research. It's okay for Sophie to ask questions that she already knows the answer to, but I'm not sure I can pull that off.

The Plough's humming with customers now and for the next thirty minutes I'm kept busy serving drinks. I don't even get the chance to round up empty glasses, meaning I can't sidle past Owen's table and hear what they're saying. But I do notice that he and Jasper leave after that one drink.

'So?' I say to Sophie when they've gone. 'What do you think? Isn't he amazing?'

Sophie wrinkles her forehead. 'I don't know,' she says. 'He seems fine.'

'Fine?' I repeat, stressing the 'F' so she'll know I'm dissatisfied with that answer. 'He's like a dream come true. I can't believe he's back. Here. In Saffron Sweeting. In my pub.'

'It's not your pub–' Sophie begins, then raises a hand as I shake my head. 'Okay,' she says. 'So he's back. But I don't think you should read too much into it.'

'I'm not reading too much into it,' I protest, though I know I won't sleep a wink tonight as I replay our conversation.

'What's so amazing about him, anyway?' Sophie asks. 'I mean, after all this time…'

'Oh, Soph,' I say, my mind already on rewind. 'He's just so brilliant. He was so intense, you know? We'd stay up all night, sometimes, just talking.' In fact, we were so broke in the early days, we couldn't actually afford other forms of entertainment. 'I could tell he was going to change the world of medicine and he said he wanted me right there, beside him.'

'But he hasn't changed the world,' Sophie says with

trademark frankness.

'Well, no, not so far.'

She's kind enough not to mention the other bit, about me being there beside him.

'And I could tell he was glad to see me,' I say.

Sophie looks at me, then swirls the whisky in her glass. How she can drink that filthy stuff, I don't know.

'What?' I ask.

She looks up. 'I'm sure Owen's talented,' she says, 'but... Bell... he didn't come back here to see you.'

I fold my arms. 'What do you mean?'

She shrugs. 'He's here for work. He didn't even know you're in Saffron Sweeting.'

'I know,' I say, dipping my chin. 'I know he was a bit shocked to see me. But now he's here...'

Sophie takes a long drink and exhales as she puts her glass down.

'You're sure you want him back?' she asks. 'I mean, he did leave you and go off–'

'Yes,' I interrupt. Now that I've seen him, it's as if I've drunk three Baileys-laced chocolate mochas in quick succession. It's sweet, giddy, and energising. I'm on an Owen high.

'Yes,' I repeat. 'He's all I've ever wanted. I just need him to see it too.'

Chapter 8

For the rest of the week, I have permanent stage fright. Having met Owen in the flesh, I'm a bundle of nerves. As I go about my daily activities in the village, I'm constantly on edge with the thought I might see him again. Thanking my lucky stars I looked half decent that night in the pub, I am following Amelia's advice to the letter. I've banished my remaining ratty clothes to the back of the wardrobe and wear my new blue coat whenever I leave the house. I'm washing my hair every day and am never without mascara and lip gloss. Well, except for in bed and in the bath.

My anxiety isn't helped on Friday when I get a hurried phone call from Lorraine, who runs the bed and breakfast. We're supposed to host our monthly supper club tomorrow. One day, I might start my own catering company, but for now the dinners quell my urges to entertain.

'Sorry. Off to Devon,' Lorraine gabbles. 'My daughter's gone into labour.'

'Oh.' This is premature. 'I hope everything's okay.'

'Don't cancel supper,' she says. 'Have it here at Oak House, like usual.'

'Okay...'

It would indeed be a shame to disappoint people who've registered for dinner. And using the dining room at the bed and breakfast will be much easier than squishing them all in at my house. We don't advertise, so our guests come through word of mouth. And we're not supposed to charge, since we're not licensed for alcohol. Instead, we have a suggested donation and so far nobody has even murmured a protest.

Still, dinner is a heap of work for one.

'Call Sophie,' Lorraine suggests. 'She'll help.'

'Sophie can't cook to save her life.' I picture bits of fingernail in the carrots.

'No,' Lorraine laughs. 'But Tom can.'

~ ~ ~

'So you haven't seen Owen again?' says Sophie on Saturday, as we set the Oak House dining table for nine. I love this room: its deep red walls and latticed window seem to nourish conversation and confidences.

'No. Not a glimpse.' I try not to sound despondent.

Admittedly, early March isn't a time when people linger in the street in Saffron Sweeting. In fact, the High Street is ideally positioned to channel the east wind which apparently leaves Siberia and doesn't stop until it reaches us here in the Fens. Brian invested in a couple of tables and chairs outside his bakery to encourage people to sit and chat, but those are deserted for the winter. So aside from the pub, the only other village gathering spot is the old bank. That now houses Mary Lou's nearly new shop which has a tiny coffee area, but it's mainly frequented by mothers and their broods. Owen's hardly likely to hang out there for fun.

'You should have asked him to dinner.' Sophie's boyfriend, Tom, arrives from the kitchen with four upside down wine glasses in each hand.

'I couldn't do that,' I reply. 'Far too forward.'

'But you lived with the guy–' Tom begins, then stops as I shake my head.

Please, not the six year thing again. I busy myself putting fresh candles in their holders.

Tom shrugs in the way he does when he's pretending not to understand our mysterious female ways. But in fact he understands Sophie wonderfully, better than anyone, except possibly me. He's been so good for her, I might forgive him for stealing my best ever housemate. She's calmer these days, and much more confident. Plus, she now has a relationship with her mother which borders on functional.

As for Tom, I'm embarrassed he knows about my quest

to win Owen back. But naturally, confiding in Sophie meant Tom heard all of it too. Not that I don't like Tom – I do – but I'm shy around him. Heart-stoppingly good-looking, he manages a family business and also finds time to pilot small planes. And he's just the kind of person you'd want behind the controls in a crisis: level-headed and reassuring. If I weren't totally in love with Owen, I might have a little crush on Tom instead.

'Still.' Tom's helping Sophie fold a linen napkin, his fingers guiding hers. 'Cooking's your magic weapon, Bella.' He looks up at me. 'Maybe you should use it.'

~ ~ ~

Tonight's guests are a mellow bunch. One couple is American, sent to us by Amelia to experience an English-style dinner party. They introduce themselves as Ted and Betsy and hand me a bottle of port.

'A small gift,' Betsy lays a manicured hand on my arm, 'to thank you for inviting us to your home.'

I decide not to explain that this isn't my home and that Lorraine is away helping to deliver twins. But I'm relieved when Ted slips me a cheque too: they haven't got the wrong end of the stick about paying for dinner.

Ted and Betsy would call the next couple African American, except they aren't American, and probably not African. 'We've just moved to Cambridge, from Shrewsbury,' says the woman, who's wearing a draped dress in an amazing shade of ochre. Her husband gives me a dazzling smile and says how much he's looking forward to dinner. 'I cook a little,' he confides, 'but am always looking for inspiration.' He sniffs appreciatively at the rich aroma of roasting meat coming from the Aga.

I'm in the kitchen when the final couple arrive, so I only have time for a quick hello while offering canapés.

'Really sorry we're late,' says the woman, Caroline,

who's slim and near my age. Her hair's in a ponytail and she has wide set eyes. 'I was held up at work and Leo forgot.'

Leo says nothing, just nods and shakes my hand while I balance the nibbles carefully in the other. Either he's a man of few words, or she's dragged him out on a Saturday night against his will. But beyond his olive skin and dark hair, I don't have time to weigh him up before moving on.

~~~

'It's a lot like flying a plane,' Tom says later, when I compliment him on the main course of tender lamb chops, buttery mashed swede and crunchy English cabbage. 'You just do all the right steps in the right order. Except you don't have to account for wind. Usually.'

I laugh. 'If that's the case, how come Sophie can keep an entire plane in the air but can't prevent a soufflé from crashing?'

Tom looks at his girlfriend, who fortunately is talking to someone else, and grins. Oh, I think, if only I could find a man to look at me like that. 'Okay, Bella,' he says. 'You've got me.'

Having left a suitable pause after the main course, I prepare to serve dessert: lemon drizzle cake with raspberries. After that, I can relax. I love these dinners but am always anxious until I see that people are enjoying themselves and that the food is a hit.

'Are we ready to move around?' I ask.

The guests – a well-mannered lot tonight – nod agreement.

Lorraine and I came up with this plan a few months ago, after we realised that her long narrow table meant the group as a whole had difficulty conversing. So now, half of us move to a new seat after the main course, meaning everyone gets a chance to chat with someone new.

'It's like the Mad Hatter's tea party,' Tom said, when I

first explained it.

'I like it,' Sophie said. 'It means if you're stuck with a complete prat for the first two courses, you can escape.'

With the lemon drizzle cake served and conversation bubbling happily around the table, I move the requisite number of places and find Leo on my right.

'I'm sorry I was in a rush before dinner,' I say. 'I hope you didn't find me rude.'

'Not at all.' He glances at me. 'You were busy. The food was delicious.'

That sounded like a compliment, but he still doesn't smile, which is a waste because he'd be quite attractive if he wasn't glowering. I notice he has dark eyes, which makes any expression there hard to read, especially in the candlelight. The rest of his face isn't mean, just guarded.

'So...' I'm glad I only need to make polite conversation for a few minutes. 'You heard about tonight through Violet? At the post office?'

'Yes,' Leo replies, cutting into his cake with a fork. 'At least, Cazz did. She loves meeting new people.'

And you clearly don't, I infer. Still, I press on. 'You live in the village?'

He nods. 'Just moved back. My father has plenty of space and I'm not sure how long I'll be here.'

'Your father?'

'Kenneth Chadwick. You might know him – he runs the library. It's not ideal to live with dad, but rents are expensive so...'

He's right about the cost of accommodation in Cambridge. After the fire at my bedsit, it didn't take me long to work out that house sitting for my Uncle Mike would save me a fortune. And I do know Kenneth, a pompous man who likes everyone to acknowledge how brainy he is. Did his son inherit the aloofness?

'You're not staying permanently?' I'm distracted, looking around the table to ascertain that dessert is a hit. Sophie's eaten her slice already, and Ted and Betsy have almost finished theirs as they talk animatedly with the couple from Shrewsbury. But I notice that Caroline is pushing hers around her plate, picking at the raspberries. She's not wearing a wedding ring, and from curiosity I check Leo's left hand too. Also bare.

'I'm working at Saffron Hall,' Leo replies, a piece of the lemony cake poised on his fork. 'Restoring the wood panels in the ballroom. I'm a carpenter.' Unlike his girlfriend, he's making steady progress with his food.

'Oh, right,' I murmur, wondering if his wooden personality has been influenced by his work. I revert to my hostess role. 'Is the dessert not okay, Caroline?'

'Oh.' She looks up, embarrassed. 'It's fine. Very nice. But I'm trying to avoid refined sugar.' She shrugs, as if spurning sugar is as common as preferring your water without anthrax.

'You can't talk, Bell,' chips in Sophie from across the table. 'You've hardly had any.'

Darn, she noticed. I cut myself only a slither and have been taking sips of water between every citrusy nibble. Every. Single. Nibble.

I frown at her, wishing she hadn't drawn attention to the cook's failure to eat her own creation. 'I'm watching my weight, remember?'

I'm not just watching my weight. *Watching* implies I'm lying on the settee, martini in hand, contemplating the rolls of fat around my waist. *Watching* suggests I'm mildly entertained by the number I see on the scales each day. *Watching* hints that I don't much care if that number goes up or down. And I do care. I care passionately. It's absolutely vital that if – no – *when* Owen puts his arms around me again, he doesn't feel any blubber.

In the week after I heard he was coming back, I lost a bit. Then – after the CrossFit wobble – a bit more. This week, it's back. All of it. It's not like I stopped being careful – although there was that time at work when Professor Palin brought in brownies. And the other night I may have had a small mishap with a container of ice cream while rewatching the first season of *Downton Abbey*. But in general I've been really careful. Yet despite my new haircut, new clothes, and new jewellery, I'm carrying the same old fat.

'Oh! So you are,' Sophie says.

Shut up, I pray silently. I just charged people a pretty penny to eat a dinner I cooked which contained butter, cream and full-fat cheese. And yes, sugar. I love you to bits, Soph, but now *shut up*.

But she doesn't. Sophie, who has never been on a diet in her life, puts her head on one side. 'How much have you lost, then?'

A sigh jumps out before I can help it. I look at the ceiling. Fortunately Leo, who clearly has no interest in diet conversations, is now talking to Betsy, on his other side.

Finally, Sophie catches on and changes the subject. 'Hey! Great idea: you should join Caroline's group.'

Caroline, who's next to Sophie and opposite Leo, looks our way when she hears her name.

'What group?' I have to say, out of politeness.

'Caroline has a running thing starting. Don't you?' Sophie looks at our dinner guest, who nods.

'Yes. It's called Couch to 5K.'

'What's that?' I ask.

Caroline puts down her fork – she wasn't using it anyway – and dabs her mouth with her napkin.

'It's an eight week programme to get people who, er, don't exercise to be able to walk or run a five kilometre race.'

'That's about three miles,' Sophie adds, thinking she's being helpful.

Caroline, who's so slender she probably jogs that far as a warm-up before her twenty mile run, nods. 'We're raising money for leukaemia research.'

Sophie grins at me. 'See! It's for a good cause.'

I shake my head. 'Sorry. I'm not really the active type.' What I mean is, after CrossFit, I am never doing anything involving lunges or squats again. Ever.

'That's the whole point,' says Caroline. 'We take it very slowly. We'll be gentle with you, I promise.'

Yeah, I think. Gentle means forty burpees instead of fifty.

'And Caroline's the coach,' Sophie tells me helpfully.

I wish she'd kept on about my weight, instead.

Caroline nods. 'We volunteer our time, and then on race day we run with you, every step of the way.'

'We?' I ask, reluctantly drawn into the conversation.

'Me and Leo,' she replies, as if it's obvious.

Great. So Mister Grumpy gets to make me do press-ups too. From the look of him, he'll put a foot on my back for good measure.

'I really don't –' I begin, but Caroline talks over me.

'Leo, do you have any of the leaflets on you?'

Leo, who's finishing his dessert, exhales through his teeth. The candle in front of us flickers violently. 'No. You hustled me out of the door without even a jacket. Of course I don't have any leaflets on me.'

Ooh, he really is grouchy. Although I suppose it is going to be chilly out there, if they're walking home. His shirt, brushed cotton in a graphite shade, is hardly adequate.

Then he turns to me, his voice a bit softer. 'It's for a worthy cause. We've done it before. And we want people to enjoy it, not suffer. The training's very gradual.'

So, he guessed I was picturing burpees.

I nod to Sophie that she can help herself to more dessert. She does so, and passes the cake plate around the table. To my gratification, I notice several people cut second slices.

'What do you get out if it?' I ask Leo.

'My sister had leukaemia. When she was twelve.'

'Oh.' I grapple for what to say. 'I'm sorry. Is she –' It's too late to cover my clumsy reaction.

'She's fine now.' Leo reaches for more lemon drizzle cake too.

Relieved, I smile at him, and am amazed when he

smiles back. It makes such a difference to his face, like a whole cloud has lifted. I drop my eyes first.

'We'd love to have you in the group,' Caroline says. 'It starts next week.'

Sophie's staring at me meaningfully. I recognise that look: it's the same one I used on her, when she was trying to wriggle out of tackling her fear of flying.

'It sounds brilliant,' she says, waving her fork for emphasis. 'You'd really get in shape.'

I gaze disconsolately at the lemon drizzle cake on Sophie's fork and think about the flab I want to tame. I recall the atrocious CrossFit class as I compare my wings with Caroline's toned arms and shoulders. I look at the couples around the table, and the empty chair at the other end. And I'm filled with renewed resolve, that at next month's supper party I want Owen to be occupying it. Maybe I *will* do as Tom suggested, and invite him.

But before that, I need to lose some weight. I'll never be as lean as Caroline or even as trim as Sophie, but I can at least ditch a few pounds. And three miles isn't far – only a couple of circuits around the village. I'll manage that in no time.

'Okay,' I say, thinking that now I've decided to start running, I can reward myself with a normal helping of dessert. 'Where do I sign up?'

Chapter 9

As I shuffle from foot to foot at the edge of the school playing field, there's a crunching of frost. The moon has sensibly found somewhere warmer to hang out, and the quaint but low wattage Saffron Sweeting streetlights aren't helping much. It may be March, but spring still seems like years away.

'Bloody hell, darling, how did I let you talk me into this?' Amelia slams her car door shut and strides towards me across the grass. She only lives half a mile away but clearly found it necessary to drive here.

'I didn't talk you into it,' I reply through teeth which threaten to chatter. 'As I recall, you said it sounded like a blast.'

Amelia adjusts her fake fur earmuffs. Well, I hope they're fake, and not the result of a collision with a badger. 'Blasted cold, I meant. Crumbs, Grace, you too?'

Grace steps forward from the shadows. In the dark, under what looks like a knitted ski hat, I barely recognise her. 'I don't mind,' she says. 'I'm always talking about taking up jogging. I thought I'd keep Bella company.'

'James not coming?' Amelia looks around for Grace's husband.

'No, he's all tucked up in bed. He said he might join in once we can do ten miles.'

I squeak at this, shoving my hands in my armpits to keep them warm. Now that we're out here in the pre-dawn chill, I want to get going.

'Brilliant, you're all here!' Caroline arrives, looming from the darkness. She's wearing a dinky light strapped to her forehead and I realise she must have run here. Behind her another figure is all in black, like an SAS agent: Leo.

'Quick introductions.' Caroline squints at a sheet of paper then shoves it back into her zip-up jacket. 'Just your name's fine.'

'And whether you've done any jogging or running before.' Leo steps forward. 'Remember,' he says, looking straight at me, 'we're not here to judge.'

With the sky towards Newmarket finally showing signs of dawn, six of us give our names. Grace says she's done a bit of jogging 'but not for a few years', while Amelia declares she only ever breaks into a sprint for the Harrods sale. An older man admits he needs to walk three miles to keep his doctor happy, which makes a tall, pale woman laugh. She says she wants to raise money, and 'a marathon seemed a bit ambitious'.

The final group member is a man in his forties. 'I used to run fast,' he says, in a faintly Russian accent, 'but I give up after snowboarding accident. I want to get back in it.'

Leo nods. 'These are all great reasons. And you?' He looks at me and I realise I haven't explained why I'm here.

'Well, you know, just want to get a bit... fitter.'

I sense Grace and Amelia each take a breath, and I hope they're not going to reveal that I am, in fact, running after a man. I'm not ashamed of trying to win Owen back, I just don't want the whole village to know it. Gossip spreads staggeringly fast around Saffron Sweeting.

Fortunately, Leo continues, giving us a one minute lowdown of the charity and the good we'll be doing for others as well as ourselves.

'Enough of the chat!' Caroline's keen to get started. 'These good folk are getting cold.'

She's right, the group is shuffling and swaying as if trying to stay upright on the deck of a lurching ship. My fingers by now are numb, but at least my legs are toasty. To avoid any danger of malfunctions in the wardrobe department, I'm wearing two pairs of leggings and my sturdiest knickers underneath. I could sit on an iceberg and probably not feel it.

'Warm-up!' Caroline says and I brace for lunges, but all we have to do is walk briskly to one end of the playing field and back. And I'm not last: the man who's here on doctor's orders is the straggler, marginally behind Amelia who was texting as she walked.

Then Caroline and Leo make us march on the spot, swinging our arms. Even in this light, I'm acutely aware of how slender she is compared with me. I suspect my thighs are twice as wide and three times as wobbly. I bet hers don't rub together, either.

'The programme's really gradual, obviously,' Caroline says. 'You'll do jogging mixed with walking. As you get stronger, we decrease the walking and increase the jogging.'

I wonder how far I'll have to jog to get a body that's half as good as hers.

Leo shows us some stretches, finishing with standing on one leg with the other ankle grasped behind us. Grace and the wannabe marathon runner have decent balance but the rest of us wobble and wail before clinging to each other for support. Caroline, I notice, is standing perfectly still with her toes so far up behind her, she could tickle them with her own ponytail. *I want to look like that*, I think. Not just skinny and pretty – although those would be great – but poised, strong, and confident. Like nothing can knock her over.

Finally we begin, walking for a minute then jogging slowly for the same duration. And after just ten repeats of that, as the sun peeks over the roof of the school, we're finished. The frosty grass has been thoroughly pummelled. Caroline makes us do a few more stretches, before praising us and promising more of the same on Thursday. With a farewell wave, she and Leo set off running, at a considerably faster pace than our laps of the playing field. I give a wry smile when I see they're heading away from the village, not towards it. Of course. This truly was only their warm-up.

'Well?' Grace plants her hands on her hips and breathes deeply. 'What did you think?'

Amelia takes off her furry ear muffs. 'Bloody awful,' she says. 'To think I could be tangled up with a hot man in a warm bed instead.'

'Which hot man?' I ask.

'Never you mind,' she says, and I'm still not sure if she's joking. 'How about you, Bella? And come to that, what *are* you wearing?'

I ignore the second question as the morning light reveals the added bulk on my bottom half. 'It was okay,' I say. 'A million times better than CrossFit.' I may discover grumpy muscles tomorrow, but at least nothing is screaming at me yet.

'Tell you what, though,' says Grace, 'I'm awfully hungry.'

'Oh, lord, yes,' agrees Amelia. 'I could murder a fry-up.'

My stomach gives a thunderous rumble. 'What time does Brian open?'

Grace peers at her watch. 'Dunno. Eight? But he'll be there, doing the bread. I bet he'll sell us some.'

I'm salivating at the suggestion. 'I have eggs,' I say. 'Come back to mine, I'll make us fried egg sandwiches.'

I can be a bit late for work. Gerty often doesn't saunter in until ten.

Grace hesitates. 'That's really kind, but...'

Amelia smacks her lips. 'I'm in. Definitely. But what Grace is too polite to say is, is troughing on a cooked breakfast compatible with Project Owen?'

I pause to consider. 'What – too greasy? Scrambled, then? I could grill a tomato too.'

And maybe pop some parsley on the side. That makes it a balanced meal, right? After all, I must have burned a thousand calories. I totally deserve it.

Chapter 10

'You spend far too much time staring out of that window,' says Shirty Gerty from across the office on Friday.

'It's for eyestrain, Gert,' I reply. 'It's important to take regular breaks from the screen.'

She harrumphs but I ignore her. Lurking behind her own monitor, there's every chance she's downloading needlepoint designs. She sends those to the colour printer when she thinks I'm not paying attention.

But she's right, I do like to linger here at our tall, narrow window. There are few offices in England, surely, with a more inspiring view than the one we have at Trewe. I love the symmetry of it, the huge green lawn bisected precisely by paths, the roughened stone of the buildings, the college clock in its little tower above the Porters' Lodge. It's simply gorgeous. One of the nineteenth century's big breakthroughs in mathematics was at Trewe, when some chap called Turlington was contemplating the angle of the path and the lawn. And more recently, one of our professors shared a Nobel prize for economics. His decades of work were done mostly in his office, over there across the court.

There are a few students mucking up the perfect vista before me, but that can't be helped. They scuff along in their jeans, laptop bags slung over their shoulders. And in the far corner, an awestruck cluster of tourists has made it past the stony welcome from the Porters at the college entrance. They tread carefully, keeping their feet well away from the edge of the lawn, since stepping on the grass at a Cambridge college is almost as bad as treason. Now I come to think of it, several students did commit treason in the 1930s by spying for the Russians. So stepping on the grass is worse.

I sigh contentedly and am about to heed Gerty's glowers when a couple of men in dark suits catch my eye. They're too smartly dressed to be students or tourists – or faculty, for that matter. They're not here for an admissions interview – wrong time of year. I look more closely and whoop in surprise. It's *him*.

Pressing my nose to the window, I confirm the sighting. Yes. It's Owen. I whirl around, look at Gerty, then at the door.

'Back in a minute,' I call, already half outside our office. But as I start to clatter down the stairs, I jerk to a halt and look down at what I'm wearing. Not good: the boring grey skirt which barely made it past Amelia, and an equally boring jumper. Drat.

I turn a hundred and eighty degrees, leap back up the stairs two at a time, and hurtle into the office, where I grab my new coat and fling it on. As I do, I catch sight of Gerty's startled face. I think she asks what's got into me, but I'm not sure, as by that time I'm beetling down the stairs again. That CrossFit woman should see me now, I think. Still, I have the sense to slow when I reach the bottom of the staircase. I don't want to pelt up to Owen like an Olympic sprinter and then have to bend double to get my breath back.

I look around the courtyard but don't see them. After a moment's indecision, I choose left, towards the main entrance. If they're leaving, I need to catch up fast, and if they're not, then I have more time to search the college.

Thank goodness for mobile phones and our modern love of checking them every five minutes. There they are. The man Owen's with – I see now it's his boss, Jasper – has stopped to make a call. Beside him, Owen's thumbs are moving over his phone too.

'Gosh.' I march up to him, trying to look as if I was en route to somewhere else, despite the fact I'm carrying nothing. 'Fancy seeing you here.' Inwardly I berate myself for such a bland line. But it's appropriate, after all, for an ex-boyfriend who has inexplicably turned up at one's workplace.

'Bella! What the –' He steps back and narrowly misses the edge of the hallowed grass. 'Oh. I forgot. You work here.'

I tuck my hair back and smile engagingly. It's the middle of the afternoon and I suspect my make-up is long gone, but that can't be helped. There's no way I can pass up an opportunity like this.

'Well,' I say, 'what a coincidence! What are you doing here?'

For a split second I imagine him saying 'I came to see you', but of course he doesn't. He looks at Jasper, who's still on the phone but raises a hand in vague acknowledgement.

'We had a meeting. With one of the professors.'

'Gosh,' I say again, then kick myself for sounding like a schoolgirl in an Enid Blyton novel. 'Right. Of course.'

There's an awkward exchange, during which we both ask how the other is, then Owen says, 'My mum says hello. I told her I bumped into you in the pub.'

'Oh! How nice.' Naturally, I enquire after Sarah Rigby, who, although she indulged Owen a fraction too much, would have been a super mother-in-law. She made top notch puff pastry – something I've always struggled with – and we had many cosy chats in her kitchen. Unlike my own mum, Sarah listened more than she talked, occasionally murmuring a mantra like *least said, soonest mended*. I had a couple of Christmas cards from her after Owen moved to California, but then they stopped, and after a few years I gave up sending mine.

'She moved to Cheshire,' Owen tells me now, and I decide that explains the lapse in correspondence.

We look at each other for a moment and I'm glad that the coat is hiding most of my bulk. I was supposed to have lost at least a stone before seeing him again. Owen, on the other hand, is drop-dead gorgeous in a grey suit with faint pinstripes. He's even wearing a tie, in a deep indigo. Just last night, I added some gorgeous bridesmaid dresses in that shade to my Pinterest collection. The thought gives me a delicious frisson. I try not to look too long at his neck, nor to imagine kissing his throat.

'I haven't seen you in a suit for ages,' I say, which is daft because I haven't seen him at all for five years. But what I mean is, when we were together, a suit was a rarity. I think the last time was at his niece's christening, when the catering was done on the cheap and everyone got food poisoning afterwards. But I enjoyed it at the time, especially the heavy hinting from his Aunt Alice.

'Top hole, these family occasions when everyone dresses up,' she declared in her deep, strident voice. 'P'raps you'll be next with a little nipper, eh?'

'Er, we're not married, Alice,' Owen replied.

'Don't be so old-fashioned, my boy!' Alice boomed. Then she poked my arm. 'Anyway, that's easy to fix.'

I decided this was another Rigby family member I liked. If Owen needed a nudge, Alice was on my side.

'I dunno, Alice.' Owen looked wan. He must have been coming down with the shrimp already. 'I'm pretty fond of my sleep, you know?'

This was true. At the weekend, Owen could easily snooze for ten hours straight. His snoring had long since ceased to trouble me.

'Bah! Still, I'll hand it to you, boy, you're honest. I respect that.'

I smiled fondly at Owen as Alice said this. His integrity was one of his best qualities, even if we did have the occasional tiff when he told me a new clothing purchase wasn't flattering.

Now, at my suit comment, Owen frowns. He doesn't put his phone away, but twists it in his hands. I cast around for a better conversation topic, but am saved by Jasper finishing his call.

We say hello, and I reintroduce myself since Jasper has clearly forgotten and Owen doesn't supply my name.

'I work here,' I say to Jasper. 'What a coincidence, eh?'

Jasper turns to Owen. 'You didn't mention that, dude.'

I don't have time to ponder whether it matters that Owen forgot where I work, when I can recite his entire curriculum vitae. Instead, I say to his boss, 'I hear you were at Trewe for a meeting.'

Jasper shakes his head. 'That was the plan. Professor Grayling, you know him?'

'A little.' Grayling is one of the more eccentric faculty members. Sometimes when I pass him in the college he'll ignore me completely, and other times he'll greet me effusively and bow down as if to kiss my hand. I don't see him much; I think he works in a lab most of the time. I do know that three years ago there was a scandal when two female students from Newnham College tried to poison him, and Trewe hushed it all up.

'Well, he stood us up.' Jasper scowls. 'Real annoying.'

'Oh,' I say. 'Sorry.' Although, of course, it's nothing to do with me. 'What were you meeting about?'

Owen looks at Jasper, as if checking for permission. 'We were hoping to collaborate. On some research.'

Now I understand. Professor Grayling's field is biochemistry. He might indeed have professional overlap with Marin Genetics.

'And what do you do here, Bella?' Jasper looks at me appraisingly. 'You're not going to tell us you're Grayling's assistant?'

'Lord, no,' I laugh. 'I work with the alumni. And development stuff.'

'Development?' repeats Jasper.

'That's what we call fundraising,' I say, distracted. Did Owen just stifle a yawn?

'Oh, really?' Jasper's eyebrows go up as if I've said something surprising, or interesting, or both. 'Well, maybe we should meet with you too, Bella.'

Owen looks at his boss, clearly confused. I'm flummoxed too but am not going to look a gift horse in the mouth.

'Oh?' I stall.

'Yeah,' Jasper says, apparently thinking aloud. 'We've been saying – at Marin, I mean – we have a foundation, you know? Anyways, we might want to fund some research. Or a

– what d'ya call it – a chair. I think maybe we'd like to talk with Trewe about that.'

I glance at Owen, who meets my eye. I can tell he's not heard this mentioned before. But if Jasper's being upfront, and Marin Genetics does have a charitable foundation, then Gerty might want to pursue it. The mention of 'a chair' potentially means supporting a professorial position. Big money. Huge.

'Oh, right,' I say, as if I have conversations like this every day. I don't: that's Gertrude's area. She's the one who schmoozes with rich alumni, concocts proposals, and browbeats the faculty into showing up for long boozy lunches with prospective donors. And sometimes, after a suitable amount of time, and claret, the donor gets their cheque book out.

I, on the other hand, make tea, plug numbers into spreadsheets, and update our database when people graduate, get married, or die.

'Well, of course,' I say airily, 'we'd love to talk with Marin.' I don't actually have the first clue about convincing an American charitable foundation to sponsor genetics research at Trewe, but Jasper clearly doesn't realise that.

'Cool,' says Jasper. 'Let's set something up.' He reaches for his phone again, which is buzzing, and turns, striding towards the Porters' Lodge. 'Owen,' he says over his shoulder, as Owen's a couple of paces behind, 'call Bella and set something up.'

And there it is. As I stand in the fading afternoon light, an electric thrill runs from my left foot all the way up to my brain, across my forehead and back down my right side.

Owen's received a clear order from his boss to phone me.

Chapter 11

The next Thursday, I almost don't make it out of bed in time for running. I finally relinquish my duvet and arrive at the playing field at the same time as Leo. The tall woman and Grace are there, but none of the others. A wood pigeon calls repeatedly from near the river, but otherwise we could be the only creatures in the world.

'The alarm clock's tough,' Leo says, beginning the stretching routine. 'We know that.'

Too right. Sophie came over last night and we emptied a bottle of red wine with the bangers and mash I made. Morgan was out on yet another date.

'Where's Caroline?' I ask.

'She had to go to Birmingham.' Leo demonstrates a stretch for our calf muscles. 'For a meeting. Her store manager's ill, so Caroline's covering.'

We learnt last week that Caroline works in a fancy fitness shop in Cambridge. No wonder she has such trendy gear. I looked up their website and a pair of Lycra leggings is fifty pounds.

'How did you feel after last time?' Leo switches legs. 'Any aches?'

'A few,' Grace says, and I nod. But overall, it didn't hurt too much. Certainly nothing like the CrossFit aftermath, when I could barely put my shoes on.

We're standing on one leg, grasping each other like novice flamingos to stretch our thighs, when Amelia turns up with a thermos of coffee. My aunt's closely followed by snowboarding guy, and finally the overweight older man arrives, apologising. During the brisk warm-up walk, I learn his name is Sid and he's a regional finance manager for a cleaning supplies company.

'Too much time in the car,' he pants. 'Too many pub lunches.'

I make sympathetic noises, although I'm concerned that driving and pub lunches don't mix well. But I'm preoccupied this morning, still thinking about bumping into Owen at work.

Warm-up over, Leo makes us jog twice around the playing field.

'Walk when you have to!' he calls, probably aimed at Sid and me. The tall pale woman is out in front, with snowboarding man behind her. Sid, in fact, gives up after one lap, meaning I arrive back last, on my own. How can this be so hard? My chest heaves, lungs stinging from the cold morning air.

'Good,' says Leo to the group. 'Well done.'

I'm coughing now, as unused parts of my respiratory system creak into action. He can't mean me.

The main activity today turns out to be a relay, which I haven't done since primary school. But we dutifully split into two teams and I notice stirrings of competitiveness as I scurry back and forth. Until exhaustion sets in, that is.

After ten minutes, Leo calls us back together. Some people appear exhilarated; others, like me, only shake our heads and pant. Poor Sid looks like he might be sick.

'Nice work,' says Leo. 'That's what we call interval training. You go all out for a minute or so, then recover before the next time.'

'I don't call that recovering,' says Amelia. 'I call a nice massage recovering.'

'You can do that too,' Leo half smiles, 'later.' He looks around. 'The point is, it's not how fast you can go now. It's that you're asking your body for a bit more than it's used to. We all start off at different stages' – he looks at me – 'but with time, you'll get faster and fitter.'

'If it – doesn't – kill us first,' pants Sid.

'It won't kill you,' Leo says, then backtracks. 'Sid, you did get a check-up from your doctor, didn't you?'

Sid nods. 'He was the bastard that sent me.'

'Good,' Leo tells the older man. 'Show that bastard what

you're made of.'

We all laugh, and even Sid cheers up a bit.

'So.' Leo's tone is businesslike. 'In addition to Tuesdays and Thursdays I want you out at the weekend. Use your legs, for at least half an hour. You don't have to jog: walk if you need to. But get some miles in.'

The group murmurs.

'Try it,' Leo says. 'Sid, you do twenty minutes, all right?'

Sid nods.

'Does beetling around Selfridges count?' Amelia asks.

Leo grins. I think how much nicer he'd seem if he just smiled more. 'Make that an hour, Amelia. And I mean *walking*. Take the stairs between floors. No stopping at every handbag.'

So he does have a sense of humour.

'Now,' says Leo, 'nutrition.'

I recoil. Apparently, he's noticed my flab.

'You're asking a lot from your body,' he continues. 'You need to give it fuel. Drink plenty. And not coffee or red wine.'

I flush, thinking of last night's merlot with Sophie.

'Eat lots of lean protein, whole grains, with fruit and veg. This is no time to try to diet.'

'But –' I say, before I can stop myself, then feel obliged to continue. 'I need to lose weight.'

Leo frowns. 'Says who?'

'It's why I signed up...' I trail off as he looks me up and down.

Grace gives me a sympathetic smile, but snowboarding man yawns.

'Chances are you will lose a bit, Bella.' Leo's face is inscrutable. 'But the focus here is on getting stronger and fitter. Don't punish your body.'

I look at Sid, who's perked up at these words, while Amelia has her head on one side.

'But that doesn't mean a fry-up for breakfast.' Clearly, Leo's read my mind. 'Keep it healthy, yeah?'

I nod, but I'm thinking, what does he know, he's a man, and built like a greyhound. He's probably never had a pancake craving. This morning was fun, but I'm not going to win Owen back by lolloping around a school playing field twice a week.

I need a stronger game plan.

Chapter 12

'I can't stand it,' I wail over the phone the following week. 'I'm going to kill Gerty. I mean it.'

'Steady on, Bell,' says Sophie. 'We'll think of something.'

'We can't think of something!' I shoot back. 'It's now. They're meeting *now*.'

It seems my game plan had a serious flaw. Owen didn't phone me, as instructed by his boss. And with hindsight, I missed the opportunity to thrust my business card into his hand outside the Porters' Lodge. Instead, he called the college switchboard, who put him through to the Development Office. I was out, buying salad for lunch and trying to get a peek at the period drama which Joey told me about.

So Gerty took the call. While I was straining for a glimpse of film star Tasmin Fellows, my boss set up a tentative meeting time, checked it with Professor Grayling's assistant, emailed Owen and Jasper to confirm, and did background research into Marin Genetics. All without breathing a word to me. I only found out yesterday.

'I've tried everything I can think of already,' I tell Sophie. 'I offered to attend to take notes and she said I wasn't needed. I offered to create a funding proposal and she said it was too early. I even suggested I bring them tea and sandwiches –'

'That sounds truly desperate,' Sophie says. 'Haven't you got ambitions beyond being the tea lady? Don't you want Owen to respect you for your contribution, not your Earl Grey?'

'But I am truly desperate! Shirty Gerty didn't even want me to be tea lady. She said Mrs Widdicombe would serve refreshments, like usual.'

'Good,' says Sophie. 'You're better than that.'

'But it means I'm stuck in the office with no excuse for seeing Owen again!'

I'm pacing now, the phone cord at full stretch. The bucolic Cambridge view doesn't sooth me today.

Sophie clicks her tongue. 'They're talking about – what – cold research?'

'Yes.'

Even if Owen did once work on curing cancer, his current focus is more lowly. Professor Grayling, it seems, was employed at the Common Cold Research Unit, which was set up after the Second World War to try to find a cure for the miserable but mundane affliction. People actually volunteered to go away on holiday to a remote part of Wiltshire, and be infected with a cold virus for experimental purposes. The researchers did make some progress, but the project was ultimately shut down as a failure. According to Gerty, the Professor's had a chip on his shoulder ever since.

'All I can think of is suggesting they infect me with something,' I say miserably. 'But I can hardly knock on Grayling's office door and go in with my sleeve rolled up.'

'Hmm,' says Sophie. 'So they're meeting this Professor – Grayling? In his office at the college? Now?'

'Correct.' From what I can make out, Grayling never got over the professional humiliation. He's convinced he'll get a Nobel prize, if they crack it. 'And if I could somehow represent Trewe, instead of Gertrude, I reckon I'd be able to meet with Owen and his boss at least a couple more times. I even considered poisoning Gerty,' I admit. 'I thought if she was off sick today, I could step in.'

'That's brilliant!' says Sophie. 'Why didn't you?'

'Come on, Soph...' Although if I'd had access to a test tube of cold virus I would have been tempted.

'Still, that's the answer,' Sophie says. 'We need to get her out of that meeting, and you in it.'

'How?' They've been underway for fifteen minutes already.

'Who's your biggest donor?' Sophie asks. 'No, wait,

second biggest?'

'I dunno.' I pace faster. 'The supermarket guy, maybe?'

Lord Butterson, grandson of the founder of the Butterson chain of grocery stores, attended Trewe in the 1960s. With a massive family fortune behind him, he's now a philanthropist with particular interest in the arts and education. Trewe has benefitted enormously from his gifts.

'Right,' says Sophie. 'Get out your Rolodex, or your database, or whatever you have. Find out who his assistant is.'

'Why?'

But I sit down at my desk, and enter my screensaver password.

'I'm going to be her,' Sophie says. 'Assuming it is a her, not a him. She's going to call with a pant-piddlingly urgent need to speak to Gertrude.'

'My God.' I suck my breath in. 'That's genius.'

~ ~ ~

Three minutes later, I'm climbing the staircase leading to Professor Grayling's office with shaking legs. Sophie's now on my mobile.

'I could get sacked for this,' I hiss.

'It'll be fine,' Sophie replies calmly.

'Aren't you nervous?'

'No,' she laughs. 'I miss the old days of making things up as I go. And I totally owe you some subterfuge.'

She has a point. There was a time not so long ago when Sophie's life was a tangled mess of false stories, and I covered for her like a trooper. Maybe she does owe me this.

I took two minutes in my office to look up Lord Butterson in our database and tell Sophie everything I could glean. Last gift. Second wife's name. Other charities he supports. The grandson who's currently an undergraduate at Trewe, admitted to the college largely because of the patriarch's cheque book. All this I relayed in the time it took me to gallop down our staircase and across the courtyard to Grayling's staircase. Everything revealed to Sophie, despite being marked in our computer as highly confidential information.

'Okay.' Last of all, I give her Gerty's mobile number. 'Here goes.'

~ ~ ~

Knuckles trembling, I knock on Grayling's door and go in without waiting for an answer.

His office is surprisingly crowded. There's the Professor himself, of course, stationed behind his walnut desk. He doesn't look up, but Gerty does, along with Owen, Jasper, and another man I don't know. Either he's from Marin Genetics, or, possibly, the university group which deals with intellectual property and patents. Although it's early to involve them: as far as I know, nothing's been invented yet.

My mouth goes dry when I see Owen, who's sitting near the window. The light's on one side of his face, making him look like a sultry hero with a brooding past. He's wearing another dark suit and could go straight from here to dinner at an expensive restaurant. I wish.

'What is it, Bella?' Gertrude barks.

'I'm sorry to interrupt...' I'm blushing now. 'Gertrude, it's, um, Arabella Alderton.' I lower my voice as Gerty looks blank. 'Lord Butterson's assistant? She says it's vital she speaks to you.' I cough. 'Now.'

Oh, God, this is never going to work. I've made an absolute fool of myself. I stop, my eyes drawn from my boss back to Owen. Much to my surprise, he smiles at me. He has a dazzling smile, with perfectly white, even teeth. Did they used to be so perfect, I wonder?

'I'll call her back,' snaps Gerty.

I hesitate, but the smile from Owen gives me courage.

'She said now,' I say, looking at him, not Gertrude. 'She's going to call your mobile. Sorry.'

Right on cue, Gerty's phone starts to vibrate in her lap. My boss huffs to her feet. 'Excuse me,' she says, making her way to the door. Then, 'Arabella, it's so nice to hear from you,' as she steps outside.

Before I can chicken out, I take her seat and open my yellow notepad, pen poised. 'I'll cover for her,' I say brightly. *Good luck, Sophie*, I add silently.

Professor Grayling, who as far as I can see has been looking into the fire the whole time, reaches for his teacup. 'It's all damned inconvenient, you see.' He takes a slow, deliberate sip. 'My sabbatical, you understand.'

'Sabbatical?' Jasper asks. 'You're going away, sir?'

Grayling nods. 'Vancouver, in September. Wife's coming too.'

I look from Grayling to Owen, in time to see his jaw clench. Then he recovers. 'That's a terrible shame, Professor. You see, we're convinced that with our recent findings, and your previous work in this field, we'd make giant strides.'

Jasper leans in. 'Marin is prepared to put considerable resources behind this project.' He looks at me meaningfully.

Dutifully, I write *resources* on my yellow pad. What does that mean? Is that industry speak for lobbing sackloads of money at the college, in return for access to the Professor? I'm way over my head here.

Grayling treats us to a long sigh, not unlike something you'd hear in an advanced yoga class. 'Yes, yes. But Mrs Grayling has her heart set on Vancouver, you see. We're taking a cruise to Alaska.' He doesn't look all that excited himself and sets his teacup down again. 'Illuminate me – quickly, mind – what's so salient about your approach?'

Jasper nods. 'It's the VP4 protein, sir. The interface between the capsid and the RNA genome wasn't understood, back in the eighties.'

'You were stymied by the sheer number of serotypes,' Owen adds.

'But we know now that VP4 is highly conserved.' Jasper's leaning forward, totally animated.

Meanwhile, I've totally given up trying to take meaningful notes.

Grayling raises his eyebrows. 'Go on.'

Jasper looks at me. 'We'd be thrilled to fill you in, sir, we just need everyone to sign the appropriate non-disclosure agreement.'

Is he suspicious about the sudden change of cast in the meeting?

'I'll sign!' I say immediately. 'Absolutely. I'd love to sign.' For goodness sake, I'll write my name in blood if it keeps me in this meeting.

'Maybe,' says the man I don't know, 'the Development Office could come up with examples of how this has worked in the past. Previous successful collaborations?'

I haven't a clue what he means, but eight male eyes turn to me.

'Absolutely,' I say. 'I'll get right on it. Glad to.'

Owen tilts his head to one side and gives me an appreciative look. His blue eyes go a bit crinkly at the edges and I feel my stomach flip.

'And I'm sure we can sort something out with the Professor's schedule,' I say, emboldened. 'It really would be a marvellous, er, collaboration.'

Grayling nods thoughtfully and I sense he's at least a little interested in the project. Jasper's forehead relaxes, and Owen sits back in his chair. He glances at me and nods, a definite smile playing on his lips. My heart swells.

And then the door flies open as Gertrude strides in. 'Bella,' she bites out, and even from this distance I can tell she's furious. 'You're needed.'

There's nothing for it. I excuse myself, and face the music.

Chapter 13

'Ooh, that sounds bad,' Grace says. 'Was it?'

'It wasn't good.' I trade looks with Sophie. 'Soph did really well. Gertrude – my boss – knew something was up, but she's not sure what.'

It's Amelia's birthday and we're gathered in the pub to celebrate. She said she didn't want a party, but would buy drinks for everyone at The Plough instead. Her swarm of friends has taken over half the main bar, and she's making new pals by the minute, especially as there's a magnum of champagne on her table. Joey's darting around with his camera, although why he needs shots of ruddy-cheeked Sweeting villagers is beyond me. Morgan, who doesn't usually bother with village events, is lounging at the bar, talking to Fergus. Even Mungo, Violet's spaniel, is here, although I suspect he's more interested in the food than the bubbly.

Sophie grins. I'm worried how much she enjoyed committing fraud, or whatever it's called when you impersonate a VIP's assistant.

'I'm pretty sure she rumbled me,' she says, 'but there was enough doubt in her mind that she couldn't say anything. You need to be careful, Bella.'

'I know. Gerty was in a right strop afterwards.' She told me through clenched teeth that she smelled a rat and was fed up with my devious ways. Which was unfair, really.

'Until this week, the most devious thing I've done at work is to pretend that reading *Cosmo* is legitimate media research,' I say. 'Well, you never know when an alumna of Trewe will invent the next generation of control knickers, do you?'

'Are you seriously discussing panties in public?' Morgan chooses this moment to perch on the edge of our table.

'No,' says Grace, with a slight edge to her voice, 'we're

discussing *knickers*. And this isn't public, it's our pub.' She looks at me. 'I wish all this running would hurry up and work, then we wouldn't need control underwear.'

I groan. 'Tell me about it. I was supposed to lose all this flab before Owen caught sight of it.'

'Well,' says Sophie, 'as long as you're seeing him, that's the main thing.'

'I suppose so. But I've made no real progress.'

'You need to take the initiative,' Morgan says. 'You can't just sit around, hoping he'll call.'

Easy for her to say. She's so assertive, one day she'll invade a small country by mistake.

Joey sidles into the seat next to me, shooting Sophie a wary look. They normally avoid each other, although she claims she doesn't hold a grudge. Tom, on the other hand, will rarely stay in the same room as Joey, and says the only thing he's ever done right is to botch things with Sophie.

Happily, my former housemate decides it's time for another round of drinks and takes herself off to the bar. Morgan wastes no time in taking the empty seat and starts chatting easily with Joey. She assumes, rightly, that he remembers their only previous meeting. I watch her flick a long strand of hair over one shoulder and laugh at something he says.

I have so much to learn.

'You'll get your moment,' Grace says to me. 'If he's the one, I mean.'

'Who's the one?' asks Joey. So, he's not completely mesmerised by Morgan. 'Oh, your ex, right?' Bless him, he manages to seem interested. Probably because he has all those sisters. 'Did you cook him that beef thing yet?'

'I haven't had a chance.'

Sophie arrives back with our drinks and we shuffle up to make room for her.

'But I thought he was staying in the village?' Grace's face implies that means we all spend the whole time nattering in each other's kitchens.

'Yes, but I can hardly turn up at his fancy executive flat and say I happened to be passing with a platter of rump steak.'

In fact, I'm irritated that I haven't had the luck to bump into Owen in Saffron Sweeting. I've spent hours wandering the quiet village streets – no fun in March – buying stamps from Violet, rolls from Brian, and borrowing stacks of books from the library, only to return them unread. But there's been no sign of Owen.

Joey frowns, as if he's thinking it would be perfectly reasonable for me to knock on his door with a dish of the day. 'You could invite him over,' he suggests.

I wince. 'Too obvious.'

'Well, how about one of your dinner party things?' Sophie says.

'The supper club? I could try, I suppose.'

I recall the last supper club, and my hope that Owen would be a future guest. Then I'm distracted by Joey's camera flash.

'Oh, must you?' Grace shields her face with her hand.

'Yes, knock it off, Joey,' I say. 'Most of us hate that thing.'

'You shouldn't,' he says, eyes flicking in my aunt's direction. 'Amelia doesn't.'

I glance across at Amelia, looking stunning in a jade green wrap dress, and clearly in her element as the centre of attention tonight. She's currently twirling a shoe in time to *Dancing Queen*, but earlier, she confided that she was having boudoir shots taken to mark her birthday.

'You're kidding,' I said, as my jaw dropped.

'Not at all,' she replied. 'When I'm ninety-five I want to look back at how gorgeous I was. I plan to be draped in feathers and nothing else, darling.'

'But...' my voice tailed off as I tried and failed to phrase my question. Instead, I settled for saying, 'Well, if I wasn't carrying all this weight...'

Now I jump up. 'That reminds me. I baked a birthday

cake and stashed it behind the bar with Fergus.'

Joey looks delighted, and Sophie perks up too.

'Amelia,' I call, 'shall I fetch your cake?'

She looks up and I catch my breath as I see the tall, fair-haired man beside her: Scott, one of my few one-night stands. His arm's draped casually along the back of her chair and he looks completely at ease. I wonder if he'll be seeing the boudoir photos.

'Darling, that sounds scrumptious.' Amelia blows me a kiss.

Oh well, I think. Everything happens for a reason. If Scott had stuck around with me, instead of fleeing in the opposite direction, I might not be single now that Owen is back. And I wouldn't want to miss out on this.

I retrieve the cake, position it in the middle of the table next to Amelia, and we sing an appallingly flat version of Happy Birthday while she blows out the solitary candle. She expressly warned me not to use the correct number.

'You cut it, Bell,' she says. 'I'll only make a pig's ear of it.'

There are many practical things I can't do. I've never wired a plug, and changing the battery in a smoke detector has been known to fox me. But I've had lots of practice at cutting cakes. I busy myself creating wedges of Victoria Sponge for everyone present, using plates borrowed from the pub. Fergus is too generous to charge us for bringing in a cake, and since he's just sold Amelia h er third bottle of champagne, he's not doing too badly tonight.

I hand out a dozen or more pieces and hear appreciative comments from all directions. Mungo, stationed next to the cake, is drooling uncontrollably.

'Did Ellie ask you to make the cake for her wedding?' Amelia asks. 'Joey's doing their photos.'

I shake my head. With an unworn Vera Wang in my own cupboard and no one to go to the ceremony with, I've been trying not to think about it.

Pushing that aside, I allow myself to inhale the

heavenly smell of vanilla. The classic scent is mixed with my homemade strawberry jam, silky red and laden with fruit. I picked the berries myself, at a farm on the Gog Magog hills last June. The jam, together with a decadent half inch of whipped cream, is holding the two layers together. Bliss. As the queue of cake eaters subsides, I look left and right before sliding a thin wedge of sponge onto a plate. Well, I slaved over this. I deserve a sliver, don't I?

'This is so yummy,' Grace says, as I make my way back and sit next to her and Sophie.

'Umm,' agrees my former housemate, her cheeks bulging. 'As usual, delish, Bells.'

I balance my plate on my lap and look down at it. Mungo sits beside me and does the same.

'Forget it,' I tell him. 'Too rich for you.'

He sighs and lies down, his head on his front paws.

But my attention's on the cake, not the dog. I force myself to breathe – once, twice – before digging in. I've been trying so hard with my diet, and apart from the odd lapse late at night, have denied myself so many tasty things. I lick my index finger, then, determined to make this last, dab first at the crumbs. Inch by inch, I lower my nose and surrender to the scent of the cake. It did turn out well. It's moist but firm, the rich yellow colour coming entirely from the eggs kindly provided by Lorraine, or, I should say, her chickens. Carefully, I break off a morsel and bring it to my lips. With eyes half shut, I savour the first tantalising bite, barely a nibble. I allow it to dissolve in my mouth before I swallow.

And then, I can't help myself. I lift the plate, seize the piece of cake, and chomp it down. *It's better than sex*, I think, then feel guilty as I realise that reflects badly on Owen. Well, maybe I've forgotten how good it was with him, whereas the cake is wrapping itself around my senses right here and now.

'Hello.' A voice interrupts my reverie on the sensual merits of home baking.

I look up, mouth still stuffed with cake. It's Caroline,

with Leo right behind her.

'Oh!' I say, because there's not much else I can enunciate. 'Hello.'

Grace, who finished her own wedge of carbs a few seconds ago, introduces them to Joey and Sophie. 'Meet our running coaches,' she says. 'They're whipping us into shape, right Bella?'

I nod, chewing frantically, my private erotic cake moment fading fast. The others are all saying hello, including Mungo who's greeting Leo and Caroline like old friends.

'Amelia invited us,' Leo says, his eyes flickering to the cake, 'for her birthday.'

'Great!' Grace replies, making room on the pub's antique wooden bench. 'Would you like some cake?'

I half stand, preparing to cut more for the new arrivals.

'Oh, no thank you.' Caroline smiles but her cheeks are rigid.

She's wearing a silver polo neck sweater: sleeveless, with a bit of shimmer. Leo's nowhere near as muscular as Owen, but next to him, she appears as fragile as an elf.

Caroline looks me up and down, presumably taking in my dark jeans and Monsoon tunic in a muted mulberry hue. She's judging me, I think. She's looking at me and thinking, Bella's fat because she jogs twice around the school playing field, then goes home and stuffs herself with cake.

I flush. 'It's a special treat.' I gesture to the cake on my plate. The rest, inside my stomach, is suddenly twice as heavy as it was just minutes ago. Dense, not fluffy. Cloying, not tantalising.

'Good,' says Leo, looking at Caroline. 'Treats are important, right, Cazz?'

'Of course,' she says, although clearly she means *once in a million years.*

Joey doesn't sense the change in mood. 'Bella made it,' he says, making me flinch further. 'She bakes brilliant cakes. And desserts. I've told her, all she has to do is slap together a sticky toffee pudding, and that bloke she's after won't be able to resist.'

'Is that so?' Leo's patting Mungo now. Unlike Caroline, his party outfit looks well worn. He's in a long-sleeved T-shirt from the Berlin Marathon. His jeans are faded, which is probably a good thing, judging by the spaniel's trademark slobbering.

'Shut up, Joey,' I say through clenched teeth, remembering why Sophie declared him a tactless idiot. I hope he shows more discretion around his film star clients. If he's taking photos of Brendan McKinley and Tasmin Fellows, he needs to learn about confidentiality.

'What bloke?' Caroline says, winding hair around her finger.

'No one,' I say, at the same time as Grace, Joey and Sophie chime, 'Her ex.'

Terrific allies they make.

I decide the cake was, after all, the safer subject. 'Anyway,' I say hastily to Leo, who's the only one not intrigued by my pursuit of Owen, 'I really am being careful about food. Honest. You said nutrition was important. I've been trying so hard.'

'Have you?' Caroline purses her lips as her eyes go to the cake again. 'Because you need to treat your body with respect, Bella.' She stretches her arms above her head, revealing a slither of toned midriff. 'Obviously, it can only perform if you feed it the right fuel. Whole grains, protein, not...' she wrinkles her nose, 'well, you know.'

My face is hot. 'Look, I've eaten nothing but salad since Tuesday. I had cottage cheese and pineapple for lunch. It's my aunt's birthday, I was up until one o'clock last night making her a cake. I had a *tiny* piece, okay?'

I put the remains of the cake on the table, all pleasure lost now. I wasn't fibbing: I really did stay up until the wee hours. I wanted it to be perfect. Tears prick at the back of my eyes.

'Steady on, Cazz,' Leo says. 'Bella can have a piece of

cake if she wants.'

'Too damn right she can,' chimes in Sophie, looking crossly at Caroline. Joey, meanwhile, is eying my abandoned cake as if adoption is on his mind. Mungo clearly has the same idea.

'It's fine,' I say. 'I don't want it. I'm trying to lose weight.'

Leo looks at me. 'But you love food?' he says. 'Baking and so on?'

I nod. It's my hobby, my talent, my comfort, my solace.

'Okay.' Leo, who's only just sat down, stands up again. 'Come with me.'

Chapter 14

I stare at Leo for a moment, unsure what he said. But he simply jerks his head. 'C'mon. I won't bite.'

Now, I look at Caroline, to see what she thinks of this strange request. As his girlfriend, does she have some insight into this? When she shrugs, I climb to my feet.

'Where are we going?' I ask.

'The library,' he replies, leading the way through the throng of Amelia's friends.

Once again, I'm not sure I heard correctly. But I follow. As we pass the table where the birthday cake – now decimated – sits, Leo pauses, then picks up a piece that's crumbled onto the serving platter. Popping it into his mouth, he chews, swallows, and licks his lips.

'Yeah.' He nods slowly.

'Yes what?' I fold my arms, braced for further persecution of my gift to Amelia.

'Absolutely delicious,' he says, completely wrong-footing me.

Then he strides over to the heavy pub door, tugs it open, and holds it for me.

'Did you say the library?' I ask, as I find myself on the pavement.

'I did.'

'Why?'

'C'mon,' is the only answer I get. He really is a strange character, taciturn to the point of rudeness. But he was nice about my cake.

We walk the short distance to the library in silence. I left my fancy blue coat at the pub – hopefully I'll be back in plenty of time to rescue it – and the evening air has a distinct bite to it. But the sky is clear, and I can make out stars above us.

'Would you mind filling me in on what we're doing?' I

say, as we come to a halt outside the library entrance.

'There's a book I want you to see. Stay here, I have to fetch the key.'

He disappears up the narrow street at the side of the library and I remember he said he's living with his dad, the intellectually stuffy Saffron Sweeting librarian. I've never taken any notice before of where Kenneth lives, but apparently it's close by. As I wait, a fox trots down the opposite side of the road, tail jaunty with unknown purpose. By the time it turns the corner where the bank used to be, Leo is back.

'Does your dad know you've got those?' I eye the keys in his hand.

'Nope. He's at his bridge club in Saffron Walden.' Leo unlocks a padlock, then the large main door. 'This won't take long.'

'I've looked at the books here already,' I say. 'On dieting and stuff.'

'This just came in,' Leo says. 'I was helping dad and noticed it.'

He flicks on a couple of lights, and the black skeletons of the shelves become normal. I'm glad we're not creeping around in the dark like book thieves. After hours, though, the smell of the books is a lot more noticeable, as if they've been marinating in the still air since the library closed.

'D'you like reading?' I ask.

He goes behind the front desk, bending to a couple of large boxes there. 'Don't tell my father,' he says, dragging one out, 'but yes.'

Leo crouches to dig into the box. I pause, then kneel too. 'Why shouldn't he know that?'

He's silent for several seconds, lifting books out and making haphazard piles on the floor. I think he hasn't heard me, but then he says, 'He tried to shove literature down my throat, when I was a kid. Ransome, Salinger, Defoe, all of it.'

I wait. Leo's emptied the box, hasn't found what he's looking for, and begins to put the books back. Then he drags the other box out. 'I rebelled.' He's unloading fresh books. 'Didn't want anything to do with it.'

Fair enough. Being the son of a zealous librarian could put you off. I think back to my eccentric primary school teacher, Miss Campbell, and how she gently, insidiously, got several of us hooked on reading at a young age. I still get a thrill when I open a brand new paperback, handling it carefully so I don't crack the spine.

'Then I opted to study carpentry and he went ballistic,' Leo surprises me by continuing.

'Because he wanted you to do something more...' I prompt, 'more bookish?'

Leo shrugs. I take this as a yes.

'What did your mother think?' She'd be more supportive, surely.

'Mum died when I was fourteen.'

I gasp. 'I'm so sorry.' Seconds tick by. My own mother is a chatterbox who drives me demented, but I can't imagine her not being around. I swallow. 'But carpentry is extremely intricate. Very skilled, right? You said you're working at the Hall?'

'I specialise in old buildings, traditional techniques. Restoration, usually.'

'Well, that's great.' I'd like to say more, but the moment passes.

'Rats.' Leo's stacked the contents of the second box in wobbly piles on the floor. 'Must have been shelved already.'

He sits back on his heels, balancing expertly. If I tried that, I bet I'd fall on my bum.

'Look, it's kind of you...' I start to return books to the box, '...but it really doesn't matter.'

I've just picked up the new hardback by Marian Keyes when Leo puts his hand over mine.

'We're here now,' he says.

I freeze, a tingle running from my arm to my neck. I should be a little frightened to be with a man I hardly know, in the library after hours. But I'm not. He's gruff and economic with his words, but he's far from creepy. In fact, if I liked my men dark and reed-like, instead of blond and hunky like Owen, I might even say he was attractive. His warm fingers are a little rough... from all that woodwork, I suppose.

Leo doesn't seem to notice my awkwardness. He hops easily from crouching to his feet. 'Come on.'

This time, he catches me lightly by the sleeve and tugs me along past the shelves of romances and mysteries, past travel and biography, to cooking.

Leo lets go of my sleeve to run his hand along a shelf, his lips moving, then he ducks to the shelf below. 'Six-forty, six-forty-one...' he mutters, looking at the Dewey numbers. 'Here.'

He pulls a book from the shelf and I reach to take it, but he holds it to his chest.

'Don't be offended,' he says, which is usually a cast iron guarantee that I'm going to take exception to something. 'It's just I can see how much you love food,' he continues, 'but it doesn't seem to be making you happy.'

Something about the shadows of the library, with only the lights in the main area on, makes it easier for me to meet his eye. 'Well, look at me,' I say. 'There's someone, er, special, and I know I'm not exactly alluring at the moment.'

Leo does look at me, and I immediately want to protest, to explain I wasn't being literal. I didn't expect him to look down to my knees and then all the way up again. I stiffen, wishing I was anywhere but here, and pull a piece of hair down over one eye. Maybe, if I can't see him, he won't see me either.

'Forget it,' I say, and turn to go.

'Wait,' Leo says from behind me.

I pause at the end of the row of books.

'Someone special?' he says.

I turn, then give a tiny dip of my chin.

'Your ex? That's what your friends said at the pub, right?'

I sigh. 'Yeah. I've been trying to trim down a bit... you know...' Stupid thing to say, of course he doesn't know. He's never yearned for a wedge of cheesecake in his life.

'How much weight have you lost?' he asks.

I say nothing, studying the books beside me. It's the pet section: *Reptiles for Dummies* and *Puppy Training Made Easy*.

'I'll take that to mean none,' Leo says gently.

'No!' I defend myself. 'I've lost three pounds.'

He waits.

My shoulders sag. What the hell does it matter? I'm not trying to impress Leo. He already knows I'm fat and can't run more than two hundred yards without retching. I need to focus on Owen. 'But every time I make even a tiny slip, it goes straight back on again.'

He looks down at the book he's holding. 'So that's why you joined our 5K thing.'

'Yeah. I thought –' I catch myself and give a half laugh. 'Well, you know, Caroline is so gorgeous...' Of course he knows that, he's seen every inch of her. 'I thought it would help.'

'It will help,' he says. 'But you can't expect to look like Cazz.'

I redden, hoping he can't see my face in this light. Of course I shouldn't have implied I could ever look that lovely.

'What I mean is,' he says, 'Caroline pushes herself far beyond what most people would consider normal. When she wouldn't eat your cake, she wasn't being bitchy. She never eats cake, or puddings. Hardly touches bread. Practically lives on salmon and broccoli. When you hug her, there's nothing there.'

'Oh.' I can't disguise my dismay.

'She's a competitive runner, Bella. Regional standard, hoping for national. She's trying to shave seconds, not minutes, off her pace. She's had offers for speciality modelling too.'

Modelling? Of course she has, I think. Of course she

bloody has.

'It's not realistic for most people,' Leo says. 'I don't think it would make you happy.'

I study the floor. We both know he's right.

A book nudges into my vision. He's holding it out to me. 'So I thought you could use this. If you stick with the 5K programme, and make small changes in your eating, you will see results.'

I look at the book, curious, but can't make out the title.

'My job as your coach is for you to enjoy the running,' Leo says. 'Not for you to turn into a miserable, hungry shadow of yourself.'

Salmon and broccoli do sound dire. I take the book and glance down. *Wholesome Junk Food.* Great. 'You're implying I eat junk food?'

He shakes his head. 'I told you not to be offended.'

I snort. 'That's like telling someone not to think about horses. They immediately picture Red Rum, or New Forest ponies.'

Still, I flick through the pages. It's a cookbook. The recipes look tasty.

'So...' I consider carrot muffins and breakfast macaroons, '...you're saying I can have my cake and eat it too?'

'Not quite.' Leo grins, and it brightens his whole face. 'But you might be able to bake your cake and eat it.'

My 5K training is supposed to include a long walk on Saturday as well as the early sessions. I admit I haven't been the model of perfection with this, but this morning Grace and I dutifully stroll across the fields towards Anglesey Abbey.

'I love this walk by the river,' she says, apparently oblivious to the mud. We're now in early April and it rained heavily during the week. Undeterred, a horde of daffodils dances next to the path, bobbing yellow faces to us in greeting.

'Don't you miss America?' I try to keep from sinking into the sludgy ground as we negotiate a stile. Landing heavily on the other side, a generous spattering of mud decorates my tracksuit trousers.

'A teeny bit,' she says. 'But things didn't go well for me there.' She pauses. 'It put... my marriage under pressure.'

We hold onto each other for balance as we hop across the worst of the mud. From a nearby tree, a chaffinch trills encouragement.

'I'm lucky,' she says, as we continue on the path, 'that James was such a sport about moving back here.'

'He seems lovely,' I say, careful to keep envy out of my voice. James is a bit of a geek but always considerate towards Grace. Then there's Sophie, with her hunky pilot, Tom. And Morgan, of course, is never short of a guy on her arm.

'He is.' Grace looks at me. 'You'll find someone lovely too.'

'I thought I *had* found someone.' My efforts to insert myself into the discussions between Trewe and Marin Genetics hit a brick wall when Gertrude took me off the project. And in all my glammed up hours hanging around the village, I haven't managed to bump into Owen there, either.

'Maybe,' Grace says gently, 'you could consider someone else?'

I know she means kindly. But I haven't waited this long to give up now. 'No,' I say as we turn for home. 'Owen's the one. Always has been, always will be.'

~~~

Our route back to the village takes us past Oak House, then the duck pond. I don't know how far we've walked, but it's probably three or four miles. My cheeks are pink, my hair's been whipped by the wind, and my legs are pleasantly achy.

'I know you're watching calories,' Grace says as we pass the pub, 'but I promised James I'd bring back croissants for breakfast. Sorry. I need to go to the bakery.'

'That's okay,' I say. 'I'll come too. Treat myself to a coffee.'

Normally, I would cave in and buy a large pastry – or two – but I have organic muesli waiting for me at home. Some of the recipes in that book Leo foisted on me aren't bad. But even with all the healthy ingredients, I've been paying attention to the calories in the recipes.

'Don't hate me,' Leo said, that night in the library, 'but you should know you have to run or walk roughly a mile to burn off a hundred calories.'

Since then, I've been reading the nutritional information for everything I buy or make. My mental translations tell me a sandwich can equate to four miles, a cookie is easily three, and so on. A small pizza, garlic bread and ice cream would apparently require I march halfway to Canterbury.

We turn right, towards the bakery, and are outside my favourite cottage, the terracotta-coloured Old Forge, when I stop dead. 'Oh-my-God.'

Coming towards us, swinging a white paper bag from

one hand, is Owen.

~ ~ ~

Grace stops too. 'Is that him?'

I don't have time to answer. I look around desperately, but it's not yet nine o'clock and none of the other shops in this little road are open. Anyway, I don't want to hide: I've been waiting over a month to bump into him. But why now? Why today, when I look like a mud-spattered gypsy? Instead of my blue coat, my seductive cashmere, and a strategically positioned necklace, I'm in trackie bottoms and a sweatshirt. True, it's a flattering sweatshirt – Amelia purged the others – but my face is bare, flushed, and my hair is hanging wildly.

'Hi.' Owen stops mere feet away from us and takes off his sunglasses.

'Hello,' I stutter, my pulse already faster than at any point on that morning's walk.

'You're up early,' he says.

I nod. There's no clever answer to that – we're clearly not on our way home from clubbing. If we were, I'd be wearing something more alluring.

It's only when Owen and Grace introduce themselves that I realise my rudeness. 'Sorry,' I say, 'forgot my manners.'

'That's okay.' Grace smiles and turns to Owen. 'Bella and I are just back from a walk.'

He looks at me and I know he's taking in the mud and ratty hair. Marvellous. He hasn't shaved this morning, but the stubble is sexy, not scruffy.

'We were on our way for coffee.' I find my tongue and gesture towards the bakery.

'Oh,' Owen replies. 'I just came from there.' He pauses. 'But coffee sounds good.'

My eyes widen in speechless surprise. Thank goodness for Grace.

'Great!' she says. 'Although I can't stay. I promised my husband I'd be back.'

I could kiss her.

Since it's officially now spring – although you wouldn't guess it from the weather – Brian has reinstated the tables and accompanying chairs outside the bakery. By mutual agreement, I park myself at one table, while Grace goes in for her croissants and Owen purchases two coffees. This gives me a couple of minutes to collect my thoughts and drag my fingers through the rats' nest on my head.

Before I know it, Grace has excused herself with a meaningful squeeze of my shoulder, and Owen is sitting down opposite me. He throws a baseball cap on the table and places his phone more carefully beside it. He's wearing sweat pants and a navy T-shirt featuring a bear silhouette.

'Looks like we were both working out,' he says. I nod, although I'm not sure a trek across the fields counts. 'You look well,' he adds, and I busy myself stirring my coffee.

When I look up, he's still studying me, then he blinks. 'I wanted to thank you for your help with Professor Grayling. He's warming up to the idea.'

'That's super,' I say.

Owen blows on his coffee before taking a cautious sip. He makes a slight face.

'What's wrong?' I try mine.

'Oh, it's fine,' he says. 'I guess I was spoilt in the States.'

Poor Brian, I think. He's tried so hard to please all the Americans in Saffron Sweeting, but I suppose they're used to six different flavours and strengths, brewed from beans grown by Guatemalan monks. Still, most of the village shops have tried to make adjustments for their new clients. And Owen isn't American: he should be happy with a mug of builder's tea and three sugars.

'So... the Professor,' I say. 'You think he'll share research with you?'

'Not sure.' Owen leans back in his chair, almost slouching. 'It's so frustrating. The idea is sound, but we need help proving it. He'd bring so much credibility to the process.'

'Right. Makes sense,' I say, although I'm thinking that Grayling's track record of scrutinising paper hankies doesn't exactly guarantee success. Owen once read a biography of the leader of the Cold Research Unit and regaled me with the highlights during a wet weekend in Derbyshire. Even now, I remember the researchers obsessively collected snotty tissues from their human subjects to analyse. Yuk.

'I thought you were working on a funding proposal.' Owen interrupts my reverie. 'We haven't heard anything.'

He reaches for his phone, swiping the screen a couple of times, as though news from Trewe might have just arrived.

'My boss, er, took me off the project.' I grimace at the reminder of my attempt to worm my way in.

'Why?'

I shrug. What an idiot I made of myself. He must think I'm ridiculous.

'So...' To my relief, Owen puts his phone down again. For a minute I thought he was going to sit there and play Candy Crush. He stretches out his legs, and I notice he's not wearing any socks. Is that a fashion thing, maybe?

'How've you been?' He's drinking his coffee now.

'Oh, fine.'

Immediately, I reproach myself for the banal answer. 'Fine' covers the spectrum from *I had a horrific car accident but only lost one leg* all the way to *I won the lottery and bought the mansion next door to Kate and Wills.*

And sure enough, he's tipping his cup all the way up to drink. Considering the coffee wasn't up to par, he's drunk it awfully fast. Then again, he always did eat and drink quickly. Although I loved cooking for him, it used to exasperate me that a three hour steak and kidney pie could be gone in three minutes.

I clutch at a fresh new topic while there's still time. 'Will you live in Saffron Sweeting for long?'

He shakes his head. 'It's handy for work, but once the company stops paying for the apartment, I'll have to find something else.'

Since I'm off the project at Trewe, if he moves away from the village, I won't have any excuse to see him.

'And anyway,' Owen continues, 'Sadie wouldn't like it there.'

Sadie? I stiffen. 'Uhh... who's Sadie?' I aim for a casual voice, but feel like I'm biting on a knife. Why did I not consider the possibility he might have a glossy Californian girlfriend in tow?

'My dog.'

My shoulders detach from my ears.

'Or I should say, I'm her human.' Owen grins. 'She's great. Loves to surf. We met at the beach, actually.'

He picks up his phone again, taps the screen a few times, and shows me a photo of a perky-eared brown mutt, tongue lolling over pointy little fangs.

'What kind is she?'

'Not sure. Part lab, part pit bull. Who knows what else. She's about three.'

I study the photo, more benign now I know Sadie has four legs.

'And you rescued her?'

'She hung out with me one day, we played in the waves, then I went home and didn't think any more of it. But the next time I went down there, she was waiting. In the exact same spot.' His voice is warm and there's an endearing wrinkle to his brow. 'She guzzled two burgers, and that was that. Poor baby.'

I don't know what to say. I had no idea Owen was a dog person. I mean, yes, he'd pat a pooch that was friendly in the street, or pop a pound in a collection for Guide Dogs, but he never showed an inclination to adopt genetically confused strays from beaches.

'So, where is she?' I look around as if Sadie might be tethered to a nearby lamppost, or be roaming the village at will, like Mungo does.

'In quarantine.' Owen's forehead wrinkle deepens. 'I miss her so much.'

My gosh, he's smitten. Well, that's okay. It makes him seem... vulnerable, in need of comfort. I can do that, take his mind off Sadie's detention. And when she's cleared by doggie immigration... well, I can be a dog person too, right? After all, I get on okay with Violet's crazy spaniel.

'You'll need a place with a garden, then?' I ask, and he nods. 'Maybe Amelia could help. You remember my aunt? She's an estate agent.'

'Right. Yeah.'

Naturally, I'll make sure Amelia only shows him local rentals.

We sit in silence for a moment, and I contemplate his long fingers wrapped around his coffee cup. Those fingers used to wrap themselves around me, on a regular basis. The flashback is so clear, I catch my breath. Surely he must sense I still have feelings for him? And he did suggest coffee. That's got to be a good sign.

I'm so distracted by thoughts of Owen's fingers, I don't notice Morgan approaching. When she speaks, she's right beside me. 'Hi guys! Having breakfast?'

'Oh. Hi.' I have no alternative but to introduce them. Owen makes a thing of getting half out of his chair – do men still do that? – and she sits down, uninvited.

'Morgan, were you going to buy something at the bakery?' I say pointedly.

She shakes back her beautiful hair and I notice Owen's head turn. In total contrast to me, she looks like she stepped out of a Gap store, in skinny jeans and a long, slim-fitting sweater. She's even wearing lip gloss, darn her. How can I have been so lucky as to bump into Owen, and then so unlucky that she shows up too?

'Maybe.' She leans back on two legs of her chair, balancing perfectly. 'But I wanna hear from Owen first that he's gonna come have dinner.'

'What?' This comes out between my teeth, the way a poodle might growl.

Owen's eyebrows lift. 'Sorry?'

'Bella does these dinner things,' Morgan says. 'They're great.'

My God, she's barely sat down, and she's come straight out and asked him. I can't believe her audacity.

'Oh?' This is from Owen.

'It's... a supper club,' I say. This is never going to work.

Morgan nods. She and I both know she has no clue what a supper club is.

'You'll come, yeah? When's the next one, Bella?'

'Next weekend,' I mutter. 'Saturday.'

Owen, who's been staring at Morgan, glances at me. 'Are you cooking?'

I nod. Is he considering it? Next to me, Morgan says nothing, but rocks gently on her chair.

'Who else is invited?' Owen asks. 'Are you coming?' He's not looking at me when he says this.

Morgan shrugs. 'Sure.' She reminds me of a cat that's trapped the mouse.

I gulp. If she can be bold as brass, maybe I can too. 'How about I invite Professor Grayling and his wife? Then you two can, er, talk.'

Owen's eyes flick towards Morgan again. 'Okay. Thanks.'

Really? He's coming? I try to catch Morgan's eye but she's smiling enigmatically at something further down the street. Instantly, my mind races off into recipe land. Maybe Joey was right. I mentally abandon the menu I had been planning, in favour of Owen's most loved dishes.

Then I think of a book I saw at the library, the night I was there with Leo. I didn't take much notice of it then, perched on a display ledge at the end of a row of shelves, but I remember its curious title. And immediately I know I'm going back for it today, as soon as Kenneth opens the library doors.

Owen stands, looks awkward, then puts his hands in his pockets. I pick up his empty cup and stack it with mine. I have a daft, teenage urge to take it home with me.

'I'll mention the house thing to Amelia,' I say. 'Why don't you give her a ring?'

'All right,' he says.

'And we'll see you Saturday,' Morgan adds.

'Right. Saturday,' Owen says. 'Bye, then.'

'Bye.' I try to keep my voice light, as if this coffee wasn't the highlight of my entire weekend.

But what I want to say is, after you call Amelia, why don't you give me a ring too? Any kind of ring. The phone, of course, would be lovely. Or failing that, maybe the platinum kind? With a flawless, cushion cut diamond. That would do just fine.

Chapter 16

At our running session the following Thursday, I'm more interested in telling Grace about my coffee with Owen than I am in moving my feet. After a prolonged winter, we're finally enjoying milder weather, so the imperative to keep moving is reduced.

'Come on, Bella.' Leo moves fluidly past us with strides twice as long as mine. 'Get that heart rate up.'

'How d'you know it's not up?' If only Owen were jogging alongside us, and not Leo, my heart rate would be plenty high enough.

'Your breathing,' he says, 'and the fact you can chat comfortably with Grace. But that's good: it means your body's handling this more easily.'

With three weeks to go before the race, we're now supposed to be able to jog for twelve minutes. Then we walk for a minute to recover, before doing it again. Leo's right: it is getting a bit easier. When we started this, I was struggling after ninety seconds. But I'm not sure I'll ever be able to run continuously for three whole miles.

After stretches, we gather back at our small pile of belongings. I reach into my rucksack for a Tupperware box, ignoring the beady gaze of a nearby crow.

'I brought snacks,' I say, 'if anyone wants to try.'

'Ooh.' Amelia cranes her neck. 'Did you make them?'

'Yes.' I catch Leo's eye and look away, unaccountably shy. 'Chocolate cherry bites.'

The rustic appearance of my first try needs some work. Sure enough, Caroline looks sceptical. But the sweet, fudgy smell persuades the others to take one.

'Mmm,' says the pale woman, who we now know is called Tracey. I mentally named her Racy Tracey before I could stop myself. 'These are wicked.'

Leo steps forward. 'I'll try one.'

I try to pretend I'm not watching, but in reality I'm looking sideways for his reaction.

'From the book?' he asks quietly.

I nod. 'Dried cherries, oats, and almond butter. With chocolate chips. I know they're a bit calorific, but since we've all just run I thought –'

But he doesn't let me finish. 'They're good,' he says. 'Well done.'

Grace and Amelia return for seconds, then, to my amazement, Caroline sidles up. 'Can I try?' She has the decency to look a bit sheepish. 'I'm fuelling up for a race on Sunday.'

'Oh?' Grace overhears. 'What kind of race?'

'The London Marathon.'

Murmurs and whistles greet this news. Sid asks Tracey how far that is, and she answers, 'Twenty-six miles.'

'Twenty-six point two, actually,' Leo supplies. 'Which reminds me: field trip for anyone who's interested. We'll cheer Caroline on and you lot can get a feel for a big race.'

'We don't have to run it, do we?' Sid finishes a second chocolate cherry bite.

Leo shakes his head. 'No, mate. We'll stay in one spot. You just have to make lots of encouraging noise.'

I look at Grace. 'Sounds like fun,' she says.

'Okay,' I nod too. I haven't been able to find some of the ingredients in the new recipe book, so this would be an excuse to snuffle around the Harrods food hall afterwards.

Amelia says she'll be in London anyway on Saturday, but will try to meet us on Sunday. Snowboarding man – I shouldn't keep calling him that, his name is Petric – says, 'Why not?'

Caroline nods appreciatively. 'Thanks, guys.'

Leo smiles fondly at her, then looks at us. 'Nice. Meet at Cambridge station at eight.'

What a great boyfriend, to round up a support crew. Did Owen ever do something like that for me? Of course he did. I'm sure he did. I just can't come up with a precise example right now.

~ ~ ~

'Tom's mum's popped round. Again.' Sophie has one foot on the doorstep as she speaks. 'Can I lurk here, with you?'

For once in all the years I've known her, I hesitate, holding the door firmly at forty-five degrees. 'It's... not really a good time, Soph.'

With Morgan safely out of the house at a college function, I wasn't planning on being interrupted.

'Why? What are you doing?' Sophie knows full well that my Friday night social life is rarely noteworthy.

'Uhh, getting ready for tomorrow. The supper club.' But I open the door a fraction wider.

'Fine. I'll help.'

She leads the way to the kitchen, where Whitney Houston is belting out the chorus of 'Didn't We Almost Have It All'.

Sophie takes in the closed blinds and red candles. 'Why's it like a boudoir in here? What are you doing?'

'I told you. Getting ready for tomorrow.' But my eyes flick to the book, face down on the kitchen counter.

'What's this?' Sophie seizes it. '*Magick Made Easy*?'

I resist the urge to grab it back as she flicks through the pages. I need to stay calm and centred. The book said that was important, to get the desired effect. Along with the lighting and music, of course.

'Oh my God!' Sophie claps a hand over her mouth, then removes it with a flourish. 'You're casting a spell!' Her eyes fly around the room, as if searching for a cauldron in the corner.

'I'm not.' I glare for a moment, then relent. 'It's called *wishcraft*.'

'Wishcraft?' Sophie's at the stove now, lifting the lid on a pan, but carefully, as if a frog might leap at her. 'Is that why you've got all these candles?'

I nod, hoping that if she stirs that sauce, she does so in a clockwise direction. If she hasn't noticed, I'm not going to admit to having symbolic items placed at the northern, eastern, western and southern points of the kitchen, either. Nor will I mention the deep, rose-scented bath I took before I began, or the reverent minutes spent stroking the Vera Wang dress. We've been friends since we were six, but it's hard to know how someone's going to react when they catch you halfway through your first attempt at magic.

Sophie refers to the book's subtitle. 'Charms, spells, potions and power?'

I shouldn't have answered the door tonight. Not in the middle of the most important part. My confidence ebbs, not to mention any magical aura I'd managed to summon.

'You're working on something to get Owen back?' she asks.

'No, for England to win the cricket.'

She looks hurt. There's a pause. I shrug. 'What else would I be wishing for?'

Sophie frowns, crossing to the table and the ingredients there. Fortunately, she finds honey, ginger, raspberries, and vanilla pods. No newt eyes or dog tongues.

'I can't just sit around and... wait,' I say eventually. 'I have to *do* something.'

She taps the book on the table. 'This is so cool, Bell!'

'Really?'

Sophie rolls up her sleeves and peers at her fingernails. 'Or as your aunt would say, bloody marvellous.' She goes to the sink and begins scrubbing her hands. 'Tell me what to do. I'll help.'

'Uh, okay.' I wasn't looking for her approval, but it warms me nonetheless.

'Yes. And when we've made your love potion, can we whip up something to repel Tom's mother?'

Chapter 17

As the first supper club guests arrive at Oak House on Saturday night, I'm optimistic. The whole menu has been devised with love and passion in mind, with extra components representing other beneficial elements. Plus, I was delighted to find that the ancient oak tree is associated with blessing and luck. This is the perfect venue to bewitch Owen.

'I've never seen you take so long preparing for one of these,' Lorraine says, as we greet our guests.

Little does she know, I had to make everything twice. Once for Owen, in my red-candled Whitney-infused kitchen, and once for everyone else.

Then, of course, I had to get myself ready. I mustered my bravery and tugged on a dress I've only worn once before. In deep pink, it's a vintage style, with a halter neck. Sophie made me buy it and until now it's always seemed a bit girly. But trying it on this afternoon, and finding it snug but not unbearably tight, I decided to gamble.

Professor Grayling is surprisingly prompt. 'Wife was busy,' he says, half bowing to me on the threshold of Oak House, 'so I brought Palin instead. Hope that's all right.'

'Of course,' I say, secretly pleased to find kindly Professor Palin instead of the severe Mrs Grayling. The positive energy is working in my favour already.

'You look very fetching, my dear,' Palin says as I show him into Lorraine's lounge.

Well, good, at least someone's noticed.

Owen and Morgan arrive together, which doesn't worry me because I sent her over there specifically to make sure he didn't forget. He's thrillingly stylish tonight, far more than he ever was when we were together. His shirt's a striped linen, with a trendy Nehru collar. And is that intentional stubble, or the beginning of a beard? The whole effect is casual but deeply alluring.

'I'm looking forward to a good meal,' he says as I take their coats.

Then, just as I turn away, he leans down and brushes my cheek with his lips. It's over in a moment but a long forgotten charge rushes through me, from my face to my toes and back up my spine. I'm probably glowing to match my dress but I don't care.

'I hope you like the menu,' I murmur, offering celestial thanks to the Magick universe.

Apart from Sophie, no one else knows about my crafty cooking. Lorraine is a wonderful co-host but a bit traditional in her views. I'm not sure she'd react well to incantations. Nor has she any idea I chased her tortoiseshell cat around earlier, in a vain attempt to make it sit still so I could meditate with it. As for Morgan, I was hardly likely to tell her. She's chatting casually with Owen as they move into the lounge, but I can't risk her letting something slip. Not with such a promising start to the evening.

~ ~ ~

It's a good thing the Magick book says knots are a symbol of binding love and unity, because as the meal progresses, the muscles in my neck grow ever tighter. Not that dinner isn't going well, but as the palpitations from Owen's kiss finally subside, I'm watching like a hawk to make sure the right food reaches the right people.

We start with a vibrant basil and carrot salad, representing love and passion respectively, sprinkled with flaked almonds as I figured I might as well go all-in and include an ingredient symbolising marriage.

The main course is bold: venison with rosemary and orange segments, paired with piping hot scalloped potatoes. I wanted to do something with rabbit, which apparently stands for feminine power and passion, but I wasn't sure feasting on bunny pie would go down well with my guests. So I settled for venison – no special powers, sadly, although it does smell divine. I comfort myself that love, happiness, and perspective are all accounted for by the side dishes. I arrange each plate artfully in the kitchen, mark Owen's with an extra sprig of rosemary, and deliver them to the dining room myself. So far, so good.

Around the table, conversation has flowed well. We're eight again tonight – Lorraine and me, the two professors, Owen, Morgan, plus a couple I haven't met before. Peter is Violet's son, but he's easy-going and charming, not bristly like her. His girlfriend, Nancy, is American, but not the loud or glamorous kind. Instead, she's down-to-earth with gentle manners, and thinks carefully before she speaks. But I can tell she's incredibly intelligent, and does something scientific for work, which is another piece of wonderful luck. I think Lorraine knew this, as she seated Nancy next to Professor Grayling. With Owen on his other side – my doing, of course – the Professor has been conversing happily about viral proteins, clinical trials, and goodness knows what else.

The only problem with the seating arrangement is I've barely been able to talk to Owen. Still, with him busy chatting to either Grayling or Morgan, I've been able to gaze blatantly over the top of the rose and orchid centrepiece and do precisely what the Magick book recommends: project my wishes in his direction.

Professor Palin, meanwhile, has been flirting enthusiastically with Lorraine on his left side and Morgan on the right. I think you could add the women's ages together and they'd still be younger than Palin, but he's a sweet old boy and has enthused over every dish.

'Bella,' he says, as he samples the hearty meat and rich sauce, 'this is out of this world.'

If only you knew, I think. I let my eyes slide back to Owen, who's showing Grayling a photo of his adopted dog.

Meanwhile, Peter, who is clearly unable to hold his own

on the topic of clinical trials, has been ferrying dishes to and from the kitchen.

'You're not supposed to be working,' I say, as he arrives at the sink with a stack of empty plates. 'You're a guest.'

He smiles. 'I don't mind. You and Lorraine are working so hard to feed us all in style.'

Lorraine's cat chooses this moment to slink into the room and weave around my ankles. Another excellent sign.

'Shall I take these through?' Peter asks. 'For dessert?'

'Oh, I can manage,' I say hastily, but as I turn from the sink I find my feet tangled by cat.

'Please. I insist.' Peter picks up three dainty plates.

For the sweet course, I considered Owen's favourite, treacle tart, but rejected it as too obvious, afraid he'd see through my attempts to recreate old times. And its ingredients aren't particularly magical. So instead, I went for individual ginger and honey cakes (passion and faithfulness), shaped like a ring (obvious, yes?). Each has a perfect mound of raspberries in the centre, representing forgiveness, since I am, after all, miffed with him for leaving for America in the first place. But the dusting of icing sugar and creamy vanilla sauce should set the seal on happiness.

'All right, thanks.' I nod. 'Why don't you serve the ladies first?' As long as he doesn't touch the plates nearest this end, I'm good. And I should start the coffee brewing. With two Americans – and Owen – at the table, I don't want the meal to fail its final test.

Lorraine appears in the kitchen, picks up three more desserts, and doesn't question me when I whisper that I want to serve Owen myself. She knows tonight is a special dinner, she just doesn't realise I'm aiming for supernatural results.

Finally relaxing a smidgen, I measure out the coffee, make sure the filter paper is secure, and flick the switch on the machine.

But when I get back to the dining room, Owen's dessert in one hand and mine in the other, I find my plan is unravelling.

'I changed to jazz. You don't mind, do you?' Morgan's next to Lorraine's Bluetooth speakers, holding my phone. My carefully selected soundtrack has been replaced with what sounds like strangled trumpets.

'Oh, jazz, first class!' Professor Palin grins. 'Well done, dear.'

I'm distracted by the music long enough for worse to happen. My dinner guests, in a show of careful politeness, have redistributed the dessert plates down the table so that the people furthest from the door have been served first.

'We passed them along,' Nancy gestures. 'No need for us women to be first.'

Only two empty places remain, for Lorraine and Peter.

'Oh, but –' I grapple for a reason to shuffle them. 'I left out the nutmeg on this one. You don't really care for nutmeg, do you, Owen?'

In fact, there's no nutmeg in the precisely-spiced cakes at all, but they don't need to know that. Thank goodness, no one has started. Quick as a flash, I whip Owen's plate away and plonk it down in front of Peter. Then I lower the magical gingery cake in front of my beloved, turning it so it's presented perfectly. 'There,' I breathe, before moving to serve the final portion to Lorraine. Then I sit, noting the murmurs of appreciation rippling around the table.

Except at one place. 'Nutmeg?' Professor Palin says. 'Oh, dear.'

At the same time, Owen mutters, 'I don't mind nutmeg.'

'What's wrong?' Morgan asks Palin, whose face has fallen tragically.

'I'm allergic to nutmeg,' the Professor says glumly. 'What a pity.'

'Here,' says Owen, 'have mine.'

Palin beams. 'Oh, you are kind!'

I let out a strangled yelp, pushing back my chair.

But it's too late. With a cheery flourish of plates and camaraderie, they swap.

I freeze, every muscle tensed. No one notices. All around me, forks are seized and clever conversation pauses as the guests dig in.

'Mmm,' says Peter on my left, 'first class.'

'Ambrosial,' says Professor Grayling, as Nancy nods agreement.

'Very tasty.' Owen smiles in my direction, which earlier tonight would have felt triumphant, but now leaves me numb. I can't smile back at him; all I can manage is a frigid nod, as my stare fixes on Professor Palin.

He's chewing carefully, his eyes shut, but tilted rapturously towards the ceiling. Then he swallows, opens his eyes, and looks adoringly at Lorraine. 'My dear,' he says, 'did you make this?'

'No.' She hardly glances at him. 'Bella did.'

'Ah.' Palin dabs his mouth with his napkin, his gaze not wavering from Lorraine. 'Well, it's enchanting. Absolutely enchanting.'

Chapter 18

Unfortunately someone has put a spell on the train operator too. Saturday night's engineering work has run over and as a result, our service to London crawls along.

Leo checks his phone for about the tenth time. 'Unless Amelia's coming, it looks like it's you and me.'

'Oh.' I say. 'Okay.' But I'm thinking, that's awkward, me and Mr Grumpy for a whole morning. As if I didn't have enough problems.

It seems that the others weren't as enthusiastic about travelling to London to support Caroline in her marathon as they first appeared. By Friday, Sid backed out, saying he was unaware of something his wife had arranged. Racy Tracey apologised: she was double-booked for a christening. Then, this morning, Grace texted that she'd come down with a stinking cold and was staying in bed, while snowboarding man – Petric – emailed Leo saying he'd met someone the previous night. We decided this meant he was staying in bed too, but in a different way.

Gamely, I refresh my messages, but there's nothing from Amelia. She must have had a better offer. I sigh. After last night's magical disaster, I could have used her company. I can hardly confide in Leo that I tried to cast a charm on Owen and instead bewitched an esteemed Cambridge University Professor. A married one, at that, who was last seen kissing Lorraine's hand and declaring the evening to be 'simply spellbinding'.

'I guess we won't be needing all these cheese scones, then,' I say.

Leo looks up from his map. 'Sorry. It was nice of you to bake. I'll have one a bit later.'

I decide to make the best of it. Even though the magic was a let-down, I'm here now, and I've never been to a marathon. 'So, what's the plan?'

Leo's squinting at his phone and the map, side by side. 'Limehouse.'

'Limehouse?' I've barely heard of it. I expected him to say Greenwich, or Tower Bridge, or the Mall.

'The course does a loop. We'll catch her twice, if we're in time.'

'Not at the finish, then?'

Leo shakes his head. 'She won't need us at the finish. She'll need us around twenty-one or twenty-two. That's when it bites.'

As our train finally pulls into Liverpool Street station, we're almost fifty minutes late. Leo swears under his breath.

'Can we still make it?' I ask, as we join the other passengers jostling for the door.

'Maybe.' His mouth has a determined set to it, then he looks at my feet. 'Are your shoes comfy?'

~ ~ ~

We pelt along the platform and through the ticket barrier before galloping towards the entrance to the Underground. I don't think I've ever run this fast before, but I still end up lagging behind by several yards. Leo's in trainers, as usual, but my new Chelsea boots weren't meant for this.

'Sorry.' I finally catch up when Leo's delayed by a family wheeling luggage.

'You all right?' Not waiting for my answer, he steers me to the escalator, then bounds down, two steps at a time.

My legs simply aren't long enough for that and I don't care enough about Caroline's race to break my neck. I canter down as best I can, but I know I've held him up. At the bottom, a tiled corridor stretches before us.

'Go on,' I wheeze. 'I'll catch you up.'

'That's okay. We'll jog it.' This time he takes my hand, but even at a lope, his pace far exceeds my ability.

We're still far from the platform when a whoosh of

warm air tells us a train is arriving. As we hurtle around the final corner, the doors are closing.

'Damn!' Leo drops my hand.

I sag against the wall. I can't believe I risked a heart attack and we still missed it. 'I'm sorry,' I pant.

Leo looks up at the indicator board which claims the next train will be eight minutes. We both know that could mean fifteen.

'Can't be helped,' he says. Then he glances at me. 'Oh, cripes Bella, I'm sorry. I forgot I was with you and not –'

He comes over and takes me by the elbow, guiding me to a seat. 'Are you okay?'

I fold over, clutching a stitch. 'Yeah.' My breath is, in fact, returning to normal.

'Hey, you did really well.' He crouches beside me. 'You moved pretty fast!'

I don't have the breath for a decent retort.

~~~

'So, this is Limehouse?' I say, as we hurry from the Tube station, in search of a vantage spot for the race. I'm breathing hard but the pace is more sedate than at Liverpool Street.

'Sorry it's not very scenic,' Leo replies.

I've visited this part of London once or twice before, but have never been able to picture myself living in one of the regenerated Wharf areas, taking the funny electric train to my high-powered job in the financial district. Then again, a six-figure stock trader bonus isn't me either. I'm definitely better off in Saffron Sweeting.

'Have you ever lived in London?' I ask.

He shakes his head. 'Hell, no. Can't stand the place.'

'Why not?'

He shrugs. 'Too many people, not enough air. It's fine to visit. But it's a bit like dating someone versus settling down. I couldn't live in London.'

Hopefully, Caroline feels the same way.

Dozens of spectators have already bagged their spot beside the marathon course, many with flags and banners draped over the railings. With a bit of nudging, we claim a few feet of crash barrier. The atmosphere is festive, and runners are already streaming past.

'Are we in time?' I ask. 'Have we missed her?'

'Dunno. We've missed the wheelchair athletes, and the elite runners. This lot are moving at a fair lick. Hopefully they started before her.' He reaches for his phone 'Let's find out.'

'What do you mean?' I crane my neck to see the screen.

'The runners wear a chip, for timing.' Seeing my frown, he continues, 'Because it takes so long to get across the start line, the actual finish time for most of them is useless. So they have a chip, either on their bib or shoe, and it records when they pass certain points.'

This is far easier to grasp than Owen's research.

'Some bright spark's linked that to an app,' Leo continues. 'So I can track her on my phone.'

'Wow,' I say. 'Really?' I consider the possibilities for tracking Owen, and popping up – as if by coincidence – when he's out and about. That would be better than relying on magic, surely.

Leo swipes the screen, muttering calculations under his breath. 'The signal's lousy.' He looks up at the sky, as if a lazy satellite might be visible. 'According to this,' he says, 'she's doing great. Past mile twelve. But I don't trust it. Keep your eyes peeled.'

'Why are they going in both directions?' I ask. The runners coming from the right look considerably fresher than those approaching from the left. But most are travelling easily, long legs apparently chewing up the miles.

Leo pulls a crumpled sheet from his back pocket and, keeping one eye on the competitors, shows me the race route. 'We're here, see?' He points to the map, where two red lines run alongside each other. 'On the outbound, they're on the far side of the road, coming up to mile fourteen. Then, when they go past us from left to right, they're between twenty-one and twenty-two.'

A minute or so passes. Leo's eyebrows knit more tightly together as runner after runner rolls by.

'I'm so sorry,' I say. 'I feel awful we missed that Tube train.'

'We're here now.' Leo exhales. 'Let's give it a bit longer.'

A scrawny boy on my right has been listening. 'You missed the *best* runners,' he informs me. 'You were late.'

'That was my fault,' I tell him. 'Who are you here for?'

'My dad,' he says proudly.

I smile at his mother, who tells me her husband is doing his third marathon today. Then I produce the tin of scones from my rucksack, and they're greeted with much enthusiasm.

'Yum!' says the little boy. 'They're crusty and cheesy and chuggy! Can I have another, mum?'

Leo keeps his word and eats one too.

'Mmm,' he says, chewing. 'Light but satisfying. Really good, Bella.'

'Do you think Caroline will want one? I can hold one out as she passes.'

He reacts as if I was joking, then pauses as he sees my face fall. 'Sorry. But runners are very picky during a race.' He finishes the last of his scone and dusts crumbs from his fingers. 'My first marathon was in New York. I had no clue what I was doing: walked miles around the Expo the day before, wore a cotton T-shirt. Then I had a bagel for breakfast.'

That sounds perfectly logical. He'd need sustenance for such a long race, surely? I wait.

Leo goes on. 'Disaster. Totally indigestible. I puked up in Brooklyn, finished in four hours thirty-five.'

I've no idea whether that's good, bad or indifferent, but from his face, I understand it wasn't the plan.

'How do we spot her?' I ask. 'Assuming she hasn't already passed us, I mean.'

The flow of runners is getting thicker, in both directions. To see Caroline on this part of the course, we need to look beyond the runners on our side of the road.

'She said she'd wear green.' Leo's leaning on the barrier now, absorbed by the race.

I focus too, but it's hard to make out individuals in the throng.

'There!' exclaims Leo suddenly, and cups his hands to his mouth to roar. 'Go on, Cazz! Looking good!'

I join in too, though, to be honest, I can't see her. But I look at Leo and follow his gaze, and I think I see Caroline disappearing with the pack, one hand raised in a wave.

'How did she look?' I ask. 'I couldn't see.'

'Fine, I think.' He consults his watch and nods. 'Yeah, her time's good. But she's only halfway.'

She's already run fourteen miles – *fourteen* – and yet she's covered little more than half the distance. Good grief.

'How fast is Caroline hoping to do?'

'She's talking about three-twenty, maybe three-twenty-five. The Boston qualifying time's three-thirty-five, so she's got to get under that.'

These numbers mean nothing to me, but the young commentator on my right is better informed.

'The man who wins it is gonna do it in, like, *two hours*.'

'That's right.' Leo nods to him. 'Or a tiny bit more, maybe.'

'Those guys're *really* fast,' says the boy. 'Faster than the British guys. They're from, like, Kenya and Ethiopia.'

Leo grins. 'You know your stuff.'

'Are they faster than the Brits?' I ask softly.

'Yep,' Leo says. 'They're incredible, if you ever get a chance to watch them. Maybe next year, if our train isn't late.'

There's a pause while I do the sums. 'So, my 5K race...' I look down at the pavement. 'That means they'd complete that in fifteen minutes?'

'More or less.' Leo leans over the barrier to focus on the street.

I'm silent.

'Hey,' he looks back at me, waiting until I meet his eye. 'This is meant to inspire you, not depress you. Everyone's different.'

'Okay,' I say. 'Anyway, I'm not exactly built like them.'

I regret it as soon as I've said it. Any idiot can see that. But Leo just gives the faintest of smiles and tactfully consults the map.

~ ~ ~

With the help of our new friends, we polish off the scones while the kaleidoscope of runners streams by. When the little boy's dad passes, Leo hoists the lad up so he can see his father continue down the road. For such a small person, his cheers are ear-splitting.

'I had no idea it'd be like this,' I say, when the kid's stopped yelling. 'Such a big deal.'

Leo laughs and deposits his precious cargo safely on the ground. He's smiled more this morning than in all our previous encounters. He must be excited for Caroline. 'It's really good of you to come today.'

I smile back. He looks so much more pleasant when he's not glowering. 'I'm enjoying it.'

And I am.

'We've got a good half hour before she'll be back,' Leo says. 'Shall we find a coffee?'

'I'd love one.' After that morning sprint, I'm parched.

We relinquish our spot by the barrier and walk to a tiny cafe.

'How did you and Caroline meet?' I ask, as we perch on barstools, facing the window. 'You're so well matched.'

He's silent for a moment, giving me a bit of a strange

look. Have I been too nosy? But then he answers. 'We were on a train, both with bicycles, trying to get to Cambridge. A swan had nested on the line, so everything was disrupted. They kicked us off at Audley End, supposedly to take a bus. Obviously that wasn't feasible with the bikes.'

'And so...' I prompt.

'So we decided to ride it together. I didn't know the way, fortunately she did.'

'Nice,' I say. They must have discovered they were both fitness addicts, although what flirting you can do while you're toiling up hills in Essex, I can't imagine. But it's more romantic than my first encounter with Owen. He was stung by a wasp while we were both inspecting peaches in Cambridge market.

'Bella –' Leo starts, but at that moment my phone rings.

'Sorry,' I say. 'It's Amelia.'

'Darling!' she says as I answer. 'I couldn't talk sooner, I was in bed with a fabulous Kenyan chap. Gangly as can be, but incredible stamina.'

At this, I start to giggle, but notice Leo shift on his stool. Catching his eye, I jerk my head towards the door of the cafe; should we walk back? As we go, I press my phone to my ear, so that I can still hear Amelia.

'He said he's in London for some race,' she purrs, 'but he was still sleeping at ten o'clock this morning, so I think that was a porky pie.'

I cover my mouth to stifle the laugh.

'Anyway,' Amelia says, 'tell me about last night. Did Owen fall at your feet?'

'Not exactly.'

Despite my escalating anticipation through the evening, Owen didn't repeat the kiss on the cheek when he left Oak House, much less sweep me into his arms as I had fantasised. And although my aunt would probably find my misdirected magic a complete hoot, I'm not going to relate it with Leo beside me. 'I'll tell you when I see you.'

'All right, we'll chat in the week,' she says. 'Must go.'

While I've been talking, Leo has been nudging and excuse-me-ing to make room at the barrier. We're crammed in tightly this time.

'You'll never guess what Amelia's done.' I put my phone away, failing to keep a straight face. 'I think she's shagged one of the elite runners.'

'No way,' Leo says.

I nod, giggling. 'She said he was Kenyan and had amazing stamina.'

Leo's face creases and he gives a deep belly laugh. I join in and we grin at each other.

Once we calm down, he says lightly, 'And you? How's it going with your guy?'

Either it's the coffee, or the excitement of the race, but I find I'm longing to tell Leo about Owen and ask his advice. But instead I smile vaguely and say, 'Oh, you know... fine...'

I don't sound convincing, but Leo seems to accept the statement. 'I'm pleased for you,' he says.

There's a long pause and I think he might say something else. But as I look at him to check, he gives a wry smile. 'Just be sure to ask about his stamina.'

'Will do,' I say, and together we turn back to the race.

Chapter 19

Gerty must know my mind isn't fully on the job the next day. 'You're sailing close to the wind, Bella,' she says. 'Have you done those database updates yet?'

'Almost,' I say, which is stretching the truth appallingly. We've had a stack of alumni magazines returned to us by the post office, and I've only marked a tenth of the addresses as defunct.

Instead, since arriving at Trewe this morning, I've been devouring accounts of yesterday's marathon and studying race photos. We didn't go to see Caroline at the finish: Leo said it would be total chaos and that she was meeting her mum there instead. I found that strange, but he assured me the hard part was over and in any case, she'd cover those last few miles way faster than we could.

Now, I check Caroline's time: three hours and twenty-two minutes. Words cannot describe how awed I am by that. She even pulled off what Leo called negative splits, running the second half of the race faster than the first. No wonder he's smitten. I wonder if Owen would be impressed, if I ran a marathon? Then again, maybe I should see how the 5K goes, first.

And I need a bit of recovery time from my own marathon shopping trip yesterday. After the race, I walked miles around Harrods food hall, then Fortnum and Mason's, and finally a speciality shop in Primrose Hill. I lugged my loot home on the train and stayed up late trying new recipes.

Gerty, though, has been in a foul mood since she came back earlier from a meeting with Kathleen Russell in Human Resources. I don't know why, and I don't want to know.

Fortunately, Professor Palin spends quite a bit of time in our office. Ostensibly, he's giving a lecture in Lyon next week and needs help getting special characters – like é and ê – into his PowerPoint presentation. But he's asked after

Lorraine twice, which is particularly alarming as I happen to know his wife's away at her sister's in Penzance. His socks don't match and his shirt is blatantly creased. Thank goodness men of my generation know more about taking care of themselves. Owen was good with the washing machine at least. Clueless with Tupperware, and cling film, and making beds, but super with the Persil.

And of course the thought of Owen doing laundry is all I need for my mind to start churning like the rinse cycle, as I wonder what on earth I can try next.

~~~

On Easter Saturday, I'm careful to complete my long walk and be strolling through the village near the bakery at precisely the time I bumped into Owen before. It's not too obvious, I tell myself. It's perfectly reasonable that someone's exercise routine would be the same.

But there's no sign of him.

So later that afternoon, when there's a knock at the door and I open it to find Owen there, I barely believe it.

'Gosh,' I gasp, 'it's you.'

He retreats a step.

'Come in!' I recover and check him covertly for signs of enchantment. 'Come on in.'

Could it be that something in the magic dinner worked after all? The book did warn the effects are not always immediate.

He follows me into the living room. 'Nice place,' he says, conversationally.

Fortunately, there's no danger of him spotting *Magick Made Easy* lying around. Sophie ran off with it, in the hope of quelling Tom's mother. Lucky, too, that my laptop is closed, so he's not going to glimpse a Pinterest board with two hundred wedding images, most featuring cornflower, indigo or Prussian blue.

'I'm house sitting.' I explain about Uncle Mike, and his divorce from Amelia. 'I have a housemate too. Morgan.'

'Ah,' he says, 'is she here?'

'Not at the moment.' Is that a good sign, that he wants to know if we're alone?

'Right.' He clears his throat.

I take a deep breath. Then, with more poise, I ask, 'Would you like a cup of tea?'

He hesitates. 'I should –'

Should what? He only just arrived. How odd.

'And a hot cross bun? I baked some earlier.'

'Okay.' He smiles. 'Sounds good.'

Owen sits, checking his phone while I make our tea. With shaking hands, I slice two buns and put them under the grill to toast, then surreptitiously tidy my hair. I didn't realise he knows where I live. Unless he's asked someone. That thought amplifies my excitement and I almost tip boiling water over my hand, then whirl around as the first whiff of smoke alerts me to the buns.

'Here we are,' I say, setting two mugs of tea on the coffee table and going back to the kitchen for the food. I considered a tray, with teapot, cups and sugar, but decided I shouldn't appear to be trying too hard. And of course I know how Owen likes his tea. But I don't mention that, I simply place the mug with a dash of milk and one sugar in front of him, then settle in the opposite armchair. And I hide my satisfaction when he pockets his phone, turning his attention to the hot cross bun.

I pretend I'm not watching as he picks up his plate and inhales the fragrant spices. I added just the right amount of butter, which has now formed a glistening coating on the crispy toasted surface. My own mouth watering, I allow myself a hearty bite of my own bun, and am rewarded with its plump, zesty comfort. There's silence while we both savour the butter-laden satisfaction of cinnamon, cloves and currants.

'So,' I say eventually, in the time-honoured way of

starting a sentence when, in fact, you have no idea what to say next. I'm dying to ask what he's doing here, but if Owen needs a few minutes to work up to it, that's fine. Still, I struggle to fill the gap. He's now sporting a definite beard, but a short one. I'd give anything to know how it feels under my fingers.

'How are you liking being back in England?' I manage.

He shrugs. 'It's okay.'

I wait politely.

'My mum's over the moon, obviously. The weather's not as dire as I remembered. But the roads and parking are driving me nuts. And why the shops all have to close at five...' He reaches for his tea. 'Stuff's expensive too. Like, in pubs, you know? Daylight robbery for an orange juice. Then, when it arrives, it's tiny, no ice. And the beer. Ugh. I like my beer cold, now.'

Ouch. I feel wounded on behalf of Fergus, his pub, and half of England.

'Well,' I say, 'that would explain why I haven't seen you in The Plough, after that first time.'

'I mean,' he says, 'I know the history's great, and Cambridge is amazing. I've found some good walks for Sadie. Even Saffron Sweeting's quite nice.'

Quite nice? This village is adorable. I love every inch of it, from the noble church to the whiffy duck pond to the crumbling malt house. Owen used to have more appreciation for the English countryside and villages: one of our first dates was a picnic in the grounds of Wimpole Hall. After lunch we walked across the fields towards the ruined folly, and our first kiss was beside a five-bar gate. Funny, I don't remember much about the kiss, but I remember the picnic vividly. We had Scotch eggs, local cider, and homemade Battenberg cake.

I realise I've let our conversation lapse. 'Any luck yet with somewhere to live?'

'Not yet. Rent's bloody ridiculous.' Then he shrugs. 'Still, the food's okay. I've missed bangers and mash, and pork pies and stuff. Dinner last week was great, by the way.'

Great? Perhaps he really means entrancing, bewitching or irresistible. Maybe it's worth me pursuing this food angle further. Should I invite him to come back later, for steak, like Joey suggested? That would give me a chance to put on something flirty, shave my legs, and whip up a treacle tart.

'How are you, then?' Owen gestures with the last of his hot cross bun. 'How's work?'

Damn, he's changed the subject. Why didn't I jump in and ask him?

'Oh, fine, I suppose. How about you?'

He sighs, and my heart twists with empathy. In the old days, if his work was going badly, he'd come home and lie on the settee with his feet in my lap, and I'd rub his ankles while he talked about it. I rarely understood the scientific terms he used, but it didn't matter. I nodded and murmured and pretended. Then I'd make dinner, and open some wine, and before long we'd be in bed and he'd say how much better he felt.

But I can hardly go over there now and grab his foot. 'Go on,' I say instead.

'Jasper had a family emergency, he's gone back to the States for a few weeks. I'm stuck reporting to his boss, who's a wanker. He basically only cares about the numbers. Keeps asking if I've made the big breakthrough yet. I can't make him understand, this isn't some Hollywood movie where the scientist mixes the green test tube with the blue test tube and shouts Eureka.'

I laugh, then catch myself. He wasn't trying to be funny.

'What happened to the cancer research?' This has been niggling at me. 'You know, when you moved to America, I thought you...' I don't voice the rest. *I thought that you were going to do something really important, work that could save millions of lives. Transform our world. Something worth leaving me for.*

Owen shrugs. 'Oh, that. The funding got pulled.'

He sounds casual, but maybe because I know him so

well, I sense there's more. I wait.

Sure enough, Owen leans forward, puts his empty plate on the coffee table, and sits, nudging the remaining crumbs with his index finger.

'It came down to me or my lab partner.' He doesn't look up. 'Neither of us saw it coming. We'd just tested a promising hypothesis and the stats were decent. We were stoked.'

I murmur to show I'm listening.

'The project lead called me into his office and explained the budget had been slashed. But he said he was going to keep me, instead of my buddy, because the last test had been my idea.'

'Right... so...?'

There's a long pause. 'That was the problem. It wasn't my idea.' He stops tormenting the crumbs and pushes the plate away.

I catch my breath as I infer the rest: the experiment hadn't been his brainwave, and he'd confessed. Owen let the other guy keep his job and he was out on his ear with only his integrity for company. My heart swells with renewed admiration.

'So you went to work for Jasper?'

He nods, then gets to his feet and paces in front of the fireplace, checking his infernal phone again. Sure enough, he's not wearing any socks. That really must be a thing in America.

'And... Professor Grayling?' I say hesitantly. 'Any luck there? You two chatted quite a bit, at dinner.' Not that I was gawking, or anything.

'We did talk. I thought it was going well, but the guy's stalling.' He shakes his head, hand on the mantelpiece now. 'I need to follow up with him, keep pushing.'

'Another meeting?' I suggest, thinking that this time I won't take chances. I really will have to poison Gerty.

Owen shakes his head. 'Something more casual. Like, I don't know, on the golf course or something.'

I didn't know Owen played golf. I open my mouth to say so, then close it in case he was being figurative. I don't want to look silly. That was one of the problems, when Owen and I were together. I was always half a step behind, no matter what the conversation.

He's fingering things on the mantelpiece now, not in a nosy way, just absent-mindedly. His hand runs over a candlestick, a Busy Lizzie pot plant, a photo of Morgan's parents. He picks up the dreaded wedding invitation but puts it down again without reading it.

'Oh, my gosh,' I say, as the most brilliant idea hits me.

He turns his head.

'You could be my plus one.' I don't pause for even a second, in case I wimp out. 'At that wedding.' I nod towards the invitation and he picks it up again, frowning.

'I –' he begins.

'No, wait,' I jump up. 'The bride is my cousin. I sort of have to go, but don't really want to. But the guy she's marrying – Eddie, Edgar?'

Owen glances down. 'Edwin.'

'Well, you'll never guess who he is.' I'm beaming now. This solves my plus one problem, helps Owen, and gives me the perfect excuse to see him again. Now who's the clever one?

'Who?'

He's wary, but I don't care. I know I'm holding, if not the trump card, a King, at least.

'He's Grayling's godson. The wedding's at Trewe, and the Professor will be there. I'm sure of it.'

Chapter 20

'Darling, I'm frightfully pleased, but it's not really a date, is it?' says Amelia as she hustles me into Cambridge on Easter Monday.

I phoned her, begging for fashion assistance, as soon as Owen left.

'Well, all right,' I say, '*date* might be a slight overstatement, but it's clearly more than a casual cup of coffee.' A wedding! We'll be standing there, side by side, as the happy couple say their vows. 'How can that not lead him to consider his own situation?'

'Crikey.' Amelia pauses in the entrance of the Grand Arcade. 'Steady on, old thing.' Then, as I set my mouth in a peeved line, she gestures towards John Lewis. 'Well. We can't control what Owen's thinking, but we can make sure you look delectable.'

'What are you wearing?' I ask, as she whisks me up the escalators and begins investigating ladies' fashions like a sniffer dog. 'You are going, aren't you?'

'Oh, God, I suppose so. I find weddings so boring though, don't you?'

Boring? *Boring*? No, I do not find them boring. I think an English wedding, especially in spring, is possibly the most romantic thing ever invented. I accept every invitation, I watch all the reality TV programmes, and although I claim I'm only flicking through the wedding magazines at the hairdressers, I'm actually devouring every square inch. If I'm feeling really down, I sometimes buy a bridal magazine to read at home, under the covers, like a guilty teenager with *Penthouse*. And then there's the small matter of my already purchased wedding dress.

'Oh, never mind.' Amelia tuts. 'I can tell by your goofy look you quite like them.'

She's yanking dresses off racks, surely too many for the

fitting room limit. Her arms are full of silks, chiffons, and taffeta. Some are full-length, some strapless, some sleek, some frilled. There are pastel florals, bright abstracts, navy polka dots... and one that's cerise tartan.

'Whoa,' I say. 'Now who's getting carried away?'

Amelia tosses her head in the manner of an artist who knows exactly what she's trying to create, but accepts she may only be famous after she dies. 'Lucky for you I don't charge by the hour. You can buy me lunch afterwards. Now tally-ho!'

I pretend to grumble, but deep down I trust her. She did such a lovely job with the other clothes she picked for me, I'm excited to see what she has here. And weddings are so tricky. Gone are the days when a simple pink suit would do. Nowadays, one has to navigate bizarre dress codes, including fascinators, evening outfits, and shoulder coverage. I blame those young royals.

Despite my dieting, my dress size hasn't budged. This is demoralising because until the setback yesterday with a Thorntons Easter egg, I was doing well. Mum insisted on buying it for me, despite my protests, and to my shame, I demolished it by mid-morning.

But, amazingly, the hefty chunks of milk chocolate I guzzled have not wrecked things entirely. Amelia's picks do fit better and hang a fraction looser. There's less straining across my stomach and hips as I wriggle into dress after dress.

Amelia leans against the fitting room wall, eyes narrowed.

'No,' she says, to the navy dots.

'Doesn't work,' to the black strapless.

'Nice, but not for you,' to the green chiffon.

'Bloody awful,' she laughs to the cerise tartan, to my absolute relief.

My posture sags more with each rejected frock. I wanted to find the perfect outfit to knock Owen off his feet, and these are all hideous.

'Are you tired?' Amelia detects my low spirits.

'I didn't think this would be so impossible.' Maybe the chocolatiers at Thorntons *are* to blame. 'I'm not that fat and ugly, am I?'

'No, darling, you're lovely. These dresses are cut for a different shape.'

'You mean skinny.' I hang my head.

'No. I mean women with no waist and no hips. You have both. Like me, actually.'

'Well, *you* always look fabulous.' I try to keep resentment from my voice. 'Where do you shop?'

'Here,' she says, her forehead wrinkling. 'Hang on.'

She bustles out again, returning with another crop of garments. 'Separates,' she says, slapping the heel of one hand to her temple. 'I was looking for a dress. That's where I was going wrong.'

~~~

Thirty minutes later, we're seated in The Oak Bistro, wineglasses in hand, menus on the table.

'To you,' I say, raising my pinot grigio. 'You're a genius.'

She says nothing, just bows her head like the style goddess she is.

Beside me, in a posh shopping bag, is a beaded top and long matching skirt. In a gorgeous blue-grey, the skirt is cut on an angle so it skims over my too-ample hips and too-chunky thighs. The top has a low, cowl neckline – 'Definitely what you want to flaunt', said Amelia – and there's clever draping at the waist which miraculously minimises my stomach. The whole outfit makes swooshing sounds as I move. It's absolutely perfect.

'Do you have shoes?' Amelia says now. 'Silver sandals, maybe?'

I shake my head. Oh, no. More to buy?

She swirls the wine in her glass. 'Your feet are much

smaller than mine. Not to worry, we'll borrow off someone. Daphne, maybe.'

So her metaphorical Rolodex doesn't only contain cashmere wholesalers, but a designer shoe library too? Not that it matters, if she can rustle some up for me.

'Thank you,' I say again. 'You really are the bee's knees.'

'Nope,' grins Amelia. 'In that outfit, *you* are.'

~ ~ ~

The running group grumbled so much about the early mornings that Leo and Caroline agreed to move the Thursday sessions to after work. The clocks changed a few weeks ago, so we're benefiting from lovely light evenings. And it's not as nippy at the end of the day. Caroline has thawed considerably since I turned up to her marathon, and she's even sampled some of the treats I've made.

The group, however, has diminished in size. Snowboarding man, Petric, found that once he regained his stamina, our training was too gentle. Caroline found him new running buddies and made him promise to sign up for a longer event, later in the summer.

Meanwhile, not long after her Kenyan conquest, Amelia drops out. 'Sorry, all,' she says. 'I don't think I'm made for this kind of exertion.'

Leo catches my eye and I try not to laugh. Whatever exertion Amelia prefers, her boundless energy suggests she's doing something right.

'But I'll see you at the malt house tomorrow, Leo?' Amelia is oblivious to our smirks. 'With the surveyor?'

My aunt is still spending every spare minute on saving the old building, and her group has now raised enough money to hire a surveyor. First step, apparently, is to prepare a plan and costing for renovation. When Amelia got wind of Leo's carpentry knowledge, the surveyor agreed to bring him in as a specialist to assess the condition of the timber frame and roof.

'I'll be there.' Leo nods. 'Might take a while to determine, though.'

When he hears Amelia's excuse, Sid tries to wimp out too. To my amazement, Caroline takes him to one side and spends most of the session convincing him not to quit. Then Leo adjusts his training plan, so that Sid can realistically aim to walk the 5K instead of jog.

This means the wannabe runners are reduced to Grace, Tracey, and me. On a few previous occasions, Mungo has joined us, but he has no discipline for training. He either gallops ahead, diverts randomly to the bakery, or spends ages with his head down a favourite rabbit hole.

'Okay,' says Leo, 'ten days until the race. That means twenty-five minutes of continuous jogging today.'

Grace sucks in her breath. She's still getting over her cold and I know she's been sneaking into the bakery more often than she should. But Tracey gives a determined sniff.

'Don't worry, Grace,' Leo says kindly, 'you can do this.'

I say nothing, but I'm willing to give it a try. Spurred on by the marathon – not to mention counting down the days to my date with Owen – I've stuck religiously to the training plan. My weight, annoyingly, has levelled off, but I'm seven pounds lighter than I was on Valentine's Day.

The three of us set off, Leo just behind us.

'Remember, Bella.' His breathing's barely affected by the effort. 'Don't start out too fast.'

I adjust my stride, letting Tracey, who's naturally more speedy, go ahead. Grace is panting already so I slow beside her.

'In theory,' Leo continues, 'you should be able to hold a conversation. But we won't worry about that today.'

Daylight running has the added advantage that our routes can be more adventurous. This evening, we do a loop of the village which takes us across the little footbridge at the ford, past Amelia's house and the duck pond, then up the slight hill by the church. Someone's cut the grass in the graveyard and my nostrils devour the unmistakable scent of spring. From there, a footpath takes us across a couple of fields and I spot a kestrel wheeling above us. Then it's an easy lope back down to the village, past Grey Stoke Farm. I think Grace tells me she used to live near here, but her breathing is so laboured, I'm not sure.

And twenty-six minutes later, we're back at the school. Tracey beat us, of course, and is stretching, her head near her toes. Mungo lolls next to her, panting proudly, although I suspect he was scrounging chips in the pub until just a few minutes ago. Meanwhile, Caroline and Sid are finishing their more sedate walk, returning together from the direction of the malt house.

'Nice work,' Leo calls, as we trundle to a halt next to the football goal posts. 'Well done, all of you.'

Grace starts coughing but waves away offers of water. 'I'm alright,' she puffs. 'I think.'

'How about you, Bella?' Leo asks. 'You okay?'

I'm breathing hard, hands on hips. 'It was good,' I manage. 'I liked it.' But I'm not being entirely honest. I feel strong, energised. I think I want to do it again.

Leo looks me up and down, nods, then says something in a low tone to Caroline, who immediately purses her lips and looks at me too. But before I can work out what they're discussing, Leo begins our stretching routine, followed by Caroline recapping our mileage assignments for the weekend.

'And don't forget to make a last push for sponsorship,' she says, from her crouched position with one leg stuck out. She reminds me of that bit in the Nutcracker, where the Russian dancers come on.

As we're gathering our things, Tracey asks, 'Didn't you bring a treat for us today, Bella?'

Darn it: I forgot the snacks. In the last couple of weeks I've been trying out recipes on the group.

'Oh, I was looking forward to a morsel,' Sid echoes.

'Well –' I begin, but Leo interrupts.

'It isn't Bella's job to feed you greedy gannets.'

'I don't mind,' I say. 'Actually, I did bake, but they're at home. You can all come over, if you'd like.'

There's a brief discussion as they weigh up the short walk against the promise of sweet things. It doesn't take long for the treats to win. So, the six of us – me, Grace, Tracey, Sid, Leo and Caroline – troop the minimal distance from the school to Uncle Mike's house. Mungo, not understanding the mission, scents a squirrel and hurtles off in the direction of the ford instead.

Once home, I find myself offering my guests hot chocolate too.

'You only jogged three miles,' Caroline warns, 'that doesn't mean you can feast all night.'

'It's for morale,' Sid protests.

'And team spirit,' adds Tracey, which, considering she runs alone these days, doesn't quite ring true.

'Sid's right,' says Leo, as they crowd into the kitchen, 'you all did great. Lighten up, Cazz.'

'This one's apple and walnut cake,' I explain, as I lift the lid from a large, square tin. 'I hope it doesn't crumble. And these are Nutella energy truffles.' I transfer little chocolatey blobs onto a plate and pass them around.

The kitchen goes quiet as people sniff, lick and munch.

'Mmm.' Tracey waves a piece of cake. 'Scrummy. Really moist.' She pauses. 'Aren't you having any?'

I shake my head. 'I have a big date coming up.' I can't resist mentioning his name. 'With Owen.'

Grace offers to help make hot chocolate and I put her in charge of heating milk on the stove.

Then Caroline takes me to one side, putting her arm around my shoulder conspiratorially. 'Bella,' she says, dropping her voice, 'I'd like you to come into the shop next week.'

'What for?' Surely Amelia hasn't told her to glam up my running outfits?

'A sports bra,' she replies. 'Now you're running further,

and faster, support is important.'

I glance down at my chest. Okay, so my boobs were bouncing around today, and they were pretty uncomfortable. But I'm surprised she noticed. 'How do you know?' I say. 'You were with Sid the whole time.'

Then I catch her look towards Leo. 'Oh, God,' I say, under my breath. 'Really?'

To hide my scarlet face, I go to the stove and elbow Grace out of the way, asking her to find mugs instead. She lives up to her name and doesn't comment on her job changing so abruptly. A few minutes later, we serve the hot chocolate, then another helping of cake. I offer fairy cake cases for those who want to take an extra truffle home.

'Those really were lovely,' Caroline says on her way out, perhaps trying to placate me for the bra suggestion. 'Could you work out the nutritional content, do you think?'

'I'll try,' I say.

Other people follow her: first Tracey, then Sid, and Grace, carrying two extra truffles for James.

Thinking everyone's left, I close the front door and jump when I find Leo behind me in the hall.

'Sorry,' he says, 'I'm just going.'

I lean back against the front door. 'It was you, wasn't it?' There's a distinct edge to my voice. 'You told Caroline to invite me to her shop.'

He nods. 'Yeah.'

Embarrassment mingles with my annoyance. 'I can't believe you were looking at my boobs.' I fold my arms over myself.

Leo's eyes flick to my chest and then immediately back up. He takes a step backwards.

'Look,' he says, 'firstly, I'm your running coach. It's my job to make sure you're comfortable. And clothing... is... important.'

Two small dots of colour appear on his cheeks: he feels as awkward as I do. I unfold my arms, then think better of it and cross them again, the other way.

'And secondly?' I prompt.

'What?'

'Secondly. You said firstly, so there must be a secondly.'

'Give me a break, Bella. I was trying to help.'

There's a pause so long, I decide that's all I'm going to get. Still rattled, I open the front door.

Leo shakes his head, and steps over the threshold. Then he turns and gives a half smile. 'Secondly,' he says, meeting my eye, 'I'm a guy. You're an attractive woman. Of course I looked.'

The Magick didn't exactly go to plan last time, but surely it's worth one more try.

The night before Ellie's wedding, I spring-clean my room and change the sheets before luxuriating for thirty minutes in a perfumed bath. Then I lock the bedroom door, light a dozen white candles, and shimmy into a new satin kimono.

With reverent precision, I lay the Vera Wang dress on my bed, sighing at its perfection. Alongside, I place my photos of Owen, the cards he gave me, and the wedding invitation.

'Please...' I whisper, taking deep, intentional breaths, 'all-powerful universe, bring me my one true love.'

~ ~ ~

The taxi drops me off outside Trewe at half past four. The wedding is at five: late in the day, in my opinion, to commence nuptial festivities. But, knowing how much the college charges, perhaps Ellie and Edwin are saving money with a shorter rental. I left Owen a message yesterday suggesting we travel from Saffron Sweeting into Cambridge together. He didn't call me back and I began to get worried. Then, last night, a text arrived, saying he'd meet me there. Fine, I thought. I'm a big girl.

I smooth down my skirt, which is entirely unnecessary since the beaded folds don't show creases, and decide to wait for Owen inside Trewe's main gate. People are already arriving. Couples and small groups trickle past me, dressed in colourful finery, strolling in the direction of the chapel.

A few minutes pass. I'm not wearing a watch because it

didn't look right with my outfit, so I keep glancing up at the college clock tower. The big hand is lazy but relentless in its progress. If I listen hard, I think I can hear it tick.

Then I brace myself as I spot a familiar – and familial – group trouping along the pavement.

'There she is!' The first cry is songlike: my mother tends to get musical when she's excited. She's dressed in maroon and looks surprisingly chic.

'Beaky!' The next greeting is from my brother Gordon, although I don't know why I still answer to that ghastly nickname.

'All right, Beaks?' My other brother, Keith, equally gruff. Together, they resemble a pair of bouncers, fidgeting in their suits. Undoubtedly, they'd rather be playing rugby. I hope for Ellie and Edwin's sake they don't have an open bar: these two may drink it dry and still be more sober than the rest of the guests put together.

My father, bringing up the rear, leans down to squeeze my arm and give me a kiss. A large, stocky man – the Beecham genes – he's the strong, silent one in the family.

'So, where is he?' Mum gets straight to the point. She looks around, her nose raised as if trying to scent prey.

'Owen? He's not here yet,' I say, stating the blooming obvious. I can't help looking up at the college clock. Twenty to five.

Mum's lips draw into a line. Even though I played it down, she knows how disappointed I was when Owen went to America. And despite making only the tiniest mention he'd be my date today, she's onto me.

'You sure he's coming?' Keith shoves his hands in his pockets.

'Of course,' I say, as the first doubts creep into my mind. 'He just had... something to do first.'

'Righto. Well, are the rest of us going in, or what?' Gordon yawns.

Mum opens her mouth, but dad beats her to it. 'Yes. Come on, you lot. Bella, we'll save you a seat.'

I nod, my smile tighter than it should be.

At quarter to five, I acknowledge my shoes – borrowed from the enormously kind Daphne Pennington-Jones – aren't as comfortable as I first thought.

At ten to five, the groom's party arrives on foot, ravishing in grey morning coats. I spy hyacinth blue waistcoats, my first clue as to the colour scheme for the wedding. It's a pretty shade, but of course I wouldn't want the same as Ellie, when it's my turn. I don't know Edwin, but have no trouble picking him out: he's the one other people keep clapping on the back. They too head off towards the chapel. I swallow and check my phone. Nothing. Does it have a signal? Battery? It does. I realise my dad said they'd save a seat. Singular.

At five to five, a pedicab squeaks to a halt in front of the gates. From the back, Amelia tumbles out, hooting with laughter. 'What a divine way to travel! Young man, we must do this again.' She thrusts a ten pound note into the cycling chauffeur's hand, and shakes out her hair.

'Hello, darling!' she hugs me.

I hug back, hard, my hands sliding over the silk of her sumptuous apple green trouser suit. 'Hi,' I say, at half her volume.

She steps back, holding me by both shoulders as she inspects me. 'You look bloody gorgeous. Well done!'

'Thanks,' I reply, without enthusiasm. My shoes are definitely going to be trouble.

She checks her diamond-encrusted watch. 'Ah,' she says, 'I see the problem.'

'I'm sure he's just a bit held up.' My voice trails off.

'Yes,' Amelia agrees brightly. 'That'll be it.'

Above us, in its haughty tower, the clock reads one minute to five.

'Do you think –' I stop and blink a couple of times. 'Do you think we should go in?'

Amelia looks up and down King's Parade. I swear I hear the clunk as the clock heaves its big hand up to the hour.

There's a moment's pause, then it begins to chime. Bloody, mocking thing. I pull out my phone again.

'Anything?' Amelia asks, as a vintage Rolls Royce comes into sight.

I shake my head. If we don't move now, we're going to be scuttling in behind the bride.

'Okay.' My aunt is impassive. 'In that case, darling, yes. In we go.'

~ ~ ~

I honestly do try to concentrate on the marriage ceremony. After all, I love those seconds when the groom and his best man step from their seats to the head of the aisle, when everyone else starts looking over their shoulders, whispering, when the fill-in music ends, when every single person in the chapel holds their breath, allowing the organ to draw in enough air for the wedding march.

But today, only half my brain is at this wedding. Yes, I smile with everyone else as the bride glides up the aisle. I stand and sit and kneel in all the right places, and I belt out a few lines of 'I vow to thee my country' along with the rest of the congregation.

But the other half of my brain is dancing a jig, like an evil kelpie, delighting in the news.

'He stood you up!' it squawks. 'You fool! Did you really think Owen was going to come to a wedding with you? A wedding! The boy's allergic to weddings! Didn't you know that?'

I press my hand to one ear, temporarily quashing the kelpie. This enables me to catch a few phrases from the sermon, words like solemn journey, lifelong partners, sunny hillsides and deep ravines. The best man fumbles for the ring in the traditional fashion, and we all hold our breath once again. The tiniest bridesmaid sneezes for the tenth time and the congregation titters indulgently.

And the kelpie prattles on. 'Look at you,' it says, 'in your stupid new outfit. What a waste of money – he was never going to show up. What made you think he'd be your date at a wedding. A *wedding*!'

I bite my lip, hard, as the college chaplain pronounces Edwin and Ellie man and wife.

Next to me, Amelia leans in. 'He may still show up,' she whispers, 'if he was delayed.'

I nod. Owen could be waiting outside, apologetic about an unavoidable hiccup.

Except he's not. As we emerge from the college chapel to watery sunshine, I station myself near a wisteria-draped wall and scan the crowd. My eye runs over the bride, groom, bridesmaids in blue, mothers in hats, the chaplain. There's Joey, working at warp speed to take group photos before the littlest guests get bored. And I spot Professor Grayling, stiff in his formal suit, his expression so solemn he might as well be at a funeral.

But as the sun disappears over the westerly college rooftops, there's no sign of Owen.

~ ~ ~

As we're ushered into the Great Hall, and I see the rows of round tables with their white linen and blue chair sashes, I balk.

'Could I leave now?' I mutter to Amelia, who's behind me.

'You could...' She gives the question serious consideration. 'But you'll miss a five star feast. If I were you, I'd guzzle some lobster, drown your sorrows in chardonnay and then duck out when things deteriorate.' She consults the seating plan. 'Chin up, darling.' Then she drifts away.

I attempt to slip invisibly into my chair at the table for eight which also contains my mother, father, brothers and two bird-eyed, stiff-haired women.

'Bella, you remember Hettie and Betty?' my mother says, by way of introduction.

Of course I don't.

'Why, yes,' I reply, 'how nice to see you both.'

Who are they? Cousins? Nannies? Cleaning ladies? I have no clue and I don't care. At this moment, all I want is to get my wine glass filled, and to make the empty chair on my right evaporate.

'Your chap didn't show up then?' says my brother Keith.

I don't need to shake my head.

'Course he didn't.' Gordon ogles a bridesmaid.

I'm about to ask why 'Of course', but change my mind. I don't want to hear the answer.

'What a shame,' chimes in Betty.

Thank goodness, here's the waitress with wine. I give a tight smile.

My mother leans in. No, I think. Please, no.

Too late.

'It's Owen, you see,' she tells Hettie and Betty. 'You remember? He and Bella were together for *ages*. Then he flitted off to America, the rascal, and left her in the lurch.'

'Mum –' I eye the delphiniums in the middle of the table, and make a note to remove similar images from my Pinterest board. I don't want any reminders of today.

'Anyway, he's back in Cambridge and she thought he was coming, didn't you, pet?'

I say nothing, relishing my first glug of wine.

'He's obviously run a mile,' says Gordon.

'All right, Gordy,' says my father. 'Het, how are your bunions?'

~~~

And that's how it continues. The empty chair lurks beside me, reminding me that Owen should be in it. We should be talking and laughing and falling in love again. Instead, for two long hours, I endure blunt wit from my brothers, sharper comments from Het and Bet, and informative but hurtful anecdotes from my mother.

'Never mind, it'll be your turn next,' simpers Betty, over the lobster mousse.

Later, 'She had no idea, poor thing. Didn't even wonder why he'd bought a new suitcase,' says my mother, prodding the beef en croute.

And later still, 'You won't be eating that, will you, Beak?' My brother's spoon is poised as individual toffee apple crumbles are served. 'You know, considering?'

And all the while, I alternate between twisting my napkin, staring at the table, and draining my glass.

Chapter 22

Finally, after I feel like I've endured dental surgery, a school reunion, and a cervical smear test all in one day, we applaud the speeches and the cake is cut.

As people start to move from their tables to socialise, Joey slides into the empty seat next to me.

'God,' he says, slinging a single camera bag over the back of the chair. 'I'm knackered.'

'Hard work,' I agree, 'weddings.'

'Sorry?'

I repeat myself.

'I thought so,' he says. 'You're sloshed.'

'A bit.'

'No,' he says, helping himself to wine from my glass, 'a lot.' He puts his head on one side to look at me. 'Nice, er, frock.'

'You're supposed to say that to the bride,' I slur. 'Not me. I'm just a guest. A spinster guest.'

Every 's' in my sentences is a sloppy mess.

'What's up with you?' Joey asks.

'Her chap didn't turn up,' supplies Gordon. 'Stood her up.' Darn him, he's been knocking back the booze all night but his voice is as clear as a BBC newsreader.

'Wow.' Joey surveys the untouched place setting. 'Which guy?'

'Owen,' Keith answers helpfully. 'The one that strung her along for years and then didn't marry her. She thought tonight might give him ideas.'

I hate him, I hate him. Next time he brings a girlfriend to mum's for Sunday lunch, I am totally getting out those Kajagoogoo-era photos.

'All right, lads. Beaky doesn't need any more of that.' Dad's trying to be helpful, but even he's calling me by that loathsome name.

I reach for my bag and simultaneously grope for my shoes, which at some point I kicked off under the table.

Dad surveys Joey. 'What's your name?'

Joey tells him.

'Well,' says dad, 'if your photographer duties are finished, why don't you ask Bella to dance?'

Great. Now my *father* is trying to help get me a man. If only he knew Joey isn't reliable boyfriend material.

'I'm fine,' I say. 'I think I might leave now.'

Joey stands up too. 'I'll walk out with you. How are you getting home?'

'Dunno.' I have one shoe on, but the other no longer fits. Fine, I'll carry it.

Obviously, it's my uneven footwear that causes me to lurch as I stand, so that I have to grab onto Joey to avoid falling. It can't possibly be the alcohol.

'Come on,' he says, 'this way.'

I notice he's got one lone camera slung around his neck. 'Where's the rest of your fo-fograph stuff?'

'The college let me lock most of it up for tonight. I'll come back with my car in the morning.'

We should say goodbye to the bride and groom, but as I look towards the small dance floor, it appears Edwin has his tongue down Ellie's throat. Well, good, I think. Better her than one of the bridesmaids. Or the bride's mother, which I read about once in an online wedding forum.

As we step outside, the night air hits me like a bucket of cold water. 'Oof. Chilly.'

Joey puts his arm around me, as much for support as warmth. 'Sorry about Owen,' he says.

'Don't be,' I say, wishing I could check my phone one more time but knowing there will be no new messages. In any case, the battery's dead from repetitive refreshing. 'I should have known he wouldn't fancy a fat ugly cow like me.'

'You're not a fat cow,' Joey says, as we make our way across the court, carefully avoiding the grass. 'And I fancy you.' Then he adds hastily, 'A bit,' in case I get the wrong idea and throw myself at him.

'Thanks very much.'

'Hang on a minute, can I park you here?' Joey lowers me to a bench before I can answer. He's reaching for his camera, preoccupied.

I look up; it's dark now, of course, and Trewe is bathed in silver highlights and charcoal shadows. I suppose the creeper inching up that wall, towards the leaded Tudor windows, is pretty. And the half-moon above the clock tower is attractive. Joey takes a few shots of the college, fiddles with the focus, takes a few more. Then he turns the camera on me.

'You're not ugly, either,' he says, snapping a couple of photos.

'Hah,' I answer, deciding I'm going to lie down on this bench to see if that makes the stars stop moving.

'I mean it,' he says, still clicking. 'Those beads on your dress look great in the dark.'

'Put that thing away,' I say mildly. But I've had such a crappy evening, those few kind words from a lech like Joey are better than nothing. I take a deep breath. Behind me, there's a plant wafting a sweet, heady smell, like jasmine.

'Just wait,' he says. 'When you see these, you'll want to pay me for them.'

'I bloody won't.' I giggle, then stretch my arms above my head and make a tiny frame with my hands, to help me focus on one star at a time. 'You do talk bollocks, Joey.'

He laughs and stops taking photos. 'Can we go down to the river? Do you mind?'

Why should I mind? Maybe I'll take off these beautiful, pointless clothes and drown myself. Or get in a punt and cast off, and see where I end up. I frown, trying to picture where the river will take me. Is there a weir? Jesus Green perhaps? Or will I end up somewhere like Ely by dawn? I should find out.

'Full moon,' Joey says. 'I bet the water looks brilliant.'

He's ridiculously excited about taking artsy-fartsy shots

of the River Cam.

'Haven't you taken enough photos for one day?' I ask, heaving myself up to sitting. 'Haven't you run out of film yet?'

'You're showing your age, you daft thing.' He pulls me to my feet and starts to steer me towards the river.

We don't get far before I decide to remove the other shoe, although I do have to cling to Joey to accomplish the manoeuvre.

Trewe has a pleasant bridge over the Cam; not a scientific masterpiece, like the Mathematical Bridge, nor a copy of something from Italy, like the Bridge of Sighs, but a stone arch with pleasing pillars at each end. I lean against one of these, while Joey scrambles around, on the bank, under the bridge itself, standing back, then practically wading into the water, to get his shots. He's right, the moon skimming the surface is beautiful, and when a swan glides into view, even I can see that these pictures could be calendar-worthy.

Then I remember my punting plan and look around. Ah, there they are: four Trewe punts, moored side by side, next to the bridge. Excellent.

'Whoa,' says Joey, as I stumble and slide down to the bank, almost pitching head first into the river, 'what are you doing?'

'I'm going home by punt,' I announce. 'Obviously.' I have difficulty with the word *obviously*. It apparently has more syllables than I previously realised.

I teeter on the rear platform of the punt – the barefoot decision now the luckiest part of my evening – and then collapse inelegantly into the punt itself. 'See,' I call, from my reclined position, to Joey, who's now above me on the bank, 'piece of cake.'

From the darkness, a duck erupts in a flurry of quacking before flying off up the river.

Joey laughs, watches it go, then points the camera at me. 'Nice one,' he calls, then crouches down to take another.

And another.

'Wow,' he says. 'You look amazing.'

My response is an alcohol-infused snort.

'No,' says Joey, fiddling with the camera with more urgency now, 'I mean it. This is incredible. Like the Lady of Shallot.'

I have no idea what he's talking about, but the punt is now rocking gently on the water and I find it pleasantly calming. I stretch serenely, knowing that if I want to float home I'll have to cast off at some point. But there's no hurry. In any case, Joey's talking to himself now, using words like *beautiful* and *gorgeous*. I like those words. A lot. They're soothing words, words that make me think I'm not a useless, frumpy spinster whom no one will ever date, let alone marry. Those words are taking the sting out of the worst evening of my life. I want to hear more of them.

'Bella,' says Joey, coming all the way down the bank and putting one foot on the back of the punt. 'Could you take your top off?'

The soothing evaporates. 'No!' I start to cough, and sit up. 'No, I bloody couldn't, you pervert.'

'Not like that,' he says hurriedly, 'not so we'd see anything. I'll make sure the punt hides it. I mean, them. Just stretch out, on your front, and face me.'

He jumps into the adjacent punt and demonstrates what he's describing. It doesn't look comfortable but I can see, lying like that, there wouldn't be much on show.

'It is two parts, isn't it? Your dress, I mean?' He sits up in the next door punt, examining my outfit.

I, in return, fold my arms. What is it with men and boobs?

'Please,' he says. 'I promise, they'll be really, really tasteful. But seriously, you look absolutely stunning.'

I admit it. I'm curious to see what he sees in me, in this flat wooden boat on this flat, stealthy river, that's so special. Owen clearly sees nothing in me whatsoever, and after tonight, I'm not sure I do, either.

'Trust me, when you see the pictures, you'll be blown away. Please, Bella. You look so beautiful.'

Looking up at the moon, I don't say anything. The only sound now is the river lapping gently against the punt when I move.

'You liked the other photos, didn't you? The ones from Amelia's birthday?'

I shrug. I did like those pictures. They were subtle, classy and ridiculously flattering; my aunt looked like the proverbial million dollars. And sexy too.

'Well, these will be ten times better,' Joey says. 'But if you don't like them, I'll delete them. I promise.'

'You promise?' I say slowly.

'Cross my heart and hope to die.'

Chapter 23

It takes me a minute to realise the pounding isn't solely in my head. There's someone outside, acting like my front door is the only thing that stands between them and a lifetime's supply of chocolate truffles.

'Go away,' I mutter, and pull both pillow and duvet over my head. Surely Morgan can deal with this.

My room is at the front of the house and now I hear calling too.

'Bella! Wake up!'

It's a male voice. As that detail penetrates my hangover, I sit up in bed. Owen? Could it be?

'I know you're in there,' comes the next holler.

I swing my legs out of bed. It doesn't sound like Owen, but I can't take the chance. If it is him, he's clearly in total anguish about missing the wedding and is desperate to explain himself. But as I reach the top of the stairs, I pause. I probably look fiendish: hair like a scarecrow, face creased and smudged. Maybe I shouldn't open the door after all.

Too late. I hear the letter box rattle and before I can retreat, the voice is triumphant. 'I can see your legs. Get down here!'

I waver. I don't think it is Owen, after all, and I'm torn between relief and disappointment. There's still no sign of Morgan.

'Bella! Move your stumps! It's me. Leo.'

Oh, God. I remember. The 5K. I lumber down the stairs and open the front door.

Leo takes half a step back. I glimpse myself in the hall mirror and see why: mismatched pyjamas, beehive hair, one set of false eyelashes in place, the other stuck to my cheek.

'I'm not doing it,' I say, before he can gather himself.

He takes a good look at me before speaking. 'Are you ill?'

'Yes,' I say. 'Alcohol poisoning.'

His eyebrows go up.

'And bastard ex-boyfriend poisoning.'

'What?' He surveys me, as if trying to detect whether I'm messing around.

'Forget it.' I shake my head. 'But I'm not coming today. Sorry.' I start to close the door.

'Wait.' He puts a hand out, as if to touch me, but changes his mind at the last moment and presses lightly on the door instead. 'Was it the wedding? Yesterday?'

I duck my head and look at the flower bed next to the front door.

'Wait,' he says again. From the corner of my eye I see him pull out his phone. 'Cazz? Go on ahead. You can drive it, yeah? Okay. We'll see you there.'

As I hear this, I look up, and see he's watching me as he speaks.

'We hired a minibus, remember?' Leo puts his phone in his back pocket. 'They were all waiting for you.'

I lean against the door post. All I've done is totter out of bed and I'm exhausted. 'Sorry,' I say again. 'I can't.'

'What happened?'

I shake my head. Conversation is too much effort and I think I might be sick.

'Look –' he pauses, then gestures to the front step. Good idea. I sit, lowering myself without grace. 'Whatever happened last night, you have a race this morning.'

'No,' I say slowly, 'I don't.' I do feel a bit better now I'm sitting down, but although my headache is subsiding, the crushing humiliation is not.

'You made a commitment,' Leo says gently.

'I don't care,' I say, then feel guilty about the leukaemia research. 'I mean... sorry. I'll pay the sponsorship money myself.'

'I'm not talking about that,' he says. 'I'm talking about the commitment you made to yourself.'

I squeeze my eyes shut and lean forward to wrap my

hands under my legs and rest my chin on my knees. 'I don't care,' I say again.

'Yes, you do. You've worked so hard, this is your reward. The race, I mean.'

'I don't give a stuff about the race,' I say. 'Yesterday was the most excruciating day of my life, I got dreadfully drunk to get through it, and now I want to crawl off into a hole until Christmas.'

'What did he do?' Leo asks. 'Owen, I mean?'

'It's more what he didn't do.' I'm tricked into answering. 'He stood me up. No message, no excuse, not a sausage.'

'I'm sorry.'

I try to say something else, to explain how years of hope fell around my feet like the wedding confetti, how the giddiness of my romantic fantasies only sharpened the swooping descent into despair. I want to explain that when you know you've found your soul mate, yet you don't even make his shortlist, that when the highlight of your evening is a few pathetic compliments from Joey, then living itself, let alone running, seems entirely pointless.

But I don't. I simply start to cry.

I feel a hand on my back. Not a pat, not a rub. Just a hand – a solid, stable presence.

'Don't you see?' I gulp after a minute. 'Look at the state of me. Running today is the absolute worst thing I could do.'

There's a pause. The warmth from Leo's hand feels nice. He's not an insensitive guy; he understands.

Or so I think.

'Actually,' he says, with a long inhale, 'that's where you're wrong.'

I'm so surprised, I look across at him, wiping my eyes with my forearm.

'That's precisely when you run,' he says, with a small smile. 'When it seems like the whole world is against you. When your dreams have come crashing down around your ears. When the people you trust the most betray you. When you think you'll never, ever look in the mirror and smile again.'

Leo's speaking with an intensity I could never have foreseen. I'm amazed by his accurate description of my despair. As he gets to his feet, I allow him to pull me up too.

'That,' he says, 'is when you haul yourself up, dust yourself down, lace up your shoes, and run.'

~ ~ ~

I try to resent Leo, I really do. I do a good job of grumbling as he makes me go back inside and put running gear on. I do a passable impression of someone about to throw up in the kitchen sink, until he makes me drink half a pint of water and tells me to pull myself together. And I am mutinously quiet as he drives – in my car, incidentally – towards Milton Country Park, the start point for the race.

But the moment we join the throng of nervous, excited runners, the atmosphere sucks me in. My pulse quickens and my muscles twitch as I'm surrounded by people stretching, adjusting headphones, pinning on race numbers, and craning their necks as they jostle into position.

'We're late,' Leo says, pulling me over to one side of the path. 'Get warmed up.'

'Shouldn't we find the others?' In this melee, we're going to have to phone Caroline, or Grace, and pick a landmark to meet.

Leo looks at his watch, a huge black thing which has GPS capabilities to tell him his pace, distance, and other statistics. It can probably put dinner in the oven too. 'No time. They'll be starting any minute.'

I make vague attempts to stretch my calves and thighs, then take the race number and safety pins from Leo.

'You're organised,' I say, trying not to stab my stomach.

'I've played this game before,' he replies, fiddling with his watch, which beeps obligingly. He's already wearing his number – neither wonky nor crumpled – on the front of his shirt.

At that moment, there's a huge cheer from the start line. Around us, the crowd turns in that direction, like an army ready to march.

'Oh!' I pull my head up. 'Are we off?'

'In theory,' Leo says. 'Could be a slow start.'

He's right. Because of my tardiness, we're nowhere near the front of the pack, and are surrounded by other novices. My fellow 'runners' include hefty women with bum bags and Costa Coffee cups, men with pushchairs, and a group of eight dressed in a yellow centipede costume and all linked together. Together, we shuffle our way towards the start line, jostling with British politeness and apologising whenever someone bumps into us.

As we get closer, I see the digital clock overhead, already approaching two minutes.

'We haven't even started yet,' I wail. 'That's going to wreck my time!'

Unlike Caroline's marathon, this event is too short to bother with chip timing. There'll be no proof of how long I took.

'You've changed your tune,' Leo answers wryly. 'For someone who vowed they wouldn't run today.'

'Right. Well.' I sniff. 'Now that I'm here, you know.'

But the truth is, I'm absorbing the buzz of the race. I'm grasping the distraction from being stood up by Owen. And I'm loving the possibility of proving I'm still good for something.

'Well,' Leo says, 'I'll time you.'

'What?' I'm concentrating on the start line, which is finally getting near. Some people are attempting a comedic, slow motion jog.

'I said I'll time you.'

'But – I assumed, once we got going, you'd want to do your own pace.'

'No need.' He shakes his head. 'Not my first time. And

I'm not fit enough to break a personal record today.'

'Right,' I say, as we pass under the starting banner and a tiny space opens in front of me.

'Besides,' Leo says, pressing a button on his watch, 'someone's got to make sure you don't spot an old flame and veer off course to chase him.'

I attempt a dirty look, but then shake my head and turn back to the course. I have a race to run.

~~~

The first kilometre is crowded. I'm concentrating on not stepping on anyone, and on weaving my way around the walkers, who are making determined progress, with elbows out, up the precise centre of the course.

'Remember,' Leo's voice comes from behind my right shoulder, 'don't set out too fast.'

'Am I fast? I can't tell.' I twist sideways to squeeze around a pair of youngsters who've stopped to take selfies.

'A bit,' Leo dodges the obstruction, then falls into step beside me. 'Nine-forty.'

It takes me a few strides to process that he's talking about my pace per mile. I ease off, and glance at him before returning my focus to the space ahead of my feet. He looks completely comfortable, a long, rolling gait propelling him forward smoothly. By comparison, I'm scuttling like a rabbit.

'You're doing great,' he says, as if reading my mind. 'Glad you came?'

'No,' I pant, 'it's horrible.'

But I know he knows I'm smiling.

~~~

We've passed the first kilometre marker when we spot Caroline and Sid, walking. But they're doing a good pace and are keeping politely to the right of the course.

'Sid!' I call as I jog past. 'Good work!'

Sid, who's grinning from ear to ear, raises both hands in an extremely uncool wave. Over my shoulder I see that Caroline is beaming too. Leo drops back to talk with them, and I carry on by myself until he catches up again.

Boosted from seeing Sid, I'm aware of the wind in my hair and sunlight on my face. The blood is pumping around my body now, my legs have loosened up and I'm starting to feel alive.

I'm also benefiting from the extra comfort of my first ever sports bra. Smarting with shame that Leo and Caroline had been discussing my chest, yet longing for more support in that area, I snuck into her fancy sports shop on a day I suspected she wouldn't be there. I left thirty pounds poorer with the least glamorous undergarment I've ever owned. The straps alone are as wide as a motorway. But it's done the trick. Now, I find myself able to get on with the business of running without worrying about what's bouncing in front of me.

'Is Sid okay?' I ask Leo, when he rejoins me.

'He's fine. I think he's enjoying himself.' From the corner of my eye, I know he's giving me another of his looks. Has he twigged that Sid isn't the only one?

At two kilometres, I ask how long we've been going. When Leo answers – twelve and a half minutes – I start mental calculations. For some silly reason, it occurs to me I might be able to complete the course in under thirty minutes. I don't know why I care, but it's a nice round number.

~ ~ ~

There's a water station near the third kilometre. I don't want to stop, telling Leo I'm fine, but he's insistent.

'You're hungover, remember? I don't want you bonking a hundred yards from the end.'

'I beg your pardon?' I'm so surprised, I only narrowly miss the back of the centipede, which has slowed for the drinks. 'What did you say?'

'Never mind, running term.' Leo reaches out a hand and guides me past the yellow furry hazard to the far end of the water table. 'I'll tell you later. For now, drink this.'

The cup he thrusts into my hand contains liquid of the most lurid shade of blue I've ever seen.

'Bloody hell,' I say.

'Looks like they made the Gatorade a bit strong.' He reaches for a cup of water as well. 'Here, drink both.'

I do as I'm told, then we set off running again. I scrunch the cups and hurl them in the vague vicinity of a bin, where they join a hundred others strewn on the ground. I can't help grinning at the mess. 'Now I'm a real runner!'

Chapter 24

Leo and Caroline want us all to meet at the Sweeting pub for an after race celebration. At first I refuse, knowing that now I really *do* want to plod home, dive into bed, and not emerge for several months. But this time it's Grace who persuades me to show up.

'You have to be there, to wish the others well, if nothing else,' she says. 'Sid's like a kid who's mastered the potty, telling the time, and tying his shoelaces all on the same day.'

I tell her, briefly, about Owen standing me up.

Grace listens, her face softening. 'Okay,' she says, 'I know how that feels, to be the biggest fool and to lose the man you love.' She pauses, then reaches for my hand. 'Later tonight, you can get into a hot bath, drink a cocktail of melted ice cream and vodka, and bawl your eyes out. But for now, plaster on a smile and come to The Plough.'

I do as I'm told. I go home, shower, then find some comfy trackie bottoms and a grey hoodie which were in the wash during Amelia's wardrobe annihilation. I forgo make-up and scrape my damp hair into a scraggly ponytail. Then I trudge the short distance to the pub.

Usually, when I step over The Plough's oak threshold, my spirits lift. The cosy bar, smell of beer and peanuts, and rumbling conversation of the regulars typically give me comfort. But not this afternoon. Spotting my running buddies in the corner, I squeeze in between Grace and Leo, who appear to be in cahoots and have saved me a seat. Only now do I realise everyone has brought their other half. There's Leo and Caroline, of course, and on Grace's other side is her husband James, doing his usual thing of not saying much but smiling a lot, especially at Grace. Sid is next to a woman who – there's no kind way of saying this – is even more overweight than he is. And Tracey is turning frequently to a wiry man with russet hair and round glasses.

Introductions are made, but I confess I don't remember any names. I let someone buy me a drink and sip it morosely, heeding Caroline's warning that if we're dehydrated, we'll get drunk faster than we realise. Then again, maybe that's a splendid plan.

'Well done for coming.' Grace squeezes my arm. 'Have you eaten anything proper since the race?'

I shake my head. I hadn't noticed.

She pushes her plate of scampi and chips in my direction. 'No wonder you look so glum. Help me with these.'

The plump, golden chips do look comforting. I take one and chew slowly, savouring the smell as much as the taste.

'And I'm going to order you something,' Grace adds. 'Do you fancy fishcakes? Or shepherd's pie, maybe?'

I shrug. 'Either. Thanks.'

'You okay?' Leo asks.

I nod, but my shoulders sag. 'I wish Amelia were here.'

'Amelia? Why?'

'Then I wouldn't be the only singleton, and she could regale us with outrageous stories, like how she ended up in bed with that entire centipede team.'

'Nice one.' He laughs. 'But what do you mean, singleton?'

Surprised at his poor vocabulary of relationship statuses, I start to explain, but Caroline knocks on the table to get our attention.

'You all did a super job this morning!' she announces. 'I was immensely proud of each and every one of you.'

She runs through our race times, measured by the course clock, or our own watch if we had one.

'First was Tracey, in a brilliant time of twenty-four minutes!'

We applaud dutifully. Tracey bows her head modestly, but her husband beams around and nods as if he had a lot to do with her pace.

'Bella took thirty-one minutes. Well done, Bella.'

Caroline graciously doesn't mention the extra twenty-eight seconds on top of that. Though I was disappointed not to break my arbitrary half hour goal, and the last kilometre hurt my lungs like crazy, I smile as I remember the elation of crossing the line and the satisfaction of accepting my cheesy medal and goodie bag.

'Grace was just behind, at thirty-two minutes,' Caroline continues. Grace's time was slower than mine, but we didn't pass her on the course because she started sooner. As the others clap, I turn to her and we hug briefly. James, on her other side, squeezes her thigh.

'Ouch,' she squeals. 'Honey, don't.'

I'm not the only one with angry legs, then.

But the biggest cheer is saved for Sid.

'Fifty-nine minutes!' Caroline announces.

'Bloody well done, mate.' This is Leo.

Sid looks so proud, he might cry. I feel tears welling up too, and scrabble for a tissue in the pocket of my hoodie. Grace was right: it is gratifying to see the others celebrate. Especially Sid, who was probably heading for a heart attack before he started walking four times a week. But although I'm happy for them, there's a cloak of gloom around me which is getting heavier. As Caroline goes on to announce what she calls our 'brilliant' fundraising total, the voice inside my head is vying for my attention.

'Now,' Caroline is saying, 'you've reached a wonderful goal today. But after you go home and get a good night's sleep, I want you to think about your next goal. It might be exercise – maybe Sid, you want to keep up with your walking routine, or Tracey, you should consider a 10k, obviously. It might be a fundraising goal. Or maybe you'll combine the two.'

Goal? I think. I had a goal: it was to get Owen back. And I've failed miserably.

'Sorry, everyone,' Grace says a few minutes later, 'but I'm dying for a long bath.'

As she and James leave, Caroline slides into the empty

seat beside me. I'm nursing half a pint of lemonade, prodding at the lemon slice and watching it bob up again.

'Will you consider it, Bella?' she says, as if we were already part way through a conversation.

'Sorry?' The lemon slice refuses to drown. Resilient bloody thing.

'It would mean a lot to Leo.' She drops her voice. 'He's been so down since last weekend.'

I've missed something. Why's Leo been down? I slide my eyes sideways; he looks all right to me.

But I'm distracted by the arrival of my shepherd's pie, its bronzed ripples of mashed potato promising rich minced lamb oozing underneath. Beside it on the plate are a mound of tiny peas and a small pot of baked beans. I count to two before seizing my fork.

'So, we were hoping you might be able to help,' Caroline continues. 'Weren't we, Leo?'

'Help?' My mouth is full, but I look at him.

'I'm organising a half-marathon,' Leo says. 'Or at least, trying to.'

Oh, blimey. I was right. Just because I did a 5K and raised a couple of hundred quid, they think they can bully me into thirteen miles. *Thirteen*, for goodness sake.

'I don't think –' I begin, but Caroline interrupts. 'Leo's having some bother with logistics,' she says.

'Logistics?' I swallow another mouthful, amazed by the comfort three forkfuls of food can bring.

'There's a hell of a lot of details,' Leo admits. 'I've taken part in plenty of races, and organised a lot of construction projects, but this is a different kettle of fish. I'm having trouble with the city council... they're stalling on everything from portaloos, to permits, to packet pickup.'

'And we thought,' Caroline puts in, 'that since you do events for the university, you might be able to help.'

'When is it?' I ask.

'End of June, so not long,' says Leo. 'I've got two hundred runners signed up, and eight thousand of my own money invested.'

'Wow. Why so much?'

Caroline answers. 'You have to pay for stuff before the entry fees come in. And insurance, and marketing expenses, obviously.'

Obviously. I'm starting to hate that word. Then I look again at Leo: he does indeed seem dejected. He's never a smiley person at the best of times, but there are extra creases across his forehead today.

I realise now he did me a favour this morning, when he hounded me out of bed and peeled me off my doorstep. And he ran the whole course with me, though he could have completed it much faster. Then at the end, when my hands were so sweaty I couldn't even open my bottle of water, he'd calmly done that for me without uttering a word.

Then I think about Owen. It seems I'm not going to be busy rekindling our romance, let alone planning our wedding. I can't binge on ancient movies alone every night, and with the running group disbanded, there are only so many homemade recipes I can eat on my own. Unless I want to wallow unconditionally, I'm going to need a distraction. It doesn't really matter what.

'Okay,' I say, slowing my assault on the shepherd's pie. 'I'm not sure what I can do, exactly. But count me in.'

~~~

Despite putting on a brave face at the pub, once home I crawl into bed with a whimper. The satisfaction of completing the race has worn off, adrenaline pushed out by reality. They didn't give out foil blankets today – the race was nowhere near long enough to need them. Instead, I feel as if someone draped lead around my shoulders as I crossed the finish line.

But although my legs, back, and – strangely – my arms are bone tired, my inner voice is on top form.

Okay, it says, you ran a daft three mile race. Whoopee-do. But in case you forgot, missy, Owen doesn't love you any more. He doesn't even like you enough to turn up for free food and booze at a wedding.

I recall Caroline's pep talk from the pub. 'If you set your mind on something,' she said, 'I promise you can achieve it.'

Balderdash, I think, and my inner voice agrees.

Yeah, it says. Total bollocks. Better get used to that empty seat beside you. You're pathetic. In fact, you're worse than pathetic. You're also alone.

~~~

The next week is like wading through scone mix. Heavy, over-kneaded scone mix. Not only does my body ache, but my head throbs from the moment I wake in the morning until I lose consciousness at night. I sleep fitfully, waking at intervals to remember that Owen wants nothing to do with me.

Monday, thank goodness, is a bank holiday, mostly spent shrouded in my duvet. But the claustrophobic self-reflection makes my skull pound. I open Pinterest out of habit, only to close it again immediately.

When I venture into the kitchen, Morgan is there, pacing like a caged lion.

'I can't believe it's raining *again*.' She scowls at the drops streaming down the window pane. 'What is it with this island?'

'It's a three day weekend.' I grunt and open the fridge. 'It always rains then, didn't you know?'

It's a standing British joke, after all.

'And what's with you?' she asks. 'You look like death.'

I spy eggs and milk. Pancakes it is. 'Owen stood me up. At that wedding.'

'Jeez. What a jerk.' She fixes me with her feline stare. 'You're not moping, are you? He is *so* not worth it.'

Fine for her to say. I think I'll mix a double batch of batter. I haven't stepped on the scales since the day of the wedding and have no intention of doing so today.

On Tuesday, I lug myself into Trewe, stopping at Boots on the way to buy the biggest pack of paracetamol they'll allow without a prescription. Gerty, however, piles on ludicrous amounts of work. I catch her watching me several times, often when I'm staring out of the window with glazed eyes. She probably thinks I've taken up drugs.

Joey emails to say the photos he took of me are 'ace', but I delete the message without responding. When I next see him, I'll ask him to delete the pictures too. I'm positive they're hideous and I don't want to be reminded of that terrible, tipsy evening.

But on Wednesday afternoon, I am reminded of it. Jolted out of my gloom by a text from Owen, I jab the screen so hard, I fear I might crack my phone.

I am so sorry. I'll make it up to you.

Finally! I choke back my triumphant whoop, ignoring Gerty's piercing gaze. All is not lost! I hold my breath and wait for more.

I'm still waiting on Friday, although fortunately I gave up on the breath holding much sooner. I've refused social invitations from Grace, Amelia, and even Sophie, so I can stay home and pace. I'm convinced Owen will turn up, or at least call, at any moment. But the only time my phone shows any life, it turns out to be my mother and I have to feign nonchalance.

'Honestly, mum, it was a misunderstanding. I thought we'd made definite plans and we hadn't.'

'So are you all right, Beaky?' she asks.

'Totally fine!' I give up on the pacing to sink onto the sofa, where I land in half a dozen soggy tissues. 'Everything's super.' Crumbs, I'm starting to sound like Amelia.

But I know I'm not fine. I know it's not reasonable to cry at every little thing, from a dead bird in the road to an earthquake on the television. I know it's not appropriate for the woman in Boots to know my name and to reach for the heavy-duty painkillers before I ask. I know it's not healthy to eat nothing but pancakes for four whole days.

And I especially know it's not normal to sometimes skip the part of the recipe which involves heat and a frying pan, and instead eat the batter straight from the bowl.

Chapter 25

By Saturday morning, I see I can't go on like this forever. I've watched every weepy film in my DVD collection, including *Casablanca*, which Owen loved, and *Pretty Woman*, which he hated. I've run out of eggs, so making more pancakes, or any other cake, is out of the question. And, now that my legs have stopped screaming obscenities each time I rise from a chair, I admit I miss the fresh air and scenery of running.

Not that I feel like running, of course. Leo might have some misguided idea that jogging a dozen miles is the cure for all evil, but that's because he's been shacked up with Caroline for too long. I'll go for a walk instead.

~~~

An hour later, I grudgingly concede I feel better. May is a pretty month around Saffron Sweeting: the hedges have filled out, the emerald grass is lush, and cowslips paint swathes of yellow. It rained heavily last night, but apart from a few lingering puddles, the ground has dried up well. I breathe deeply as I make my way past the church, up Damson Lane and on to the fields beyond. It's past lambing season, and the sheep I pass are sedate, but the birds are warbling with the vigour of spring.

As I turn for home, I realise I can go back through the village and buy a few bits to restock the fridge, or I can turn left and take the footpath towards Grey Stoke Farm. I haven't been that way since they converted Grey Stoke House into apartments for short-term executive stays. For people like Owen.

And then it hits me. Why have I been mooching around,

feeling sorry for myself, wondering when I'll see him again? He stood me up. One measly text does not constitute an explanation. I pivot so suddenly, my boot skids on the soft earth.

The poshed-up entrance to Grey Stoke House still smells of fresh paint. With a choice of six doorbells, none of them labelled, I do the logical thing and start with the top left buzzer.

'Yes?' A female voice crackles over the intercom.

'Hi, I'm looking for Owen? Owen Rigby?'

There's a pause. 'The Irish guy?'

'Er, no.'

'The other one? Try number four.'

The connection clicks off before I can thank her. I take a breath and press gingerly on the bell she suggested.

There's a long pause, then, 'Hello?'

'It's me. Bella,' I say.

A longer pause. 'Bella?'

'What the hell happened?' This comes out before I remember to play it cool.

'Oh, God,' comes the reply. 'I'll come down.'

I wait, studying the manicured bay trees in smart copper pots on either side of the porch.

Owen appears in the doorway, wearing a V-neck sweater and jeans. His feet are bare. 'Bella!' He claps both hands over his eyes, then takes them away again. 'I am so, so sorry.'

He's scanning my face anxiously.

'What happened?' I repeat, in a monotone now.

He steps outside, under the little gabled roof which makes a feature of the door. Make it good, I think. Really good.

'I got stuck,' he says, 'in Paris.'

'In Paris?' I'm so surprised, I echo the information.

He nods. 'Well, not at first. We were in the Channel Tunnel, for about three hours.'

'Start again.' I narrow my eyes, but my curiosity grows.

He coughs. 'I went over on the Friday,' he says. 'Jasper found out Grayling was speaking at a conference and we thought it would be the ideal time to grab him.'

'Professor Grayling? At a conference? In Paris?'

'Yeah, yeah,' Owen says quickly, as if all that was obvious. I'm reminded again of my inability to keep up with his mental gymnastics. 'So we went, and spoke to him, and went with him to get dinner. And we decided to come back on Saturday.'

I assume 'we' is him and Jasper, but that hardly matters.

'Saturday, the day of the wedding?' I try, but fail, to keep my voice neutral.

He nods. 'And there was some huge engineering problem in the Chunnel. Like I said, we were stuck. Literally. For hours. No mobile signal. Then by the time they towed the train back to France, my phone had died.'

I have a flashback to waiting at Trewe, all dressed up, not knowing he was, in fact, stranded in the Channel Tunnel. Grayling must have flown back, since he made it to the wedding.

'And then?' I prompt.

'Well, we decided to go back to Paris.'

'Right.' I nod. But my mind pictures planes, and ferries, and hovercraft, and all the other ways of crossing the English Channel, if you really want to. Except he didn't want to. He'd already had a useful dinner with Grayling on Friday; there was no need to make the effort for Saturday.

'You didn't call me.' I hate the catch in my voice.

'Like I said, my phone was dead by then. I didn't have your number anywhere else. I'm really sorry,' Owen repeats. 'I felt rotten.' He reaches for both my hands and, dumbly, I let him. He gives me a small, boyish smile and squeezes my fingers.

It feels like heaven.

'When... did you get back?' I ask.

He frowns. 'Uh, Monday.' Gently, he releases my hands.

Monday. Despite being glued to his phone every time I've seen him, he didn't text me until Wednesday. If I hadn't come jangling random doorbells, would he have done anything else?

Still I say nothing. I just stare distractedly at his gorgeous face, less tanned now than when he first came back. But his eyes are as blue as ever, his lips as tempting. Why am I clinging on to hope?

Behind me, a woodpecker lets out a barking laugh as it swoops from one tree to another.

Then Owen says softly, 'I'll make it up to you,' and I feel my knees tremble.

But before I can speak, a phone rings.

'Sorry.' He reaches for his back pocket. Then, glancing at the screen, 'It's work.'

On a Saturday? Great.

With a sigh, I step back, mouthing *Ring me* in the knowledge that he's unlikely to be stuck in the Channel Tunnel two weeks on the run. I'm not sure whether Owen understands, but he lifts a hand in a half wave before closing the front door to Grey Stoke House.

And although the building conversion is elegant and spiffy with the right blend of architectural details, they clearly didn't invest in a particularly heavy front door. Because as I turn to leave, I can hear Owen inside as he takes the call. And try as I might to come up with another explanation, I have a funny feeling the first word he utters is *Babe*.

~~~

Although it's the last thing I feel like doing, I promised Leo I'd look at the logistics for his race.

We meet at the bakery, where I accept his offer of coffee and a date slice, and settle ourselves at an outside table. The sky to the north is draped with clouds, but for now, at least, it's dry.

'Where'd you come from?' Leo recognises Mungo the spaniel, who trots up to our table and thrusts his nose into Leo's lap. 'Are you on your own?'

'Don't worry,' I say, 'Mungo rampages around the village at random. There's no knowing where he'll turn up.'

Mungo waves his plumy tail at the mention of his name, but keeps his big eyes firmly on the date slice.

'Cupboard love.' Leo fondles the dog's ears. 'Just when I was thinking he liked me.'

'Hmmph,' I say. 'Tell me about it.'

Leo's eyebrows move but he says nothing. Instead, he takes a bite of date slice before he speaks. 'I like your apple cake better.'

With a practised eye, I assess the proportions of dense, sticky dates and flaky oat topping on Leo's plate. 'Brian's a legend in these parts. There's no way anything I bake is superior.'

Leo shrugs, and feeds a piece of date slice to Mungo. From the way the spaniel wolfs it down, he clearly has no problem with the quality of Brian's cakes.

Once I see Leo's list of all the logistical parts which make up a half-marathon, I start to worry. Yes, I've loads of experience with events at Trewe, but there, honestly, all you need is a room, some food, and a not-yet-dead faculty member, and everyone's happy. A half-marathon, on the other hand, has hundreds of moving pieces. Literally.

'No wonder you're freaking out,' I say, as we finish a second coffee and survey page after page of notes. 'There's no doubt. We need more manpower.'

~ ~ ~

I'm sure Leo notices that the volunteers who gather around my dining table the following week for our first meeting are the same posse he and Caroline trained for the 5K.

'Okay,' he says, 'thanks for coming. Where shall we start?'

Caroline isn't here this evening and I suspect he's more comfortable leaving this kind of thing to her. I'm surprised she isn't pitching in to help. Or maybe she is, behind the scenes.

'How about we talk through everything that happens to a runner from the moment they register to when they leave the after race party?'

It's a big help that we've all done a 'real' race, although, since this one's so much longer, Leo explains details like chip timing, prizes, and facilities for the runners to store gear.

'And then there's stuff you hope you don't need,' he adds, 'like medical assistance.'

With luck, I think, my restless dreams featuring Owen are going to be replaced by nightmares about sweat check, portaloos, and goodie bags.

Grace claims she's hopeless at organising, but is happy to do a bit of marketing. And she's brought James, whose job is something convoluted with computers, so he can help with the website. It turns out Racy Tracey, who was never especially friendly during our training, manages a youth club in Chesterton.

'I'll make the kids help on the day,' she says in her blunt drawl, 'and any grunt work you need beforehand.'

I've been scouring my contact list. Trewe does most of its events on college property, but I do know a few people in the hospitality business. I'm hoping we can do our packet pickup at the Corn Exchange.

The only person who hasn't said anything is Sid. He sits quietly at the corner of the table, unobtrusive despite his size.

'And you, Sid?' I say now. 'Where do you fancy helping?'

'Oh, I don't know I'll be any use to you,' he says. 'I wanted to show my support, though.'

Grace smiles at him. 'I can't remember, what's your day job?'

'Finance. I'm a management accountant,' he says, then bristles as we all laugh. 'What?' he demands.

'Sid,' I say, 'it's obvious. We need to keep track of our budget, and expenses, and registration fees. Leo's paid for stuff with his own money, so we have to see he gets that back. An accountant is just what we need.'

I glance at Leo, who gives me a sideways smile, then at Sid, in time to see him flush and sit up straighter.

'Oh!' he says, grasping a pencil. 'Right. Right you are.'

'And my most important job,' I say, getting up and walking the few steps to the kitchen, 'is to keep you lot well fed. An army marches on its stomach.'

The general murmurs of approval escalate when I return with a new version of the energy truffles. 'I added oats,' I say, 'to release the calories more slowly. And this other one's a courgette and pistachio loaf.'

The others munch for a minute. I bite my tongue and wait.

'Well?' I say, when the silence stretches on.

'These are amazing.' Grace reaches for another truffle.

Sid licks a finger. 'Did you say courgette? The vegetable? Goodness me.'

Tracey grins. 'We should cancel the half-marathon and have a cake sale. We'd probably raise more money.'

The others laugh, but Leo's frowning.

'Don't you like them?' I ask. 'I can change the recipe back –'

'No,' he says, 'they're terrific. Far better than the packaged snacks I buy. Even Caroline would approve, I'm sure she would.'

'So why the face? You looked like you hated them.' Honestly, he's so serious all the time. Just when I think he's finally lightening up, he goes back to being Mister Sullen.

'Did I?' He looks down at the half truffle in his hand. 'Sorry. No. I was thinking.' Then he looks up at me again, his brow more furrowed than ever. 'Thank you,' he says slowly, his eyes on mine.

'For what?' I feel a tingle I can't explain.

But Leo doesn't answer. He merely gives one of his rare smiles, before popping the remaining truffle in his mouth.

Chapter 26

'What do you mean, you've lost them?' I'm so stunned, I can't take this in.

Joey studies the river gloomily. 'They were on a flash drive. On my desk. I nipped out for a sandwich. When I looked for it the next day, it'd gone.'

He called me at work this morning, saying he needed to meet urgently. So, since my social calendar is hardly overflowing, here we are at The Mill pub, sitting outside on the wall along with the other lunchtime patrons.

'Joey.' I try to breathe deeply but suspect it's only a matter of minutes before I throw him – or myself – into the water. 'Let me get this straight. The photos you took of me at Ellie's wedding were on one of those USB thingies?'

He nods, still not looking at me. 'Along with some of Tasmin Fellows.'

He's talking about the sexy actress who's been in Cambridge to shoot that period drama.

'What, from the film? The publicity shots?'

Tasmin Fellows sells newspapers just by appearing on the cover, even if she's only buying baked beans at Tesco. A sneak peek at her new film would be a scoop.

'Not exactly...'

'What do you mean, not exactly?'

'She wanted some... personal shots. For, er, her boyfriend.'

My eyes widen. 'You're not saying –'

Joey cowers like a stray dog. I understand what kind of photos they must be.

'Oh, Christ, Joey. You kept raunchy photos of Tasmin Fellows and me in the same place, and they've gone missing?' There's a metallic taste in my mouth.

'I'm so sorry,' he says. 'I don't know what happened.'

'Did you lose it?' I say. 'Maybe it fell down the back of

your desk? Have you looked?' How can I have been so stupid? Good grief, I was topless. 'Well, have you? Do you *know* someone took them?'

He shakes his head. 'I don't know for sure. But I have a bad feeling. You know, given the subject.'

'Shit.' I say, then repeat it under my breath: shit, shit, shit. Nearby, a cluster of French schoolchildren start to giggle. 'Sheeet,' one of them sings, while the others mutter 'merde' to each other in translation.

'We have to go and search. Now, at your studio.' I jump off the wall, my glass of Pimms forgotten.

'Bella –' He tugs my sleeve. 'I've looked. I promise.'

I shake him off. 'Well, we have to look again! Joey, for crying out loud!'

'I'm really sorry –' he says again, but I'm not listening.

'I can't believe I let you take those photos. I should have known you'd do something clueless. Sophie was right, you *are* the biggest plonker ever!'

Joey hangs his head. 'I know. But you *did* look beautiful.'

'Well, that's not much bloody comfort now, is it?' I hiss. 'Now, for the last time, don't just sit there. Come *on*!'

~~~

We can't find the flash drive.

I phone Gerty to say I won't be coming back to work this afternoon. She grinds her teeth when I claim I was taken ill during my lunch hour, but I can't help that. I force Joey to drive us straight to his studio in Cherry Hinton where I tear the place apart. The studio is messy, but after two hours of fingertip searching, I admit the missing USB stick is nowhere to be found.

After that, I go home, eat a dozen spoonfuls of honey straight from the jar, and call Sophie.

She, in turn, recommends confiding in Amelia, so here

we are, the three of us, gathered around Amelia's kitchen island where I've finished relating the sorry tale. Amelia's home started life as the Saffron Sweeting fire station, and I'm hoping this is one fire we can put out fast.

Sophie, though, is far from cool. Her volley of expletives begins with 'wanker' and ends with something the French school kids hopefully would *not* understand.

'I told you Joey's a catastrophe waiting to happen,' she sputters. 'He may be a talented photographer but the collateral damage is breathtaking.'

I nod. She still hasn't forgiven him for suggesting they get married, immediately after she found him conducting a nude photo shoot in our kitchen. 'I know. But that doesn't help me now, does it?'

After the initial disbelief and fury, oppressive doom has settled on me. I turn to Amelia, desperate for her advice.

My aunt pours three large shots of Tia Maria. 'Okay,' she says, in her low, steady voice. 'Joey's lost raunchy photos of Bella, along with explicit shots of a famous actress, which every tabloid would kill for.'

'Tasteful raunchy photos,' I correct. Oh, please God, let them be tame.

'Well.' Amelia inhales. 'Look on the bright side, darling. Hopefully they *are* tasteful. And even if they're not, it's not as if you're engaged to a vicar, is it? I mean, is it so disastrous? This is the twenty-first century. We're not in Saudi Arabia, thank God.'

'It might up your street cred a bit.' Sophie swigs her drink.

'Is that the best you can do?' I say. 'If they get out, I'll be a laughing stock.'

Sophie puts her arm around me. 'Sorry,' she says. 'but you're lovely. The pictures can't be all that bad.' She angles her head. 'How much did you say you took off?'

I catch Amelia's eye. At least, thanks to her, I was wearing both a skirt and a top. If it had been a dress, I might have been completely starkers.

Sophie tries again. 'What about legal action?'

We look at my aunt, hoping her expertise on real estate transactions translates to mislaid photos.

'Worth a try,' she says, with a face that suggests it's not worth a try at all. 'But look, Bella darling, it's hardly a scandal. You're not royalty, or trying to get elected. The newspapers are unlikely to bother with artsy photos of an unknown girl next door.'

'No.' I sip my Tia Maria and try to appear calm. 'That's right. Why on earth would they bother with me?'

But I'm not fooling anyone: I'm sick to my core about the pictures. In the time since Joey broke the news, I've admitted to myself that the reason I let him take them was because I wanted to feel beautiful, and desirable. I wasn't all *that* drunk. I was intrigued, tempted, flattered.

And now they're lost, out there, for anyone to find and publish. What's worse, I'm bitterly aware that alongside Tasmin Fellows, I'm going to look like a baby hippo.

Chapter 27

'You look as pleased to be here as I am,' Leo says on Wednesday night. He has to raise his voice to be heard from the adjacent table, over the hum of anticipation in The Plough.

All I can offer in return is a weak smile. He's right: I can't believe I let myself get dragged out for a pub quiz. But it seems that Sophie, Amelia, and possibly Grace have made a pact that I'm not allowed to languish at home. There's been a steady stream of texts, phone calls, and in person visits, which as far as I can see are intended to cheer me up and check on me simultaneously. So far, the only good thing about the vanished photos is I've lost the pounds I put on after Owen stood me up. The gnawing trepidation, no doubt.

But I'm not sharing this with Leo. 'What about you?' I ask. 'Quiz not your thing?'

He shifts on a velvet-covered stool and stretches both legs. 'I wouldn't mind,' he says, 'if some people didn't take it so seriously.' He jerks his head towards the bar, and I see Caroline and Kenneth making their way towards him with their hands full of drinks and crisps. Well, Caroline's carrying drinks; I can't imagine she'll be eating any crisps. And I remember what Leo told me about the pressures of having a fanatical librarian for a father.

'Well,' I lower my voice, 'I doubt your table will come last.' I'm rubbish at quizzes: I can never remember the answer until after it's all over, then it comes to me, crystal clear. Not only that, but our team tonight is all female: my aunt, plus Sophie, Grace, and Violet from the post office.

'She gets lonely in the evenings,' says Grace, when Amelia hisses a protest about this last team member. 'Sorry.'

'Shouldn't we have a man?' I suggest, as we settle at our table and the others begin discussing their strongest subjects. 'You know, to round out our knowledge a bit?'

'Of course we don't need a man!' comes the chorus from Amelia, Sophie, and, surprisingly, Violet, all at once.

'You old-fashioned thing, Bell.' Sophie cracks her knuckles. 'We're modern women, with a full spectrum of interests.'

'Anyway,' says Violet, 'we've got Mungo.'

Right on cue, the dog flops down, squarely on my feet. At least my toes will be warm.

But by the halfway point, we're struggling. True, Amelia knows her fashion designers, Sophie can name the capital of Antigua and Violet has surprisingly good recall of Mrs Thatcher's years as Prime Minister. But Grace struggles with American politics and I fluff the main ingredient of a Singapore Sling. None of us knows anything about snooker, the Apollo missions or eighteenth century Dutch art. It's a pity they haven't asked about mobile phone coverage in the Channel Tunnel: I've researched that topic to death.

'It's not lack of a man,' Amelia insists. 'The questions are rubbish.'

I turn and catch Leo's eye.

'How are you doing?' He shuffles his stool closer to be able to hear me.

'Awful,' I say, leaning that way. 'You?'

He shakes his head. 'My dad's making me feel about thirteen again. Grim flashback. He didn't know the date the Titanic sank, but somehow *I* was expected to.'

'Never mind,' I say, 'maybe in the second half they'll ask who won this year's London Marathon.'

'Or the secret ingredient in your chocolate cherry bites.'

Beyond him, I see Caroline watching us, her head to one side. I can't read her expression, but I suspect she doesn't approve of me fraternising with her team mate and boyfriend. 'Good luck,' I whisper, and turn back to my table.

Fergus, who is both quiz master and bar tender, makes the last call for drinks before the second half. As the teams settle again, I look up and see Owen. He's clearly just come into the pub and is surveying the crowded tables. The next moment, those grey-blue eyes land on me and I feel my face light up. Then, as he starts to push his way through the pub towards our table, my heart jolts.

'Hi.' He speaks first.

'Hello.' From my seated position, I'm dwarfed by his physique. In fact, my eyes are level with his waist and I avert them hastily.

Owen nods hello to the others at the table. Sophie's eyebrows are up, but she's keeping quiet, while Grace has a quizzical look. Amelia opens her mouth to speak, but is distracted by a question from Violet. Mungo, unusually, doesn't move from my feet.

'It's quiz night,' I say, in case that isn't obvious. 'A matter of life and death.'

'Ah,' he replies, 'silly me.'

I can't sit down here any longer with him up there; I'm getting a crick in my neck and his groin, in blue jeans with just the right amount of wear, is terribly distracting. I stand and step away from the table.

'I only came in for a celebratory drink.' There's a grin tugging at Owen's lips. 'I should buy you one too.'

'Oh?'

'Grayling's agreed to work with us. A formal partnership. We're chuffed to bits.'

'Oh, my gosh,' I say, 'that's brilliant!'

Owen rolls his shoulders. 'We heard today. And I know you helped, gave him a nudge...'

'Oh, well, I...' I didn't do much at all, but if Owen thinks I was helpful, I'm hardly going to correct him. Not when he's looking at me so appreciatively.

'Okay, you lot, settle down,' calls Fergus. 'Next round is history!'

A groan emanates from the quiz participants. Glancing around the pub, I make brief eye contact with Leo. He's looking serious, brow furrowed, probably getting his brain into gear. I smile, but he doesn't smile back.

'Maybe you should join our team?' I suggest to Owen,

loud enough for the others to hear.

Sophie rolls her eyes and Violet promptly folds her arms.

He glances at my frosty friends. 'I can't stay.' Then, as my shoulders sag, he adds, 'But I would like to buy you a drink. Or something?'

'Okay.' My voice is squeaky. 'That would be nice.'

I sink onto my barstool as Owen, apparently giving up on celebrating in The Plough tonight, heads for the door.

'And what was *that* about?' Amelia wants to know. She's twirling a moccasin on the end of her foot, a sure sign her brain is in overdrive.

'I'm not sure.' I fan myself with my answer sheet. 'But I think Owen just asked me on a date.'

Chapter 28

The following day, I decide to turn up for our – now unofficial – running group. With the light evenings, we've fallen into the habit of meeting at six at the school playing field. Those who want to run together do, while those who want to go faster, or further, do their own thing.

I'm still demented about the missing photos, but since I now have a potential date with Owen, I need to burn a few calories. My thighs no longer rub together when I jog, and I want to keep it that way. Plus, although I hate to admit that Leo's right, the exercise does calm my mind and improve my mood.

Racy Tracey arrives, stretches with us, and then sets out on a longer run.

'Where do you want to go?' Grace asks me.

'Dunno.' I shrug. 'Not far. It looks like it could thunder.'

'Shall we just do laps of the field?'

As we set off, she says, 'I hope you don't mind me saying...'

I look across at her. 'What?'

'Well, we're a bit worried about you.'

I adjust my stride, which is longer because I'm taller, to match Grace more closely. She doesn't know about the wayward photos – at least I don't think she does – so what does she mean?

'You said Owen... asked you out again?' She's puffing already.

I nod happily. 'He did.'

'Oh.' Through her heavy breathing, I sense the undertones.

'What?' I ask.

'It's just... Owen's treated you so badly up to now... we're not sure you should get your hopes up.'

'Not you as well,' I mutter. Last night, after the quiz,

Sophie said much the same thing, only with stronger language which included *tosser*.

'He hasn't treated me badly,' I say, as we turn the corner near the river.

'Bella –' she slows to a walk and I consider continuing to run. But after a few paces, I slow too. 'He sodded off to America, came back, showed hardly any interest in you, and then stood you up at a wedding.'

'He explained that,' I retort. But she's only voicing the thoughts which have been whispering to me for weeks.

'Which part?' Grace shoots back. Then she clears her throat. 'Look, sorry, it's none of my business. But Amelia says...'

There's nothing like knowing people have been talking about you to make you curious. 'What does Amelia say?'

'Well, we all agree, really: you can do better.'

'Fine.' I say. 'Let's run.'

We've only completed a couple more laps when Leo arrives. 'Hey,' he says, his face even more brooding than usual, 'don't stop on my account.'

'How are you?' Grace asks him, apparently not sensing his dark mood as he falls into step alongside us.

'I've been better.' He puffs out a long breath which I suspect is not to do with the exercise.

'Join the club,' I mutter, giving Grace a dirty look. Why can't she be happy for me, now that Owen's finally making a move?

'What's up?' Leo looks at me. 'You seemed okay last night. With your chap.'

'Owen asked me out,' I reply, 'and certain people are giving me grief.'

'I wasn't giving you grief,' Grace protests. 'We're just protective of you.'

'Will you go?' Leo asks. 'After what happened before?'

'Don't you start,' I say, and he glowers. Clearly, he's had a bad day.

'Grace is right,' he replies, as the three of us jog together down one long side of the school football pitch. 'Don't trust him. Men are cads.'

I'm about to protest, but have second thoughts. No matter how I feel about him, Owen did not behave well over the wedding. Then there's Joey, taking raunchy photos of me and losing them. Even my last few dates have failed to show men at their best.

I settle for saying, 'You're not a cad.'

Leo doesn't answer, just harrumphs and keeps his eyes on the grass ahead of us. I realise we haven't asked about his bleak mood.

'So what's up with you?' I say.

He slows to a walk. Surprised, I do the same and Grace stops too.

'Oh, stuff,' Leo says. 'Race headaches.'

'Like what?' I ask.

'The snack sponsor pulled out.' We must look puzzled, because he continues. 'There's supposed to be a muesli bar in each goodie bag. But they've had to recall one of their other products, and now they say they can't afford to give us the bars.'

'So, what will you do?' asks Grace.

'We'll have to buy them.' Leo sighs. 'I know it's trivial, but it's more cash out of my pocket.'

We make sympathetic noises.

'What does Caroline think?' I ask.

'Dunno. She's gone to France.'

'Why?' Grace and I speak simultaneously.

'She got selected for a running camp. They'll live and train at altitude. It's in the Pyrenees somewhere.'

'How long for?' asks Grace.

I expect him to say a week or two.

'Not sure.' Leo shrugs. 'Six months maybe?'

'And she upped and left, just like that?' What kind of girlfriend does that?

Leo looks at me. 'I'm happy for her.'

But I can tell he's trying to play it down.

'So now you're organising the race on your own,' Grace says.

'Yeah.' Leo stops walking. 'Sorry. I'm not really in the mood for running tonight.'

I'm about to chirp that this is precisely the time when he should run, but I think better of it.

'Don't worry, we'll help you.' Grace shows her kind side once again. 'Won't we, Bella?'

I don't answer at first. I'm pondering the Pyrenees. Then, as Grace nudges me in the ribs, I say, 'Help? Oh. Of course we will.'

But I'm not thinking about Leo's race. Instead, I'm beginning to see that Caroline and Owen have a lot in common.

Chapter 29

I wake on Saturday to the insistent buzzing of my phone. Although set to silent, it's dancing around like it's caught rabies.

'It's me,' comes Sophie's voice. 'They're on the web.'

I don't have to ask what. 'Bugger,' I mutter sleepily. It's barely a week since Joey lost them. Looking at the phone, I see a flurry of text messages too, most likely from Amelia. Although what she's doing up this early, I don't know.

'Where?' I haul myself out of bed and reach for a dressing gown, then pad downstairs to the lounge and my ancient laptop.

'Pretty much all over,' Sophie says, and I hear her conversing with Tom in the background. 'Tom saw a hashtag trending. Looks like it started on some French tabloid site, but they've spread.'

'Oh, merde,' I mutter, but I don't sound funny, even to myself.

'But so far it's only the ones of Tasmin thingummy.'

'Fellows,' I supply. 'Not the ones he took of me?' I will the computer to boot up faster.

'No. At least, not that we can find.'

'Thank God.' I sink onto the settee.

'But they're quite explicit,' Sophie adds. 'Just google *Tasmin photos*, you'll find them fast enough.'

'Hold on,' I say, 'I'm trying to get to a browser.'

Sophie waits. I hear her making that trademark clicking with her tongue.

'Oof.' I finally get Firefox to respond. 'Crumbs.' I tilt my head. 'You can see what she had for breakfast.'

Poor Tasmin Fellows. Whatever the purpose was of her photo shoot with Joey, I'm not sure she intended these to be released.

'Are the ones he took of you... like that?' Sophie asks

hesitantly.

'No!' I reply, trying to recall the drunken punt evening. 'At least, I bloody hope not.'

~~~

The morning descends into chaos. Amelia arrives first, wearing a black linen dress and enormous sunglasses. 'Darling!' she says, air kissing me vigorously. 'Don't worry, don't worry!' But she's barely sat down before she whips out an iPad and starts jabbing at the screen.

Then Sophie and Tom show up. He's carrying a laptop while Sophie swings a bulging Waitrose bag. 'We brought sandwiches,' she declares. 'I wasn't sure you'd feel like cooking.'

Good old Sophie, never one to overlook the food.

And last but not least, pounding on the door as though the mafia are after him, comes Joey.

'Can I hide out here?' He falls over the threshold. 'They're outside my studio, and at mum and dad's.'

'No, you cannot,' I protest, as he heads into the lounge. 'You're to blame for this mess.'

Joey, however, is white as a sheet. Having yanked both sets of curtains across the windows, he sits down on the carpet as if to evade sniper fire.

'I've been phoning you, you moron!' I plant my hands on my hips.

Joey shudders, reaching across the coffee table to commandeer my computer. 'So's half of Europe.' He throws his head back in despair. 'I am so screwed. She's gonna sue.'

'Who?' ask Sophie and Amelia at once, then supply their own answer. 'Tasmin?'

He nods. 'Her lawyer emailed already. She's livid.'

'Understandably,' Tom puts in.

'Joey,' I say urgently. 'The photos of me, they don't – er – show as much, do they?'

I was pretty drunk and although Joey claimed the pictures would be tasteful, I'm not sure how much the camera could see.

He shakes his head. 'Yours were different. Anyway, don't panic, they're not online.'

The other three look up, but it's Amelia who pulls a face and says what we're all thinking.

'Yet.'

~ ~ ~

The day crawls by, with the four of them hitting refresh on their screens like they're bidding in an online auction.

Amelia, having located Tasmin's photos at a reasonably good resolution, is amusing herself by zooming in to look for cellulite. 'She's only twenty-eight, but look, that's a wobble right there,' she says.

'Please,' I say, '*that's* not a wobble.' I don't need to finish what I'm thinking.

'Has she had her breasts done?' Amelia squints at the screen.

'Yes,' says Joey emphatically.

'Stop it!' I hurl a cushion in his direction. 'Stop looking at them.'

Sophie keeps consulting Twitter to see if the pictures are still trending. 'Oh, goody,' she says, 'there's been a mudslide in Los Angeles. Tasmin's dropped to number two.'

I'm ashamed of the relief I feel that people may have been buried alive in sludge, knocking Joey's seedy photos out of the limelight. He, incidentally, keeps telling us how many hits are coming back on Google, taking perverse pleasure in the worldwide reach of his work.

Morgan, thankfully, has been upstairs all morning. She strolls through the lounge at eleven, long hair damp, and returns from the kitchen with a smoothie.

'What are y'all doing?' she asks idly, the drink in one

hand, her phone in the other.

'Fundraising,' I say, quick as lightning, silently willing the others to play along.

Joey, who for once is smart enough to keep up, lowers the lid of his laptop.

Morgan notices him. 'Hey down there, Joey.' She chugs the smoothie and wipes her mouth.

Here we go, I think. The Italian charm will be unleashed and we'll never get rid of her.

But Joe, bless him, senses this is no time for flirting. 'Hi.' He looks up blankly.

Morgan gives a small sniff. 'Right,' she says, as though that decided matters. 'I'm off to Antwerp.'

'Have fun,' says Tom, as if popping across to Belgium for a long weekend is perfectly normal. Oh, wait, he's a pilot. For him, it is.

As soon as Morgan leaves the room, five heads snap back to our screens.

~ ~ ~

'I can't stand it.' At three o'clock, I clamber to my feet. 'I'm going to bake something.'

But none of them respond. They're sitting there, in a squashed line on the settee, nudging each other and leaning across to see each other's devices.

'What?' I say.

'Is it only Spain?' asks Amelia.

Tom shakes his head. 'Canada.'

Joey looks at Sophie and points. 'This is German, right?'

Sophie nods. 'Bollocks,' she says. '*Dazzle* just went live with it.'

'What?' I ask, surely the most pointless question ever.

Amelia shakes her head. 'Darling, I'm so sorry.' She bites her lip as she turns her iPad around.

I barely recognise myself. Though I'm half expecting this, it's like an out of body experience to see the sultry, moody, black and white shot. I'm leaning over the edge of the punt, my eyes look huge and I'm showing acres of flesh. Above me, in the most massive font I've ever seen, is the headline:

Mystery nude puts Tasmin in the shade.

Chapter 30

It doesn't surprise any of us that after the photos of me appear on *Dazzle*, other websites publish them too.

I barely sleep on Saturday night, alternating between refreshing my screen and running to the bathroom, where I hunch over the sink, trying but failing to be sick. For years, I've hated glimpsing my own body naked in the mirror, and now the *entire* world can see it.

By Sunday lunchtime, I'm wrung out. I huddle on the sofa, refusing food and drinking nothing but warm milk, which Sophie supplies every hour. I haven't met Tom's eye at all today and can't bring myself to speak to Joey.

'You must admit, though, the general tone of the captions is positive.' This is Amelia, who has remained defiantly upbeat.

'You just haven't shown me the ones which are calling me a fat blob,' I mutter. 'And Tom hasn't let me look at Twitter at all.'

But on the sites the others do allow me to see, the words underneath my mug shot include *voluptuous*, *mysterious*, *sensual*, *enigmatic*, and *womanly*.

'They're being ironic,' I scoff.

'No,' says Sophie firmly, 'you look beautiful.'

I blush. 'Don't be daft. Joey found... a good angle.'

Still, I put my head on one side to consider the photos again.

By some miracle, you can't actually see anything you wouldn't see on Bournemouth beach on a July day. You can definitely tell I'm topless, with my shoulders and acres of cleavage revealed, but in most cases the camera didn't go lower than that. There are, however, a few where my arms strategically cover my bare breasts. And some are taken from the back, with me looking over my shoulder, showing an expanse of moonlit skin.

Joey, who may or may not have slept here last night – I really don't care – looks up from his sprawl on the carpet. 'I keep telling you, you looked great.'

I dig my fingernails into my palms and say nothing.

Amelia, though, is still studying the photos. Considering how interested she was in Tasmin's cellulite, I dread to think what she might be about to point out.

But all she says is, 'Right. Let's make you harder to find.'

She makes me take down my Facebook page, and remove my photo from LinkedIn, and even scrub pictures from the simple website Lorraine and I have for our supper club.

'But why?' I protest, as she marches over to the phone and unplugs it.

'Darling, I know you haven't scrutinised all the pics, but there's something here which stands out.'

'Stands out? What?' Alarmed, I peer again at her iPad. The picture on the screen is remarkably tame, only my head and shoulders peeking over the edge of the punt. 'I don't see anything.'

'Bella, love, here.'

She points at the corner of the photo and I gulp at the single word clearly visible, painted on the side of the little boat: *Trewe.*

'Oh, crap,' I say.

On Sunday night, I suggest this is an ideal time to claim the measles and stay home from work.

But Amelia won't hear of it. 'Of course you're going to work,' she says. 'This will all blow over in a day or two.'

Sophie is more gentle. 'They might not realise it's you. I know it seems like the end of the world, but it isn't.'

Fresh nausea surges through me. Every instinct is to retreat, hide, roll myself into the smallest possible ball and pretend I don't exist. If Uncle Mike's house was old enough to have a priest's hole, I would climb in there and hibernate.

'Come on, Bella. Chin up, darling.' Amelia tosses her

head, as if to show me what defiance looks like. 'And remember,' she says, 'you've done nothing wrong.'

~~~

I arrive at Trewe an hour earlier than usual, figuring that if I have to be there, I'm going to sneak in before anyone else arrives. I'm wearing my jacket collar turned up, a beret and the inevitable dark glasses.

Sophie drops me off on Kings Parade. 'Remember,' she says, 'the rest of Cambridge hasn't spent Sunday looking at the gossip sites.'

I nod, relieved there are no media vans parked outside the college gates. Then I scuttle inside with my head down, barely acknowledging my friends in the Porters' Lodge.

Once settled in front of my computer, I launch my email and scan the weekend's messages for signs of trouble. Just the usual stuff: alumni trying to find each other, someone wanting to know how to donate a work of art, a complaint about a faculty dinner where the wine ran out by ten o'clock. No voicemail: that's good. I've no appetite, but I boil our office kettle for tea, then, peeking through my fingers, I bring up a web browser and start working my way through the news.

At first, things look promising. The main article on BBC News is about elections in Greece, while CNN leads with the latest in the Middle East. Their entertainment sections are dominated by JK Rowling and by a teenage country music star. I move on to the *Guardian* and *Times Educational Supplement*, although I'm hardly expecting trouble there. But then I steel myself to click from *Femail* to *Cosmo* to *Hello!* And there they are: front page news.

Mostly, the photos of Tasmin still dominate: she is, after all, the celebrity, and her photos are way more scandalous than mine. But as I click from site to site to site, I see more mentions of the other woman, the mystery girl, the unknown model. My heart sinks as some websites have labelled me the *Cambridge University Student*, mistakenly believing that every female who lolls around in a punt must be enrolled on a degree course. *Brains and beauty too*, suggests one blogger. *Can Tasmin compete?*

Beauty? I think. Hardly.

Who is the Trewe College student, asks another site, *and how did her May Ball photos get mixed up with Tasmin's?*

They're way off the mark with that one. I'm ten years older than most of the Cambridge undergraduates, and the May Balls aren't even held until June. However, the fact they've made the link with Trewe, as Amelia predicted, makes my mouth dry.

It's horribly addictive, reading about myself. My tea goes cold in its mug as I quail at the *Daily Mirror's* crudity, then giggle at the description of Joey as photographer to the stars. But I admit I read the commentary on *FemUK* twice. This site, admittedly a left wing squawk box, suggests that *the mystery girl is more real, and a far better role model for women, than an anorexic Hollywood twig.*

I suppress my involuntary smirk as the office door opens and Gertrude arrives.

'Morning,' she says, with the enthusiasm you might expect if she was off to clean the college toilets, rather than sit at her computer, drink coffee and browse needlepoint ideas.

'Hi,' I squeak.

Then, as Gerty shrugs off her coat and collapses into her chair with a blank face, I begin to relax. She can't possibly have seen the photos or she'd be hopping around like Rumpelstiltskin.

'What?' she asks, noticing that I'm watching her.

'Nothing.' I inch down in my chair so she can't see me as easily over the top of her monitor. 'Er, good weekend?'

She grumbles something about her daughter's friends, and I allow myself to breathe. She has no clue that I'm plastered topless all over the interwebs, in a punt painted in Trewe's colours.

Is there a chance I'm going to get away with this?

~~~

For an hour, nothing happens. The clock on the wall ticks in slow motion. I brew more tea for both Gerty and me, and I make half-hearted attempts to answer alumni emails.

Then, at nine-thirty, my desk phone rings.

'Bella? It's mum. The most extraordinary thing happened.'

'Hi, mum.' Already my voice is a weak wobble.

'I popped round to Mrs Worthington to buy some of her jam and she said there are naughty photos of an actress on the internet and that Trewe College is involved.'

'Uh?' I can't manage more.

'So then she got them up for me on her computer and, Bella dear, they look awfully like you!'

'Uh, really?' I look in Gerty's direction to check her antennae aren't twirling.

'In fact, I could swear it was you. They're soft focus, mind, taken at night. And what's more –' mum pauses, as if this part takes special effort to enunciate, '– they're topless!'

My whole body deflates. In all the panic since Saturday, I hadn't thought about my family seeing them. My mum... my brothers... oh, crikey, my father. Perhaps I'll phone Amelia and ask her to mediate.

'Mum. I can't talk now.'

'Good God, Bella, are you admitting it?'

I take a breath. 'Yes. I have to go.'

And for the first time in my life, I hang up on my mother without saying goodbye.

If she's seen them, what about everyone else I know? What about Owen? He never used to spend much time idly browsing the web... but you never know.

The phone rings again and I jump.

Except it isn't mine, it's Gerty's. Instinctively, I hunch in my chair as she gives her usual greeting. Then there's a pause and her tone gets sharper.

'Who is this?'

Another pause.

'I never heard anything so ridiculous,' Gerty says. 'Of course our female undergraduates –'

During this pause, she taps frantically on her keyboard. I get up and go to the window, my back to her.

'No comment,' Gerty snaps. 'No comment. Thank you.' She slams the phone down.

I don't turn around, staring resolutely out at the smooth green lawn. From behind me comes more typing, and I tense my back. I'm so still, my senses so heightened, that I can hear the manic clicks of her mouse.

Then she utters one word: 'Jesus.'

I'm pretty sure she's not referring to our rival college.

As if on cue, the office door flies open. I glance over my shoulder for a split second. It's the Bursar. I whirl back around, wishing our room had curtains so I could hide behind them.

'Miss Finch,' he booms, formal as usual. 'I had the most outrageous telephone call from the *Daily Mirror*! And my secretary says our good name is all over the world wide web. Photographs! Filthy photographs!'

I grip the windowsill, briefly considering opening the window and throwing myself out.

Gertrude rallies quickly. 'Bursar,' she says, 'I just heard the same thing. And I'm shocked, extremely shocked.' From the change in her voice behind me, I can tell she's stood up.

'Well, it won't do. It won't do at all. We must take out an injunction immediately.'

Yeah, I think. Good luck with that. Look what happened to Barbra Streisand, who tried to suppress an aerial photo of her house. It went global. I know this because we talked about it at length last night, after my desperate pleas that there must be *something* we could do.

'Yes, of course. I'll look into it, Bursar,' Gerty murmurs. Total sycophant.

'And who is this young woman, this – this hussy?' the Bursar splutters. 'She must be sent down at once.'

And that's when the dread swirling in me begins to solidify. He wants to expel the presumed student in the photos. I turn around. It's like a car crash. I can't bear not to watch.

'I haven't...' begins Gerty, pulling her glasses off her head and back onto her nose. She leans down to look at her computer screen, frowning, clicking, frowning more.

'Well?' growls the Bursar. 'Is it that Spanish girl? The one reading economics? I never liked the look of her. Sly eyes. Or that blonde one? With the brother at Kings? Total tart.'

I see the recognition, then the shock, cover Gertrude's face. She gapes at me, then the Bursar, then her screen, and finally back at me. And the shock in her expression falls away, replaced with something else entirely. I hold my breath.

'No, Bursar,' says my boss. Her voice is clipped, professional. 'It isn't the Spanish girl, or the one with the brother.' In her eyes is an unmistakable gleam of malice. 'It's Bella.'

Chapter 31

They send me home. Compassionate leave, the Bursar calls it, which is a joke as compassion is blatantly absent from the discussion.

But as I reach the main gate of Trewe, and see the first photographers gathered on the pavement, I realise it's best I'm leaving now. I shrink back against the wisteria-covered wall, wondering whether to backtrack and leave through the river gate instead. Then I reach for my dark glasses, square my shoulders, and stride briskly past the Porters' Lodge, turning left on Trumpington Street.

'Hey!' Behind me, a shout goes up. 'Who was that?'

'Was it her?' Another voice, with a foreign accent.

I don't look back, just pray they don't have motorbikes as I break from my march into a trot. Thank God for Caroline and Leo. Without them, I wouldn't be able to put this distance between myself and Trewe so quickly. At the corner of Mill Lane, I take advantage of a group of tourists blocking the pavement to dart behind them and look back. Is that guy following me? The one in the black jacket?

I set off again, running now down Mill Lane, desperate to make another turn before the photographer reaches the street corner. I pause at Millers Yard, considering hiding out there, but then dismiss it: it's a dead end, I'll be boxed in. Instead, I pelt the last few yards to the tiny lane that runs behind The Anchor. As I turn the corner, I glance back: no sign of the guy in black. Still, I daren't stop. Within moments, the lane brings me to Silver Street. I swerve left and cross the bridge, weaving around more tourists, accelerating now. By the time I reach the peaceful safety of the Mill Pond, I suspect I've broken the record for my fastest ever mile.

Then, not waiting for my breathing to slow, I pull out my phone and call Sophie.

~ ~ ~

Over the next few days, things go from bad to worse.

By the time Sophie's driven into Cambridge, scooped me up and returned us both to Saffron Sweeting, I've been named online as the mystery woman in the photos. There's a blurred picture, too, of me dashing out of Trewe with my head down and collar up.

Within minutes, my phone lights up with calls and texts. Amelia, smart cookie that she is, calls Sophie's mobile instead.

'All right,' she says on speaker phone, 'so the hounds have scented the fox. Now the real fun starts!'

'Fun?' I mouth at Sophie, not relishing for one moment being the prey in this scenario.

'Get her out of there,' is Amelia's next command.

'What? I'm not going anywhere!' I exclaim. 'I thought you said I haven't done anything wrong?'

'Where?' asks Sophie. 'Tom's mother is staying. Can she come to you?'

'Of course.' Then Amelia tuts. 'But she'll have to share with Oscar.'

Oscar's my cousin, taking an extended break from university. I think that means he's lying around, getting drunk, and sponging off Amelia. I shake my head vehemently at Sophie.

'Well, where then?' she says, half to me, half to Amelia. Then she clicks her tongue. 'How about Oak House?'

'Quick,' agrees Amelia, 'before the press catch up.'

So that's how I find myself hurriedly installed at Lorraine's bed and breakfast, with a single suitcase containing eight pairs of knickers and no bras.

Lorraine, it must be said, does a wonderful job of fussing over me, declaring the whole debacle to be a 'silly storm in a tea cup'. Then she distracts me expertly by setting me to work making scones.

But, short of going into business to rival Brian, the process of mixing, kneading, cutting, rising and baking can only keep me going for so long. Sophie stays a few hours, but says Tom's mum will get uppity if she's away much longer.

'Duty calls.' She rolls her eyes and hugs me.

In the evening, Grace stops by, apparently part of the secret circle trusted by Amelia to know my whereabouts.

'Gosh,' she says, looking around Lorraine's expansive kitchen. 'Seems like yesterday I was hiding out here myself.'

'What were you hiding from?' I ask.

'I, er, ran away from James for a bit.' She looks sheepish.

'James?' My eyebrows lift.

She smiles now. 'We got it sorted out. But believe me, this is a perfect bolt hole, when you need one.'

'Do I need one?' I say. 'It's not that big a deal, is it?'

She looks sceptical. 'Well, you're the talk of the pub.'

'Really?'

'It's an awfully small village, Bella. Last week they were all lit up about squirrels nesting in the malt house roof. This week, it's you.'

I'm silent. I love Saffron Sweeting, but I realise how conservative most of the residents are. They don't approve of people landing themselves in the papers, let alone topless.

'Who's leading the gossip?' I ask eventually.

Grace looks uncomfortable. 'Well, you know...'

I keep my eyes on her.

'You can probably guess. Kenneth from the library, obviously. And the man who runs the parish council – you know, the one who looks like a potato.'

I smile. 'And Violet?' That consummate busybody, she'll be having a field day.

'No, actually,' says Grace, 'she told Kenneth to put a sock in it, said the female form was nothing to get offended over. Then she threatened to make him watch *Calendar Girls* on DVD.'

~ ~ ~

The next day, Tuesday, I help Lorraine with the guests' breakfasts, then volunteer to tackle a mountain of ironing. But I keep out of the way otherwise, staying in my room and staring at the flowers on the duvet cover. I try to stay off the internet – best not to know, as Lorraine says – but can't resist a bit of quick googling. I'm comforted that the story is subsiding. Trewe have put out a press release, saying this is a private matter and that the staff member concerned has been placed on leave. But that's all. Joey, thank goodness, has refused all interviews and word has it that Tasmin Fellows has checked into a spa in northern Mexico. With no fresh news, the press are getting bored.

I phone my mum, who alternates between concern for my well-being, and reprimands for my foolishness. 'You've ruined your reputation!' she keeps saying, as though I'm Tess of the d'Urbervilles and the only possible fate now is the hangman's noose. I give up trying to defend myself, and she puts dad on the line instead.

'Never mind, love,' he says calmly. 'No use crying over spilt milk.'

But mum's words trouble me. Not that I really believe I'm a ruined woman, but I'm aware that appearing topless in national media may be hard to live down. And it's now almost a week since the pub quiz, when Owen mentioned having a drink. Does his silence mean he's come across the photos? Or has the drink merely slipped his mind? Should I ring him?

I take myself to the end of the garden, where Lorraine's chickens are pecking at microscopic delights in the shade of the oak tree. I twist my phone around a few times, while summoning courage to make the call.

After two rings, that courage sags. After four, I decide I might be more comfortable sitting on the grass. After six rings, I let my back slide down the tree until I meet the earth with a bump. And that's where I stay, my face turned to the blue spring sky, long after the phone has lapsed into silence beside me.

~ ~ ~

Wednesday passes slowly. I like Oak House, but being sequestered here is strange, like the time I was nine and caught German measles while we were on holiday in Llandudno. Mum and dad made me stay in our hotel room so I didn't frighten the other guests and get us kicked out.

Lorraine does her best to keep me occupied, encouraging me to plan an elaborate menu for our next supper club. I start a new Pinterest board for recipe ideas, carefully ignoring anything that resembles wedding cake. Then, feeling guilty about the time I've spent, I embark on polishing Lorraine's silver. I even get down on my knees to scrub the black and white tiles in the hall, buffing them until they shine and trying not to laugh when the cat promptly skids. But my aching back doesn't prevent the time dragging horribly.

Yesterday, when I realised Owen wasn't going to answer the phone that never leaves his side, I called back and left a cheery message, mentioning the drink and suggesting – casually – that he ring me.

He hasn't.

On Thursday, as it's getting dark, Grace arrives.

'Lorraine's gone for a soak in the bath,' I tell her.

'No, no, I'm here to see how you're holding up.' She looks furtively over her shoulder.

'You're acting like you're afraid of being followed,' I say. 'I doubt MI5 are interested in me yet.' Unless Joey's lost raunchy pictures of a cabinet minister too.

'I told him to wait on the pavement until I asked you,' she says.

'Who?'

'Leo. Is it okay if he comes in? I know your location's supposed to be secret.'

'Leo? What's he doing here?'

Grace takes this question as permission, and turns again to give the least subtle signal I've ever seen. Leo promptly emerges from the shadows of the hedge and, with a few long bounds, joins us at the front door.

'We mustn't stand here!' Grace flaps her arms until I retreat into the large hall. She and Leo jostle in together, both looking delighted with the conspiracy.

Grace sniffs the air. 'Ooh, shortbread.'

'Come into the kitchen.' I'm secretly glad to have visitors.

They settle at Lorraine's big table while I locate her buttery shortbread and put the kettle on. After they've made small talk and I've made tea, I sit down with them. But I can't meet Leo's eye. All I can think about is the photos, and that he's probably seen them. Seen me, topless. And Caroline: oh, God, what must she make of my naked torso, all flesh and wobble compared with her own? I must be a laughing stock.

I stir my tea, then stir it again. And a bit more, for luck.

'We thought you might want company.' Grace is holding a stick of shortbread by the ends, using the thumb and forefinger of each hand. She looks like she might be about to play it, like a harmonica, but settles for inhaling the aroma.

'Thanks.' Finally, I glance at Leo, who's said little since arriving. His brow is more furrowed than usual.

I've already dropped my eyes when he speaks, but I can tell he's looking at me. 'You missed training.'

'It's Thursday,' Grace supplies.

There's silence. Will I ever get over this? Will I ever stop obsessing that people are picturing me in the buff every time I talk to them?

I take a breath. 'But I'm not training for anything.'

Surely Leo doesn't think I'm going to do his half-marathon?

'Doesn't matter,' he says, looking at the table and fiddling with his shirt sleeves.

Oh, no, is he feeling awkward too? He's seen the photos, I know it.

Then Leo seems to rally, his eyes meeting mine. 'It's good for you. Good for the soul.' If there's a message in his expression, it's supportive.

'Yeah, well, I've had a lot going on,' I mumble, gesturing around the kitchen as if the room is evidence of my busy-ness. Then I take a piece of shortbread too. My weight's back up – *again* – but who cares?

'So... how've you been?' Grace says brightly, looking from Leo to me and apparently concluding that she's going to have to keep the conversation going.

I shrug, savouring the velvety biscuit. 'Okay. Lorraine's been really kind. But I'm hoping maybe I'll go home in a day or two. You know, if things have... blown over.'

Lorraine's kitchen table is wonderfully smooth. I rub my fingers back and forth along the edge.

'Have you... looked at the internet much?' Grace asks.

'No. Yes. A bit,' I admit. I don't look at Leo.

'Most of it's been nice, you know. People feel sorry for you. Popular opinion is that you're an ordinary girl who got caught in the celebrity spotlight.'

Which is true. 'Yeah. I could have done without that light, though. It's sort of blinding if...'

'If what?' Grace prompts.

I draw small circles on the table. I was about to say, 'if you don't have the body for it,' but am too embarrassed by Leo's presence. 'If you're not used to it.'

'Have you heard anything from work?' she asks.

This is a more comfortable subject. 'They've asked me to come in tomorrow. Maybe I'm out of the dog house.'

'Oh, good!' Grace reaches for a second piece of shortbread. 'Isn't that good, Leo?'

Leo's eyebrows are knitted together but he nods.

'Sounds great. Yeah.'

I realise I've been so wrapped up in my own woes I've neglected common courtesy. I make an effort to tear my mind away from everyone in Saffron Sweeting knowing what I look like with my kit off. 'Anyway, how about you two? How's the race planning?'

Grace wrinkles her nose, letting Leo answer. 'Troublesome,' he says.

'Gosh,' I say, 'I'm sorry. With all... that's been happening, I completely forgot to contact the Corn Exchange.'

Leo nods. 'I've – we've – got to nail down a place for packet pickup. We can't afford to post them out, no way.'

'Okay. Sorry,' I say again. 'I'll phone them tomorrow.'

'Any luck with a new snack sponsor?' Grace asks Leo. I wonder if she realises she's gesturing with a piece of shortbread.

As he shakes his head, I say, 'Maybe you should ask Lorraine to make them.'

'What?' Leo looks blank.

'Never mind.' I feel foolish. 'Just joking, ignore me.'

But foolish or not, it's a relief to discuss something other than those wretched photos. We make more tea, and talk moves to the malt house.

'The timber frame is mostly sound, but the roof is worrying,' Leo reports. 'I'm still figuring out how bad it is.'

'It's nice of you to look at it,' Grace says.

Shortly thereafter, my guests start yawning. They haven't had the luxury of lying in bed for half the morning, like me.

I see them to the door and as Grace opens it, Leo looks at me again. 'I meant it,' he says. 'No matter what else is going on, you should run. It'll help.'

'Okay,' I say, in the way that you do when someone makes a vague invitation and you both know there's no obligation whatsoever to follow through.

'Good,' he says. 'Sunday, then. I'll come and get you.

Either here, or at yours.'

'I –' My mouth falls open as I try to say that wasn't a definite commitment, and certainly not for Sunday.

But he's already stepped through the open front door and, with astonishing speed, has disappeared into the darkness.

Chapter 32

When I arrive at Trewe early on Friday morning, Gertrude is already there.

Tentatively, I park my bag in its usual spot and switch on my computer. There are probably dozens of emails from alumni waiting, unless Gerty's answered some of them, which is unlikely.

'Good morning.' She picks up her phone. 'She's here.'

But I don't register that, because I'm doing battle with my password. 'Are there network problems?' I check caps lock and try again. 'I can't log on.'

Gertrude just looks at me, her mouth in a line.

'I'll, er, make tea, then.' I get up, but find my path to the kettle blocked by my boss.

'Bella,' she says, 'I'd like you to come with me, please.'

'What? Where?' This isn't business as usual: Shirty Gerty never arranges meetings before her second cup of tea.

Gertrude jerks her head, and leads the way out of our office, down our staircase, and across a couple of the courts to another staircase where further administrative offices are located. I trail behind, up the first flight of winding stairs, then the next, until Gerty opens the door of what turns out to be a small conference room.

Seated at the table are the Bursar and Kathleen Russell from Human Resources. My heart sinks: they're clearly going to give me a formal dressing down. Oh well, best get it out of the way.

'Bella, please come in,' Kathleen says, which is a bit pointless as Gertrude and I are already standing in the middle of the room.

Trewe's HR manager gestures to me to sit and as I take my place, I notice Gertrude goes around to the other side of the table, next to the Bursar. Three against one. I smooth out my trousers and wait.

The Bursar clears his throat. 'I'll get straight to the point. Miss Beecham, it has come to our attention that you have brought the good name and reputation of Trewe College into extreme disrepute by appearing in certain offensive photographs.'

My stomach flips. He drops his gaze and begins shuffling papers on the table in front of him. Upside down, I recognise several of the incriminating pictures, printed so they each take up a full sheet.

'Do you deny this?' Gertrude asks, in the pause.

'No.' How can I deny it, when the Bursar has my boobs – so to speak – spread out on the table?

'And you admit this incident took place on college property?' The Bursar selects a photo featuring the Trewe punt. 'In one of our boats, moreover?'

I nod. 'Yes.'

They're waiting for me to say more, so I take a deep breath. 'I apologise sincerely for the impact on the reputation of the college.' Lorraine made me rehearse this last night.

'It's fair enough they might want an apology for Trewe,' she said, after Grace and Leo left. 'But you shouldn't apologise for the photos, or your body, Bella.'

Easy for her to say, I thought: her rolls of fat haven't gone viral online. But I liked the wording she came up with, nonetheless.

'I really do regret the involvement of Trewe,' I add now, trying to keep my voice from shaking.

The three of them are looking frightfully fierce, so I fold my hands in my lap and look down, waiting for what comes next.

It isn't good.

'See,' says Gertrude, 'she doesn't deny it. Any of it.' She exhales loudly, as if it pains her deeply to say this. But her eyes are as animated as if she'd won first prize in knitter of the year. In fact, she's making an effort not to grin.

'In that case,' says the Bursar, 'I believe we must

proceed.'

Proceed? My heart thuds as I start to understand I'm in huge trouble. I look now to Kathleen, who hasn't said anything. 'Ms Russell? I really am very sorry.'

Kathleen takes off her reading glasses and clasps her hands together on the table. She leans in and addresses me kindly. 'Bella, I'm here mostly as an impartial observer, and to clarify anything that's... needed. The decision is the Bursar's, and Gertrude's.'

'Decision?' My voice is growing fainter.

The Bursar looks pointedly at Gertrude, who folds her arms and nods back at him. He clears his throat again before addressing me.

'Miss Beecham, in a case of gross misconduct such as this, you leave us no other choice. We're obliged to terminate your employment.'

'What?' I heard him perfectly clearly, and yet I don't believe my ears. 'What do you mean?'

But I know what they mean. They're sacking me. My insides give a massive lurch; I think I might be sick. No wonder I couldn't log on to the network this morning.

After what seems like minutes but must only be a matter of seconds, Gertrude speaks. 'Bella, do you understand?'

She wants to make sure I know she's won. She's never liked me, not since the day I got this job. Well, she's certainly triumphant now I've lost it.

I suppress the nausea and try again, looking at Kathleen. 'You're telling me I'm fired?'

Kathleen nods. 'I'm sorry, Bella. Yes.'

So that's why she's at this meeting, it's so I don't hurdle the table to strangle Gerty, or accuse the Bursar of putting his hand on my bum. She's here for legal protection for the college.

'But... I thought there were warnings and things? Don't you have to give me a written warning, first?'

Kathleen's face softens. She's not much older than me; I

bet she doesn't have to sack people often. She's wearing a sombre navy jacket, and I wonder if she knew, when she dressed this morning, what her day would hold. Gerty, by contrast, is in bright red.

'Usually, yes, we follow a lengthy procedure,' Kathleen says carefully. 'But in cases of... gross misconduct... then the college is within its rights to let you go immediately.' She pauses, looking at me expectantly for signs of comprehension. When I gulp and nod, she consults her notes before going on. 'You'll receive a month's pay, Bella, which I think you'll agree is very generous. That's on condition that you sign an agreement not to discuss the matter with the media.'

Mutely, I nod. Talking to the media is the last thing I want to do. Anyway, they appear, thank goodness, to have lost interest. Nobody was lurking outside the college gates when I arrived this morning. I'll have Sophie or Amelia check at home for me, then I can move back. For all the comforts of Oak House, I'm more anxious than ever to get back to my own bed.

~~~

'Screw it,' says Sophie. 'We're going to the pub.'

I raise my head from my pillow to protest, but she's already rummaging in my wardrobe, flinging clothes at me. Lorraine must have phoned her, no doubt sharing news of my latest crisis.

Having dragged myself back from Trewe to Oak House, it was late morning when I arrived at the bed and breakfast. Lorraine wasn't there, so I left her an apologetic note and then moved my stuff back home. To my relief, but not necessarily surprise, there wasn't a single reporter lurking. The last couple of days had brought fresh news stories, including flooding in Dorset and a young politician caught in bed with his wife's sister, so the world's attention, fortunately for me, had moved on.

I did the only sensible thing, under the circumstances, and went to bed.

'What time is it?' I ask Sophie now.

'About six,' she mutters, holding up a pair of boots then tossing them aside to delve again.

Once she's located some blue high-heeled wedges, she has the audacity to pull the duvet off me. 'Come on: shower for you!'

'Jeez, Soph, I've just been sacked. I don't want to go out.' I close my eyes and curl up in a foetal position, tempted to stick my thumb in my mouth.

'Yes, you do. It's Friday night. Fergus has a new guy helping. He does cocktails, apparently.'

'Cocktails?' At The Plough? I open one eye.

~~~

Despite my protests that I don't feel like mixing, Sophie has her phone out as soon as we close the front door. Her thumbs move faster than Caroline's legs on race day as we walk the short distance to the pub. As a result, we've been there less than twenty minutes, tucked into a discreet corner of the smaller bar, when we're joined by Grace, Amelia and Joey.

'Sometimes,' Grace tells me, 'the best place to hide is in plain sight.'

'Is that right?' I say, already part way through my first cocktail. It's creamy, pale yellow, served with a bendy straw and wedge of pineapple.

They've seated me carefully, my back to the other regulars. There was some nudging as we came in, but so far, none of the village busybodies has approached our table.

'You're already yesterday's news, darling,' Amelia says matter-of-factly. 'Your moment of fame's been and gone.'

'A pity Trewe didn't see it that way.' I swizzle my drink

with the straw. And it's easy for her to say: she doesn't have to face people. Maybe I should move to somewhere nobody knows me.

'Bella, I'm so sorry,' Joey says. 'I feel like a shit.'

'That's because you *are* a shit,' Sophie tells him cheerfully. 'Honestly, Joe, I don't know whether I'm more pissed off about Bell's job, or because this has propelled you to fame and fortune.'

The leaked photos have done Joey's career no harm whatsoever. Taken at face value, they were excellent shots. He's been contacted by a London gallery and several B-list celebrities.

'Okay, okay.' Joey shrinks away. 'I've said I feel awful.'

'It's all right, Joey,' I say. My drink must be mellowing me. 'At least one of us is coming out of it well. You can bung me a few quid when my dole money runs out.'

'Or buy the drinks, at least,' Amelia suggests, waving a hand around the table where the contents of five glasses are now dwindling.

'Right,' says Joey obediently. 'Gotcha.'

Armed with our drinks orders, he heads towards the bar. I notice Morgan there, all long legs and skinny jeans, and turn away fast. I don't want her caustic sympathy tonight.

'I still can't believe they sacked you.' Grace shakes her head. 'That's really mean.'

'They are mean,' Sophie says immediately. 'A bunch of stuck-up gits.'

Amelia nods. 'I remember my college. Ridiculously pompous.'

'But you didn't *love* it there, did you?' asks Sophie. 'Gertrude was a cow, right?'

I consider this, my head on one side. Maybe it wasn't my dream job, but I didn't want it yanked out from under me so swiftly. 'It wasn't so bad,' I say. 'Some of them were nice.'

'Yeah? Like who?' This is Sophie again.

'Professor Palin was a sweetheart. I'll miss him.' I inspect my empty glass, the shock wearing off and pain nudging me instead.

Grace, perceptive as ever, clears her throat. 'Maybe we shouldn't talk about Bella's job tonight.'

'Good thinking,' Amelia agrees, looking towards the bar as Joey starts to make his way back with a laden tray. 'It's Friday night! Cocktail night!'

'Who's this new bartender, then?' I ask, as a second drink – this one pink – lands in front of me. Perhaps losing my job means I won't have to buy a round tonight.

'Some guy from up north,' Joey says. 'Fergus says Ingrid wants him to have more time off.'

'Aww,' says Sophie. 'How cute.'

By the fourth drink, a classy one with mint in it, my limbs have loosened. I see Amelia, opposite me, nudge Grace and jerk her head. Grace glances in the same direction, and then they look at me.

'What?' I ask.

Grace pauses before speaking. 'Not a what... more of a who.'

Amelia sucks on a slice of orange. 'Someone who might cheer you up a bit.'

I swivel around. Owen is leaning against the bar, bank note in hand as he waits for his drink. Finally, something is going right today.

''Scuse me.' I squeeze past Sophie clumsily.

'Ow!' she retorts. 'Are you sure that's a good –'

But I'm too busy running my hands through my hair and pulling back my shoulders. Thank goodness Sophie made me wear this flirty peasant top, and the high-heeled blue shoes. And hooray for those cocktails and the resulting surge of courage. I wipe my mouth to make sure there's no strawberry daiquiri lurking.

'Well, hello there,' I say, as I reach Owen's side.

He seems startled, drawing back for a second. Then he collects himself. 'Hi!'

'We keep meeting like this.' I speak slowly, my voice low and hopefully purring, like Amelia's. Tilting my head, I give him a slow smile.

'Right, yeah,' Owen says.

'And last time,' I continue, 'I recall you promised me a drink. Want to do it now?'

He hesitates.

I lean in, emboldened by a blend of rum and vodka. 'Or, if you like, we could go somewhere more... intimate?'

'What?' Either he's frowning with one eyebrow, or I'm not seeing straight.

'You know,' I say, reaching up a hand to adjust his shirt collar, 'get reacquainted.' I let my hand linger on the soft cotton near his neck.

'Hey, Bella.' Morgan arrives beside Owen. Has she no sense of timing? 'I hear you had a rough day,' she continues. 'Wanna walk home together?'

I make an attempt to swot her away, as you would a horsefly. 'No, Morgan. I'm heading off with Owen.'

'Bella.' He swallows. 'That's not going to happen.'

I take my hand away, but my smile lingers. 'Okay,' I say, 'if you'd rather stay here.'

'Look, I'm sorry.' He shakes his head. 'I think you've got the wrong end of the stick.'

'Let's go home, honey.' Morgan reaches for my arm, and I give her a look which would freeze lava.

Then I turn back to Owen. 'Last time we bumped into each other, you invited me for a drink.'

His eyes dart away from me. He's not looking at Morgan, is he? 'I'm sorry. I'm not having a drink with you. Not since...'

Despite the mist of alcohol, I'm catching on. 'Not since what?'

Owen shuffles his feet. 'Since those... photos. And Trewe... letting you go.'

I go cold. 'You saw them?'

I've been holding out hope he hasn't, but of course the

chances were slim.

He nods.

'Oh.' I moisten my lips, wishing I'd had the sense to bring my drink with me. 'But you know what I look like,' I say, trying to sound light. 'You had first-hand viewing for six years. Surely that needn't stop us getting reacquainted.'

'Reacquainted?'

'Yes. Like, when you came to dinner at Oak House. And then you came over to mine, to see me.'

'I didn't come to see you.'

My vision is wobbly but I concentrate and look directly at him. 'Yes, you did.'

'I came to see –' He stops, but I see where his eyes go. To my housemate.

'And I only came to dinner because Morgan asked me.' He's still looking at her, like there's a secret pact between them.

I feel like I've been slapped. 'Morgan?' I gape. 'Really?'

'Hey, don't look at me,' she says.

'I thought you were chatting me up,' Owen says to her.

'Oh, pur-lease.' She rolls her eyes. 'I was helping Bella out.'

'Jesus,' Owen mutters.

Despite the daiquiri dancing around my bloodstream, I see now that he wasn't looking for me when he came to the house at Easter. After all, the week before, at the magical supper I slaved over, he chatted to Morgan most of the night.

'Oh, God.' I lean heavily on the bar.

'Bella, if you thought we were picking up where we left off, I'm sorry, but you've got a screw loose.'

Then, leaving me in no doubt as to my insignificance, he reaches for his damned phone. Maybe he has an app on there to banish ex-girlfriends.

'I didn't come back here to pick things up with you.' Owen recoils at the thought. 'Especially now you've made a fool of yourself and are persona non grata at Trewe.'

I blink, unable to speak. I'm pretty sure he didn't just wallop me in the solar plexus, but there's a stabbing pain there nonetheless.

'I came back to Cambridge to work on the project of a lifetime.' He's looking at me with distaste. 'For the chance to collaborate with Grayling and his team. There's no way, now, I can be seen having anything to do with you.'

My fingernails dig into the wooden bar top. They're holding me up, because I can no longer feel my knees.

Owen turns for the door. He rams his hands in his pockets, looking past me. 'I'm sorry, but I thought you knew. You and me were finished a long time ago.'

I don't remember which cocktails I drank after that, or how many. I don't know who else was at the pub, and I have no idea how I got home. And I've no recollection of raiding the bathroom cabinet for sleeping pills, or painkillers, or both. But I assume that's what I did. Because when I wake up, it's not Saturday, but Sunday.

My mouth feels sticky but I'm ravenous too. Creeping downstairs in the dawn light, I knock back a huge glass of water. Then I gobble breakfast cereal directly from the packet, shoving it in my mouth and not caring that half of it scatters on the floor. From there, I stagger to the settee, pausing only to grab my laptop. Before I can change my mind, I log onto Pinterest and delete my wedding board. Then, I curl up. My head pounds, my eyes sting and my heart is splintered.

I fall asleep again, but am woken rudely around nine o'clock by the doorbell. Turning towards the back of the settee, I ignore it.

Unfortunately, Morgan comes tripping down the stairs. 'Are you expecting company?'

I can't believe she's got the nerve to show her face.

When I ignore her pointedly, she flings open the door. Through my hangover, I hear a chorus of greetings.

'We're here for Bella,' comes a voice, which might be Grace.

'Time to run!' Another female, but I'm not sure who.

I snuggle deeper into the settee, pretending to be invisible. But then I hear Morgan, much closer.

'Hey, Bella! Apparently you made a running date?'

'I didn't,' I grumble. 'Leave me alone.'

'Yes, you did.' This voice is male. 'With me.'

Oh, sod, I think. Leo. He *did* say something about running today.

'No way,' I say. 'Sorry.'

There's a long pause, then someone pokes me in the bum.

'Oy!' I sit up. 'Which of you was that?' Despite my blurry brain, I have enough awareness to hope it wasn't Leo. I squint up at him and am relieved when he points at Morgan.

'How dare you,' I hiss. 'First, you steal Owen, then you assault me.'

Morgan steps back. 'Pur-lease,' she says, just like Friday night. 'I don't want him. The guy's a jerk.'

I'm still glaring at her in mute outrage when I hear Leo stage whisper to Grace, 'Is he?'

Grace doesn't hesitate. 'Yes.'

'Will you all bugger off and leave me alone?' I feel a sob rising. 'Can't you see I'm busy?'

Busy being jabbed by bits of broken heart every time I move. Busy feeling like the biggest fool this side of Bury St Edmunds. Busy wishing I'd taken Owen's bloody phone and dropped it in a Bloody Mary.

'On the contrary.' Morgan puts her hands on her hips. 'You're keeping these people waiting.'

Grace and Tracey – she was the other person, then – are standing by the fireplace, looking awkward. Leo, who's next to Morgan, rubs his chin.

I swing my feet onto the floor but then droop forward, my head on my knees.

'Sorry everyone. I'm not coming out today. Carry on without me.'

'No can do,' Leo says, his voice neutral.

Then Grace chimes in. 'Bella, we sort of need you.'

I see her look at Tracey, who adds, 'To measure something.'

I pretend to mishear. 'Yeah, my head *is* thumping, actually.'

'Oh, quit messing around.' Morgan tuts.

'Like you were messing with Owen?' I snap. 'In case you

hadn't noticed, I just got dumped.'

But Morgan just does her eye rolling thing. 'Too bad.'

Leo appears at my side with a pint glass full of water. 'Down the hatch,' he commands.

I'm so thirsty, I obey.

'Still, we do need your help,' Grace says again. 'It might, er, take your mind off things.'

'For bloody hell's sake,' I say, 'what kind of help?'

'Measuring the course,' Leo says. Then, when I look blank, he adds, 'For the half-marathon.'

I drink some more, the water blissfully cool against my scratchy throat. 'Does it have to be today?'

'Yes,' say all three of them together, which would strike me as suspicious if my brain wasn't impersonating a washing machine.

'You just have to come with us in the car,' Tracey says brightly. 'And –' she looks at Grace, 'take notes.'

I look at Leo. 'I don't get it.'

'Perfectly simple,' he says. 'Come on, we haven't got all day.'

Leo leans towards Morgan now, whispers, and she leaves the room.

Meanwhile, Grace nudges my left elbow at the same time Tracey materialises on my right. They have the nerve to haul me up and towards the door.

'You've both gone nuts.' I dig my bare toes into the rug. 'I told you, I'm broken-hearted. I want to stay here and wallow.' And throw up, probably.

'Fine,' says Leo from behind. 'Help us for twenty minutes, then you can wallow all you want.'

'Come on, Bella,' Grace says. 'Leo needs a hand. For his race. Be a sport.'

I sniff, looking sideways at Leo. He gives a half smile, eyes questioning as he jerks his head towards the door.

'Twenty minutes?' I say. 'Then you'll leave me alone?'

'Not even twenty,' Tracey says, 'then you won't see me all day.'

I'm too light-headed to realise she says me, not us.

'Okay,' I reply. 'Whatever.'

I let them march me out of the front door and into the passenger seat of Leo's waiting car. As Tracey and Grace hop in the back, I see Morgan throw a plastic bag in with them. But my head throbs, my stomach's heaving and I think no more of it as my housemate returns to the front door and waves us off.

~ ~ ~

We drive down one of the narrow, hedge-lined roads leading out of Saffron Sweeting. At the first crossroads we come to, Grace leans forward and hands me a paper bag.

'Here,' she says, 'breakfast.'

'I'm not hungry,' I say, but my nose is on alert.

'It's from Brian,' Grace replies. 'He says you like it.'

I peek in the bag and find a chunk of barmbrack. Brian has a good memory: it's ages since I had this.

'Humph.' I take a nibble, then another. 'Thanks.' The sweet bread is made with tea and fruit. It's moist, but not sickly. I might have a go at making it myself, one day soon.

'You should drink more too,' Leo says. Although he's driving, he reaches down with one hand and produces a water bottle, which he throws into my lap.

'Why,' I say, 'if we're only going to be out a few minutes?'

Nobody answers as we drive on. It's a beautiful spring morning, and Leo opens the windows a couple of inches. Involuntarily, I turn towards the breeze, closing my eyes and trying not to think about Owen: his face, his arms, his mouth... and how he looked on Friday night when he broke my heart. Again.

'Okay!' Leo brings the car to a sudden halt. 'Four miles.'

I open my eyes. He's pulled off the road into a gateway, the engine still running.

'Great!' Tracey opens her door.

'Thanks,' echoes Grace, and they both get out.

I look back over my shoulder, bemused, as the doors clunk shut. 'What are they doing?'

Leo checks the rear view mirror, and puts the car in gear. 'They're running back,' he says. 'Four miles.'

'Oh,' I say.

'Want to join them?'

I give a startled sputter. 'Hell no.'

'Fine,' he says. 'Onwards, then.'

Leo turns the car back onto the road and we continue at an unhurried pace. He glances at the dashboard more than strictly necessary, as the road winds and becomes narrower.

'Is this the course for the race?' I ask, thinking he's checking the mileage.

He shakes his head. 'Not exactly.'

'Well, where are we going?' My curiosity grows.

There's no answer as he navigates a sharp bend, then a crossroads, then another corner.

'Leo, where are we –'

'We're here.' He pulls the car off the road, onto the verge. 'Six miles.'

Beside us, the cow parsley is so high, I can't see a thing. I gesture impatiently. 'What, we're measuring the route? Okay, six miles.'

Leo turns off the engine. 'Six miles from Saffron Sweeting. Get your stuff on.'

'What?'

I sit there as he gets out of the car and lifts his sweatshirt over his head, tossing it on the driver's seat. Now I realise he's wearing shorts and running shoes.

'What are you doing?' I ask again. Then, as he pulls one foot up behind him, 'You look like you're warming up.' For the first time, I notice the powerful muscles in his thighs.

'Correct. We're running back home.'

'You what?' I choke on nothing. When he doesn't answer, I jump out of the car and slam the door. '*What* did you just say?'

Leo gestures to the plastic bag on the back seat. 'We're running back to Saffron Sweeting. Your gear's in the bag. Get changed. I won't look.'

My eyes fly to the bag. Holy smoke, did Morgan pack that? I glare at Leo across the roof of the car. 'You've got to be bloody joking. I'm not running back.'

He shrugs. 'Suit yourself. You can walk if you prefer.'

I blink twice, hard. 'What about the car?'

'I'll pick it up later.'

'But... but it's six miles!'

He shrugs again, maddeningly nonchalant. 'We'll take it slowly. You're perfectly capable. Lovely morning for it.'

'It is *not* a lovely morning for it! I'm hungover, in case you hadn't noticed.'

Not to mention nursing a broken heart.

'I did notice. Well done with the water.' His voice is perfectly level, measured, as if he had planned this. Wait a minute, he *did* plan this. Were Grace and Tracey in on it too? Good grief, they must have been. Grace brought me a snack, for heaven's sake.

'You tricked me!' I squawk. 'You all sodding well tricked me.'

'Yup.' He stretches his arms high above his head, leaning to one side, then the other. 'Come on, chop chop.'

'Chop chop? Chop bloody chop? You toad!'

'Don't get mad, Bella, get running.'

'Give me the keys!' I make a dash around the front of the car, but he's too quick, nipping around the back so we end up swapping sides.

'All right,' Leo says, 'that counts as warming up, I suppose.'

'Leo, give me the damn keys!'

We repeat the choreographed trot around the car. For a second I glower at him, then, with a howl, I hurl myself across the bonnet.

Leo stops dead, stands his ground, and catches me as I

sprawl off the car on his side. Grabbing me by both arms, he steadies me, pulling me against him until I regain my balance. I'm breathing heavily, not seeing straight, as the world sways. Despite myself, I lean in, one hand finding the warm comfort of his T-shirt, my cheek pressed against his chest. He smells of – what? Herbs? Trees? Bark, maybe?

He says nothing, just waits, holding me.

He's Caroline's boyfriend. The thought comes from nowhere. I pull back.

'Bella,' he says gently. 'I know you're hurting.'

I don't answer. I'm on the brink of tears.

'But you have to trust me,' he continues. 'The best thing you can possibly do right now is to run.'

'What would you know about it?' My voice cracks. 'What would you know about losing someone? About waiting for them for five years, all for nothing?'

'I know that you'll get over him.' He looks me in the eyes. 'I know that you're a wonderful person and you *will* find true love. And I also know that the pain you're feeling this morning is up here.' He lets go of one of my arms and taps me lightly on the side of my head.

'No –'

'Yes,' he says. 'Even if you think it's here' – he touches his hand to his torso – 'it's mostly in your head.'

I take a ragged breath, not sure now whether I'm more angry or upset. I'd like to pull away, but I don't.

'And I know, for absolute certain, that the best cure is to move your legs.'

'No.' I look down as nausea rolls through me. 'I can't do six miles. Not today.'

'I'll be with you,' he says. 'Every step. You're going to take your pain, your anger, your humiliation –'

He pauses, waiting for me to look back at his face. When I do, I see something that could be empathy.

'Take all that hurt.' Leo squeezes my arms softly now. 'And take it out on the road.'

Chapter 34

Over the next week, I run more than thirty miles. I run at dawn, at noon, at dusk. I run when the sun beats down on Saffron Sweeting's thatched rooves, when rain streams down the main street and fills the duck pond, and when the moon is peeking over the malt house. I run alone, or with Grace and Tracey. I startle deer, rabbits and, once, a puzzled hedgehog. I run until my calves cramp, my thighs burn, and my feet blister. I run until the stabbing in my heart disperses. I run until my sides ache and my shoulders stiffen.

Sometimes, I run through tears, stumbling on uneven pavements and tripping over tree roots. Once, I fall, and am lucky to miss a thicket of stinging nettles as I plunge to the ground. But I pick myself up, take some ragged gulps, gingerly test my ankles, and keep going.

I run because with every step, I feel a little better. Every time my heel hits the ground, and I push off for another stride, I'm reminded I'm still alive. And that I'm strong. When I feel angry, which is often, I push harder, focussing on an upcoming tree and striving to reach it sooner. When I think about Owen, and how I wasted six years with him and then another five apart, I pick up my pace and sprint for a hundred yards, or maybe two hundred, until all I feel is the pounding of my feet and the crashing of my lungs.

And afterwards, watching the mirror fog up while the bath runs, I bypass the scales. I don't need them at the moment. Regardless of the number, I feel leaner than I have in months. Nor do I have the urge to sink into a vodka bottle or bucket of ice cream. Instead, I lower myself inch by inch into the steaming tub of water, until it laps at my chin and the pain begins to float away.

~ ~ ~

On Sunday afternoon, I arrive home after a three mile dash to find Leo on the doorstep. I slow to walk up the gravel driveway, sweat trickling down my forehead. 'What are you doing here?'

'Wanted to see how you're getting on. And whether you're speaking to me yet.'

'Hmmph.' I put my hands on my hips, not because I'm still furious with him, but so I can twist and stretch my midriff.

The day he made me run six miles home, I was so livid I did most of it in defiant silence, a monologue in my head about how I would report him, or sue, or both, once we got back to civilization. But even that day, after a couple of miles, I realised I felt better. By the third mile, I was learning to take out my frustration on the solid earth of the footpaths beneath us. Some time after that, I began to answer him in monosyllables. The fifth mile was tough: I was tiring and wondered if I could make it back. Leo had switched by then from wry remarks to genuine encouragement, but grunts were all I could manage in return. By the last mile, when I spotted the Sweeting church spire, I was secretly thrilled with the distance I'd covered. I was also bluntly aware that his ridiculous subterfuge had rescued me from drowning in heartbreak, that instead of the pits of despair I was now on something resembling a runner's high.

But there was no way I was going to let him know that, no way I would give him the satisfaction. With our six miles completed, I called him a weasel and shut the door in his face.

'Still running, I see?' Leo says now, as I bend to grasp one ankle and relieve the tightness in the back of my thigh.

'Apparently,' I reply, to the gravel on the driveway. I don't look up, but I sense his feet shift. I reach across and grab my other ankle.

Behind me there's a white lilac bush, probably planted by Amelia, and its perfume fills my lungs as I take deep, invigorating breaths.

'Feeling better?' he persists.

After a few seconds, I stand up straight and use one hand to pull the opposite arm all the way across my chest. But I give a small nod before looking away at a blackbird, tugging at a worm in the flower bed.

There's a smile in Leo's voice. 'How many miles have you done this week?'

I shrug, like I haven't been keeping careful, proud count. Then, my mouth tugging at the corners, I tell him.

'Bella! That's incredible.' He's genuinely pleased. 'You're not overdoing it, are you?'

I don't answer and he frowns. 'Don't increase your mileage too quickly. Even if the running's helping, you need to rest too. Otherwise you'll knacker your knees, or worse.'

I bite my lip. 'How did you know about my knees? They have complained a bit, actually.'

For some reason, I press on. 'Come to that, how do you always guess what I'm feeling?'

He doesn't answer.

'Well?' I stretch both arms above my head, one hand clasping the other wrist.

Leo's eyes go even darker than usual. 'I was twenty,' he says. 'My teenage sweetheart announced she was sick of going out with a glorified carpenter. She ran off with my best mate, the day before I was going to propose.'

My hands flop to my sides. 'And?' I breathe.

'I bought a pair of running shoes.' His voice is flat, but I sense his pain, like a clone of my own.

There's a long pause, then a look passes between us. He knows he saved me, that day we ran six miles. He knows I've forgiven him.

Leo's expression clears. 'Just take it easy, that's all I'm saying.'

'Yeah, well, I've had some time to kill, you know...'

'I know. And I was hoping with some of that time, you might be willing to pick up where we left off with the race plans.'

Guilt slams into me. I've done nothing to help with his half-marathon. 'Oh, God, I'm sorry. I've been wrapped up in my – never mind. Look, do you want to come in?'

He steps back and I unlock the front door. 'I'll just jump in the shower,' I say. 'Then I'll be right with you.'

~ ~ ~

The next evening I meet Leo and the others for a race planning session at the pub. I hesitate as I walk in: it's only been ten days since the disastrous conversation with Owen and returning to the scene rattles me.

'Are you okay?' Tracey asks.

I nod, but grit my teeth. I could swear the regulars nudged each other as I arrived. Today, there was a piece on the *Huffington Post* about me losing my job and the unfair treatment of women whose private photos end up online. The (female) writer was vigorous in my defence, but I'd much rather the whole thing was forgotten.

'You look better,' Grace says, then looks around the The Plough, following my darting eyes. 'Why don't we sit outside?' she suggests.

We find a secluded table in the garden, the scent of honeysuckle wafting on the slight breeze. It's June now and it'll be light for hours yet. Leo joins us and a few minutes later, Sid turns up.

'I'm sorry,' I say to the group, 'for going AWOL.'

Sid looks embarrassed – a sure sign he's seen the photos – and this makes me blush too. No one will ever look at me the same again.

'Don't be daft,' Tracey says. 'Anyway, I feel bad about that six mile trick.'

There's a pause. Beside me on the bench, Leo shifts. I

wait, letting him sweat. Then I say quietly, 'No apology needed.'

I'm out of touch with plans for the race: the others bring me up to speed. Marketing is going great guns and finances aren't too bad. That leaves logistics.

I take a swig of white wine. Better get this over with. 'Bad news,' I say. 'I thought I could get us a discount on the Corn Exchange, for the packet pickup and Expo.'

Leo waits, but Sid reaches for his calculator. 'And?'

I look down. 'It appears none of my former contacts are willing to help.'

I called four different people today: two on the city council, plus a hotel manager and even a wedding planner. Two claimed their bookings are so healthy, they unfortunately couldn't offer me any discount. One coughed a lot, then said special rates were only for members of the university. The fourth told me I was a laughing stock and would be better off leaving town.

'I'm sorry,' I say.

Leo sighs. 'It's not your fault.'

I sense his sudden distance. And despite the insults I hurled at him last week, letting him down makes me deflate more.

'So we've nowhere for the packet pickup?' Tracey confirms.

I shake my head.

'Can we afford to post them?' Grace asks Sid.

He sucks air through his teeth. 'Not if we want Leo in the black.'

I glug the rest of my wine. This is awful. 'Maybe, since I can't help, I'll leave you to it. I really am sorry.'

I half stand, trying to untangle myself from the picnic table. My legs are stiff from running; Leo was right, I should take a day off.

'Don't be daft,' says Sid, at the same time as Tracey and Grace chime, 'No, stay.'

I pause, one leg over the bench. To complete this

manoeuvre, I need Leo to lean away, but he's studying his messy folder of papers.

'We want you here,' Grace repeats, 'don't we, Leo?'

Leo looks up finally, first at Grace, then me. 'We do,' he says, with the kind of smile that, if Owen had given it, would have melted my heart to a puddle. Then he reaches out a hand, puts it on my shoulder, and presses firmly until I sit down again. His hand stays there for several more seconds before he takes it away.

I'm starting to see what Caroline sees in him.

'The packet pickup,' Tracey says. 'Does it have to be in Cambridge?'

They all look at Leo, who frowns. 'It's –' he stops to chew his pen. 'No.'

'Where were you thinking?' Sid asks Tracey.

'I dunno,' she admits, 'just thought it might give us more options.'

Leo gives a small laugh. 'Pity the malt house is a wreck.'

'But it could be in the village?' Grace seizes on this.

'Yeah, but where else –' Leo begins.

'Saffron Hall,' Grace blurts. 'The Hall would be okay, wouldn't it?'

'Oh!' I say. 'Saffron Hall would be brilliant!'

Leo looks at Grace. 'Would they let us?'

Grace grins. 'I know the caretakers. I think they might. Daphne's such a sport.'

She's talking about the charming woman who lent me shoes for the wedding. Mrs Pennington-Jones also insisted I take a pearl choker, saying she no longer wore it and her daughter had no interest. My hand goes to my neck, bare of jewellery since the night Owen dumped me. It's too warm now for my pretty cashmere, but I could at least make an effort with a necklace. It's not as though I'm in mourning.

Leo brightens. 'Ask them,' he says.

I smile at Grace too, but I'm aware how pathetic my own efforts are in comparison.

'Jolly good!' Sid raises his glass. 'What else? Any luck

with the snacks?'

Leo shakes his head. 'I've tried a couple of other sponsors, but it's too late to negotiate now. I'm going to have to buy them.'

'Shame,' Tracey says. 'What will you get?'

Leo names a couple of inexpensive brands which are met with zero enthusiasm from the others.

Sid looks down at his sheet. 'I liked the treats Bella made...'

'Me too.' Tracey sounds wistful.

I smile at their kindness. Then I feel eyes on me and look to my right: Leo's fixed me with a gaze I can't read.

'Of course,' Grace says, from across the table.

'What?' I look at her in time to see agreement pass between them.

'Your treats,' Grace says, 'would be perfect.'

'Mine? What do you mean, mine?'

Grace shakes her head, as though I'm being exceptionally dense. 'You could make the snacks, Bella.'

I stare.

'You *have* got some free time now,' she says.

I turn to Leo, who's watching me. 'How many do we need?'

'Three, maybe four hundred.'

I swallow. Four *hundred*? When I usually make two dozen at a time? I open my mouth to refuse, then close it again.

This group has been so kind to me. They stuck by me when I was a public spectacle, and helped me begin to accept I've lost Owen for good. Thanks to Leo, I'm stronger and healthier than ever before. I love to bake, and they need my help. Grace is right, what else am I going to do with myself? How hard can it be to come up with snacks for a few hundred people?

'Will you make them, Bella?' Leo reaches out a hand to mine, but then at the last second withdraws it.

I look at him, wondering briefly why he changed his

mind. 'Of course,' I say, as I realise my answer was never in doubt. 'If you really want me to, of course I will.'

Chapter 35

With less than two weeks to go before the half-marathon, I fly into action.

At first, I'm paralysed with indecision over which snack to make. This gives Grace, Sophie, and Amelia a perfect excuse to volunteer as taste testers.

Gathered around my kitchen table, with official looking notepads and glasses of water for palate freshening, we consider the apple and walnut cake and the Nutella energy truffles.

'Love this cake,' Amelia says, '*almost* as much as custard tarts. Ooh, could you do custard tarts, darling?'

'No.' I try not to laugh. 'Not fresh eggs and pastry for four hundred people.'

'Besides, they'd get squished,' Sophie adds.

'I'm not sure this cake would stay fresh, would it?' Grace balances a piece on her fork and peers at it. 'I mean, you can't bake them all the day before, can you? You'll have to start ahead of time.'

'You're right.' I prod the cake. 'No good.'

Morgan sidles into the kitchen behind us, puts the kettle on, and stands quietly to one side. We've spoken only a few sentences since the awful night in the pub when Owen announced he was more keen on her than me. For all her bravado, she's had the sense to keep out of my way.

'Maybe the truffles?' Grace suggests.

My English friends all take a truffle, sniffing like judges at a food show. I join them, pretending I don't know precisely how they taste and that I didn't sneak two when I made them earlier.

'To die for,' Sophie says. 'Will you make some for my birthday?'

'Sure,' I say, 'but aren't they too gooey to go in the race bags?'

'But I love that they're gooey.' Sophie pops another in her mouth. 'That's the best part. Want one, Morgan?'

Morgan hangs back, then comes over and takes a truffle. 'Yeah. They're awesome,' she confirms. 'Great job, Bella.'

For the first time in days, I meet her eyes. 'Thanks.'

And that's when I know I believe her, that she didn't lead Owen on. In fact, what was it she called him? A jerk? I give her a tentative smile.

'Still...' Grace is concentrating on the task at hand. 'We don't want people to end up with a sticky mess.'

We sip our water solemnly.

'What about those things you did ages ago?' Amelia says. 'With the cherries?'

'Oh, I liked those,' says Grace. 'Flapjacks, weren't they?'

'Flapjack's yummy.' Sophie looks interested, although, frankly, she thinks everything's yummy.

'You mean, a pancake?' Morgan is clearly doubtful.

'Flapjack?' Why haven't I thought of flapjack? 'Stay there,' I say, 'talk amongst yourselves.'

Everyone loves my first attempt at a flapjack based on the chocolate cherry bites, although Grace has to explain to Morgan that an English flapjack is nothing like a pancake, but a baked bar of oats and golden syrup. But I'm not happy. I make three more batches that evening, finally hitting the right combination of ingredients at one in the morning. By that stage, I'm so fired up, and have consumed so much sugar, I have psychedelic dreams.

~ ~ ~

Nonetheless, by eight the next morning, I've delivered samples to Grace and James, and have pushed a little bag through the letterbox at Hargraves & Co for Amelia. Then I eye the sorry-looking timber framed building across the road and reach for my phone.

'Sorry to call you at work,' I say, when Leo answers, 'but I want you to try something. Are you at Saffron Hall, or the malt house?'

He meets me three minutes later, in the High Street outside the malt house. He's wearing a hard hat, jeans and a flannel shirt sprinkled with dark sawdust. Of course, I think: the woodsy smell I always sense when I'm near him.

'How's it going?' I nod towards the malt house, unsure what his work there actually entails.

'Not bad.' His tone is guarded.

'Do you think it can be saved?'

'Structurally? Yes.' From his face, you wouldn't think so.

'Good.' I smile. 'I'll look forward to a proper tour.'

Leo's eyes narrow and he draws back a little. What did I say?

'There's an awfully long way to go before that. The economics might be different.'

'Well, that's Amelia's problem. But I have faith in your work.'

He doesn't say anything, but I notice the slight lift of his eyebrows.

'I do,' I say again, not sure why this conversation is so weird. 'I have faith in you.'

After a long moment, his jaw relaxes. 'I thought... you were taking the mickey.'

'No! I wasn't kidding – I'd be thrilled to see the malt house restored.' I step closer, putting my free hand on his arm, trying to convey sincerity.

Leo shifts his feet awkwardly and I jump back again, embarrassed to have invaded his space.

'Sorry,' he says. 'Dad... still gives me grief, you know?'

Wow, his father really is a crusty old pillock.

'I wouldn't tease you about your work, Leo. Not when you've helped me so much.'

Finally, he gives me a slight smile.

I take a breath. 'Anyway, the reason I phoned...' I

gesture to the box I'm carrying. 'I've been trying out snacks. For the race.'

'Okay.' He pulls off his sturdy gloves. 'What've you got?'

I open the box proudly. 'Chocolate cherry flapjacks. With extra protein, plus flaxseed.'

'They look great.' He looks down at the bite-sized squares, but hesitates.

My face falls. 'What's wrong?'

'My hands are filthy.'

'Oh! Is that all?' Without thinking, I choose a flapjack square and hold it up.

His eyes widen for a second, then he opens his mouth and I pop the treat in.

I wait, tapping a foot. 'Well?'

Leo swallows and licks his lips. 'Dunno,' he says. 'Another?'

This time, he opens his mouth before I've picked up the chocolatey square. As I bring it to his lips, he looks me straight in the eye and winks. I fumble, nearly dropping the flapjack, and end up brushing his warm cheek with my fingers.

This time he chews slowly, then laughs. His demeanour has changed completely from a few minutes ago. 'Sorry,' he says. 'I was pulling your leg. They're absolutely delicious.'

I'm too relieved to be cross with him, and too excited by the recipe to question what just happened. It's eight in the morning, after all, and Leo has a beautiful girlfriend, albeit currently in the Pyrenees.

'Can you make enough, in time?' he asks.

I nod. 'I think so. They'll keep well – the ones I have to make first, I mean – and we think they'll survive being jostled in the goodie bags.'

'Bell, you're a superstar.'

I can't remember anyone telling me I'm a superstar before. As for *Bell*, only my closest friends call me that. Grinning, I reach for a piece of flapjack, and lob it into my own mouth.

~ ~ ~

When it becomes clear that, with my home kitchen and limited equipment, there's no way I can make enough flapjacks in time, Brian comes to the rescue.

'I close at half five.' He leans over his counter when I fall into the bakery the next afternoon, wailing with fear and frustration. 'So you could start around six, if you like.'

'Really?' A lump of gratitude swells in my throat. 'You'd let me bake here, in the evenings?'

He nods. 'It's for a good cause, isn't it? I'll stick around tonight, show you how everything works. Don't want you burning the place down.'

'Oh, Brian,' I say, 'thank you so much.'

Then he closes one eye, trying to look beady. 'But I might make you share the recipe, if it's a hit. I'll flog it to the masses as the famous Sweeting Flapjack.'

'You're too late,' I say, 'Amelia's onto that idea already.'

After seeing Leo yesterday, I went home, cleaned up the devastation in the kitchen, but then couldn't settle. So I walked back into the village to Hargraves & Co to seek my aunt's opinion.

Amelia, widely known as the sharpest businessperson in these parts, took one bite of the chocolate cherry flapjack and then flung herself into her office chair, where she twirled an orange wedge sandal on the end of her foot.

'So how many races – half-marathons – give away artisanal snacks?'

I shrugged. 'No idea.'

The sandal twirling sped up. 'Find out, darling, would you?'

Within hours of me reporting that I'd found a Hot Chocolate Run in America and a wine tasting half-marathon in Bordeaux, but no other English races with gourmet treats, my aunt called an emergency marketing summit. Grace, who was finalising press releases, and her husband James, who was the only one who knew how to update our website, didn't argue. And just like that, Amelia re-branded us. We were henceforth known as The Sweetest Race in Britain.

~ ~ ~

'She's a bloody genius,' Leo says, as we meet for a final planning session at the pub, four days before the race. 'It's all over Twitter. Registrations have rocketed.'

Sid nods in confirmation. 'Excellent numbers, excellent.'

But I go pale. 'Oh, God. How many runners?'

Leo checks his phone, calling up the online registration report. 'We did it, guys: we've sold out. I'm going to increase first aiders and portaloos. Tracey, can you get a few more volunteers?'

Tracey nods and says something, but I'm not listening. I'm downing the rest of my drink and reaching for my bag.

'Bella, where are you going?' Sid asks.

'Isn't it obvious?' In my haste, I almost knock over my chair. 'I have baking to do.'

Chapter 36

'The Expo's really important for the sponsors,' Leo told us at the pub. 'Access to keen athletes who haven't just run thirteen miles. They're more inclined to spend. And it's easier on us if people pick up their timing chip in advance.'

So the day before the race, hundreds of runners descend on Saffron Hall for the warm-up act. Anticipation hums in the air.

'This is super fun.' Daphne Pennington-Jones stands with her husband at one side of the ballroom, next to a section of wood panels recently restored by Leo. 'I've never seen so many agile young fellows in one place.'

As she speaks, one of them passes, face hidden by the box of volunteer T-shirts he's hefting.

'He mended my washing machine too, you know,' Daphne continues. 'Didn't charge me a penny.'

'Who?' I look at the legs below the box, clad in ripped jeans but undeniably attractive.

'Your charming young man.' She nods at the jeans. 'Leo.'

With a start, I realise whose bum I was admiring. 'Oh!' I flush. 'He's not –'

But Daphne's eyes dance. 'Maybe next year we should host a Saffron Sweeting half-marathon, Bernard.'

Bernard Pennington-Jones, a grave-looking man in a vermilion bow tie, passes a hand across his brow and sighs heavily.

I gather my wits and make a note to invite them to dinner, to thank them for their kindness. Maybe Daphne's washing machine repairer would like to come too.

~ ~ ~

The Sweetest Race in Britain begins at 8am sharp, and a little over an hour later the first runner crosses the finish line.

'My gosh,' I say to Sophie, 'can you believe how fast he was?'

'I suspect,' she replies, craning her neck to see the winner accept congratulations from the Mayor, 'he'd keep up with me on my bike.'

There's a lull, then a trickle of other runners come through, and then another pause before the stream becomes a steady torrent of finishers.

We're stationed on Parkers Piece, which marks both the start and end of the race. With a small army of Tracey's youth club teenagers, we're handing goodie bags to the runners. Once they cross the finish line, they move along narrow lanes – or chutes, as Leo calls them – where they're also grabbing bananas and bottles of water. Then they get to us, the proud bearers of sponsored bags which contain promotional leaflets, a Lipsyl from the leukaemia charity, and four bite-sized pieces of chocolate cherry flapjack. After that, the runners can reunite with family and supporters, pick up their gear from sweat check, and even take advantage of mini massages for tired legs.

'Now I truly understand the logistics headache,' I murmur to Sophie, after we all cheer the first female finisher. I half wonder if Caroline might put in a special appearance, but Leo hasn't mentioned her recently. And in this throng it's unlikely I'd spot her.

'Yeah, right,' Sophie says. 'No wonder Leo always looks so worried.'

So she's noticed his habitual frown too. I smile. 'You'd look worried if you had to manage chip timing, the ambulance service, a live band, and a mascot dressed as a peanut.'

I understand now why stamina is vital for those

organising half-marathons, as well as those taking part. We were all up at four and by ten, I'm flagging.

'How many more are there?' Sophie grabs five more bags from our table and holds one out as yet another grinning runner passes. A few are in costumes – we've seen a Roman gladiator as well as Superman – but all wear the glow of sweat and accomplishment.

'No idea,' I reply, wishing I'd thought to strap water to my waist like some of the competitors. There's surprising strength in the hazy sunshine. 'But we're only at the two hour mark. If any are as slow as me, we'll be here for a while yet.'

The nice thing is, as the clock ticks on to ten-fifteen and then ten-thirty, the type of runner changes. Instead of lean, focussed machines of bones and sinew, they start to look a lot like me. There are groups of women in pink leggings, couples who've run together despite differing abilities, and a troop declaring *Team Kasha* on their green T-shirts.

'Oh, look!' I point as a young man gets down on one knee in front of his running companion. She promptly transforms from exhausted to exhilarated, squealing and jumping as though her legs could easily do another five miles.

'Nice,' says a voice beside me, and I turn to see Leo. Amidst this chaos, he's calm.

I'm still watching the running sweethearts as the man unzips a pocket and produces a ring. Convinced I'm going to cry, I put one hand to my mouth. 'Leo, they've just got engaged.'

'So I see,' he says. 'I should call the guy from the *Cambridge Evening News* over.' Then he looks at me. 'Are you all right?'

'Fine,' I mutter, dashing at my eyes. 'Sorry.'

He pauses. 'Have you had a break? You should drink something, at least.'

'Oh, yes please,' says Sophie, passing a goodie bag to a kid who looks no older than twelve. 'I'm parched.'

'Stay there,' says Leo, disappearing and then returning with a crate of water bottles which he hides under our table before uncapping one each for Sophie and me. 'Oh, and Bella, you might want to get over to the information table.'

I glug back half the water before I answer. 'Why?' I wonder if I can get my hands on a banana too.

Leo shrugs. 'According to Grace, there's a riot brewing.'

'A what?' Why would I want to jump into the middle of a riot?

Leo's face is solemn but there's a gleam in his eye. 'Apparently, forty-seven runners want your phone number.'

'Sorry?'

'Or your website, at least.' He winks at Sophie, who's watching us in fascination. Then he turns back to me. 'They want to know where they can buy more of that flapjack.'

Chapter 37

The next week is a bit of a blur.

I admit to spending most of Monday, the day after the half-marathon, in bed. That's one of the privileges of being unemployed, after all. With my phone switched off, I revel in not having to weigh, mix or bake anything for a whole twenty-four hours. But I do pore over the local paper, which features several Sweetest Race photos and an eloquent sound bite from Leo, surely enough to make his father proud.

On Tuesday, though, I find myself drinking three cups of coffee at breakfast and reading the back of the cereal packet. Checking my phone, my heart sinks as I register the number of missed calls and text messages. It must be those blasted photos again. What's happened now?

But it's not the photos. One of the messages is from Brian, begging me to visit him at the bakery as soon as possible. And there's a voicemail from the *Cambridge Evening News*, which I listen to four times before I understand they're after me about flapjacks, not my topless punting notoriety.

I pick the easier of the two and trundle along to see Brian.

'What took you so long?' He pours me a coffee immediately. I don't want it, but I take it anyway. Then he says, 'I'm besieged.'

I look around the bakery: I'm the only customer. Outside, at a table with a yellow umbrella, is a lone fellow with a laptop. 'Really?'

Brian gestures with his hands. 'Well, not at this minute, but I've had a stream of phone calls and visitors. People think I'm behind the flapjack you gave out.'

I consider this. 'And?'

'They want to buy more of it, you dummy.'

'They want to *buy* it?' I repeat.

On Sunday at the half-marathon, it's true, there were plenty of runners – and their supporters – hoping to blag another free flapjack. But they'd run thirteen miles, they were understandably a bit peckish.

'They jolly well do,' Brian confirms.

'Oh.' There's a stirring of what could be adrenaline in my chest. 'So... do you think I should make more?'

Yesterday, I never wanted to look at another cherry or oat flake again. But this is... different.

'Yes, you bloody should!' Brian cries. 'Today! Now! You make it, I can sell it. I'll split the profit with you, fifty-fifty.'

Before I can answer, the door of the bakery opens and Amelia steps in.

'Darling!' She kisses me on both cheeks. 'Don't you look well!' Then, turning to Brian, she scans his pastry case. 'Any chance of a custard tart?'

'Sorry,' he says. 'I've been busy fielding phone calls for chef of the year.' He jerks his head at me.

As I go pink, he fills Amelia in on what he calls the flapjack frenzy. I drink my coffee and try for nonchalance. But my brain is racing.

'So I was thinking, if Bella makes more, I'll sell them here,' Brian finishes up.

I look at him and nod my agreement. 'Sounds like fun.' And a bit of income would come in handy just now.

'That reminds me,' Brian says, 'the local paper called, as well. I gave them your number.' He looks suddenly uncertain, as if remembering why else the media might be interested in me. 'I hope that was okay.'

I nod slowly, also wary. Then, realising Amelia hasn't said much, I notice her thoughtful expression. 'What's wrong?'

Is she going to caution me against partnering with Brian? He was so generous, letting me use his huge oven before the race. I can hardly refuse him a slice – no pun intended – of the profits now.

Amelia taps her toe. I get the feeling, if she were sitting down, she'd be twirling her shoe.

'You love to bake, right, Bella?'

I barely need to nod. Everyone knows that.

'And this flapjack recipe has been a hit?'

'I think so,' I say, as Brian chortles and adds, 'Understatement! They love it!'

'Can you come up with other flapjacks? Variations, I mean? For runners?'

'I haven't thought about it. Yes, I suppose so.' Hmm, variations? What, like dates, or pumpkin seeds, or...

I pull my attention back to my aunt as she speaks again.

'I think you're aiming too low,' she says. 'No offence, Brian, but one retail outlet is hardly going to bring in more than pin money.'

Brian inclines his head. 'None taken.'

'I think,' she says slowly, looking at me, 'we should get you online. Assuming this stuff will go through the post okay? It won't go off, or get squished?'

'No,' I say, 'it's practically bombproof. It had to be, for the runners' bags.'

'Right then,' she says. Her eyes sparkle as she reaches for her phone. 'Goody gumdrops. Let's get started.'

~~~

By Tuesday evening, Grace and James – all right, mostly James – have helped me set up an Etsy store. *Bella's Flapjacks* offers just one flavour – the original chocolate cherry – but has a Facebook page with a poll asking about future variations. I'm back on Pinterest, but not for weddings. My latest board is brimming with flapjack inspiration: ginger and coconut, honey and fig, even caramel parsnip.

Amelia, bless her, appointed herself my PR manager and phoned the *Cambridge Evening News* journalist back.

This results in an interview on Wednesday morning, after which I drive halfway to Bedford to visit a wholesaler of food packaging. With trepidation, I return home with a car full of cellophane wrappers and mailing boxes. Then I tackle Cash & Carry to buy the biggest sack of oats I've ever seen, plus enough chocolate chips to sink a battleship.

On Wednesday night, I spend six hours at the bakery, repeating the flapjack process which by now I can practically do blindfolded.

Sophie, meanwhile, has been combing my mobile phone for messages and calling everyone back with my new website address. She's been posting the info like crazy on Facebook too, and has designed a cute little *Buy Flapjacks Here* image. This, thanks to James, is now live on the half-marathon's website.

When I realise, on Thursday morning, how long it is since I ran, and that my feet even miss it, I fit in a three mile trot along my favourite village footpaths, returning home past the malt house. I wonder if Leo's still there, assessing its condition, and contemplate stopping to say hello. I haven't seen him since the race on Sunday; I bet he's tired too. But as I slow to a walk in the High Street, a battered Volvo pulls up alongside me.

'Bella!' Joey winds down the window. 'I've been looking for you!'

I narrow my eyes slightly. It's not that I blame Joey entirely for the photo fiasco, but he's far from my best friend at the moment.

'Sophie sent me,' he says, sensing my wariness. 'Said I could redeem myself a bit.'

Now I'm curious.

It turns out redemption, for Joey, consists of another photo shoot. This time, for the flapjacks, not my body. I pretend reluctance, then consent to travelling with a batch of my baked goods to his studio.

'If you're selling these online,' he says, spending an extraordinary amount of time rigging up lights and backdrops, 'you need great photos. Nothing dingy or out of focus. They have to make people drool, just by looking.'

I decide he has a point and sit quietly as he messes around with white plates, blue plates, cake stands, linen napkins and even a teapot.

'They're for runners,' I say, after he nips outside and returns with some pilfered wild flowers. 'They might not be into this stuff...'

'Okay,' he says, and disappears again. I don't know where the nearest shop is, but a few minutes later he's back with a pint of milk and a bag of fresh cherries. I open my mouth to protest, but then decide I'm glad of the rest. I watch as he pours the milk into a glass, arranges the cherries, and then spends literally twenty minutes snapping from every angle imaginable.

'Do you really think that's necessary?' I ask, as he climbs a step ladder with his camera. 'Or do my flapjacks have a double chin?'

'Shut up.' His voice bounces off the ceiling. 'Or I'll bill you at my hourly rate.'

'The nerve of it!' I retort. 'It's my naked flesh that got you where you are today, young man.'

He leaps off the ladder and pecks my cheek. 'And I'm so sorry,' he says, his big brown eyes serious now, 'for the trouble it caused you.'

Oh, those eyes look like someone stirred molten chocolate into double cream. Thank goodness I'm not daft enough to fall for Joey, not even on the rebound from Owen.

'But I'll do you some great flapjack photos, I promise,' he says. 'Tell you what, I'll drive you home, then send the images later?'

'Fine.' I glance at the flapjacks, which seem none the worse for wear. 'You can eat those ones, with my compliments. Oh, and Joey?'

He pauses in packing the camera up, a flapjack already halfway to his mouth.

'Just don't lose these pics, okay?'

~~~

'I thought getting ready for the race was the hard part,' I say to Sophie, surveying the chaos on my kitchen table.

It's now Friday morning, and she came over to show me the interview on the *Cambridge Evening News* website. But, complimentary as it is – *Bella Bounces Back: from college disgrace to new venture* – I don't have time to analyse every word.

'Thank God you're here.' I park her tablet computer in the fruit bowl, which is the only available spot in the kitchen. 'Can you help me pack these for mailing?'

The half-marathon website and Sophie's phone efforts yielded twenty orders. The baking was no problem, but now I've got packing slips, sticky labels, cellophane and boxes strewn around.

'You need a better system,' she says. 'If you're like this with only one flavour, it's going to be chaos when you add options.'

'I know,' I groan.

Together, we set up a more logical packing process, but have barely sealed the last batch of flapjack when my phone starts beeping. After some confusion and searching, I locate it in a box I'd already taped for mailing.

'All right, all right,' I try to deflect Sophie's disapproving look. 'I need to practise this a bit.' Then I look down at the phone. 'Bloody hell.'

'What?' She opens the fridge. 'Is there anything to eat that isn't flapjack?'

'Order notifications.' I scroll through the phone. 'Three more. Jeez.'

'Do you think it's because of the *Evening News*?' Sophie asks.

I shrug. 'I have no idea.'

'Do you have enough stock?'

I do some quick mental calculations. 'For now.'

'Oh, good,' she says. 'Let's have a cup of tea.'

But we've no sooner sat down with our steaming mugs when the doorbell goes. What now, I think?

Sophie, bless her, takes one look at my feet on the coffee table – a dreadful habit I'm sure I caught from her – and goes to the door. She's back a minute later, followed by a skinny young woman with blue hair. I shrink back as I spot a dictation machine in her hand.

'Soph –' I wonder why she thought it was a good idea to let this predator in. I remove my feet from the table.

'Sorry to intrude, Bella.' The young woman bounds forward to shake my hand. 'I'm Ginger Jenson. I write for the *Huffington Post*.'

I look again at Sophie, who's leaning against the doorway, arms folded like a bouncer.

'For the fitness section,' Ginger adds. 'I wonder, could we have a few words?'

~ ~ ~

The *Huff Post* piece goes live on Saturday morning:

Women everywhere were outraged when Bella Beecham was unceremoniously sacked by toffee-nosed Trewe College, Cambridge, after private photos hit national news alongside racier shots of Hollywood star Tasmin Fellows. But now everyone who thinks Bella got a raw deal can show their support for her new venture, Bella's Flapjacks. The thirty-five-year-old blonde and self-confessed running convert came up with her energy-rich flapjack recipe for a recent charity half-marathon, dubbed The Sweetest Race in Britain. Now, with her chocolate cherry runner treats flying off the shelves, Bella's showing Trewe that her future has never looked sweeter.

And my Etsy order notifications go nuts.

Chapter 38

By half past six on Saturday I've chased Brian out of the bakery and have my sleeves rolled up for what could be an all-nighter.

'How am I going to keep up with demand?' I wailed to Amelia, earlier in the afternoon. 'More to the point, how do I even predict demand? What if this is all a flash in the pan and it dies off completely?'

'Good point, darling,' she said, tucking into a custard pie which Brian had finally got around to baking. 'Maybe I should get you some real PR help.'

'No!' I squawked. 'I can't keep up as it is.'

'You're doing fine.' Her reply was muffled by custard. 'Bake on demand. If people have to wait a few days for delivery, that will make your flapjacks all the more desirable.'

But I'm not convinced. I desperately need to get a fresh batch out on Monday, to keep up with the orders from the *Huff Post* piece.

An hour later, I start to relax. The first trays look great: moist and golden. I'm getting ready to begin again when I hear the tinkling bell of the bakery's front door. Damn: in my eagerness to shoo Brian out, I must have forgotten to lock it. Still, this is Saffron Sweeting, I'm unlikely to be in danger. Nonetheless, I seize an enormous wooden spoon before I venture towards the shop.

'Hello?' I call.

'It's me.' Leo stops dead, eying the spoon.

'Oh!' I lower my weapon. 'Sorry.'

'I've been looking all over the village for you.'

'Me? Why?'

'I wanted to buy you all a drink tonight, remember? For helping with the race.'

Wow, is it Saturday already? I do remember the email

now; it was buried under flapjack orders.

'Oh, Leo, I'm sorry. It's been... a crazy week.'

Quickly, I explain the sudden interest in flapjacks.

He nods. 'Grace filled me in. She suggested I might find you here.'

'You didn't need to disrupt the celebration for me.' I use a forearm to push a stray piece of hair back, since my fingers are sticky with golden syrup.

Leo watches me. Then he says, 'Need a hand?'

I open my mouth to decline. So far, I've turned down offers of help from Grace, Sophie and – perish the thought – Amelia. Brian offered to stay late, and he's infinitely more qualified to make flapjacks than I am, yet I dispatched him categorically. But now, something makes me hesitate.

'I'm good with my hands,' Leo says. 'I'll even wash them, if you like.' He gives a ghost of a smile.

'I couldn't possibly –' I'm not sure why I'm entertaining this suggestion.

'I want to.'

He looks me directly in the eye and there's a moment which can only be described as awkward. What's wrong with me, I think? It must be that I'm still shaken from losing my job, then Owen, then the sudden thrill of people wanting to buy my culinary efforts.

But nights at the bakery have been solitary. And right now, Leo's quiet, steady company, the kind where we don't have to talk, would be as comforting as the scent of warm vanilla.

~ ~ ~

With two of us working, the time flies. To my amazement, shortly after eleven, we're done.

'Would you like a coffee?' I ask, as I slide the final tray of flapjacks onto the counter to cool. 'I could fire up Brian's machine.'

'Coffee would be terrific.' Leo leans back against the wall, arms folded. 'Did I do okay, then?'

'You were brilliant,' I say. 'You weren't kidding about being good with your hands.' For no reason, I blush, and have to busy myself with the coffee grinder to hide my face.

If Leo notices, he doesn't show it. He lets the silence settle in the kitchen and puts the last of the baking equipment away. The only sounds are the spluttering of the coffee machine and the oven ticking as it cools.

'It's warm enough to take these outside,' Leo says, when the coffee has brewed.

He's right. The late June evening is positively balmy; the moon is up and dozens of stars sparkle.

'Heaven,' I proclaim, sinking into one of the plastic chairs outside the bakery. Brian forgot to take his umbrellas down today, and we sit there under the canopy in the darkness. Letting out a contented breath, I realise my jeans feel looser, even though the scales tell me my weight has barely budged this month.

Then I remember my baking companion. 'Thank you so much.'

'It was a pleasure,' Leo says. 'I don't get the chance to roll up my sleeves in the kitchen very often.'

'Why not?'

He shrugs. 'Living with Dad, I suppose. It's time I got my own place.'

'Spread your wings a bit?'

'Something like that.'

I feel compelled to mention her. 'What does Caroline think? About where to live, I mean?'

'I dunno.'

My coffee has cooled enough now to drink. 'Shouldn't you talk to her? For when she comes back?'

In the half light, he gives me a strange look.

'She *is* coming back, isn't she?' I'm struck again by the parallel with Owen and me. What if Caroline decides to stay in France, or move still further away? What if she breaks

Leo's heart, like Owen broke mine?

'I expect so,' Leo says easily, 'eventually.'

'Good.' I exhale on his behalf. 'She must know how lucky she is.'

He watches me over his coffee for what seems like ages. 'Lucky?'

'Absolutely.' An evening breeze tugs at the umbrella above us, bringing with it the scent of jasmine from one of the nearby cottage gardens. I roll my shoulders appreciatively. 'She'll come back to the perfect English village and a perfect English summer.' I gesture at the clear night sky. 'And a wonderful boyfriend who spends his time helping others and is incredible with his hands.'

For a moment I think Leo's going to choke on his coffee. Oh, crumbs, why did I add that last bit? I pull a face, trying to lighten the words. But true to form, Leo doesn't return the smile.

'Bella –'

'Sorry,' I blurt. 'Never mind.'

'No, look.' He puts his cup down abruptly. 'I think –' He swallows. 'Well, for what it's worth, Caroline isn't my girlfriend.'

'What?' My heart just stopped.

Leo's taking a sudden interest in his coffee spoon. 'We're, er, running mates. That's all.'

'But...'

But she lives with you, I want to say. You're always together. Or you were, until she trotted off to croissant land. I asked how you met and you had a cute story. She's gorgeous, and sexy, and fit, and successful. *She finishes your sentences.*

Fortunately, my tongue is too tied to say any of that out loud. I wait to confirm my heart has started again, then I force myself to speak. 'Oh. Right. Running mates.'

Leo's going to bend that spoon out of shape in a minute. 'For the record, we were never... an item. We had separate rooms at dad's.'

Really?

There's heat in my cheeks. I take a long, deep breath.

'Anyway, that's... good,' I say. 'I mean, if she's in France, good that – you know.' He shoots me a look from under his eyebrows as I blunder on. 'Good that you're not, well, smitten with her. Like I was with Owen, I mean.' My heart may be functional, but my lungs are struggling.

Leo pauses as an owl hoots repeatedly from near the malt house. When he speaks, all he says is, '*Was* smitten?'

I didn't notice the tense I used. It's true, recently I've been thinking about Owen less and less. After all, even in the best days of our relationship, he was never in my corner like Leo has been. It was always me making the running. Every time.

Leo puts the spoon down. 'Bell?'

There he goes, saying my name like that again. *What's going on?* I close my eyes briefly, then force myself to meet his gaze.

'Yes,' I whisper, relying on the darkness to protect me. 'Was smitten.'

Look away, I tell myself. Look away. I can't handle this sweet, surprising rush tonight. With an effort, I turn my face to the stars, noticing for the first time some wispy clouds moving in. Involuntarily, I shiver.

Leo looks up too, then drains his cup.

'Come on,' he says. 'It's getting late. Let's lock up here, then I'll walk you home.'

For the next few nights, I sleep fitfully, not helped by the inevitable dawn chorus which starts well before five each morning. Several times, I forget to eat. Houseplants wilt and laundry piles up. I tell myself I'm unsettled because of all the recent changes in my life.

I haven't heard from Leo, and I remind myself that with his race over, we have no particular reason to talk. But on Tuesday, when I slice my finger while assembling a hasty sandwich, I admit I have to get a grip.

Reluctantly, I allow the flapjacks to command my attention. The *Huffington Post* piece triggered a few follow-up articles and a request for a feature from *Runner's World*. Thanks to that and Joey's amazing photos on the Etsy website, orders remain steady. Compensating for my restless nights, I find I can sleep late, spend the afternoon shipping orders or tinkering with new flavours, and then bake each evening. I'm quicker now, my hands conjuring flapjacks without much involvement from my head. Which is good, as my brain still whirls off in another direction given half a chance.

On Thursday afternoon, I'm deep in thought on the relative merits of date and apple or cinnamon orange, when my phone rings.

'Bella? It's Kathleen. Kathleen Russell.'

The cinnamon stick snaps in my other hand. The Human Resources manager from Trewe? What can she possibly want?

'I wonder...' she says, 'if we might be able to meet.'

'Meet?' It's not usual, surely, to sack someone and then ask for a chin wag a month later?

'If it's not too much trouble,' she says. 'I drive through Saffron Sweeting on my way home.'

'Uh, okay.'

'Shall we say The Plough? Five-ish?'

Neutral ground. 'The pub will be fine. But I can't stay long.' I have baking to do.

I know it's unlikely that Trewe wants to place an order for a dozen cases of flapjack, but I can't think what else this would be about. I haven't talked to the press about the college, or done anything else they could object to. Still, I find myself staring at my ingredients as the afternoon ticks away.

~~~

The pub has just opened when we get there. Fergus, embracing Saffron Sweeting's international population, has decked the place out with Stars and Stripes for Independence Day. But he's added several dozen yards of Union Jack bunting too, presumably to keep Violet's crowd happy. At Kathleen's suggestion, we find a table in the garden. I've always liked her but can't tell, from her face, whether she's here as an ally or foe.

'You might have guessed,' she begins, sipping gin and tonic and choosing her words carefully, 'that this isn't an entirely official visit.'

I swirl my glass of white wine and wait.

'But, Bella, certain members of the college thought it would be a good idea for us to have a chat.'

That sounds sinister. Isn't that what villains say, before they take you out to the car park and shoot you in the kneecaps?

'I haven't done anything,' I blurt. Damn, I was planning to be more aloof.

Kathleen smiles. 'No, sorry, I wasn't trying to imply you have. The thing is' – she leans in – 'the Fellows feel they may have been a little... hasty.'

'Hasty?'

'In terminating your employment.'

I blink. 'You mean –'

Kathleen rubs a hand over her face, possibly irritated that I'm making her spell it out. 'They're thinking maybe they shouldn't have let you go.'

I was not expecting this. I thought I was in for a dressing down, or a gentle reminder not to discuss my previous employment with the media. At a stretch, maybe, landing a flapjack order for someone's leaving present.

Before I can react, she carries on. 'I know you've been extremely busy since we parted company, and perhaps you've not been keeping up with the news.'

No, not unless you count those first two weeks where I was googling my name every twenty minutes.

'Between you and me,' she says, 'Trewe got appalling publicity for how you were treated...'

Humph. She put that in the passive sense, as if my sacking was a lightning bolt from the heavens, and not something she had anything to do with.

'...and in particular, certain... constituents were extremely displeased.'

'Constituents?' That's a fancy word. 'Who?'

She wriggles her shoulders as if she couldn't possibly say, and studies a bumble bee which is apparently trying to mate with a striped beer mat.

'Professor Palin?' I always knew he was a chum.

'Oh! No, I didn't mean him. Although he *was* very upset and gave me quite a lecture.'

I smile. Good old Palin.

Kathleen sighs. 'Oh, all right then. No, I meant, er, a certain large donor. Or, specifically, his daughter.'

I narrow my eyes. I don't know any large donors. Not personally. 'Who?'

'Mindi Butterson.'

'Never heard of her.'

'Ah, I might as well tell you.' Kathleen takes a long drink, as if she needs courage to break a confidence. 'Mindi is Lord Butterson's daughter.'

Oh. Him.

'You'll remember Lord B. is particularly keen on arts and cultural heritage,' Kathleen says, and waits for me to nod. 'Well, Mindi's thing is sculpture. He nudged her in that direction. But she's made quite a name for herself, specialises in the human form. The *female* human form.'

'And...?' I raise my eyebrows.

'Mindi was absolutely livid that Trewe was seen to be ashamed of what she considers the purest form of female beauty. That we – I mean the college – '

'Sacked me,' I supply.

'Yes.' Kathleen nudges the bee, on its beer mat, to a safer distance.

I fight the urge to laugh. A month ago, topless photos of me in a punt were an outrageous blot on the pure, intellectual reputation of Trewe College, a despicable distraction from academic excellence. Now, the artsy daughter of a huge benefactor has her knickers in a twist, and they're suddenly sorry?

Kathleen must have read my face. 'It's not just Mindi,' she says hastily. 'The student body was up in arms too. Not to mention the *Guardian*.'

'Oh, my,' I offer, more sarcastically than I intended.

'Look, I get it,' Kathleen says. 'If I were you, I'd be brassed off too.' She looks at her watch, reminding me it's time I got along to the bakery.

Still, as I drain my drink, I shake my head. 'That's all very nice to hear, but I'm not sure I get your point?'

'The point,' she says, reaching for a leather portfolio that's lain unnoticed on the bench beside her, 'is we were wondering if you'd like your job back?'

~~~

As I push open the door of Oxfam in Cambridge the following day, I expect to feel stabs of bitter regret. But the flutter in my stomach is tiny, and reminds me of the satisfaction I used to get from tackling the shredding at work.

This first week of July has been humid, the kind of sultry weather where my brain refuses to settle. I decided on this course of action several nights ago, when I was tossing in bed and listening to the rustle of trees through the open window. Waking the next morning, I concluded I should give myself forty-eight hours in case I changed my mind.

I didn't.

'Can I help you?' The woman behind the counter looks at me over her glasses, which are strung on a gold chain.

'Hi.' Still no stabs. Barely a pang. Okay then. 'I'd like to donate this, please.' I jerk my head down to the heavy garment bag in my arms. 'You do accept wedding dresses, don't you?'

'Wedding dresses? Oh, yes, how generous!'

With considerably more enthusiasm, the woman springs out from behind her sales desk. She's in her seventies, with snow white hair, but moves like a mountain goat.

'Over here, dear, over here. Shall we have a look?' She gestures to a longer counter and I flop the garment bag down. It's a relief, actually: it weighed a tonne. In more ways than one.

'Yours, is it?' She brushes her hands together, as if to remove stray dust, then unzips the bag.

'Sort of.' I clear my throat. 'I mean, yes. It's Vera Wang.'

'Oh, my goodness, lovely. That's very generous of you.' She lifts the dress halfway out so she can see the bodice. I allow myself a tiny sigh as the gorgeous, intricate lace swishes.

'It's a few years old,' I say.

'No problem. Vera Wang's gowns are so classic, aren't they?'

I incline my head. Wait, was that a pang? No, I think I'm just hungry.

'Have you had it dry cleaned?' she asks.

'No,' I reply. 'I mean... I never wore it.'

'Oh!' Her hands freeze on the dress, but she recovers quickly. 'Oh. New. That's *very* generous, then.'

I get it. I'm very generous.

She's studying me now. I see her eyes go to my bare left hand, then she looks me up and down as if she might be able to read my history. A missing limb? A hunchback? Did I jilt him, or did he jilt me? How long before the big day?

I take a patient breath. If I'm over it, she should be. 'It's not a problem, is it? That the dress is new?'

'No, dear! Goodness, no. Some of the brides –' she stops.

'Some of them what?' I should feel irritated, inspected, judged. Instead, I'm experiencing detached curiosity.

'Some of our brides might feel it's unlucky,' she says slowly, 'but others will be ecstatic that it's brand new. Theirs and theirs alone.'

'Good.'

'Sorry, dear. I didn't mean to –. Well, it's just, a new Vera Wang, that really is –'

'Very generous?' I can't help finishing for her. Suddenly, I'm smiling. 'Anyway, you can reassure your customers it's not bad luck at all.'

'What's that, dear?' She's busy zipping the bag over the dress.

'If anyone asks, you can tell them *not* wearing that dress was the best thing that ever happened to me.'

Chapter 40

'Wow,' says Grace. 'Your job back? Did you accept?'

'I told her I'd think about it.'

'Bloody cheek, if you ask me, darling,' chimes in Amelia. 'I'd tell them to take a running jump.'

'I was tempted.'

'Still,' Grace adds, 'it's nice to have the option.' Her eyes drift over my shoulder. 'Oh, look, a coconut shy!'

Amelia's face lights up and she swivels on her heel. She's wisely wearing cork wedges, so she doesn't sink into the soft expanse of Ted and Betsy's lawn.

We're at the Saffron Sweeting Fourth of July party, a comical blend of American patriotism and British garden fete. The Yankee contingent in the village – a growing number – submitted plans back in April to the parish council, who at first were standoffish. But the Sweeting vicar, sensing a fabulous opportunity for church fundraising, did a splendid job of brokering a win for both sides. The Americans would get their festivities and the Blighty traditionalists could piggyback on the occasion with their own quirky requirements. Ted and Betsy, as the owners of a breathtaking manor house a stone's throw from the church, were swiftly pressed into service. Half the village is here and there are rumours of fireworks later. I definitely won't stick around for those.

'So, there's more going on than Kathleen admitted at first,' I add. 'I bought her another drink and she confessed they've sacked Gertrude too.'

'Who? Wasn't she your boss?' Amelia's still looking towards the coconuts.

'She was. I never liked her, but apparently she was selling confidential information.'

'Crumbs,' says Grace. 'What information? Who to?'

'Ooh, a spy!' Amelia suggests. 'KGB?'

I try not to laugh. 'You're a bit out of date, there. No, nothing so exotic. Gerty had a headhunter friend. She was scouring the Trewe alumni database, then suggesting people the friend could approach.'

Amelia deflates. 'How boring.'

'But anyway,' I say, 'she's gone.'

'So they need you back to fill the gap?' Grace asks.

I shrug. 'I dunno. Maybe. I don't know whether that makes me more willing, or more inclined to let them flounder.'

My aunt puts her head on one side. 'You could demand a whopping pay rise...'

'I thought you told me to tell them to get lost?'

'Yes, well, no point being hasty.' Amelia knows she's been caught out. 'Now, how hard can it be to topple a coconut?'

We amble across the grass to the handful of try-your-luck stalls, where we bump into Nancy. I remember her, and her soft American accent, from the supper club where my magic went haywire.

'Run that by me again,' she says to Grace. 'You pitch a ball at the coconut?'

Grace nods. 'You have to knock it off its perch.'

'And you win...?'

'The coconut,' Grace tells her friend, as if it's obvious.

We're pushed aside at this point by a hurricane of a boy, who, having paid a pound to the stallholder, begins hurling tennis balls in the direction of the coconut bounty.

'Randy!' I assume this screech is from his mother. 'Wait up! Aim first!'

The brat, however, has exhausted his arsenal and turns to me with a face like thunder. 'That sucks!' he announces. 'Where's the cotton candy?'

'The what?' I take a step back.

'He means candyfloss,' Grace says. 'Try over there, Randy. By the stables.' As he stomps off, she lowers her voice. 'Such a great advert for his country.'

'I apologise,' Nancy drawls. 'We're not all like that.'

'We know,' says Amelia. 'Watch out, though, once he gets his hands on sugar.' Then her eyes gleam. 'Right. My turn.'

The rest of us form a respectful ring, oohing appropriately as she spends five pounds in her attempts to win a coconut. 'Bloody hell!' she scowls. 'That's harder than it looks.'

The stallholder's poker face remains intact but I suspect he's in this business for a good reason. It's far more lucrative than flapjacks.

'Want to try, love?' he says to me.

I shrug. 'Why not?' It's for a good cause.

I part with my pound and then step up to the designated mark. 'Is it better to throw accurately or forcefully?' I wonder aloud.

'Both, preferably.' The voice is so close I jump, dropping my first tennis ball as I find Owen right behind me.

'That one doesn't count!' Amelia calls defiantly, daring the stallholder to disagree.

'Hi, Bella,' my ex-boyfriend says quietly.

'Hi.' I retrieve the ball then launch it like a missile in the general direction of its target. It flies wide, but I enjoy seeing Owen step back hurriedly to avoid the trajectory of my arm. 'Sorry,' I say crisply. 'Didn't see you there.'

This is a fib, of course. He's wearing tan corduroy trousers and a cream cotton cardigan, by far the most trendy man in sight. Probably in the whole village.

He looks at me. 'May I?' He gestures to the next ball.

'No,' I snap, 'that's mine. Buy your own.' I didn't mean that to sound so childish.

Behind his sunglasses, Owen's eyebrows shoot up. Then he steps forward and trades a pound coin for three balls. In the meantime, I lob another of mine with full force, my shoulder protesting as I do so. That's going to hurt tomorrow.

'Do you mind?' I say. 'I haven't finished.'

'Be my guest.' He waves me forward and I'm sure I detect his smug satisfaction as my final ball slices far to the right, narrowly missing the grand prize at the bottle stall beyond.

'Here,' Owen says, rolling a ball around in both hands, then holding it in front of his face and squinting at the coconuts.

'Don't forget to polish it on your trousers,' Amelia shouts. From the corner of my eye I see Grace grab her arm in a hushing attempt.

Owen ignores my sassy aunt and takes a few steps back, away from the target. Wow, I think, is he seriously going to bowl it, like an Ian Botham impression?

He doesn't. It's worse, resembling something you'd see in a junior baseball game.

'Howzat!' he shouts.

A split second later, a coconut wobbles, then topples. I bite my lip, hard.

'Fine,' I turn on my heel. 'Enjoy your nuts.' You bloody wanker, I think.

'Hang on a minute, Bella.'

I keep walking and he has to catch me by the shoulder before I stop.

'Here,' he says, holding out the coconut. 'For you.'

I do my best to wither it with a glance. 'Keep it,' I say. 'You earned it.'

'Look.' Owen shifts his prize from hand to hand, but his eyes are on me. 'I wanted to say congratulations.'

'What for?'

'For getting your job back. That's excellent news.' He smiles and nods, as if we're celebrating something together.

'Word travels fast,' I say. How can it be news, if I haven't accepted the offer yet?

'Can I buy you a cup of Rosy Lee?' he asks, gesturing towards the stables where a team led by Violet is doling out tea from the enormous church urn.

Great, I think. I spent months waiting for you to buy me a drink, take me out to dinner, and rekindle romantic relations, and now you offer me a mug of PG Tips? I shake my head. 'I'm fine.'

'Oh. Well.' He pauses, smiles again, and continues. 'I was thinking, if you're back at Trewe, we'll be able to work together again.'

Again? We didn't exactly work together before. What does he mean? Before I can say anything, he carries on.

'You have a great knack with Professor Grayling. He's such a dry old stick, but he likes you.'

'I wasn't aware of that,' I say. Grayling? That grump bag?

'Yes. I'd love to get him lined up for a press conference. Maybe you could help?'

'Help. I –' *Help?* He has the nerve to ask for my help? I think my mouth drops open. 'Look, Owen, I'm not sure that I will be going back to Trewe. Quite a bit has happened...'

'And I've been meaning to ask, can I get a copy of your treacle tart recipe? Thought I might have a go at it.'

Really? He barely lifted a finger in the kitchen when we were together.

'You could come over if you like, give me some tips?' Then he adds, 'As friends, obviously.'

I stare, dumbfounded. He has no romantic interest in me whatsoever, but he wants a free cooking lesson?

'Sound good?' He's still brandishing his coconut. 'I knew you'd be up for it.'

Wordlessly, I give him my best smile, and reach for the coconut. After all, he offered it to me originally. Owen hands it over immediately, presumably gratified that his peace offering has been accepted.

And then I find my tongue.

'Let me get this straight,' I say, my voice rock steady. 'When I was in disgrace at Trewe, you dropped me like a hot potato. You said it was completely over between us, that you couldn't be seen to have anything to do with me.' He steps back, but I continue. 'And now they've forgiven me, you want to be pals again? You want me to sweet-talk Professor Grump, and bolster your snivelling career? And then pop over to your place and whip up dessert while you lounge on the sofa watching the footie? Is that it?'

'Hey, Bell –' he moves towards me, holding out his arms now.

'Well, no thanks, Owen. I finally came to my senses. I don't want anything to do with you, your snot research, or your baking attempts. I have better things to do.'

With that, I let the coconut fall. It lands squarely on Owen's foot and as I turn on my heel I catch sight of him yelping and hopping.

'And don't call me Bell,' I snap over my shoulder. 'Only my friends call me that.'

Chapter 41

I don't look back as I cross the garden, passing the misshapen exhibits in the vegetable growing contest. I skirt the marquee next to the stables, where they're doing a roaring trade in teas and an old barrel organ is pealing out Gilbert and Sullivan tunes. Tom and Betsy's property is so large, there must be a secluded corner somewhere. Rounding the end of a large hedge, I find a wildflower meadow, flanked on one side by huge trees. I make my way over to their shade and discover a rough-hewn bench with a view of the church. Perfect.

I lower myself gingerly, and wait for my heart rate to slow. Once the adrenaline subsides, I'm assuming the wave of humiliation and regret won't be far behind. I'd like to be on my own for that part. Hopefully, I've got a tissue; I'm thinking I'll need it.

But I don't. As my breathing steadies and the trembling stills, I feel no embarrassment or recycled rejection. I'm just incredibly calm. I sit, watching long blades of grass waving in the breeze, and two brown butterflies flitting amongst the poppies and harebells. Overhead, there's the faint drone of a small plane, and as it fades, the church clock chimes four. I close my eyes and feel my breath, strong and even.

'I'm... sorry.' A hushed voice interrupts my reverie. 'But are you okay?'

I jerk and open my eyes. It's Leo. 'Hi. Yes, I'm fine.'

'I'm really sorry,' he says again. 'I didn't mean to make you jump.'

'Oh, no, it's fine,' I say, also apparently feeling the need to repeat myself.

'It's just...' Leo hesitates again, '...I saw you with Owen and wondered if you were okay.' He puffs out his cheeks. 'Well, sorry.' He backs away.

'You don't have to leave.' I start to push myself up. Then

I change my mind. 'Here, take a seat.'

There's plenty of space for both of us but I nudge to my right anyway, making more room.

Leo sits and I'm aware of his thighs, just inches from mine.

'I didn't mean to intrude.' He's holding a long strip of raffle tickets – fifteen, twenty maybe – and begins curling them around his fingers. 'But after you broke his toes, you disappeared and your friends didn't know where you'd gone.'

'Broke his toes?' I gape. 'Oh, my God.'

Leo shakes his head. 'I made that up. But hopefully, yeah.' He looks sideways at me now and grins. 'He certainly was yelling like a baby.'

I laugh too. 'Well, he deserved it.'

I want to tell Leo that every time he smiles, I feel like I've been given a special gift. But I don't. Instead, I say, 'Actually, I deserve to have my toes broken too, for being so pathetic about him. I can't believe I carried a torch for so long.'

Leo's still studying his tickets, folding them now like a concertina. 'How's that torch doing now?'

'It's out,' I say. 'Definitely out.'

From the corner of my eye, I see Leo look at me, but the moment I turn my head towards him, he glances away again.

Eventually he asks, 'Are you coming to the fireworks?'

I suppress a shudder. 'No. I, um, don't like them.' That's an understatement but since the accompanying story is embarrassing and involves a spark down my bra, I'm not sharing it. 'I'm going to babysit Violet's dog instead.'

'Sounds... fun.'

I can't tell if he's serious. I'm genuinely fond of Mungo, whose affections, unlike most men, are guaranteed. And he's no more keen on fireworks than I am.

'So...' I cast around for a new subject. 'Will you be planning any more races, do you think?'

'Maybe next year,' he says. 'It was a fantastic experience, but, well, a lot of work. As you know. I thought I might sign up for a couple of half-marathons, though. Something to aim for.'

'Sounds great.'

'You could enter too.'

I disguise a snort. 'Wow, Leo, thirteen miles? Hardly.'

'Well, think about it,' he says.

'Will do,' I say, shaking my head simultaneously.

'Anyway...' Leo begins, but doesn't continue.

There's another long pause. We're both so still, a butterfly lands on my hand before fluttering away on the breeze.

'Why didn't you say something sooner?' I whisper.

His voice is low too. 'About doing a race?'

'No... I mean Caroline... that she isn't your girlfriend.'

Leo shakes his head. 'You were totally fixated on Owen.'

Those six words ignite inside me. Flames leap from an ember that I didn't know was glowing. Would he have done something different if I hadn't been chasing after my ex? I scramble to process my thoughts and decipher what this means.

Before I can collect myself, there's a single chime from the church bell, marking the quarter hour.

Leo gets to his feet. 'I have to go. They'll be drawing the prizes.'

No, I want to say. *Stay. Talk.* But instead I nod numbly. 'The raffle.' I stand too, my brain still reeling, words coming without help. 'I'll walk back with you, if that's okay.'

'Sure.'

We amble back towards the house. My breath feels shallow and I grapple with normal conversation.

'So... you're gambling on winning dinner at The Plough, or Amelia's case of wine?' Feigning interest, I gesture towards his ream of tickets. 'You've invested pretty heavily.'

'Well, dinner would be fine,' he says, 'but actually, I was hoping for fourth prize.'

'Fourth? What's that?' We've reached the edge of the meadow now, and he waits to let me go first up a couple of steps to reach the lawn.

'Apparently, it's a double layered lemon drizzle cake.'

'Lemon drizzle – oh.' I stop and turn. 'Hang on. I made that.'

Still standing on the lower step, Leo's face is level with mine. He meets my eye. 'I know.'

My heart jolts. I look down at the tickets, flapping in his hand. 'You must have twenty pounds' worth there.'

'I know.'

'You must... really like lemon drizzle cake.'

'I do.'

I think back to the supper club, the first time I met Leo. We had lemon drizzle that night too. Can he possibly remember?

'I really do,' he says again. 'It's fresh and tangy and... just sweet enough.'

We stand there for the longest moment, then Leo drops his eyes to my mouth. I fight the urge to lick my lips.

My heart goes from a jog to a sprint as he reaches out and takes me lightly by the arm, then bends his face towards mine. But he simply brushes his lips to my cheek, then hops up on the lawn beside me.

'I'll see you soon, Bella.'

He squeezes my arm then lets go, heading purposefully towards the raffle.

Chapter 42

'Earth calling Bella!' Grace taps my arm. 'Are you all right?'

'She's not acting all right,' Amelia says. 'She's acting like someone dropped a coconut on her head, not the other way around.'

'It wasn't his head,' I say, 'it was his foot.'

We're in the tea tent, each of us with a paper plate containing a scone, two mini cucumber sandwiches, and a slice of Bakewell tart. By mutual agreement, we've bypassed the tea in favour of tall glasses of Pimms ladled out by Fergus.

'Whichever part of him it was, you definitely had the upper hand.' Amelia leans back, looking as satisfied as if she'd launched a coconut at Owen herself. 'Fergus, darling, I'll have another of those.'

'Well done.' Grace tucks into a dainty sandwich. 'Although you don't look very happy.'

'Of course she's happy,' Amelia says, 'and about bloody time too. Mind you,' she leans in, 'I'm reliably informed that half an hour later Bella was seen coming back from the meadow with Leo.'

'Really?' Grace drops the sandwich back on her plate. 'Honestly, Amelia, you have spies everywhere.'

I take a long glug of Pimms.

'So is there a story there, darling?' Amelia wolfs her sandwich then, balancing her plate on her lap, starts spooning cream onto her scone. 'Is that why you're acting all peculiar?'

'I'm not acting peculiar.' I examine my own scone, prodding it to see how airy it is. 'Of course there's no story.' The scone is fine but, strangely, I'm not hungry.

Grace and Amelia exchange glances.

'Do we know who won the raffle?' I ask.

Amelia shrugs. 'No idea. I was teasing Kenneth about

his marrow.'

'What?' Grace looks perplexed, then murmurs, 'Oh, you mean the vegetable contest.'

'I really would like to know.' I try again. 'I'd, er, love to congratulate them.'

'I think Lorraine won,' Grace says vaguely. 'And maybe Daphne Pennington-Jones.' With this, she waves at someone and calls across the tent. 'Daph, did you win that?'

I recognise the silver-haired woman as the kind lady who gave me pearls and hosted our race Expo at Saffron Hall. She beams at Grace and glides towards our table, carrying a large white box.

'I did!' She kisses Grace and waggles her fingers in greeting to Amelia. 'Lemon drizzle. Bernard will be thrilled. His sister arrives from Florida tomorrow; I'm doing tea in the orangery.'

'Bella made it,' Grace says, and Daphne turns to double kiss me too.

'I'm so glad you won,' I say, wishing I meant it. 'You were so generous to me, Mrs Pennington-Jones, in the spring.'

Leo was determined to win that cake. He spent a small fortune on raffle tickets. Surely he must know I'd bake him a cake any time he asked? All he has to do, in fact, is ask.

'She's gone again,' Grace says. 'Bella, are you all right?'

'Sorry,' I say, 'I'm fine.'

'She needs another Pimms,' Amelia suggests. 'Fergus, our glasses are empty here!'

Daphne decides to join us for a drink. She sits next to Amelia, whereupon they begin speculating on who might get the honour of lighting the fireworks tonight.

'Ted thinks he and Mary Lou's husband should do it,' Amelia says, 'seeing as it's Independence Day.'

'And Kenneth was adamant it should be someone from the village council,' Daphne replies. 'I can't wait to see those sparks fly.'

Grace is still watching me. 'You would ask,' she says

softly, 'if you need anything? Anything at all?'

'Thanks.' I smile at her. 'Want my scone?'

Daphne, whose glass is already half empty, turns cheerily to me. 'I must say, Bella, you're looking incredibly well. Whatever you've been doing, it clearly agrees with you.'

'Thank you,' I mumble.

'She's right,' Amelia adds. 'You've lost loads of weight. It's all that running, I expect.'

I open my mouth to tell them I only weigh a few pounds less than I did in February. Considering I was determined, then, to subtract at least a stone and gain an ex-boyfriend, I've failed completely.

'You do look much lighter,' Grace says.

She's right. I do feel lighter, although not in the way they all mean. The scales may not have budged much, but I'm leaner, toned, and stronger. And happier. So much happier.

'Oh, now look what you've done,' Amelia snorts, bringing me back from my reverie. 'She's gone all la-la again.'

I smile and shake my head, certain now that I haven't failed at all.

'Actually,' I say, standing, 'I was thinking about something Daphne said, about Bernard's sister.'

'Yes, dear?' Daphne looks expectant.

'You see,' I continue, stumbling over the words, 'all the village shops are closed and I've realised I need something desperately.'

Amelia makes a face like I've lost my marbles, but Daphne gives an encouraging nod.

'You mentioned you have an orangery. I was wondering, does that mean you might grow citrus fruits?'

'We do, dear, yes.' Daphne nods again. 'A few.'

'Oh, good.' I let out a gush of breath. 'The thing is, it's rather urgent. I've got something I have to do. Tonight. And I'd be awfully grateful if you could sell me a couple of lemons.'

~ ~ ~

It takes me three tries to get the cake right. My nerves must be jinxing my fingers. The first, I take out of the oven too early, petrified I'll overbake it. It sinks horribly in the middle as it cools. The second looks good but as I turn to place it on the worktop, I trip over Violet's spaniel and both the cake and I go flying. By the time I untangle myself and clamber to my knees, he's polished it off and is licking his chops.

'Mungo!' I shriek. 'You bloody hound!'

But that reminds me, I can't leave him here by himself. He'll go demented if he's on his own when the fireworks start. Ignoring his waving tail and beseeching look, I phone Grace.

'You did say I should ask if I needed anything,' I begin.

'Yup. What's up?'

'Could you babysit Mungo tonight?'

'Oh,' she says, her voice telling me she'd been looking forward to the fireworks. Then she rallies. 'Okay, yes, can do. I love Mungo.'

'You're a brick.'

So then I decide to make a double batch of energy truffles for Grace as a thank you, before I take Mungo over there. Especially since he might throw up an entire cake later tonight.

When I get back, I have to wash my cake tins and mixing bowls before I can make another attempt at the lemon drizzle cake. And although the third time is indeed lucky, and the cake emerges soft and springy from the oven, I've wasted so much time it's getting dark.

As I pace up and down, waiting for it to cool before I can drizzle the lemon-sugar syrup over the top, my stomach begins to churn. But not just with nervous anticipation. There's dread too. If I don't get a move on, there's a risk the fireworks will start.

Luckily, Operation Drizzle goes smoothly and, holding my breath, I slide my creation into my favourite cake tin. This, I realise, may be the most important cake I've ever baked.

Chapter 43

I go first to Kenneth's cottage next to the library, nurturing the possibility that Leo might be home. But the little house is dark and no one answers despite my repeated clangs with the door knocker. He must be with the rest of the village: over by the malt house, waiting for the fireworks. I don't know what time they're supposed to start – I planned to be at home with Mungo, with a duvet over our heads, by now – but I suspect it might be soon.

I cross the main street, cake tin tucked carefully under my arm, and make my way past a long line of parked cars. Dusk has given way now to near darkness: the antique streetlights are on and the bunting outside the pub appears black and white instead of red, white and blue.

As I approach the malt house I hear chatter and music, but nothing prepares me for the density of people in the field beside it. It's an absolute scrum. How am I going to find him?

'Excuse me, excuse me.' I begin pushing my way gently through the throng of villagers – both British and American – who've decided a mild July evening is infinitely more suited to firework viewing than a foggy November night. 'Have you seen Leo?' I ask anyone I recognise, but no one can help. My pushing gets less polite, my apologies more muttered as I pass Fergus, Brian, my next door neighbour, Ted and Betsy, and Violet. This delays me as I have to explain Mungo's whereabouts, but at least provides the direction where she thinks she saw Amelia and Sid.

'Bella!' my arm is grabbed and I whirl around, protecting the tin. It's Sophie. 'What are you doing here?' She looks up at Tom whose arm is curled over her shoulder. 'Bell hates fireworks,' she explains.

'Have you seen Leo?'

'Who? Oh, your running guy? I don't think so. Are you

all right?'

'Fine,' I mutter, continuing my quest to reach the far side of the field.

Next, I encounter Amelia, but she's not with Sid, she's with Daphne and her husband.

'Thanks again for the lemons!' I give Daphne my biggest smile, but keep going.

And then, finally, I see him. He's near the edge of the field, with Sid and Tracey. His back is to me, and I pause for a moment. I have no clue what I'm going to say.

'Why look, here's Bella!' Sid spots me first and the others turn.

In the shadowy light, I think I see surprise on Leo's face. If there's any other emotion there, though, I can't detect it.

'I thought you said you weren't coming tonight.' His voice is neutral.

I look at him and gulp. 'I wasn't.'

'Well, glad you could join us,' Sid says jovially.

'Hi,' Tracey adds.

I ignore them, which I know is rude, but I can't take my eyes off Leo. He's frowning now – nothing unusual there – but he's gone still too.

'I wanted to bring you this.' I hold out the tin.

'What is it?' He doesn't take it.

'A lemon drizzle cake.'

'A what?'

'Seeing as you were so keen to win it. I thought I'd make you one. You know, since you've been so... sweet to me.'

He raises his eyebrows.

Damn, I shouldn't have said that. I keep talking, trying to cover up. 'So, since you didn't win the raffle, I made another one.'

'You made me a cake?' Leo says slowly.

I nod. It's not that hard to understand, is it? It's not like I reached up and plucked the moon down for him. Although, now I think of it, that's not a bad idea.

Sid leans around to ogle the tin. 'Well, isn't that lovely?'

'It's for Leo,' I say tightly, not taking my eyes off the man who's shown me nothing but steadfast loyalty and encouragement since the day we met.

Leo's frown clears. He's been watching me the whole time and now I see him lick his lips. Presumably, that's in anticipation of the cake, but my heart skips anyway.

'Thank you,' he says in an undertone.

And then there's an almighty bang.

'Oh, Jesus Christ.' The cake flies from my grip as I instinctively clap my hands over my ears. When I open my eyes, Leo has caught the tin and is grinning.

'Shit,' I say, all decorum gone. 'They've started.'

They have indeed. Like any self-respecting fireworks show, they've grabbed the audience's attention with a volley of bangers, and now red and white fireworks are arching into the air, exploding over our heads. Relieved of the cake tin, I grab the zip on my sweatshirt, yanking it so high I graze my neck.

'I have to go,' I yelp.

'Why?' Leo glances up at the sky, his face briefly illuminated by hundreds of pounds worth of exploding gunpowder. Then he reaches out a hand to my arm. 'You've only just arrived.'

But I shake my head vigorously. 'I can't be here. Enjoy your cake.'

This was a huge mistake. Whatever made me think we could have a meaningful conversation surrounded by the entire village, with whizzing and crashing and – the worst part – hot sparks flying around over our heads? Whatever made me think Leo would take one look at the cake and guess that I've finally worked out what sort of man I want to be with? Whatever made me think I could lean into him, say 'You only had to ask', and he would sweep me off my feet?

Illuminated now by the flashes from above, I shake off his hand and turn. The crowd is thicker than before; everyone's attention now is upwards as they ooh and aah at the red, white and blue showers above. The smell of sulphur reaches me, evoking even more panic. I manage to wriggle through the first cluster of people, duck under the pointing arms of another group, and shove my way between another family.

'Bella!' Leo's voice is behind me as I encounter a pair of children brandishing sparklers. What are their parents thinking, letting them light those in this crush? I jolt to a halt and step backwards, straight into another human.

'Hey!'

I turn my head to apologise and find it's Leo. From behind me, he puts a hand on my arm, steadying us both. Then he circles his arm all the way around me, pulling me back against him.

'Bell.' He speaks against my ear, low and calming. 'What's wrong?'

I feel myself tremble, the cake tin bumping against my back as I allow myself a couple of deep breaths in the safety of Leo's hug. Then I turn, carefully, aware of how near he is, aware that my heart is thundering for more than one reason.

'I'm scared of fireworks.' Although I know how silly it sounds, tears well up.

'Okay.' He doesn't argue. 'Let's get you out of here.'

Leo takes my hand and starts to lead me. Half of me wants to follow, to enjoy the feel of his fingers entwined with mine, but the other half is in serious flight mode.

'We're going the wrong way!' I stumble on the uneven ground. 'The gate's over there.'

There's only one entrance to this field, from the main street. Otherwise, one long side is flanked by a dense hedge, one side is the wall of the malt house, and the final side is roped off for the fireworks display. Not that I'd go that way if my life depended on it.

'It's okay,' Leo calls over his shoulder. He's doing a much better job of forcing a path through the crowd than I did. Maybe it's because, now the first fireworks are over, people are less rapt by the sky. Or maybe it's because his voice is louder.

We reach the malt house. Its low, sloping roof overhangs the walls and Leo ducks under it, guiding me in too. I don't feel much safer, but at least there's no mob of spectators here. Building supplies are stacked against the old wall: scaffolding, buckets, and sacks.

'Hold this.' Leo hands me the cake tin and starts moving the sacks aside.

'What are you –?'

Then I see it, behind the sacks, a small door, no more than four feet high. Leo hefts one final sack, then puts his shoulder to the door and shoves. The door gives, swinging inwards. I wonder how he knew it was there, then I realise: the proposed malt house renovations. He's spent hours studying the building.

Leo steps in first, then pulls me through behind him and kicks the door shut. I can still hear bangs and whizzes from the pyrotechnic display outside, but they're muffled by the thick walls of the malt house. And in here, it's completely dark.

'Hang on.' I hear a rustle, then we're lit by a faint glow as Leo holds up his phone. 'Are you okay to wait here?'

I nod, then confirm 'Yes', in case he can't see me properly. I'm terrified of fireworks, but I'm fine in the dark. Unless there are rats. I'm not wild about rats.

'Don't move,' he says.

I stand obediently, trying not to listen to the explosions outside. I peer through the darkness but can make nothing out, so instead I sniff the air around me. It's a mix of fresh sawdust combined with something like warm muesli. Oats, maybe? Barley? Then it comes to me. Of course: the grain, from when the malt house functioned. The scent has seeped into the walls, become part of the fabric of the place. It's a comforting, homely smell and my pulse steadies a little.

Seconds later, Leo's back, a torch waving before him. 'You did say you wanted a tour of the malt house.'

Yes, but not under such hair-raising circumstances.

Still... 'You remembered,' I say.

He swings the torch beam towards my feet, so it's no longer dazzling me. 'I remember all of it,' he says softly.

His face is in complete shadow, but hope floods into me. I swallow hard, longing to know what he means.

'This way,' he says, 'but be careful. Step where I do.' He takes my hand again and I follow, him carrying the torch, me the cake tin. At the end of a narrow passage, we arrive at a flight of wooden steps.

'Up here,' he says. 'We can sit and...' he hesitates, 'wait it out.'

I follow him up the steps, which thankfully are sturdy beneath our feet.

'I've checked them,' he says, as if reading my mind. 'They're rock solid.'

And then we're in some kind of hay loft. Leo locates a light switch and a single bulb comes on.

'You have electricity.' I'm stating the obvious as I take in our cosy, rustic surroundings.

'It's only low wattage,' he replies, gesturing to a pile of pallets, which I take as an invitation to sit. 'We rig up better lights when we're working.'

As he speaks, there's another barrage of bangs from outside. It occurs to me that if one lands on the malt house roof, it could catch fire with us inside it. I stifle the panic and shove my hands into my sleeves to stop them shaking.

'Thank you.' I'm unable to look at him directly, even in this dim light.

'For what?'

I adjust my position on the pallet to make room for Leo and jerk my head to the gap I've made. When he lowers himself onto our small perch, my whole body tingles.

'For getting me out of there.' I want to say so much more than this.

'No problem.'

There's a long pause, before a faint cheer from outside reaches us.

'That's probably the end,' Leo says. 'The grand finale.'

'Oh, I do hope so.' I try to smile. Still, the knowledge that we're no longer in immediate danger of incineration is a comfort.

'And thank you for everything else.' I'm speaking in a rush now.

'Such as?'

'Everything. You made me run, even when I didn't want to. You got me into the whole flapjack thing...'

He's so close to me, I could rest my head on his shoulder.

'...and you... you helped me see what a waste of space Owen is.'

'Only because you deserve better.' Leo's voice is quiet and his words linger between us. I turn to look at him, desperate to see if I'm reading too much into this.

'You're frowning again,' I say. 'Why are you always frowning?' Unable to help myself, I pull one hand from my sleeve and reach my index finger to the spot between his eyebrows.

He doesn't flinch, but as I move my hand away, he catches it. 'If I am frowning,' he replies, 'it's because I'm exercising so much self-control.'

'Self-control?'

He's still holding my hand and now I know the tightness in my chest has nothing to do with the fireworks, which have indeed stopped.

'Yeah.' He leans closer, watching me carefully. When I don't move, he kisses my fingers.

I can't prevent the smile which spreads across my face. My mouth goes dry as his lips press again against my hand.

'Not to eat that cake, I mean.' He kisses my wrist now.

'The cake?' I manage to repeat.

'Uh huh.'

The tin is beside us on the pile of pallets, but neither of us looks towards it.

'You're... trying to resist the cake?'

'I am.' Leo lets go of my wrist and puts both arms around me. His hands are warm and firm on my back and a feeling of sublime safety settles over me. As I look up at him in the soft light, I see the frown has gone. In its place, his eyes are twinkling.

'It wouldn't do to rush.' He leans a little closer. 'I want to savour it.'

'Savour it?' If he doesn't kiss me now, I might melt.

'I want to enjoy the sweetness.' His face is inches from mine. Then he whispers, 'Properly.'

'Oh,' I say, watching his lips part.

'If that's okay with the chef?'

'Yes,' I reply, struggling with the single syllable. 'More than okay.'

'Good.' He finally bends his head and covers my lips with his.

And it truly is the sweetest thing I've ever tasted.

The End

From the Author

Independent authors like me rely on reviews from readers to help spread the word about our work. Please consider adding your review of *Sweet Pursuits* to Amazon, Goodreads and other online forums.

At the end of this book, you'll find the first chapter of *Saving Saffron Sweeting*. Set in the same village, this is the first in the Saffron Sweeting series. You can learn more and purchase it at: http://mybook.to/sweeting

I love to connect with readers through my website and social media. Visit www.paulinewiles.com for news, bonus materials and special promotions. You can also sign up for my newsletter to be notified of new releases and receive two free bonus guides: *50 British Foods to Try Before You Die* and *60 Things to Know Before Your First Trip to England*.

Saving Saffron Sweeting

Chapter 1

I was balanced on an eight-foot ladder with a mouth full of curtain hooks when I realised that my husband was cheating.

The individual pieces of the picture suddenly came together, making terrifying sense. I blinked hard, then stared at my knuckles, which were now white from gripping the ladder. But the image wouldn't subside. The picture I saw was James with another woman.

I was hanging curtains in my client Rebecca's bedroom, and the project was almost complete. This was great, as she'd been excited to give the room a whole new look after she'd recently come to the end of a long relationship.

'I'm ready to move on. Grace, I want a totally fresh look,' she'd told me when we met to discuss how I could help her. 'Something luxurious, maybe a little sensual. I don't plan on being single forever.'

I was still new in the design business and it was a huge deal for me not only to land a new client, but also one who had money to spend and some kind of clue what she wanted. My first few months had been a real struggle and I was starting to question my talents. Other business owners had stressed the importance of tapping my personal network to get things rolling, so James had spread the word around his office. Apparently, he had done a good job of promoting my abilities to Rebecca, his company's marketing manager. She had been great to work for and seemed appreciative of my suggestions. The only slight issue was that in the last few weeks she had been anxious to speed things up and get the bedroom completed.

Eager to please, I had been beavering away and attempting to charm my suppliers into hurrying. After getting the curtains up, I planned to hit the shops for accessories, and then the room would be ready for whatever action she had in mind.

My work had been interrupted by a knock on the front door of Rebecca's condo. I'd opened it to find a bubbly young woman, who presented me with a pair of pink stilettos.

'Oh!' she said. 'I was hoping Becca would be home. Can you let her know Kerry returned these?'

'I think she's at work,' I said, taking the shoes. 'I'm her bedroom designer.'

'Ooh, you mean the love nest? Can I see it?'

'Er, it's not finished yet,' I replied. 'I expect she'd rather show you herself.'

Kerry shrugged. 'Okay. I'll catch up with her.' She turned and was a few steps down the hall before she added, 'And tell her I want to hear all about Vegas and this James guy. He sounds delish!'

My mind was still on the curtains. I'd shut the door and put the cute shoes down, before returning to the bedroom.

Climbing back up the ladder, I thought, No wonder Rebecca wants to hurry this room. She's met some man in Las Vegas and needs her bedroom back. I was stretching to try to hook the edge of the curtain to the last ring on the pole when the dark feeling began to slither over me.

Did the ladder wobble? Had one of San Francisco's famous earthquakes nudged it? Or was the lurch, the sway, the feeling of my stomach dropping to the new wool rug, due to something else? I checked the new tear-drop chandelier hanging above the bed. As a British transplant to the Bay Area, I had spent the first couple of years diving under our dining table at the slightest tremor. But by now I had learned that if the light fixtures weren't swaying, the seismic jolt was all in my head. The glass drops of Rebecca's chandelier stared back at me steadily, not even winking, let alone dancing.

I had the presence of mind not to swallow my curtain hooks as I took a huge gulp and slid down the ladder. I slumped onto the new and naked mattress as I thought about my husband's recent conference trip to Las Vegas and how edgy he had been since. I remembered our paths crossing briefly in the kitchen, the first morning after his return.

'How was it?' I'd asked, digging through the drawer for my favourite cereal spoon.

'Okay, I guess.' He reached for the tea bags.

James seemed dispirited and I thought perhaps the industry analysts had given his company, a mobile security start-up, a tough time.

'Are you home this evening?' he wanted to know.

'Probably,' I called over my shoulder. I was already heading to my computer to check whether anyone had emailed for decor advice. Even at that hour, my mind was firmly on my fragile business.

But that day I'd been called by a potential customer to discuss her family room and, as was typical, she could only meet me in the evening. I was hard at work researching inspiration pictures when James came home, and within minutes I headed out to my appointment. After more than an hour of fruitless discussion on the merits of contemporary versus rustic style, I drove the forty minutes home across the Dumbarton Bridge to find my husband was already asleep.

With an uncomfortable feeling, I also recalled the previous evening, when he'd come home from work early and asked to talk to me, but I'd been flying out of the door to my women's networking group. This had been the pattern of life recently: we seemed to pass each other fleetingly, our schedules never lining up for longer than it took to brew a pot of tea.

And now I had learned that Rebecca had hooked up with someone called James in Las Vegas. My James had been acting oddly since he had returned from there. Keep calm, I told myself, it's probably fine.

But it wasn't fine. The third and ugly part of the truth was literally staring me in the face. Rebecca's favourite colour was purple and despite some reservations on my part, she had been adamant about using a strong shade of aubergine. We'd finally agreed on a sophisticated tan for three walls, painting the dramatic colour as an accent behind her bed. And although James usually showed precious little interest in any of my decorating ideas, we had been talking about Rebecca's project just before his trip, when we'd been in the kitchen long enough to empty the dishwasher together.

'How is your client list coming along?' he'd asked, shaking leftover water from a wine glass.

'Slowly,' I'd replied. 'Rebecca's bedroom is nearly finished but I don't have anyone lined up after her.'

He didn't say anything but had stretched over my head to put some plates away.

Happy to talk about my work, I'd let my brain run on. 'I hope it all comes together okay. That accent colour was such a bold choice.'

He'd pulled a slight face. 'Yeah, purple always reminds me of something my grandad would have had.'

I had dropped the topic, as I'd learned during our years together that James based most of his interior design dislikes on the vivid avocado and orange combinations in his grandfather's house. He thought any room featuring retro patterns or an accent wall was hideous.

Now, I leaped off the mattress as though it had bitten me on the behind. I was convinced I hadn't mentioned purple, aubergine or any other arty description for the colour behind the bed.

He knows what colour this room is. He's been here.

I was out of the house and into the car before I knew it. Days later, it occurred to me I should have stuffed Rebecca's hollow curtain poles with frozen shrimp. Of course, the clever moves always elude me at the time.

~~~

By the time I arrived at the Palo Alto office where James and his team were trying to create the next Silicon Valley success story, all dignity had abandoned me. I think my tears were already beginning as I lurched through the front desk area, empty because the company was too small to have a receptionist. In my haste, I then collided with the *foosball* table, which appears to be a required toy at every start-up with venture capital funding.

I spotted my husband – cropped, dark brown hair, shirt half untucked as usual – hunched over his keyboard, at the end of an untidy row of T-shirt clad computer coders. This gaggle looked barely old enough to have gained admission to Stanford University, let alone already graduated.

James looked up and noticed me. Surprise crossed his face, but was replaced with something I assumed was guilt. I could see how deep the lines in the middle of his forehead were getting these days, and how weary he looked.

'Purple,' was all I managed to utter at first. Terrific. Millions of wives over the centuries have faced this situation and all I could say was *purple*.

'Grace –' He stood and took my arm, trying to get me to sit.

I wrenched myself free. 'How did you know her bedroom is purple? How did you know?'

'Listen.' He shook his head. 'It's not what you think'.

Okay, so *purple* may not have been eloquent, but at least it was original. I saw red – as well as crimson, magenta and every shade in between.

'How could you?' I hissed. 'I know what's going on. And

all the time, I've been decorating that sodding room!'

'Please,' he glanced sideways at the line of coders. 'Calm down!'

Fingers had frozen over keyboards. Curious youthful faces were turned towards us: James was a popular boss.

'You knew her bedroom is purple because you've been sleeping with her, haven't you? You've been sleeping with my client!'

'No, look, it wasn't like that.'

'No, you look. Look at this purple and tell me you've never seen it before.' I pulled the paint sample from my purse and unscrewed the lid. Dark and liquidly sinister, I waved it dangerously close to his computer.

'Okay, okay, I'm sorry. Please – calm down and let me tell you.' By now his dark brown eyes were wide with panic.

The whole office had fallen silent, but I saw that not everyone was watching us. Instead, some of them had turned to the far side of the room, as Rebecca stood and began heading our way. I realised most of them knew she had a part in this drama. And what about Rebecca? Was she half expecting this to happen? There I was, a total mess inside and out, and she appeared to be perfectly composed.

She came closer and I caught the eye contact between her and James. He had now turned paler than I'd ever seen, including the time he got food poisoning in Turkey and couldn't stand for three days. As she walked behind the desks of her co-workers, most of them didn't seem to know whether to freeze or flee.

'Look,' she said, 'let's not do this here.' Not a blonde hair was out of place.

'Where would you rather *do it*?' I snapped back, but my voice was quivering. 'Your bedroom? With my husband?'

James reached for me again, but seemed to change his mind and let his hand drop. 'I know you're furious right now, but it was just one stupid mistake in Vegas,' he said quietly.

'I don't believe you! You've been in her bedroom!' I was

looking wildly from one to the other, sick with the thought of them wrapped around each other.

'Well, actually,' Rebecca had the nerve to put her hand on his arm, 'it's probably best that you know, Grace. It wasn't a mistake.' She glanced at me and I noticed for the first time an intense determination in her face. 'I'm so sorry, we didn't plan it this way. It happened after I hired you. But we can't help how we feel.' In her strappy beige sandals she was nearly as tall as James, and she barely needed to lift her pointy little chin upwards to gaze at my husband adoringly. 'The thing is, I care about you and I want to be with you.'

A collective gasp flew round the office, almost loud enough to drown my yelp of pain. I could sense the techie crowd reaching for their phones to post *Wild and crazy work love triangle* on their Facebook pages. I felt like I'd been whacked in the ribs with a cricket bat, but I registered through my tears that James was shaking his head in defeat. The little pot slipped from my fingers before I could think of throwing paint in their faces. Instead, it added a permanent souvenir of the demise of my marriage to the carpet and his Hush Puppies. Rebecca sidestepped smartly and her sexy sandals escaped the shower. Too bad.

Failing entirely to live up to my name, I turned and fled with as much poise as a double-decker London bus.

~~~

We spent the next two days in an ugly blur of sobbing, shouting, and silence. Not all the tears were mine: James followed me straight home and begged me to hear his side of the story. I heard but I didn't listen and I certainly didn't believe his lame attempts to blame his cheating on a drunken night of clubbing at the conference in Las Vegas. Did he really think I was that gullible?

He tiptoed around me for the first evening, then slept in our guest room and left early the next day. That was worse than the awkwardness of him being in the apartment: I knew he was going to see Rebecca and I was tormented by the thought. I wasn't even sure he'd come home again. But he did, to find me curled up on the sofa with a blanket, in pointed denial of the California sunshine outside.

'Will you please talk to me?' He approached hesitantly. 'I know this was really, really stupid but I need to tell you my side of things.'

'You mean you've got something original to say? Because up to this point, it's all looking like one big cliché to me. You cheated, you got caught, you're a lying bastard.'

He sat down at the other end of our Ikea sofa and I immediately tucked my legs under me, as if it would burn me to touch him. 'Grace, I didn't lie to you, I was trying to tell you!'

'Well, you didn't try very hard.' I could feel my eyes welling up yet again.

'Look, ever since I got back, I've been trying to get you to sit down.' He did at least have the decency to look distraught. 'But you've been so caught up in your business recently – there wasn't a good moment.'

He was staring at me intently and I could see the beginning of tears in his own eyes. He clearly hadn't shaved that morning and his shirt was even more of a crumpled disaster than usual.

'Well, excuse me for turning my back for five minutes to try and make some money.' I was firmly on the defensive, one hundred per cent the injured party. 'And in case you hadn't noticed, I was slaving away to finish a project for the woman you're sleeping with!'

'I'm not sleeping with her. It was just one time. One stupid bloody time. I'm so sorry.'

'I don't believe you. You knew about that goddamn purple wall.' I was looking around wildly, seeking my escape route. I didn't want to be in the same room with him.

'All right, so I happened to see her bedroom! That doesn't mean anything.'

'No, it means everything.' I was sobbing now. 'It means

I'll never trust you again.'

I wish I'd had the panache to storm out of our apartment in an expensive cloud of Chanel perfume. I wish I'd owned a Louis Vuitton bag to grab on my way to check into a luxury hotel, where I'd instigate a passionate revenge fling with a nineteen-year-old bellboy. Unfortunately, I clambered off the sofa with pins and needles in my legs and tripped over my blankie instead. Then I trailed soggy tissues across the floor and locked myself in the bathroom, where my only company was a dog-eared copy of *National Geographic*.

I had followed my British husband – and his job – from London to California, but my own attempt at the American dream had flopped. I'd been working crazily, had failed to see my marriage falling apart, and felt like a total fool.

I certainly couldn't afford to kick James out and stay in our apartment on my own. My so-called business was barely breathing. I had no idea how many months or years of scraping by might be ahead of me, if I attempted to build a list of design clients who weren't going to thank me by stealing my husband. Did I have the energy to move out, find a job, and rebuild my life in the fast-moving world of Silicon Valley? What the heck was I doing in this country, anyway? All I wanted was to crawl under the bed covers and hide, preferably with a packet of imported Cadbury's biscuits.

In the small, mocking hours of the next morning, I found myself unearthing a suitcase from the closet. With safety, seclusion and comfort food as my primary motives, I booked a flight home to England.

~ ~ ~

To continue reading *Saving Saffron Sweeting*, please visit:
http://mybook.to/sweeting

Glossary of British Terms

A-Z ~ Popular brand of London map.
Bakewell Tart ~ Pastry with jam, sponge, and almonds.
Bangers and Mash ~ Sausages with mashed potatoes.
Battenberg Cake ~ A rectangular sponge cake covered in marzipan, typically shows a yellow and pink check pattern when cut.
Bee's Knees, The ~ Excellent, wonderful, cool.
Biscuit ~ Essentially a cookie, but with a crunchy consistency. Frequently consumed with tea!
Blag ~ Talk your way into getting something for nothing.
Blighty ~ Affectionate term for Britain, often used by expats or those on vacation outside the country.
Blimey ~ Exclamation of surprise.
Boiler ~ Type of furnace, giving both hot water and central heating.
Bollocks ~ Expletive, or way of saying someone's talking rubbish. Don't use in polite company; literally means testicles.
Bonk ~ In running terms, to run out of energy; can also be slang for having sex.
Bonnet (car) ~ Hood.
Boots ~ British chemist (pharmacy) chain.
Bourbon ~ A rectangular chocolate biscuit, popular for dunking in tea.
Bugger Off ~ Get lost (don't use in polite company).
Bum ~ Butt.
Busy Lizzie ~ A type of potted plant.
Cadbury's ~ Famous British chocolate company.
Chat someone up ~ To flirt; make conversation with romantic intentions.
Cider ~ Hard cider.
Coconut Shy ~ Game, often found at fairs and fetes. A player buys balls to throw at coconuts balanced on posts and

wins the coconut if it tumbles.

Courgette ~ Zucchini.

Cow Parsley ~ Weed-like plant, commonly seen in summer alongside roads and hedgerows.

Crisps ~ (Potato) chips.

Crossroads ~ Intersection, especially where two roads meet at right angles.

Crumble ~ Dessert, similar to a cobbler.

Custard Tart ~ Pastry filled with custard (that is, a mix of milk/cream, eggs, and sugar) and sprinkled with nutmeg.

Dunk ~ Dip a biscuit in a hot drink to make it soft.

Estate agents, estate agency ~ Real estate office.

Flapjack ~ Fairly dense cake, usually in a bar shape, made with oats and golden syrup.

Fortnum and Mason ~ Famous (upmarket) British store with excellent food department.

Fried egg ~ Sunny side up.

Git ~ Derogatory term, used more often for men than women.

Gutted ~ Devastated (emotionally).

Harrods ~ Famous (upmarket) British department store.

Hot toddy ~ Hot water with honey, whisky and spices.

John Lewis ~ British department store.

Jumper ~ Sweater.

Knickers ~ Panties.

Lycra ~ Spandex.

Midriff ~ Midsection, abdomen.

Motorway ~ Freeway.

Oven ~ Stove.

Oxfam ~ National chain of thrift stores, supporting humanitarian relief efforts.

Paracetamol ~ Over-the-counter painkiller. In the US: acetaminophen.

Peckish ~ Somewhat hungry.

Pimms ~ Brand of alcoholic drink, the most popular of which is served as a cocktail involving gin, lemonade, fresh fruit, and mint. A summertime classic.

Priest's hole ~ A hiding place for a priest, created in the sixteenth century when Catholics were persecuted in England. Primarily found in castles and large country houses.

Pulling your leg ~ Joking, kidding around.

Punt ~ A long, low, flat-bottomed boat, popular in Oxford and Cambridge. It is propelled (and steered) by someone standing at the back with a long pole, which pushes off the river bed.

Rosy Lee ~ Cockney rhyming slang for tea.

Sausage roll ~ British snack (or light meal) of sausage meat wrapped in pastry. Can be served hot or cold.

Scotch egg ~ Hard-boiled egg, wrapped in sausage meat, then breadcrumbs, and deep fried.

Shag ~ Have sex (don't use in polite company).

Shirty ~ Grumpy, irritable.

Shortbread ~ Plain cookie, made with sugar, flour and butter. Probably originated in Scotland.

Slobber ~ Drool.

Sodding ~ Mild expletive, for example, 'I've lost my sodding keys again.' (Don't use in super-polite company).

Sticky Toffee Pudding ~ Iconic British steamed dessert, featuring moist sponge cake, dates and toffee sauce. Personal favourite of the author!

Take the mickey ~ Make fun of someone; be cheeky.

Tesco ~ Mainstream British grocery store.

Top notch ~ Excellent.

Tosser ~ Jerk (don't use in polite company).

Trainers ~ Sneakers or running shoes.

Treacle tart ~ Very sweet dessert: pastry filled with a mixture of golden syrup, breadcrumbs and lemon juice.

Tube ~ The London Underground (railway) system.

Waitrose ~ British grocery store, somewhat upmarket.

Wimpole Hall ~ A historic country estate, near Cambridge and open to visitors.